Also by Michael Thomas Ford

SUICIDE NOTES

z

Z

MICHAEL THOMAS FORD

HARPER TEEN
An Imprint of HarperCollinsPublishers

Library of Congress Cataloging-in-Publication Data
Ford, Michael Thomas.
  Z / Michael Thomas Ford. — 1st ed.
    p. cm.
  Summary: In the year 2032, after a virus that turned people
into zombies has been eradicated, Josh is invited to join an
underground gaming society where the gamers hunt zombies
and the action is more dangerous than it seems.
  ISBN 978-0-06-073758-0
  [1. Science fiction. 2. Role playing—Fiction. 3. Games—Fiction.
4. Zombies—Fiction.] I. Title.
PZ7.F7532119Zab 2010   2009044005
[Fic]—dc22   CIP
                                                              AC

Typography by Alison Klapthor
10 11 12 13 14   CG/RRDB   10 9 8 7 6 5 4 3 2 1

First Edition

For Horrible Spider, Ocho Patas, and the Mungos,

who kept me company

I

The zombie was somewhere ahead of him. Its stench—a combination of blood, dirt, and rotting meat—filled the air. It was close. Josh flipped the safety on his flamethrower and held it out in front of him, his finger on the trigger. Almost all the overhead lights were out, and the halogen light mounted on the barrel of his flamethrower had broken during a run-in with a z on a lower floor. He could see only about six feet ahead of him through the gloom.

The hospital's hallway was littered with trash; broken glass, charred pieces of paper, and twisted medical instruments were strewn around the floor. Dark smears streaked the white tile walls. Ahead of Josh a teddy bear sat propped against the wall just outside a partially open door, its fur stained with something black and sticky. Its head was torn off and lay in its lap. Stuffing puffed from the ragged neck.

Something about the bear caused a shiver to run down Josh's spine. Clearly it had belonged to a little kid. But where was the kid now? He hoped wherever it was, it hadn't already been turned by the zombies. Child zombies were the worst. Josh hated torching them.

But I will if I have to, he thought as he approached the door.

Using the end of his weapon, he nudged the door open. The only light in the room came from one ceiling fixture, and the bulb flickered as it tried to draw electricity from the hospital's ancient wiring. The room was visible for only a few seconds at a time as the light flashed on and off. Josh felt like he was watching an old movie being played on a broken projector.

Even with the limited light he could see enough to know that the woman on the bed was dead. She was dressed in a nurse's uniform, her white dress stained with what could only be blood. Her head lolled to one side so that her face was turned toward Josh. Her eyes were gone, and there was a ragged hole in her throat where the zombie had bitten her. One arm was stretched out, and the fingers of that hand were curled, clutching a clump of long blond hair that was attached to a piece of bloody scalp. On the floor below the hand, a hypodermic needle lay in a pool of liquid.

She tried to kill it with the needle, Josh thought. *But it got her.*

Part of him was glad she was dead. If she'd been alive, he would have had to torch her, since she'd obviously been bitten and therefore could infect other people. That was the First Rule of Torching: Cleanse with fire.

Suddenly something scrambled out from under the bed, heading for the far side of the room. Whatever it was whimpered like a frightened animal. Instinctively Josh raised his flamethrower. But the thing was running *away* from him. If it had been a zombie, it would have come at him. They never ran away. He took his finger off the flamethrower's trigger.

"Are you okay?" he called out. He was thinking about the teddy bear. Had the child who owned it been in the room when the zombie attacked? Maybe the kid had hidden under the bed and escaped the zombie's notice. If so, it was Josh's responsibility to help. That was the Second Rule of Torching: Save all humans.

When the light flickered back on for a moment, he searched the shadows. Huddled in the corner of the room was a little girl. Maybe six or seven years old, she was wearing a torn, dirty dress and no shoes. Her long hair hung down in her face. She was breathing quickly, and as Josh approached, she pressed herself against the wall and began shaking her head from side to side.

"No," she said softly. "Don't kill me. Please."

Josh stopped and crouched down. "It's okay," he said. "I'm not going to hurt you. What's your name?"

The little girl stared at him. He searched her eyes for any sign of the infection, but in the dim light he couldn't see well enough to tell for sure. She *seemed* okay.

That kind of thinking can get you killed, he told himself. But he had to help. He couldn't just leave the girl there.

"Vi—" the girl said. Her voice cracked when she spoke, and she tried again. "Vi . . . Violet."

"Hi, Violet. I'm Josh. You and I are going to get out of here, okay?"

"But the monsters . . ." Violet said. She looked at the body on the bed, and her mouth began to tremble.

"Look at me," Josh told her. "Violet, look at me."

When the girl was looking at him, he held out his hand to her. "It's going to be okay."

Violet hesitated a moment, then took his hand. He helped her to her feet. He could feel her shaking. *I don't blame her,* he thought. He wanted to ask how she'd survived so long in the hospital without a zombie finding her, but now was not the time.

"We're going to go into the hall now," he told Violet.

She pulled away, shaking her head. "They're out there," she said. "They're waiting for us."

"Most of them are dead," said Josh. "My friend and I took care of them."

"Where is your friend now?" Violet asked.

You shouldn't have said anything, you idiot. Josh scolded himself for his mistake. The fact was, he didn't know whether Firecracker was alive or dead. His com-link had broken during the scuffle with the zombie in the operating room on the fourth floor, and he hadn't been able to reach him since. All he got was static. He hoped his buddy wasn't dead—or, even worse, turned. Then he would have to torch him too. *The Third Rule of Torching,* he thought. *You can't bring them back.*

He pushed the thought from his mind and focused on Violet. He needed her to listen to him, otherwise both of them could end up as zombie food. "We'll meet up with my friend soon," he said, hoping that was true. "Right now you just have to trust me, okay?"

Violet looked into his eyes. Her own were barely visible in the still-blinking light. "Okay," she said softly.

Josh led Violet from the room, making sure to

keep himself between her and the bed so that she wouldn't have to look at the dead nurse. He noticed that the little girl kept her head down until they were in the hallway. *Smart kid.* "We're going to go to the end of this hallway," he said. "There's an elevator there, and we're going to take it down to the first floor and get out of here."

"Is everybody dead?" Violet asked. "The nurses? The doctors? All the people?"

"Just stay behind me," said Josh, ignoring her question.

As they reached each new doorway, Josh peered inside, always keeping his finger on the trigger of his flamethrower. But the rooms were all empty. Whoever had been in them was either eaten or turned.

Finally they came to the end of the hall. In front of them were the elevator doors. Hallways continued both to the left and to the right. Josh made a quick scan, saw nothing, and hit the down button on the elevator's control panel. He hoped the hospital's unreliable wiring would hold up long enough for them to get out. Somewhere below them came the sound of machinery grinding to life, then the *thuck-thuck-thuck* as the elevator car rose up on its heavy cable.

As the hand on the dial above the elevator doors slowly crept from *B* to *1* to *2*, Josh surveyed the hallways in each direction. If there were any zombies on the floor, they would have heard the elevator and started to move toward the sound. *Good thing they're slow,* he thought. Still, they could move when they needed to. He knew that from experience. And all it took was one bite to ruin your day.

The 3 on the dial lit up. "Come on," Josh urged the clanking machinery. "Hurry up."

As the dial hit 4 and moved past it to 5—the floor they were on—Josh felt himself relax a little bit. They were almost there. Now he just had to hope the elevator didn't have any riders in it.

"Stand back," he told Violet, moving away from the elevator doors just in case he had to put the burn on anything inside.

Violet obeyed. Then, as the door began to open, Josh heard her call out, "Dr. Rackham!"

Josh whirled around in time to see the girl dashing down the left-hand corridor toward the figure of a man in a long white coat. He carried a clipboard in one hand, and there was a stethoscope around his neck.

"Dr. Rackham!" Violet yelled. "Come with us! We're getting out!"

The clipboard fell from the doctor's hand as he suddenly lurched sideways. At that moment the overhead light came on, and the man's face was bathed in harsh fluorescent light. The blood on his cheeks was bright red—fresh—and a scalpel extended from one of his eyes, plunged through a cracked lens of his glasses.

Violet stopped, staring at the lumbering figure. The zombie reached out toward her and moaned. Blood and something darker oozed from his lips in thick strings.

"Violet!" Josh yelled. "Get down!"

The little girl looked back at him. The zombie doctor was only a dozen feet from her. If she didn't act immediately, the doctor would reach her in a matter of seconds.

"Violet, NOW!" Josh yelled.

Violet fell to the floor, lying on her stomach and covering her head with her arms. Josh aimed his gun at the zombie and pulled the trigger. A column of flame erupted from the muzzle and flew toward the doctor. His lab coat caught most of it and burst into tongues of orange and yellow that licked hungrily at the material. The zombie looked down at himself and pawed uselessly at the flames.

Josh fired another round at the creature, this time aiming for its face. The zombie's skin crackled and burst open, and the doctor swayed from side to side. One of his hands was on fire, and he waved it around like a grotesque torch.

"Violet! Come on!" Josh shouted.

The girl raised herself up and ran to him. Not once did she look back at the zombie, who had fallen to the floor and was now fully consumed in fire. Black smoke poured from him and the smell of burning flesh was thick in the air.

The elevator doors opened just as Violet reached Josh. The box held no surprise visitors, and Josh pushed Violet inside and followed after her. He hit the button for the ground floor and watched as the heavy doors slid shut. The elevator began to descend.

Violet was crying. She was crouched in the corner, her arms around her knees, breathing in jagged gasps. Josh knelt down, but when he reached out to comfort her, she recoiled.

"It's okay now," Josh told her. "We're almost out of here."

Violet rested her forehead on her knees and rocked back and forth. Josh glanced at the panel on the wall. They were passing the third floor. *Why is it taking so long?* he wondered, willing the elevator to move faster.

As the second-floor button lit up there was a heavy *thud* on the car's roof. The whole box shook. Violet screamed as the escape hatch in the elevator's ceiling opened and a face looked down into the car. The skin was peeled away on one side, exposing muscle and bone. The eyes were clouded over with a milky yellow film, and the creature's torn lips grinned horribly.

Josh felt as if he'd been punched in the stomach. "Firecracker," he whispered, his voice cracking as he recognized his friend even through the damage that had been done to his face.

But he's not your friend anymore, he reminded himself. *He's a meatbag.*

Instinctively he raised his flamethrower then stopped as he realized that he would just end up spraying the inside of the box with fire. He might destroy the zombie, but the elevator would become an oven, and he and Violet would be cooked alive. Instead he tried to shut the hatch with the end of his gun. But the zombie threw himself forward and tumbled down on top of Josh, pinning him to the ground.

Josh looked into what was left of Firecracker's face. There was nothing of his friend there—just a monster that was coming toward him with his mouth open, ready to bite. Josh raised his arm to protect himself, but he knew that even one bite that broke the skin would mean the end for him.

"Get off him!"

Violet's voice broke through the silence. Firecracker paused. Turning his head, he looked at the little girl. It was the break Josh needed. Putting a hand on Firecracker's chest, he shoved as hard as he could, and Firecracker rolled onto his back.

As Josh scrambled to his feet, the elevator shuddered to a stop and the doors opened. Josh grabbed Violet's hand. He looked for his gun, but it was trapped beneath Firecracker, who had rolled onto his knees and was trying to get to his feet. There was no way Josh could get the flamethrower.

"Run!" Josh ordered. "Run down the hall and out the front door. You'll be safe there."

Violet didn't move. She stood in the doorway, staring into the flickering half-light of the hallway. At the other end of the hall, the doors to the hospital glowed faintly as sunlight penetrated the grimy glass.

"Go!" Josh yelled, pushing Violet out of the elevator.

The girl ran. Josh turned back to Firecracker, who was on his feet and moving his head from side to side as if he couldn't see. The flamethrower was on the floor behind him. Josh considered his choices—he could leave his gun and follow Violet out of the hospital. But that would leave Firecracker in there, where he would still be able to infect anyone foolish enough to venture inside the building. He couldn't let that happen. Plus, Josh couldn't stand to see his friend the way he was. He knew Firecracker would want to be put out of his misery, even if he was no longer human and didn't know what he'd become. Josh would want the same thing if he were in Firecracker's place.

He made his decision. He dived for the gun, reaching between Firecracker's legs and grabbing the flamethrower by the barrel. Moving more quickly than he thought possible, he scrambled back out of the elevator and got to his feet. The gun in his hands was now pointed at Firecracker.

"I'm sorry, buddy," Josh said as he raised the flame-thrower and released the safety. A tiny blue flame flickered at the head of the barrel. Josh squeezed the trigger.

"Hey!" a shrill voice yelled. "It's time for dinner. Mom says to get your butt downstairs now."

Josh whirled around. His sister Emily stood in the doorway to his room. Her hands were on her hips and her blond hair was tied in pigtails. She looked past him at the computer screen, and her eyes lit up.

"Busted!" she said triumphantly. "I am *so* telling Mom and Dad."

Josh tore the virtual-reality helmet from his head and tried to turn off the computer. As he did, he heard a robotic voice say, "Mission failed. You will turn in five, four, three—"

Glancing at the screen, Josh saw his avatar on the

floor just outside the elevator. Firecracker was kneeling beside him, gnawing on his neck. Blood pooled around his body.

"Two, one," the voice concluded as Josh finally managed to turn the screen off. He knew what happened next, and he didn't want to see it.

"Damn!" Josh exclaimed. He turned to his sister. "Look what you made me do."

"They're going to ground you for forever," Emily crowed. "You know what they said *last* time they caught you playing that game."

Of course he knew. His parents had been furious, especially his mother. She'd grounded him for two whole weeks and threatened to take away his computer privileges for another two. Only after he'd apologized repeatedly and promised not to play anymore had she relented.

He'd kept his word for three days. Then the lure of the game had proved too strong, and one night he found himself logging in. Since then he'd played secretly, always careful to lock his door when he was gaming. For some reason, this time he'd forgotten to, and Emily had caught him.

Josh wanted to yell at his sister some more, but he knew that would only make things worse. Emily had him in a corner.

"I'll make you a deal," he said.

Emily crossed her arms over her chest and cocked her head. "What kind of deal?" she asked.

Although he was angry, Josh had to stifle a laugh. For a nine-year-old his sister was a tough negotiator. Just a week before, she'd managed to get their parents to up her allowance by two dollars a week by arguing that since her eighth birthday the rate of inflation had increased by 7 percent while her allowance had increased by only 5 percent.

"I'll do half your chores for a month," he suggested.

Emily shook her head. "Uh-uh," she said. "Mom would wonder why you're doing the dishes. Try again."

Josh groaned. He didn't have much else to bargain with. Then he thought of something. "I'll give you issues one through twelve of *Changeling Quest*."

He saw Emily hesitate. *Changeling Quest* was her favorite graphic novel series, but she had started reading it at issue thirteen and didn't own the first dozen. They were no longer available for download, and only people who had purchased unlocking codes could access them on their Cybook readers. As with all Cybooks, the codes could be transferred one time to a new reader, and sometimes they showed up for sale on used Cybook sites, but it would have cost Emily a year's allowance to get her own set.

She was always asking Josh if she could borrow his reader to read the novels, and he knew how badly she wanted to own them herself. He didn't particularly like the series, but he had held on to the codes in case Emily ever had something he wanted to trade for. Now she did. He just had to pretend that giving them up was a big deal.

"Come on," he said. "It's all I've got. And you know you want to have them." He tried to sound sad about possibly losing the Cybooks.

"Issues one through twelve *and* your Spider Queen action figure," Emily countered.

"No way!" Josh said, now genuinely upset. "I saved up for that for six months. They only made two hundred of them, and mine's number twenty-two. And it's not an action figure. It's a handmade, one-twenty-eighth-scale *articulated model*."

Emily turned around. "Hey, Mom!" she called out.

"Wait!" Josh said.

Emily looked at him. "Deal?" she asked.

"I'll give you the novels and do your homework for *two* months."

Emily rolled her eyes. "Please," she said. "I want to get *good* grades. Mom!" she yelled again. "Josh is—"

"Okay!" Josh cut her off. "You can have the Cybooks and the Spider Queen. It's a deal."

Emily looked at him, beaming. "Transfer the codes," she said.

Josh shook his head. "Not until after dinner," he said. "I want to make sure you don't squeal."

"Like I would go back on a deal," Emily said, sounding offended.

Josh knew she was right. Emily drove a hard bargain, but she always did what she agreed to. Still, he couldn't let her win so easily. He stared back, saying nothing.

"Fine," Emily relented. "But *right after* dinner."

She left the room. Josh turned his computer screen back on and saw the message he'd been dreading: YOU HAVE BEEN DEMOTED ONE LEVEL. REPORT TO THE BRIEFING ROOM FOR YOUR NEXT ASSIGNMENT.

"One level!" Josh groaned. After almost a year of playing, he had recently reached Torcher First Class. Now he was back to being a Torcher Second Class. It would take months to get his rank back. His only consolation was that Firecracker would also be demoted for getting turned. Still, it didn't make him feel any better.

"Great," he said as he got up to go downstairs. "Back to the minor leagues."

2

"**Y**ou gave her what?" Firecracker looked at Josh as if his friend had completely lost his mind. They were sitting in biology class, waiting for the late bell to ring.

"I had to," Josh objected. "She was going to tell my folks, and you know how they feel about the game. If they knew I was playing again, they'd put a block on my computer so all I could access is educational sites. No more gaming. At all."

Firecracker ran a hand through his red hair. "I guess you kinda deserve it," he said. "You did almost torch me."

"That's my *job*," Josh reminded him. "Besides, no one told you to go and get bit. What happened, anyway?"

Firecracker shook his head. "Man, it was Charlie again. He tricked me into following him down to the morgue. When I got there, he was hiding inside one of the meat freezers so I couldn't smell him. Jumped out from behind a side of beef that was hanging in there and got me."

"That guy is *good*," said Josh. "What level is he now, thirty-six or something?"

"I don't even know," Firecracker answered. "Whatever he is, he's the best player I've ever seen."

"Too bad he plays a z," said Josh.

"Yeah," Firecracker agreed. "I don't get that. Why would he want to play a meatbag?" He spoke the last word as if he were spitting something nasty-tasting out of his mouth.

Josh shrugged. He didn't understand it either. Most players wanted to be Torchers. But Charlie played the other side. He'd started playing only a few months before Josh and Firecracker did, but quickly shot up the rankings and was now one of the top zombie players. Even Josh had to admit that playing a z was more difficult than playing a Torcher. You had to be really good at tricking the other players and leading them into traps where you could bite them. And Charlie was a master of it. Yet no one knew much about him. *I'd sure like to meet him*, thought Josh as Mrs. Hotchkiss entered the room.

"All right," said Mrs. Hotchkiss. "Let's get started."

She punched a button on the control panel on her desk, and the lights in the room dimmed. A moment later a three-dimensional holographic image of a brain appeared in the air in front of each desk. It rotated slowly, giving the students a view of all sides.

"The human brain is a complex organ," the teacher said. "But, according to the triune brain theory first proposed by neurologist Paul MacLean way back in the 1950s, it comprises three basic sections."

She typed on her keypad, and one section of the brain—the largest—turned blue. "This is the neocortex," she explained. "This part of the brain is responsible for things such as language development, abstract thought, and consciousness."

She continued on to the second section, which was within the brain, surrounded by the neocortex. "This is the limbic system," she explained as the area turned yellow. "It's responsible for memory storage and emotions."

The hologram of the brain had been transferred to Josh's NoteTaker unit, and as Mrs. Hotchkiss spoke, the information was updated on his screen. Since Josh could always look at it later, he didn't listen too closely.

The final area, an oddly shaped section deep within the brain, turned green. It reminded Josh of a flower on a stalk.

"And this," Mrs. Hotchkiss said, "is the most primitive part of the brain. It's called the R-complex or, more commonly, the reptilian brain."

"As in lizards?" Marcus Pell asked, earning him laughs from his classmates.

"Actually, yes," the teacher confirmed. "In reptiles the R-complex makes up almost all of the brain, controlling basic functions such as body temperature, heart rate, and breathing. It does the same for us, although thanks to the other parts of our brains, most of us are slightly more advanced than lizards."

Again most of the class laughed. Josh, however, drew on the page of his NoteTaker, using the stylus to make a series of spirals. Biology was one of his least favorite classes. As far as he was concerned, it was interesting only when they were dissecting holofrogs or doing cloning experiments. Plus, Mrs. Hotchkiss's voice always made him sleepy.

"I bring this up because I understand you're studying the zombie war in Mr. Sumpana's history class," said his teacher. "Do any of you know the science behind zombiism?"

Josh was suddenly interested. No one raised a hand, but he could see that the whole class was paying attention. Even Firecracker, in the row ahead of Josh, was sitting up and listening.

"Most of you probably know that the zombie epidemic began with a new strain of the common flu virus," Mrs. Hotchkiss said. Her fingers moved over her keypad, and a small red image appeared beside the brain. It was circular, with hundreds of tiny bumps on it. It spun slowly.

"We've all had the flu at one time or another," the teacher said. "You know the symptoms: sneezing, fever, feeling tired. The zombie flu was the same. That's why at first nobody knew how dangerous it was. With the first cases, it took several weeks for the more severe symptoms to appear, and by then it was too late."

Suddenly the holographic virus penetrated the smallest area of the brain, which began to glow red. As Josh watched, the reptilian portion of the brain grew in size while the other two sections shrank.

"The zombie virus attacked the reptilian brain," explained Mrs. Hotchkiss, "making it grow larger. At the same time, it caused the other two brain areas to shrink. As the reptilian brain took over control of the body, the infected person lost the ability to think rationally and to make judgments based on right and wrong. Instead infected people began to act more and more impulsively, until eventually the only things that were important to them were eating and survival."

A girl in the front row raised her hand. "I thought zombies were the living dead," she said.

"Yes and no," Mrs. Hotchkiss answered. "As the zombie flu virus attacked the neocortex of the brain, infected people lost the ability to speak coherently. In addition, they developed a great tolerance for pain. They seemed not to be affected by injuries that would be devastating to you and me."

"You mean they couldn't be killed?" someone asked.

"Not easily," said Mrs. Hotchkiss. "In addition to affecting the brain, the virus had a peculiar effect on the blood. It became thicker and coagulated more easily. Wounds didn't bleed as much, so a zombie could be stabbed or shot and survive. Some even lost limbs but didn't bleed to death as we would, because their blood clotted so quickly. Because of this, it was first assumed that the virus killed the infected person and then somehow reanimated the corpse. In reality, those infected with the zombie flu did not die first. They simply became zombies because their brains were attacked by the virus, and it destroyed the most human parts and let the primitive part take over."

"But you just said 'yes and no,'" Josh reminded her.

"They were alive in the sense that they breathed and moved and had heartbeats," the teacher said.

"But their memories and emotions were gone. Their ability to feel was destroyed. They didn't think in any way we would consider human. But technically, yes, they were alive."

"Why didn't they just give them a shot or something?" Josh was surprised to hear Firecracker ask the question. He almost never spoke in class.

"That's a good question," Mrs. Hotchkiss answered. "Doctors didn't give them a vaccine because they didn't have one. The flu virus is a very simple one, but that's also what makes it difficult to fight. It mutates very rapidly when it's attacked, which means that what works for one form of the virus might not work for another. In the case of zombie flu, none of the vaccines they tried worked, at least not quickly enough to save those who were already infected."

"But we get zombie flu shots now," said Josh. "When we're born. So they came up with something, right?"

Mrs. Hotchkiss nodded. "There's a preventative vaccine now," she said. "It's based on the most common strain of the zombie flu virus."

"But there could be other kinds, couldn't there?" asked Firecracker.

"Theoretically, yes," said the teacher. "However, there hasn't been a documented case of zombie flu infection in over fifteen years. The possibility of a new strain finding its way into the general population is almost nonexistent. In other words, Mr. McPherson, you don't have to worry about turning into a zombie anytime soon."

Firecracker grinned. "Too bad," he said. "It sounds like fun."

The class laughed, but Mrs. Hotchkiss shook her head. "It was *not* fun, Mr. McPherson," she said, her voice serious. "None of you have seen a real zombie. But I have. Most people my age have. Your parents probably have. Those who were infected with the virus suffered horribly. The only consolation for those of us who saw them suffer was that by the time they turned, they had stopped being human. They didn't know what they were."

"Why did they torch them?"

Josh's attention was brought back to the class by the question. It had come from Elizabeth Stalin, who sat right behind him.

Mrs. Hotchkiss hesitated a moment. "The zombie flu virus was initially passed on through saliva," she said. "A zombie would bite someone, and the virus would enter the person's bloodstream. Once it was in the blood, the virus could then be passed on through that. If someone had an open cut—or any kind of wound that exposed the body to potential infection—coming into contact with zombie blood was dangerous. It was feared that the virus might become airborne next, which would have been disastrous. So it was decided that the least risky and most efficient way to destroy the virus was to burn the zombies."

"But wouldn't that really hurt?" someone asked.

Again Mrs. Hotchkiss took some time before answering. "By that point the infected people were functioning solely on primitive reactions," she said. "Almost like puppets being controlled by strings that were being pulled by their reptilian brains. They most likely didn't know what was happening."

"Still, it must have hurt," Elizabeth insisted. "They still had nerves and stuff."

Firecracker turned around and looked at her. "Who cares?" he said. "They were *meatbags*, not people."

"Yeah," said another girl. "Besides, if people hadn't burned the zombies, they would have turned a lot of other people into zombies."

"The important thing is that we don't have to worry about it anymore," Mrs. Hotchkiss said. "As I said earlier, there hasn't been a documented case since before you were born."

Josh raised his hand. "Where did it come from?" he asked. "The virus, I mean."

"Nobody really knows," his teacher told him. "Most likely it was simply a very strong mutation. As you've seen, there was nothing supernatural about zombies. They were just people who got sick and essentially devolved into primitive life forms."

"My uncle says the Russians did it," Firecracker announced. "He says they wanted to wipe us out."

"Then they didn't do a very good job," said Mrs. Hotchkiss. "Just as many people turned in Russia as did here. I think your uncle has been watching a little too much television."

"He was a Torcher," Firecracker said defensively. "He should know."

"Yes," said Mrs. Hotchkiss. "Well, I'm sure we're all very thankful to him for his service. Now if you'll access sequence 1872-A, this will show you how the zombie flu virus interrupted the messages sent from one part of the brain to the others. This is going to be on your test on Friday, so let's go over it and see if there's anything you don't understand."

Josh keyed the number into his NoteTaker and looked at the diagram that appeared on the screen. He listened as his teacher went over the various parts, but mostly he was thinking about his aunt Lucy, his mother's sister. He'd never met her, but he'd seen pictures. She was really pretty, just like his mom.

And she had turned into a zombie.

She was only sixteen when she got sick, one of the first in the country to get the virus. He'd heard the story several times from his mother, but they didn't talk about it too much because it made his mother sad. And Josh didn't talk about it with anyone else. Not even Firecracker knew. Josh wasn't sure why he didn't tell anyone. He wasn't ashamed, exactly. Having a zombie in your family wasn't the terrible thing it had once been; it just wasn't something most people talked about.

I guess it doesn't really make it any better to know that she was just sick, he thought. It was amazing that something as tiny as a virus could turn someone into a monster like that. *But she probably didn't even know it was happening,* he told himself.

Mrs. Hotchkiss continued to talk about zombies, and for a change Josh listened to every word. When he heard the bell ring, he was actually disappointed that class was over. Reluctantly he gathered up his things and filed into the hallway along with everyone else. Firecracker caught up with him as he walked to his locker.

"You up for hunting reptile brains tonight?" he asked.

"You know I am," said Josh.

"Excellent," Firecracker said. "We've got some work to do if we want to get our rankings back." He punched Josh hard in the shoulder. "And this time, try not to screw up."

"Hey!" Josh protested. "You're the one who got—"

But Firecracker was already making his way upstairs to his next class.

"Bit!" Josh shouted after him. "*You* got bit!"

3

"All right, let's do this."

Josh spoke into the small microphone mounted inside his helmet as he prepared to play. He had already put on the interactive gloves that allowed him to move his character through the holographic landscape as if he were really there. When he looked through the lenses of his helmet, instead of his room he saw the front doors of the downtown public library building.

The creators of the game had mapped the entire city, and gamers could play in holographic recreations of every building, subway, and sewer. The zombie generator was random, so any place you went into could be infested with the creatures.

Josh leaned back in his chair and took a deep breath, allowing the sense stimulators in his helmet to kick in. They allowed him to feel, smell, and sometimes even taste things he came into contact with during the game. Of course some sensations—like zombie bites or the effects of torching—were blocked to prevent players from becoming overstimulated. Still, when those things happened in a game, the sounds and sights alone were enough to make a player imagine what it would feel like.

He knew he shouldn't be playing, but he couldn't resist. Torching was exciting. Hunting for z's and wiping them out made him feel like a real soldier. He loved the way he got more and more tense as he searched for the zombies, the way his senses became so intensely focused as he worried about staying alive and saving the other humans. He especially liked the adrenaline rush that came when he finally found the z's and torched them.

He looked to his right, where Firecracker stood checking the controls on his flamethrower. "Ready?" Josh asked.

"Let's torch some meatbags," Firecracker answered. He flipped the safety on his flamethrower, which erupted in a short burst of fire.

"Easy," Josh warned him. "We don't want to burn the place down."

Josh pushed open the huge door, which swung inward with a groan, and he and Firecracker stepped into the cavernous lobby of the library. The marble floor stretched away into the darkness, while the ceiling towered four floors above them. Books, most of them torn apart, were strewn everywhere. A thick smear of blood ran the length of the circulation desk, as if a body had been dragged along it.

Josh followed the trail to the end, and saw the body of a woman crumpled among a pile of books. Firecracker approached the woman, his flamethrower held out in front of him. When he was a dozen feet away from her, he turned back to Josh. "She's gone," he said. "Well, her head is, and she's not going anywhere without it."

"Just leave her there," Josh said. "We'll clean up on the way out."

Leaving the woman behind, he and Firecracker advanced deeper into the library. Josh listened for any sound of moaning or shuffling, but there was nothing. Then, all of a sudden, a figure burst from the shadows. Josh aimed his flamethrower at it, but a voice called out, "Don't shoot! I'm human!"

"Stand down!" Josh ordered Firecracker, who he could see was itching to set something on fire. Reluctantly Firecracker lowered his weapon.

The figure came closer, and Josh saw that it was a girl. She wasn't dressed in a Torcher uniform, which meant that she was part of the game, a character generated by the system itself. These characters made the game even more fun, but they could also make it more difficult, especially if they got in the way.

The girl was wearing a fluffy black fur jacket with a white hood. The hood had two small, round, black ears on it, and around the girl's eyes were large black circles. Josh looked down and saw that she was wearing white fur shorts and knee-high boots made out of black fur. *She's supposed to be a panda bear,* he thought.

"Great," said Firecracker. "A Zooey."

Zooeys were a problem. In real life they were people who liked to dress as animals. They listened to Japanese pop music and spent their time watching horror movies and eating candy. They were freaky but harmless, and Josh had no problem with the Zooeys generated by the game. In the game, though, they were unreliable. Sometimes they gave you good information, but sometimes they just made stuff up—stuff that would get you killed if you weren't careful.

"What are you doing here?" Josh asked the Zooey.

"Nothing," the girl said. She was breathing heavily and kept looking behind her.

"Nothing?" said Firecracker. "You mean you always run around the library playing hide-and-seek?"

"Okay," the girl admitted. "We wanted to see them for ourselves."

Firecracker groaned. "Of course you did," he said. "Stupid tourists."

"What's your name?" Josh asked.

He wasn't surprised when the girl answered, "Pandy."

"How many of you are there?"

"Just two," she said. "Me and Monkey. Oh, and Rabbit. I guess that's three."

Firecracker looked at Josh. "Please just let me torch her," he said.

"No," Josh answered. "We could lose points."

Pandy came closer, and Josh saw that there was blood on the fur of her jacket. He also saw that one hand was covered in a mitten that resembled a bear paw. The other mitten dangled from a string attached to Pandy's jacket. The nails on that hand were painted bubble-gum pink.

"We were downstairs," Pandy said. "In the children's section. Monkey was reading to us from *Alice in Wonderland*," she continued. "Then one of *them* came out of nowhere. It grabbed Monkey and it . . ." Her voice trailed off as she started to cry.

"Yeah, yeah," Firecracker said. "It bit her. We know the routine."

Pandy hiccuped as she tried to stop crying. "It all happened so fast," she sobbed.

"It's all right," Josh said. "We'll find your friends."

"What about me?" Pandy asked. "Don't leave me here."

"Go outside," Josh told her. "Wait on the front steps."

"But my friends!" Pandy wailed.

"We *said* we'll find them and take care of them," Firecracker reminded her. He flicked his flame-thrower on, and Pandy's eyes grew wide.

"Go outside," Josh said again. "Now."

Pandy obeyed, running for the front door and disappearing outside. Josh checked his flamethrower to make sure it was on, then nodded for Firecracker to follow him.

"If I'd known we were going to be on a Zooey rescue mission, I would have picked the sewer assignment," Firecracker said.

"Humans are humans," Josh reminded him. "We get the same amount of credit whether we save a Zooey or the mayor."

"I know," said Firecracker. "But half the time they're just lying. It drives me nuts."

As they walked down the wide staircase that descended to the lower level, Josh looked for any signs of activity. Halfway down they came upon something that looked like a giant cotton ball. Josh bent down to look at it and saw that it was covered in blood.

"I'm guessing Rabbit didn't make it," Firecracker said.

"Looks that way," Josh agreed. "Be careful. I have a feeling we're close."

They reached the lower level. The children's section wasn't as large as the upstairs, but it was big enough that they couldn't see from one end to the other. The walls were papered with cheerful posters featuring favorite characters from children's books, and the reading tables and chairs were less than half the size of those in the rest of the library. Josh felt like a giant as he walked through the room.

Suddenly a high-pitched whistling sound broke the silence. Josh looked up and saw a zombie shuffling toward them. It was a woman wearing a blood-splattered dress and shaking a finger at them. The whistling sound came from a jagged hole in her throat.

As the zombie got closer, Josh saw that she was wearing a name tag: MRS. JARVIS, CHILDREN'S LIBRARIAN.

"A meatbag librarian?" Firecracker said, sounding disgusted.

Josh aimed at her with his flamethrower. "Sorry, Mrs. Jarvis," he said. "I'm afraid you're overdue."

"Josh!"

The noise made him jump. He ripped his helmet off and whirled around. "Emily, I thought we had a deal!" he yelled, expecting to see his sister standing behind him.

"Oh, really?" said his mother. "And what kind of deal would that be?"

Josh dropped the helmet and jumped up, trying to block the screen. "Mom," he said. "I was just—"

"I see what you were doing," she said. She walked over and turned the simulator off. The library disappeared.

"But Firecracker!" Josh protested. "And my points!"

"Josh, you know how we feel about that game," his mother said. "You were supposed to be doing homework."

"I was just playing for a few minutes," Josh argued. "I don't see why you make such a big deal about killing a few zom—"

He saw his mother's face grow pale. "I'm sorry," he said quickly. "I didn't mean to—"

"Sit down," she interrupted.

Josh sat in the chair at his desk. His mother

remained standing. "I really am sorry, Mom," Josh said.

"Just—just listen for a minute," his mother told him.

Josh nodded.

"I know that to you this is just a game," his mother said. "You're young. The war probably seems like ancient history. But for those of us who lived through it, it wasn't a game." Her voice caught.

"Aunt Lucy," said Josh, feeling horrible for hurting his mother's feelings.

His mother was quiet for a moment. When she looked at Josh, he saw sadness in her eyes. "She wasn't much older than you are now when she turned," she said. "I'll never forget coming home from school that day."

Josh didn't say anything. His mother had never shared the details of what had happened. He found himself both wanting to know and wishing she wouldn't tell him.

His mother continued. "We thought she just had the flu, so she'd stayed home for a few days. That day I'd gotten her homework assignments from her teachers so that she wouldn't get behind. When I went into the kitchen, there was a pot on the stove. My mother had been making chicken soup." She smiled. "She always made chicken soup when one of us didn't feel well," she said. "But it was boiling over, as if something had interrupted my mother while she was cooking."

She took a deep breath. "That's when I saw the blood," she told Josh. "It started in the doorway and went into the dining room. I remember following it and wondering what it could be. My brain didn't want to believe it was blood, even though I could smell it." She shook her head. "I'll never forget that smell, not as long as I live."

Josh almost told her to stop, but his mouth wouldn't work. His heart was beating more quickly, almost as if he were playing the game. He hated seeing his mother upset, but he wanted to hear the rest of the story.

"I followed the blood up the stairs to Lucy's room," said his mother. Her voice was shaky. She stopped speaking, and when she looked at Josh she seemed to be looking right through him at something only she could see. "My father was on the floor," she said. "One of his arms had been ripped off, and his head was turned so that it looked like he was staring at me, but he was dead. My mother was lying on the bed. Lucy was kneeling over her. Her face and her nightgown were covered in blood."

The room was completely silent as Josh waited for his mother to continue. She continued to look through him.

"What did you do?" Josh asked, his voice barely a whisper.

His mother shook her head. "I didn't do anything," she said. "Not for a long time. I told myself I was dreaming and that I would wake up and Lucy would be sitting peacefully in bed, eating chicken soup."

She blinked, and now she *was* looking at Josh. "Then Lucy saw me," she said, her voice harder. "She looked right at me, and when I saw her eyes, I knew my sister was gone. When she jumped off the bed and came at me, I ran to my room and shut the door. Lucy was screaming and grunting and clawing at the door like a rabid animal. I knew that if she got in, she would tear me apart. I had my cell phone, and I called 911 and told the operator that my sister had gone crazy. She stayed on the phone with me until the police got there."

"The police?" Josh said.

"The Torchers hadn't been established yet," his mother explained. "They weren't formed until things got worse. And when Lucy turned, we didn't know about the zombies yet. I really did think she'd just gone crazy. When the police got there, I heard them shouting as they came upstairs. Then I heard Lucy run at them howling. And then I heard the shots."

She closed her eyes as a tear slipped out. "A minute

or two later someone knocked on my door and asked if I was all right," she said. "I said I was, and unlocked the door. But they told me to lie down on the floor in the middle of the room, and when they came in they pointed their rifles at me until they could look at my eyes. Even then they took me to the hospital and kept me there for a week to see if I showed any symptoms of infection."

Josh didn't know what to say. He imagined his mother in the hospital, knowing that her entire family was dead, not knowing what she would do when she got out. She'd been younger than he was now. He didn't know if he could handle something like that. He tried to find a way to apologize to his mother, but everything he thought of sounded stupid.

"It wasn't just what happened to Lucy that was so terrifying," his mother said after a while. "I mean at first it was, of course. But as the virus spread and changed, the fear became something worse. It was not knowing if, or when, you might get sick. It was not knowing which of your friends might be next. It was being afraid that the world was coming to an end."

"But it didn't," Josh reminded her, looking for anything that might make the conversation less depressing.

"No, it didn't," his mother agreed. "But when I see

people—see you—treating the war like it's fun, it's very upsetting. The war was not fun, Josh. It was not a game. Torching the zombies was something that had to be done, but nobody *liked* doing it."

She paused for a moment, then continued, "I know you think the hologame is exactly the way it was. But you can always turn off a game. We couldn't turn off what was happening to us. We couldn't hit a button and get rid of the stench of burning flesh. We couldn't remove a helmet and be back safe and sound in our rooms. We couldn't hit reset and bring people back from the dead."

She looked right at Josh. "You don't know what it was like, Josh. And no matter how much you play that game, you never will."

Josh nodded. "I guess you're right," he said.

"The game is disrespectful," his mother said. "That's the best way to put it. Turning a war into a game minimizes how horrible it was for the people who fought in it, lived through it—died in it," she finished.

"I never thought of it that way," Josh admitted. "But I'm not killing people. I'm killing meatbags."

"What did you call them?" his mother asked. Her face was reddening.

"It's just what we call the zombies," Josh explained.

"It doesn't mean anything. Besides—"

"Is that what you think your aunt Lucy was?" his mother cut in. "A bag of meat?"

"No!" Josh objected. "But that's different. She was a person."

"*All* the zombies were real people," his mother said. "Every last one of them. Don't you ever forget that."

"I said I was sorry," Josh said defensively. He thought his mother was being a little unreasonable. The z's he torched in the game were not real people.

His mother sighed, and Josh waited for her to tell him he was grounded, or that they were going to take away his computer. He held his breath, hoping his punishment wouldn't be too bad.

"I'm not going to tell you not to play the game anymore," she said. "I've told you how your father and I feel about it. I'm going to leave the decision about whether or not to play up to you."

"Me?" Josh repeated.

His mother nodded. "It's up to you," she affirmed. "And I think you'll make the right decision." She walked to the door. "Dinner's in five minutes."

When she was gone, Josh leaned back in his chair. *The right decision,* he thought. He knew what *she* thought the right decision was. But what did *he* think? After hearing his mother talk about what had happened with Aunt Lucy, he felt horrible about ever having played. He understood now why the game upset his mother so much. But like he'd told her, it was still just a game. Not playing it wouldn't erase what had happened.

He wondered if this was some kind of trick, if his mother was testing him to see what he would do. She'd said the decision was up to him, but if he chose to keep playing, would she punish him anyway?

A beeping sound interrupted his thoughts, and Josh looked over at his desk. The light on his computer screen was blinking, signaling a message. *It's probably Firecracker letting me know what a loser I am,* Josh thought as he went and clicked on the message.

Josh:
Good game. Meet me tomorrow.
1600. Yancy Square Park.
Charlie

Charlie? Josh thought. *Charlie who?*

Then it dawned on him. *The* Charlie. *The best player in the game* Charlie. Charlie wanted to meet *him*? But how did he know who Josh was? Josh read the note over but couldn't make any sense of it. Why had Charlie said "good game" when Josh had blown it? Again.

"This has been a really weird day," Josh told himself as he stood up to go downstairs. "A *seriously* weird day."

4

The boy with the skull mask was the least bizarre of the people waiting on the platform when Josh got off the elevated train at Yancy Street the next afternoon. Two girls dressed identically as baby dolls, complete with pigtails tied with pink ribbons and holding oversized lollipops, turned their heavily made-up faces toward him and laughed loudly as he passed by. A man wearing a Santa suit held a burning stick to his mouth and blew a cloud of fire into the air as a small crowd watched and clapped. When he held out his fur-trimmed hat for them to put coins into it, a little boy not more than five years old snatched it from his hand and ran down the long flight of stairs. Santa followed him, cursing loudly.

Welcome to the Docklands, Josh thought as he descended the opposite set of stairs. It wasn't that the Docklands was dangerous, exactly. It was just weird.

The Docklands was where the city's street people lived—not just the outright homeless (although there were lots of them there) but also the runaways and castoffs and people who didn't fit in anywhere else. Walking around there always made Josh feel like he was at a Halloween party. He wondered why Charlie had chosen this part of town to meet in.

"Hey, guy. Want some dust?"

Josh shook his head at the person speaking to him, a boy about his own age whose skin was the light blue of a Duster. His eyes, like those of everyone who used a lot of dust, were a peculiar mix of iridescent blue and purple swirling around a gold pupil in a hypnotizing pattern. He wore only white leather shorts and a harness from which sprouted a pair of white feathered wings. As soon as Josh passed him, the boy asked the same question of someone else: "Want some dust?"

Josh walked to the corner and entered Yancy Square Park. Like the streets, it was filled with all kinds of people. Some sat or slept on benches. Others stood in small groups, talking loudly and smoking. Josh walked through the park, looking at the faces for someone who might be Charlie. Eventually he came to a large fountain. In the center was a raised cube of brushed aluminum that stood on metal legs a dozen feet tall. Water poured from holes in the cube, falling down into the deep aluminum bowl below. On top of the cube stood the statue of a man.

Josh knew who it was. Drax Jittrund, the most famous Torcher of all time. He had led the forces that had cleaned the city of zombies. He'd fought bravely alongside his men, torching thousands of zombies himself before he'd been bitten during a final mission deep in the city's sewers. He'd ordered his men to torch him.

Josh sat on the edge of the bowl. He looked at his watch. It was just past four. The school day had been torture. All he'd been able to think about was meeting Charlie. As soon as the last bell rang, he'd raced out of there.

"Waiting for someone?"

Josh turned to see a girl looking at him. Her features were Asian, her eyes as dark as her hair. She was dressed in jeans and a white T-shirt underneath a battered leather jacket. The T-shirt said MISSION OF BURMA. Her feet were encased in heavy black boots with thick heels that made her a good five inches taller than she really was.

"A friend," Josh answered. "I'm meeting him here."

"Want to see a trick?" asked the girl. She held out a pack of cards. "Take one."

Josh looked at the cards.

"Go on," the girl said. "Pick one. If I guess right, you give me a dollar. And if I guess wrong, I give you something."

Normally Josh would have walked away. But something about the girl made him want to stay. He liked her, even though he was sure she was scamming him.

"Okay," he said.

He reached out and took a card from the pack the girl had fanned out in her hand. He was surprised to see it wasn't an ordinary playing card but a tarot card with a picture of a stone tower. Lighting was striking the top of the tower, and several people were falling from it. It was a disturbing picture, and Josh found himself wanting to hand the card back.

"Hold on," said the girl. "I haven't guessed yet." She closed her eyes and scrunched up her eyebrows. She made a series of faces, moving her mouth around and seeming to get more and more frustrated. Finally she opened her eyes. "That was hard," she said. "But I think I've got it. You have the eight of pentacles."

Josh shook his head. "Nope," he said. He held the card up so that she could see it.

"The tower," the girl said. She shook her head and sighed. "That one always tricks me." Then her face brightened and she smiled. "But that means *you* win," she told Josh.

Josh smiled. "All right," he said. "So what do I get?"

"How about I tell you where your friend is?" the girl said.

Josh laughed. "You don't even know who I'm waiting for," he said.

The girl looked at him, her eyes sparkling. "Charlie," she said.

Josh stopped smiling. "How did you know that?"

"I know a lot of things, Josh," said the girl.

"How—" Josh started. He stared at her for a moment as his brain put the pieces together. "Wait. *You're* Charlie?"

"Not quite what you expected?" the girl asked.

Josh nodded. "Yeah," he said. "I mean—"

"I know what you mean," said Charlie. "You were expecting someone taller. Now come on. Let's go somewhere we can talk."

Charlie led the way back through the park. When they came to the statue of Drax Jittrund, she stopped and fished some coins from the pocket of her jeans. She tossed them into the water. "For good luck," she told Josh.

Outside the park, Charlie walked about a block

before pushing open the door of a small noodle shop. Josh followed her inside. The air was crazy with the sound of a language he didn't understand. But Charlie spoke to a woman in the same language, and the woman pointed to a table at the back of the crowded room.

"I hope you like dumplings," Charlie said when they were seated. "I ordered some for us."

"Sure," Josh said, shrugging. He couldn't help staring at Charlie.

"What?" Charlie said. "You don't like dumplings?"

"No," Josh said quickly. "It's just that I still can't believe you're a girl."

Charlie rolled her eyes. "Get over it," she said. "That whole 'girls don't game' thing is so 2010."

Josh blushed. "I know," he said. "It's just a surprise, is all."

A waiter set a small cast-iron teapot and two small cups on their table and scurried away. Charlie poured tea into the cups and handed one to Josh. The steam that rose from it smelled like oranges. He held the cup in his hands and breathed it in.

"It's easier if people think I'm a guy," Charlie said. "It might be 2032, but boys still don't like to be beaten by girls. And anyway, I like being invisible."

"Why?" Josh asked.

"It has its uses," said Charlie. "Anyway, I didn't ask you here to talk about me. I want to talk about you. I've been watching you. I like your playing style."

Josh snorted. "Apparently you haven't seen my last few missions," he said.

Charlie nodded. "You had some problems," she said. "It happens. It's not like you have the best partner."

"Firecracker?" Josh said.

"The guy has no style," Charlie said. "He just bull-dozes his way through the missions. If you weren't around, he'd be demoted to noob status in no time."

"I don't think he's *that* bad," Josh said as the waiter returned and set a steaming bowl of dumplings on the table.

"He is," said Charlie, picking up some chopsticks and using them to pluck a dumpling. "But you, you're good."

Josh tried to pick up a dumpling, but it fell. He tried again and failed. But the third time he managed to catch the slippery dumpling between the sticks and raise it to his mouth. He popped it in before it could fall.

"See?" Charlie said. "You're a fast learner."

"Thanks," Josh mumbled as he chewed the dumpling. He didn't know what else to say. Had Charlie really asked him to come down here just to compliment his playing style?

"I have a little proposition for you," Charlie said.

Josh raised an eyebrow. "What kind of proposition?"

"You've heard about the IRL games, right?" she asked in a low voice.

IRL. In real life. *Of course I've heard of them,* Josh thought. Everybody had. Everybody who played the game, anyway. Supposedly there were gamers who got together and played the game for real. The story was that there were still some places in the country where zombies turned up from time to time. When they did, gamers who were in on the secret would go and hunt them down. Only it was an urban legend, like the rats the size of dogs that supposedly lived in the sewers.

"Sure," Josh said. "I've also heard of the sandman and the tooth fairy." He started to pick up another dumpling, but it fell onto the table.

"What would you say if I told you the games *are* real and that I'm inviting you to play?" Charlie asked.

Josh poked at the dumpling, and it slid away from him. "Right," he said, laughing.

Charlie reached out with her chopsticks and expertly scooped up the dumpling. "I only ask once," she said, and put the dumpling in her mouth. "Yes or no?"

Josh stared at her. "You're serious," he said. "You play in the IRL games?"

"Keep it down," Charlie ordered. "You might think no one in here understands you, but you'd be surprised who's listening." She cast an eye at the waiter who was shuttling bowls of noodles from the kitchen to the tables. Then she looked back at Josh. "The games aren't quite what people say they are, but they're pretty close to it. And like I said, I only ask once, so what's it going to be?"

Josh hesitated. He was already pushing things with his parents by playing the online game. What would they say if they knew he was playing it in real life? *But how can you pass this up?* he asked himself. Before he could talk himself out of it, he spoke. "Yes," he said. "Absolutely."

Charlie smiled, although for a moment Josh thought maybe he saw something in her eyes that said she wasn't completely happy that he'd accepted. But then it was gone. "Great," she said. "I knew you would." She stood up. "I've got to go. Meet me in the park tomorrow. Same time."

"Wait," Josh said. He wanted to ask Charlie just *how* real the game was. Like where did the zombies come from? But that was a dumb question. Of course they didn't hunt real zombies. "What should I bring?"

he asked instead. "I mean, I don't have any gear or anything."

"Don't worry about it," Charlie told him. "I'll take care of you. Just show up." She turned to go, then turned back. "And don't tell anyone," she said. "About me or about the game."

Something about the look she gave him chilled Josh. Her eyes were hard, and she wasn't smiling. He nodded quickly. "No worries," he said. "I won't say anything."

Charlie's friendly grin returned. "Great," she said. "I'll see you tomorrow."

Josh watched her go. As soon as the door closed behind her, the waiter came over and slapped down a bill. "Pay up front," he said, frowning.

5

"**W**hat's with you today?"

Josh looked up from his lunch. "Sorry," he said to Firecracker, who was looking at him as he chewed a bite of his sandwich. "What did you say?"

"I said we need to get busy on our planetary geography project," Firecracker said. "Our presentation is tomorrow."

Josh groaned. He'd forgotten about the project. He and Firecracker were supposed to do a report on how Antarctica was becoming a rain forest because of global warming, then do a presentation to the class. But they'd done almost no work on it. Every time they started to, they ended up playing the game instead.

"Tell you what," Firecracker said. "If you do the written paper, I'll do all the presentation stuff. Maps. An animated timeline. Maybe a holographic model. How's that sound?"

"Sure," Josh said. "You're better at the talking part anyway."

"And you're the word guy," Firecracker agreed. "Between us, we're looking at an A."

"A-plus," said Josh.

"So what's going on?" Firecracker asked a moment later. "You've been weird all day."

"No, I haven't!" Josh objected. "I'm just . . . thinking."

"Don't think too hard," said Firecracker. "You'll wear your brain out."

Josh laughed. "You should talk," he fired back.

"It's your mom, right?" said Firecracker. "You feel guilty about her catching you the other night when we were playing the game." He popped a potato chip into his mouth and chewed loudly.

Josh hesitated a moment before answering. Firecracker often had a weird way of knowing what Josh was thinking, but this time he was wrong. Although it was a good guess, what was really bothering Josh was that he couldn't tell Firecracker about his meeting with Charlie. If Firecracker knew the live games were real, he would be even more excited than Josh. But Josh couldn't do anything that would risk Charlie telling him to forget it.

"I guess I feel a little guilty," he lied. "She was really upset."

"Maybe we should lay off for a while," said Firecracker.

"What?" Josh said, shocked to hear Firecracker suggest such a thing.

"Just for a while," said Firecracker. "A week. Maybe two. Long enough for her to forget about it. It's not like we'll die if we don't play." He upended the bag of chips and tapped the remaining crumbs into his mouth.

Josh was about to protest when he realized that Firecracker had just given him the perfect way to hide what he was doing—not from his mother, but from his best friend. Still, he felt like the worst friend in the world as he said, "You're sure you're okay with that?"

Firecracker nodded. "It's no big deal," he said. "Besides, you'd do it for me."

Josh's heart sank. "Thanks," he said as he got up. "I'll talk to you later, okay?"

"You got it," Firecracker said. "You want to check out the new mechaspiders at the Menagerie after school? I'm thinking of getting a tarantula."

"Sorry," Josh said. "That would be cool, but I've got a dentist's appointment."

"Gotcha. I'll call you later tonight, then."

The rest of the day seemed to crawl by, but finally the last class was over and Josh hurried out of school. He avoided his usual route to the subway, taking the long way so he wouldn't run into Firecracker. Only when he was on the train heading downtown did he relax a little bit.

Charlie was waiting for him at the statue of Drax Jittrund. She was wearing pink pants and a bright orange leather jacket over an aqua-blue turtleneck. Her hair was done up in pigtails.

"I thought we were trying to be inconspicuous," Josh said.

"In case you haven't noticed, this *is* inconspicuous in the Docklands," said Charlie. "You ready to go?"

"I don't know," Josh replied sarcastically. "I think I'd rather be doing homework."

Charlie laughed. "Well, I'd hate to lose you to the thrill of working out math equations. Come on."

They left the park and headed into the heart of the Docklands. As they walked through the narrow streets, the shops became more and more unusual. Windows filled with shoes and clothes turned into windows filled with real books and antique toys. Josh stopped to look at an old video-game system. "My grandfather had one of those," he told Charlie. "Can you believe the games used to come on *cartridges*?"

"You can find pretty much anything in the Docklands," Charlie told him, taking him by the arm and pulling him away from the window. "But that's not why we're here."

After about ten minutes of walking, they came to the docks that gave the area its name. This was where the huge ships came to unload their cargo. Josh was a little bit nervous about being in what he'd always been told was a dangerous part of the city.

"Don't worry," Charlie told him. "No one's going to bother us."

Josh started to ask her how she could be so sure about that, but something stopped him. Charlie had a confidence about her that seemed to grow the deeper they moved into the Docklands. It was like she'd lived there her whole life, and it occurred to Josh that maybe she had. After all, he didn't know anything about her.

"Down here," Charlie said, pulling Josh into a narrow alleyway that ran between two buildings. Josh, growing more and more nervous, followed her.

When they reached the end of the alley, Josh realized that one wall had a door set into it. Charlie pulled a key on a chain from inside her turtleneck. She inserted the key into the door's rusted lock and turned it. Josh heard something grind inside the door, and then it swung inward.

"After you," Charlie said with a sweep of her hand.

Josh stepped inside and found himself on a small metal platform. Stairs ran down from it to another landing, and then more stairs continued down from that. Light came in from a dirty skylight revealing a series of platforms and stairs going down seemingly forever. Josh felt a shiver of anxiety pass through him, and he gripped the railing that ran along the exposed side of the platform.

"You're not afraid of heights, are you?" Charlie asked as she stepped inside, closed the door, and locked it.

"Maybe a little," Josh admitted.

"Just don't look down," said Charlie as she started to descend.

Josh followed her as Charlie went down and down and down. "What is this place?" he asked Charlie.

"A playing field," Charlie answered. "You'll see."

Finally they reached the end of the stairs. They were in a concrete passageway. The walls were damp, and here and there water trickled down from the low ceiling. The air was cold and smelled slightly sour. Josh looked up and noticed that there were video cameras every thirty feet or so.

"Looks like someone is keeping an eye on us," he remarked.

Charlie followed his gaze. "Those are left over from

when this place was used by the shipping company," she said quickly. "They haven't worked in years."

The cameras didn't look that old to Josh, but he didn't say anything. He didn't want to get into a disagreement with Charlie over something so stupid.

They came to another set of steps and went up this time. Suddenly the narrow hallway opened into a cavernous space filled with rusted pieces of metal. Lights somewhere far above them illuminated the skeleton of a huge ship occupying the center of the room, and several other smaller ships in various stages of completion were strewn throughout the enormous space. Scaffolding covered them, although it was obvious that no one had worked on the ships in years. Tools of all kinds littered the floor, and thick chains hung from the rafters like gigantic vines.

"Cool, huh?" Charlie said.

"This is amazing," Josh said, turning around and around as he tried to take in everything there was to see. "But we've got to be, what, a couple hundred feet underground? How did this all get down here?"

"They used to build ships here," Charlie explained. "Way back when, before they invented hydrogen-cell technology."

"Yeah," said Josh, eyeing the wooden planks. "These are definitely old school."

"These weren't just regular ships," Charlie explained. "They were used for smuggling. People would secretly build and fill the ships here. Then, when they were done, they flooded the room and the ships were raised up to the surface. There are big doors up there"—she pointed up into the dark—"that open into channels that run to the ocean."

"How do you know all this?" Josh asked.

"Clatter told me," Charlie said.

"I did indeed," said a voice. A moment later a figure emerged from the wreckage of the huge ship and walked toward them. Tall and thin, he was dressed in a strange outfit consisting of a very old-fashioned black suit and a top hat. As he moved he made a strange noise, which Josh soon realized was the rattling of hundreds of keys that were sewn onto his coat. They were the old kind—skeleton keys, Josh thought they were called—with long, thin, round bodies and elaborately curled ends. *That explains his name,* Josh thought.

Clatter had long, dark hair that fell onto his shoulders in limp strands. His skin was pale, and he wore steel-rimmed glasses with gray glass lenses. His hands were encased in black leather gloves, and on one finger he wore a gold ring with a very large red stone. Josh was surprised that Clatter seemed to be only a few years older than he and Charlie were.

"You must be Josh," Clatter said. His voice was silky smooth, almost serpentine, as if the words flowed from his mouth like water. "I've heard so much about you."

"Really?" Josh said, genuinely surprised.

"Charlie says you have great natural talent," Clatter continued. "And she ought to know. She's one of the best I've ever discovered."

Josh looked over at Charlie, who was beaming with pride.

"You must be wondering what you're doing here," Clatter said.

"I hear we're going to play a game," Josh said.

"Perhaps we are," said Clatter, smiling. "As Charlie told you, she is part of a group of people who play the game in its purest form. That is to say, in real life."

Josh nodded. "Right," he said. "She did."

Clatter smiled, his mouth forming a thin line across his face. "Well, you might say that I am the . . . master of ceremonies . . . for these games. I seek out the most talented players and bring them here." He swept his hand around the graveyard of ships. "To the arena."

But what do you get out of it? Josh wondered.

"I enjoy watching players who are good at what they do," said Clatter, seemingly reading Josh's thoughts. "It's a beautiful thing, almost like a . . .

ballet," he concluded. "It gives me pleasure."

Josh looked at Charlie. She gave him a quick nod, as if to say everything was okay.

"So how does this work?" he asked.

"You're eager," Clatter said. "I like that. You're going to play in a game with the rest of the team. After I've observed you in action, I'll decide whether or not you're a good fit. If you are, you'll be asked to join."

"And if you don't think I am?" Josh asked.

Clatter smiled again. "Let's hope that won't be the case," he said.

Josh nodded. "Okay," he said. "When do we play?"

Clatter snapped his fingers, and half a dozen figures materialized from out of the ships. "As I always say, there's no time like the present."

6

The group of figures approached, their faces becoming clearer as they stepped into the light. There were four boys and two girls, all of them around Josh's age. They were dressed in black Torcher uniforms, and they each carried a flamethrower. They flanked Clatter, three on a side, and looked at Josh with unreadable expressions on their faces. Suddenly he was nervous.

"This is my team," Clatter said. He pointed to the first Torcher, a tall, muscular boy with dark brown skin and a thick, pinkish scar running diagonally across the bridge of his nose and down past his lip. "This is Scrawl, the team captain. He's been with me the longest."

Josh nodded at Scrawl, who fixed his dark eyes on Josh and didn't blink. Clatter continued with the introductions. "Then we have Seamus and Finnegan," he said, indicating a short boy with pale skin and black hair and a tall boy with equally pale skin but red hair. "Believe it or not, they're twins."

"Hey," the two boys said in unison, nodding.

"Our last man is Stash," said Clatter. A heavy boy with thick arms, thick legs, and a thick neck looked back at Josh. His fat cheeks were tinged bright pink, and his blond hair was shaved into a crew cut. As Josh watched, he took a handful of nuts out of his pocket, cracked the shell from one, and popped the nut into his mouth. He dropped the shell on the ground.

Pistachio, Josh thought, looking at it. *Stash. Very funny.*

He wanted to laugh, but he knew that would be a mistake. Whatever was happening, everyone was taking it very seriously. He flashed a smile at Stash, who nodded curtly.

"And then we have the ladies," said Clatter. "Allow me to introduce Freya and Black-Eyed Susan."

It was easy to tell which girl was which. One was slight, with long blond hair and bright blue eyes; the other was a beautiful Latina with dark hair and eyes. "Call me Bess," she said. "It takes less time."

"And of course you know Charlie," Clatter concluded. "Now let's get you geared up and get this game going." He clapped his hands together, which seemed to break the spell holding everyone in position.

Scrawl came over to Josh. "Come on," he said. "I'll show you the locker room." He turned back to the others. "The rest of you, go through the hit-and-run drill we practiced last week. I don't want any screwups this game."

Charlie smiled and waved at Josh. "See you soon," she said.

Scrawl walked through the ship graveyard with Josh beside him. Josh wanted to ask all kinds of questions, but he also wanted to look cool and collected, so he said nothing. To his relief, Scrawl did enough talking for both of them.

"So you're Charlie's friend," he said. "I hear you've got a good game going. Well, we've got the best gamers around on this team. You want to play with us, you've got to be *ready*. This isn't some weak-ass holographic game. This is the real thing."

They walked down a short corridor that ended at a wall. There were doors on both sides of the hall. "That's the girls' locker room," Scrawl said, indicating the left-hand door. "And this is ours."

He opened the door into a large room tiled all in white. Rows of lockers lined one wall, and there were long wooden benches bolted to the floor in front of them. On the other side of the room were four bathroom stalls, and through an archway Josh saw what appeared to be a communal shower area.

"I'll skip the guided tour," said Scrawl. "Your locker's over here."

He strode to one of the lockers and opened it. Inside a black uniform was hanging, a pair of black boots on the floor beneath it. "Put those on," Scrawl said, nodding at the contents of the locker.

Josh peeled off his T-shirt and hung it in the locker. Scrawl glanced at it. "You into comics?" he asked, nodding at the Batman logo on the shirt.

"Yeah," Josh said. "Are you?"

"Big-time," Scrawl answered. "Mostly the classic stuff. You ever been to the Pageteria?"

"The paper museum?" said Josh. "No.

Scrawl nodded. "My house is about a block away," he said. "It's great. They have actual newspapers, magazines, anything printed on paper from before Cybooks made them obsolete. They have a great exhibit of comic-book art up right now. You should check it out."

"That sounds cool," Josh said as he removed his shoes, shucked off his pants, and stepped into the one-piece uniform.

"This uniform may not look fancy," Scrawl said as Josh zipped himself up. "But built into the fabric are touch-sensitive threads. They send readings to a monitor back at base. Not only can the monitor read your heartbeat and body temperature, it can tell the difference between me just touching you and you falling down and you getting bit by a z."

Josh rubbed his hands over the uniform's material. The technology Scrawl was describing wasn't new, but he'd never heard of it being used in gaming before. "This is the stuff they make army uniforms out of," he said, impressed.

Scrawl grinned. "Clatter has some major contacts," he said. "Now get your boots on. We've got a game to play."

As they walked back to rejoin the others, Josh asked Scrawl the question he'd wanted to ask since Charlie had told him the game was real. "So if we're Torchers, who plays the zombies?"

"Don't worry about it," Scrawl answered. "Just worry about killing them."

"Well, look at you," Clatter said when Josh and Scrawl arrived. "You already look like one of the gang. All you need is this."

Clatter handed Josh a flamethrower. "You know how to use it, right?"

Josh examined the weapon. "No problem," he said.

"Try it out," said Clatter. "Pretend Seamus is a z. Take him out."

Josh hesitated.

"Just do it," Seamus told him.

Josh aimed the flamethrower at Seamus and pulled the trigger. Nothing happened, but a second later a buzzer sounded and a robotic woman's voice announced, "Torcher Seamus has been killed. I repeat, Torcher Seamus has been killed."

"But how—" Josh said.

"The thrower emits an electronic beam," Freya interrupted him. "If it hits you, it activates the sensors in your suit. As far as the monitor is concerned, you just fried Seamus."

Clatter laughed. "Not to worry," he told Josh, clapping a hand on his shoulder. "I'll go to the monitoring room and reset it. In the meantime, you all get ready to play." He turned to Scrawl. "Play will take place in sections one through four. There are three z's. Understood?"

"Yes."

"Ten minutes, then." Clatter looked at Josh. "Good luck," he said. "I do hope you'll survive."

"I'll try," Josh assured him.

"All right. Huddle up." Scrawl barked his orders like he meant them, and Josh and the others circled around him.

"You guys know what to do," he said, looking at each team member. When he came to Josh he stopped. "You're the new guy," he said. "But that doesn't mean you get to take it easy. This is *your* test, so I expect you to hold your own. Got it?"

Josh nodded. "Got it," he said.

Scrawl held his gaze for a long moment, then said, "Good. Here's the plan. Seamus and Finnegan, you two take section one. Bess and Stash, section two."

Stash groaned. "Not the sewer," he said. "How come I always get the sewer?"

Black-Eyed Susan punched him in the arm. "Maybe because you play like—"

"Section three is Freya's and Charlie's," Scrawl interrupted her.

Freya and Charlie high-fived. "Piece of cake," Charlie said.

Josh had been hoping that Charlie would be with him. It would have been nice to have a familiar face around during his first IRL game. Also, he knew how good she was.

"Josh and I will take section four," said Scrawl.

"What's section four?" Josh asked.

Stash laughed. "You're standing in it," he said.

"The ship graveyard?" Josh said, looking around. "But this place is huge. It will take us hours to cover it."

"Don't worry," said Bess, grinning. "The z's will find you soon enough."

A crackling sound came from out of the darkness, and Josh heard Clatter's voice. "The quarry are being released," he said. "The game will begin in three minutes. I suggest you get moving." Then the lights in the room dimmed, throwing the ships into shadow.

"You heard the man," Scrawl said. "Get your butts in gear."

As the others ran off, Charlie turned and gave Josh a thumbs-up. "Good luck," she called out. "I know you can do it."

Josh nodded. The game was beginning, and just as it did during the hologames, his heart was speeding up as adrenaline coursed through him. He wiped his sweaty hands on his suit and took a deep breath.

"It's go time," Scrawl said. "You know how to do a one-two sweep?"

"One guy goes in and drops, the other is right behind him ready to flame," Josh answered. "You use it when checking a hallway, room, or stairwell."

"Right," said Scrawl. "That's what we're going to do when we can. But a lot of this will be one-on-one. Just us and the meatbags. When that happens, there's just one rule."

"Shoot before they bite," Josh said automatically.

Hearing Scrawl call the z's meatbags made him think of his aunt Lucy and the talk he'd had with his mother, but he pushed that thought from his mind. *It's just a game,* he reminded himself.

"Good man." Scrawl started walking. "Let's head out."

They walked into the gloom, heading for the darker parts of the cavernous space first. Around them, pieces of machinery and the rusting hulls of ships rose up in twisted shapes. Josh kept his eyes and ears open. Although the hologame recreated the experience of being in a real place, this *was* real. He smelled the rusting metal and oil all around him. He felt the dirt and broken pieces of glass and metal under his boots.

He and Scrawl approached the largest ship. "This is as good a place as any to start," he said. "I'll take point."

Josh followed as Scrawl entered the ship through a large hole torn in the hull. As they passed through the ship's belly, Josh kept alert for any sign of zombie action. It was eerily silent, and even Josh's and Scrawl's footsteps were barely more than whispers.

Suddenly a sound came from their right, a noise like metal scraping against metal. Josh whirled and pointed his flamethrower. But Scrawl held out his hand, stopping him. Without saying anything, he nodded his head, telling Josh they should keep moving toward the sound.

They crossed the hold quickly but carefully. Josh scanned the floor, making sure he didn't trip over anything or give away their approach. Beside him, Scrawl moved catlike through the dark, his flamethrower moving from side to side as he looked for signs of z's.

When they reached a doorway, they stopped. Josh listened. He heard the scraping sound again, but this time it seemed to be above their heads. At first he didn't understand, but then Scrawl pointed up and moved his fingers in a walking motion. *Stairs,* Josh thought. *It's climbing some stairs.*

Scrawl motioned again, indicating that he would go first. He ducked into the stairwell, and Josh followed. As Scrawl dropped to one knee, Josh readied his flamethrower. But there was no sign of the zombie. Josh looked up and saw that the stairs went up into darkness. He heard something hit the floor above him and roll. Then there was a series of clanks as something fell between the stair railings and hit the next level.

Josh stepped back just as the item tumbled from the darkness and landed where he had been standing. He bent down and looked at it. It was a length of pipe, covered in rust. But something didn't look right about it. Josh reached out and touched the surface. His fingers came away sticky.

Blood, he realized. *One end is covered in blood.* And not just blood. A clump of hair came away from the pipe as well. Josh dropped it in disgust and looked at Scrawl. "That's real blood," he whispered. "Someone is really hurt. We have to help."

He started to go up the stairs, but Scrawl pulled him back. "No," he said quietly. "We have to play the game."

"But whoever that is—"

"It's part of the game," Scrawl said. "Understand?"

Josh began to object, but the tone of Scrawl's voice stopped him. *He's not joking around,* Josh thought.

Scrawl pointed up once more. Then he led as they climbed the stairs. Josh kept his eyes trained up, trying to see through the steps. But there was nothing. And no sound came either.

They climbed one level, then another. There was no sign of the zombie, and Josh's neck hurt from craning his head upward. He was starting to think that the game wasn't going well for him, and that Clatter would tell him he wasn't good enough to be on the team.

When they reached the third level, Josh looked

down to stretch his neck muscles and noticed that the platform was splattered with blood. Following the trail, he saw that it disappeared though a doorway. Tapping Scrawl on the arm, he nodded toward the opening. Then he held up one finger, letting Scrawl know that he would go first.

He stepped through the doorway and went into a crouch. Scrawl stepped in behind him. They were in a hallway. The blood trail continued before them. Josh stood up, and he and Scrawl began to move forward in the dimly lit corridor.

It's got to be here somewhere, Josh thought, trying not to think about how realistic the blood and hair on the pipe had looked.

The hallway ended about twenty yards from where they had entered. In front of them was a door covering a pass-through hatch. It was held closed by five thick bars of steel that radiated out like the arms of a starfish from a central wheel. Turning the wheel would retract the bars and open the door. There was blood on the wheel.

Josh turned to Scrawl. "It's through there," he said. "It must have gone through and closed the door from the other side." It was a pretty smart move for a zombie, and Josh wondered if the person playing the part wasn't being a little too clever.

Scrawl nodded in agreement. "Let's go," he said. "But be careful."

Josh set his flamethrower down. He reached out and, avoiding the blood, tried to turn the big wheel. But it was rusted shut. He put all his weight into it. Soon sweat was running down his face and his muscles ached, but no matter how hard he pushed or pulled, he couldn't budge it.

Suddenly a horrible roar came from behind him. Josh whirled around and saw a zombie standing in the doorway he and Scrawl had just come through. It was a woman. Her long hair was matted, and her face was covered with sores. Above her right eye was a huge gash. Her scalp was torn open. Blood oozed from the wound and ran down her cheek, which was streaked with dried gore. *She really looks like a meatbag,* Josh thought, impressed by all the trouble Clatter had taken to make the game more realistic. Still, Josh was kind of creeped out seeing something so gross in real life.

Scrawl dropped down and aimed his flamethrower at the zombie, who was shuffling toward them. Her mouth was open, and long strings of drool hung from her battered lips. She moaned loudly as she moved. *It almost sounds like she's trying to talk,* Josh thought as he raised his flamethrower.

He waited for Scrawl to shoot. As the Torcher closest to the z, he had first shot. But Scrawl seemed to be struggling with his flamethrower.

"It's jammed!" he cried out. "I can't fire!"

The zombie was getting closer, and the gurgling in her throat was getting louder as she neared her prey. She reached out her hands.

"Torch her!" Scrawl shouted. "Now!"

7

Scrawl flattened himself on the floor of the hallway and covered his head with his arms. Josh aimed his flamethrower at the zombie, who was only a dozen feet away now, and pulled the trigger.

Flames erupted from the end of the torch. Josh watched, shocked, as the ball of flame hurtled toward the z, hit her in the chest, and bloomed. The zombie let out an unearthly scream and began beating uselessly at the flames as they consumed her dress. She staggered back toward the door, her hair blazing and her face engulfed in flames.

Josh could only stare at her burning figure. His eyes saw that the zombie was on fire, but his mind couldn't understand what was happening. *It's not real,* he told himself. *It's just a game. The torch isn't supposed to really work.* Was it some kind of holographic trick? No, it was too real. Had he accidentally been given a real flamethrower instead of an electronic one?

The zombie managed to get out of the hallway, which was now brutally hot and filled with black smoke and the foul stench of burning meat. A moment later Josh heard a muffled *thud*.

"Come on," Scrawl said. "We've got to get out of here."

He and Josh ran for the doorway. When they exited onto the platform, Josh looked over the railing. Far below them the burning body of the z lay on the floor. Then, to his horror, the zombie moved. She pulled herself along with her hands, managing to get about ten feet before collapsing.

Scrawl scrambled quickly down the stairs. Josh followed. When they reached the bottom, they ran to the burning body. It was now nothing more than a charred mess, unrecognizable as anything approaching human. The flamethrower had done its job.

Josh heard a crackling sound. Then the robotic voice he'd heard earlier said, "The quarry has been eradicated. Please report back to the rendezvous site."

The lights went up and Josh blinked as his eyes adjusted. Scrawl turned and started to walk away, but Josh grabbed his arm. "Hold up," he said. "What just happened? That thing was real. The flamethrower is real. It's not supposed to work."

"It's a game," said Scrawl. "That's all."

He pulled his arm away from Josh's grip and kept walking. Josh took one more look at the smoking body of the zombie and trotted after Scrawl.

"*That* is real," he said. "You can't tell me it isn't."

"You did a good job," Scrawl said. "Well, except for taking us into a dead end. But you didn't know the door wouldn't open."

"And you did?" asked Josh.

Scrawl grinned. "Got you," he said. "The whole thing was set up to see how you'd do."

Josh's mouth fell open. "Then the z wasn't—"

"Cybernetic," Scrawl told him. "Clatter's a robotics genius. He builds them for fun. Pretty real, huh?"

Josh sighed. "Too real," he said. "I just about lost it when the torch shot flame."

Scrawl laughed. "I did too the first time," he said. "That's another of Clatter's tricks. He switches it on from the monitoring room."

"But I could have torched you!" Josh objected.

"No chance," said Scrawl. "Well, maybe a *small* chance, but Clatter doesn't make it live until he's sure you're in position and anyone with you is out of the way."

Josh found himself laughing with relief.

"The guy's a little bit nuts," said Scrawl. "But you've got to admit, that was intense."

"Yeah," Josh agreed. "It was."

"You liked it," said Scrawl. "I can see it in your eyes."

Josh hesitated a moment. "Yeah," he said again. "I did."

They walked in silence until they got back to the starting point. Clatter and the other team members were there. When Josh drew near they all started clapping loudly. Charlie came up and high-fived him. "I knew you'd do it," she said. Then she grinned. "Of course when *I* did my first run, I nailed the meatbag in about half that time."

"That was very good work," Clatter told Josh.

"That was a very realistic zombie," Josh replied.

Clatter laughed. "It's nothing," he said, although he sounded pleased. "Just a little hobby."

Josh looked at the others. "So you were all in on this?"

Black-Eyed Susan laughed. "Consider it your initiation," she said.

"We were all watching from the monitor room," Finnegan explained. "You really kept your cool."

"Yeah," said Freya. "When Stash did his first run,

he saw the z and just about burned my hair off."

Stash spat a shell toward Freya. "My meatbag was way scarier than his," he said sullenly.

The others laughed, and Josh saw Stash shoot him a look. *I don't think he and I are going to be best buds,* he thought.

"So, Josh, do you want to join our merry band?" Clatter asked.

Josh nodded. "But I still don't really get what you all do. This seems like a lot of work just to play the game."

"Ah," said Clatter. "That's very perceptive of you. You're quite right. But you see, this is more than just a game."

"I don't understand," Josh said.

Clatter came closer. "Before I explain further, I require your promise that whatever is said here remains here."

"Sure," Josh said.

Clatter cocked his head. "I'm very serious," he said. "Don't answer lightly. Should you break your promise, the ramifications are very . . . unfortunate."

"He means if you shoot your mouth off about this, we'll make sure your reputation in the game community is dirt," Seamus said.

Josh hesitated. They were taking everything really

seriously for it being a game. He wondered if he'd gotten himself in over his head. But it didn't seem like he could back out now. "It's okay," he said. "I don't talk."

"Excellent," said Clatter. "Because Seamus is right. I've invested a great deal in this operation, and there are people who would dearly love to know how I've achieved what I have. It's a business, and a very lucrative one."

"A business," Josh repeated. "You mean people pay to play it? To play against us?"

"Actually, they pay to *watch* you play it," said Clatter. "And they make bets as to who will make the most kills in a game."

"Gambling," Josh said.

"I prefer to call it wagering," said Clatter. "It's more . . . civilized. We hold games, and people come to watch them. They place bets on the team as a whole or on individual players."

"Or on the meatbags," Stash added.

"Or on the zombies," Clatter agreed.

Josh thought about this for a moment. "But if you make the zombies and you own the team, how do the gamblers know you haven't rigged everything?"

"The *wagerers*," said Clatter, "have generally had other dealings with me. They know me to be a man in whom they can place the utmost trust."

"And it's all legal?" Josh asked. "I won't get into any trouble?"

Clatter smiled. "I admit that not every aspect of my operation is, shall we say, completely approved by the authorities. As you know, the topic of zombies is a very touchy one. I'm afraid there are some people who—if they knew about this—would call for us to be shut down due to their own ignorance and fear. But I assure you that I take very good care of my team. You have no need to worry." He paused for a moment. "And of course you will share in the rewards of our success."

"You mean I'll get paid?" said Josh, surprised.

Clatter nodded. "As a junior member of the team, you'll receive base pay of two percent of the take. In addition, you will receive a bonus for each zombie you dispatch during a game. And occasionally a wagerer will take a liking to a particular player and tip handsomely."

"Wow," Josh said. "Getting paid to play the game. That's pretty cool."

"We generally play one or two times a week," Clatter continued. "I arrange the games so they inter-fere with your outside life as little as possible."

Josh shrugged. "I guess I don't have any reason to

say no," he said. "I'm in."

A smile spread across Clatter's face. "I'm very pleased to hear it," he said. "Welcome to the team."

The others came and one by one shook his hand. When it was Stash's turn he gripped Josh's fingers tightly and gave them a painful squeeze, smiled stiffly, and said, "Good to have you." Everyone else seemed genuinely glad to have him aboard.

After Josh had been given an electronic-reader card containing a handbook to study, he and Charlie left the building together. This time they exited through a door that led to the back of a warehouse filled with boxes marked TEA.

"There are a dozen or so ways in and out," Charlie explained as they made their way to the street. "Some of them are in the handbook, but some you'll only find out about when somebody shows you. By the way, make sure you memorize the handbook. You'll have to give it back next time we meet."

"Tell me how you started playing," Josh said.

"Bess recruited me," Charlie answered. "We played together in a hologame group."

"How long have you been doing it?"

"About a year," she said.

"And the others?" asked Josh. "Have they all been playing that long?"

Charlie shook her head. "They come and go," she told him. "People burn out or move away. The only ones still here from when I joined are Scrawl and Bess."

"Scrawl seems like an interesting guy," said Josh.

"He used to be a tagger," said Charlie. "A graffiti artist. That's how he got his nickname. Clatter caught him tagging one of his buildings and trained him to be a Torcher. He's nice like that. I know Clatter looks kind of weird, but he's been great to me."

"I don't think Stash likes me much," Josh admitted.

Charlie laughed. "Stash doesn't like anybody. Or at least he pretends not to. I think really he just doesn't know how to have friends. His family is kind of messed up. His dad is in prison for murder, and his mom is a drunk. He's the youngest of six kids. The others all left, and he's the one looking out for his mother. So don't take it personally. He's just not good at trusting people."

"It sounds like there are a lot of stories on the team," Josh said.

"There are," said Charlie. "Finnegan and Seamus had a little trouble with setting things on fire and ended up in juvie. Clatter managed to get them out. They live with him, and he's teaching them all about robotics. Freya's dad is an ambassador. She got kicked out of three or four boarding schools, so now she lives with her dad, but he's never around, and he has no idea whether she's home or not."

"And Black-Eyed Susan?"

"Bess?" Charlie said. "She's kind of a mystery. No one really knows where she lives. Personally, I think she's a runaway."

"So what's your story?"

Charlie grinned. "Mine's pretty boring. Family I like. Good grades. No sociopathic tendencies. I'm just really good at playing the game."

"Same here," Josh said. "I guess we're the token normals."

They stopped in front of a subway entrance. "This is me," she said. "Go home and read the manual. Com me if you have any questions. Clatter will let us know when the next game is."

"Will do," said Josh. "Oh, and thanks for inviting me to play. This is going to be fun."

Charlie smiled. "It will be better than anything you could ever imagine," she said.

8

Josh slipped the card into his reader and waited for it to load. Ever since he got home, he'd been dying to look at the manual, but first he'd had to sit through dinner with his family, and then he'd had to do his math homework. But now all that was done, and he could devote his attention to more interesting matters.

The first section was standard Torcher information, basically an outline of the Rules. Josh already knew these by heart, so he skipped ahead to the next section, which was a description of the various zones in the playing field. In addition to the underground area in the Docklands, Clatter had set up three or four smaller fields throughout the city. One of them used the maze of underground tunnels beneath the abandoned Central Station, another was laid out in the ruins of the Great Park at the northern tip of the city.

Josh pored over the different maps with growing excitement. He couldn't believe Clatter's operation was so extensive. *This is going to be so cool,* he thought as he tried to memorize as many details of the maps as he could. He wanted to impress the others the next time they played.

As he was looking at a map of the sewers that ran beneath the ship graveyard, the telecom sounded an incoming call. "Firecracker is calling," the machine's voice said. "Firecracker is calling."

Josh went to his desk and hit the answer key. Firecracker's face filled the screen. "How's the paper going?" he asked.

Josh wracked his brain. "The paper," he said, a sinking feeling growing in the pit of his stomach.

"Right," Firecracker said. "Did you get your part done?"

"Just about," Josh lied. "I'm still researching a couple of things, but I'm almost finished."

"All right," said Firecracker. "Make sure it's good. My presentation is going to kick major butt, but it's only half the grade. Don't forget you have to submit the written report to Darjeeling by eight tomorrow. She's going to have them graded before we do the presentations."

"Don't worry," Josh said. "It'll be done."

"Okay," Firecracker said. "I'll see you tomorrow. Firecracker out."

The screen went dark, and Josh groaned. He'd forgotten all about the paper. He looked at the clock. It was almost ten. Reluctantly he closed the manual he'd been reading and started to pull up information on Antarctica.

His computer beeped, signaling an incoming message. He opened it and saw a note from Charlie.

The next game is Saturday. Meet me at the park at 1400 hours. Study the maps for Location 4.

Saturday? That's the day after tomorrow, Josh thought. That didn't give him much time, especially since Friday night was family night, when he and Emily were forced to do something with their parents. *You can't show up unprepared,* he told himself.

He started to pick up the manual again, then remembered the planetary geography paper. *Paper first.*

He worked quickly, locating the information he needed and cobbling it into something that resembled a paper. When he was done he read it through. It wasn't his best work, but at least it was finished. Hopefully it was enough to get them a decent grade.

He glanced at the clock and was shocked to see that it was after one o'clock. He was exhausted, but he forced himself to open the manual file and start reading again. Location Four was also in the Docklands. It was an old amusement park called Happy Time that had been built along the boardwalk. Since the ocean around the city had become too polluted to swim in, nobody went there anymore, and like everything in that part of the city, the boardwalk—and Happy Time—had been left to slowly fall apart. Josh had never been there, although his parents had told him and Emily stories about going there when they were kids.

According to the manual, there were a number of buildings still standing at the park, as well as several underground tunnels that must have been used for maintenance purposes. They formed a complex maze that Josh found difficult to keep straight, so in order to memorize them he focused on one section at a time, taking in the details and then closing his eyes and trying to re-create the map in his mind.

The problem was that every time he closed his eyes, he felt himself drifting into sleep. Several times he woke with a jerk, having dozed off in the middle of trying to picture a stairwell or hallway. Then one time he closed his eyes and didn't wake up.

Josh dreamed about trying to find his way out of a

dank cellar. He'd lost his bearings and no longer knew where the stairs he'd come down were. Things were moving in the dark, and he couldn't remember how to use his flamethrower. Hands were grabbing at him, and he felt cold breath on his face. The alarm clock jolted him awake.

He sat up and looked around his room, his heart racing. The dream had been so real. There was a knock on the door, and Emily looked in.

"Are you okay?" she asked.

"Sure," said Josh. "Why?"

"You were yelling in your sleep," his sister told him.

"Oh," said Josh. "It was just a nightmare."

Emily nodded. Then she noticed the reader lying next to Josh on the bed. She came in and picked it up. "What are you reading?"

"No!" Josh yelled, grabbing the reader from her.

"Ohhh," Emily said, a grin spreading across her face. "You were looking at something *naaauugh*-ty!"

"I was not!" Josh countered. "It's just something for school."

"Okay," Emily said, giving Josh an exaggerated wink. "Sure."

"Get out of here," said Josh. "I have to get dressed."

Emily scurried out, laughing, and shut the door. Josh looked at the reader. It was still open to the map of Location Four. Close call. If Emily had seen the map, she definitely would have asked a lot of questions.

Twenty minutes later Josh was downstairs having breakfast. Emily looked at him from across the table and smiled sweetly. "Read any good books lately?" she asked.

Josh glowered at her.

"Don't forget, tonight is family night," his father said. "We're going to go play mini golf."

"Yay!" Emily said, genuinely excited by the news. Josh was a little excited too. Mini golf was super old-fashioned, but it was also kind of cool. He would never let his parents know, but secretly he was looking forward to it.

Fortunately for him, the mini golf news also made Emily forget all about the reader. On the train to school all she talked about was how much fun it was going to be. When she got off at her stop, she waved good-bye to Josh and ran to catch up with some of her friends who had been riding in the car ahead of theirs.

The rocking motion of the train almost lulled Josh back to sleep, and he was glad when he reached his stop and could get out into the cool air.

Firecracker caught up with him as Josh was opening his locker. "Did you get it done?" he asked.

"I did," Josh answered. "*And* I sent it to Darjeeling. The rest is up to you."

"Piece of cake," said Firecracker. "I'll see you later."

The day dragged on. At lunch Josh tried to perk himself up by downing an energy drink, but all it did was make him feel sick. By the time planetary geography class rolled around in the afternoon, he was both wired and sleepy. It was a horrible combination, and all he wanted to do was sit at his desk and zone out.

Unfortunately, he had to listen to the other presentations. There was going to be a test on the information, so he forced his eyes open and tried to concentrate on what was being said. Beside him, Firecracker's leg bounced up and down anxiously as he waited his turn to go before the class.

Josh listened as Veda Churling told them about the formation of the Martian Sea, then as Peter Prieboy gave a rambling account of the meteor strike that had created the Vargas Canyon. None of it was very interesting, and Josh found his thoughts wandering. He hoped the recorder built into his NoteTaker had caught everything, but he doubted it. It had been acting up lately, and he hadn't had time to fix it.

Finally it was Firecracker's turn. He went to the front of the room and started talking. As promised, he had made holographic maps to illustrate the changes taking place in Antarctica and how the resulting rise in water levels was affecting the rest of the earth. This was followed by an animation showing the Antarctic Conflict waged by the seven countries claiming territorial rights to the area, and the ultimate creation of a protected world park there.

When Firecracker was done, the class applauded. Firecracker took a deep bow, waving to his audience and hamming it up. Josh couldn't help but laugh. They were going to get a great grade, he just knew it.

With the presentations over, Ms. Darjeeling resumed control of the class. "I have to say, I'm very impressed with your work on these projects," she told them. "I'm sending your grades to your NoteTakers. If you have any questions about them, please see me after class."

She punched a sequence of numbers into the control panel on her desk, and all around the room NoteTakers made the chiming sound that indicated the arrival of a transmission. Josh clicked on his message box and looked for his grade.

When he saw it, his heart skipped a beat. He'd expected a B-plus or at worst a B. He'd gotten a D.

"I got an A," Firecracker said. "Score one for me. What did you get?"

"Not an A," Josh said.

Firecracker looked at Josh's screen. "A D?" he said loudly enough for several people to look over at them. "Our final grade is based on *both* our scores. That means we're getting a . . ."

"C-plus," said Josh as Firecracker tried to figure out the answer in his head.

"A C-plus," Firecracker agreed.

"A C-plus isn't *that* bad," said Josh, trying to reassure his friend.

"It's not an A," Firecracker shot back.

"I'm sorry," said Josh. "I don't know what happened. I thought I did an okay job."

"Yeah, well, apparently you didn't," Firecracker said, slumping in his seat. "Thanks a lot, partner."

"I'm sorry," Josh said again. But Firecracker wouldn't even look at him.

9

"What's the matter, cowboy?"

Josh looked up. Charlie was standing in front of him on the train. "What are you doing here?" he asked her, looking around.

"Relax," Charlie said. "Your friend isn't here."

"Did you follow me?" Josh said.

Charlie smiled. "Why would I do that?" she replied. She took the seat next to Josh. "Okay, maybe I did. But I'm not stalking you or anything. I just wanted to see if you could come over tonight."

"Come over?" Josh repeated.

"To my house," Charlie clarified. "I thought we could go over the maps for tomorrow."

Josh shook his head. "I can't," he said. "Tonight is family night."

Charlie raised an eyebrow. "Family night," she said. "Sounds fun."

"Yeah. Well." Josh shrugged. He didn't want to tell Charlie he was actually looking forward to mini golf. Or at least he *had* been, until he'd gotten the grade on his report. Now he didn't really feel like doing anything.

"This is a big game for you," Charlie reminded him. "And Location Four isn't the easiest field to play. Are you sure you're ready?"

Josh started to assure her that he was, but found himself saying, "Actually, no. I'm not sure at all. I tried to memorize the maps last night, but I had to do this report for school, and it got late and—"

"You're coming over," Charlie interrupted him. "Just tell your parents you have to do something else tonight."

"Like what?" said Josh.

Charlie thought for a moment, biting her lip and frowning. "Tell them you're volunteering for something," she said. "Tonight is orientation, and tomorrow is your first day. That gives you an out for both days. And whenever we have a game, you can say you have to volunteer."

"I don't know," Josh hedged. "I don't think they'd buy it."

"Tell them it's for school credit," said Charlie.

Josh thought about it. "That *might* work," he

agreed. "But I need to think of a realistic group to volunteer for."

"The homeless," said Charlie. "You're helping the homeless. That's perfect. You can tell them the group works all over the city; that way they won't ever expect you to be in any one place."

Josh knew Charlie was right that he was going to need a good excuse for spending time away from home. He took a deep breath, then dialed his mother's number at work and told her what he was supposedly doing.

"That went well," Charlie remarked when Josh ended the call.

"I lucked out," said Josh. "She was distracted. One of the gryphons bit someone."

"Gryphons?" Charlie said.

"She's a biologist," Josh explained. "A cloner. She makes imaginary animals. I mean she makes imaginary animals *real*."

"I get it," said Charlie. "Cool. What does your dad do?"

"He's a doctor too," said Josh. "The normal kind. You know, shots and checkups and stuff."

"Wow," Charlie said. "Two brainiacs for parents. Did you inherit their superbrains?"

Josh laughed. "Not so much," he said. "My sister

Emily is the smart one. She's actually scary smart. I'm pretty good at a lot of things, but not super good at any of them."

"Except torching," Charlie reminded him.

"Except that," Josh agreed. "So what do your parents—"

"This is our stop," said Charlie, interrupting. She stood up as the doors opened, and she and Josh hopped off. Charlie pointed to a train on the other side of the platform. "Come on," she said. "That's the one we want."

The second train took them diagonally across the city, going underground for most of the way and then emerging into daylight and climbing up onto the elevated tracks. Below them Josh saw the squat, brown brick houses of Old Town. The steel supports of the elevated train stuck up like the legs of giant birds from the tangle of homes.

Old Town occupied the northeast corner of the city. Most of the houses were the original ones built hundreds of years before by the settlers who discovered the land. They were all built with bricks made from local clay, which gave them their brown color. Josh had been there a few times, mainly to visit the Museum of City History on school trips. But he didn't know anyone who lived there.

"Here we are," Charlie said as the train came to a stop. They exited onto a platform high above the street and headed for the stairs.

They walked to Charlie's house, passing lots of cafes where people sat drinking, smoking, and talking loudly. Then they turned a corner and came to a house that looked just like all the other houses in the neighborhood, with one notable difference; the front gate was made of wrought iron and topped with a big black bird whose eyes—made of copper—seemed to stare at Josh menacingly.

"My dad made it," Charlie said, as if she was used to explaining the bird. "He's a sculptor. Iron, mostly."

"It's cool," Josh said, but the truth was that he found the bird more than a little creepy.

They went up a short flight of steps to the front door, and as they stepped inside Charlie called out, "Dad?"

There was no answer.

"Come up to my room," Charlie said, heading for a set of stairs.

Josh followed her. The wood of the stairs was old and well worn. Centuries of use had made the wood smooth, and there were deeper indentations in the center of each step where people had most often placed their feet.

"This is my dad's studio," Charlie said as they arrived at the second floor. It was one huge space, with bare brick walls and a floor covered with white canvas cloths. A workbench cluttered with tools lined one wall, and in the center of the room stood a sculpture made of bits and pieces of metal, all welded together to form what looked like a human figure. But something was wrong with it. It was twisted, the arms seeming to reach out to grab something.

"My bedroom is on the third floor," Charlie said, walking past the sculpture without looking at it. They went up another flight of stairs and down a hallway. "That's my dad's room," Charlie said as they passed a closed door. "This is mine." She opened a door on the opposite side of the hall and went inside. The room also had bare brick walls, and at one end, farthest from the windows, a huge bed made out of iron stood against the wall.

"Another of my dad's creations," said Charlie. She went to a console on the wall, pressed some buttons, and music began to play. It was a song Josh had never heard, with lots of loud guitars and wild drumming.

"What is this?"

"It's old," Charlie said. "A band my grandmother used to listen to called the New York Dolls. I'm kind of into it." She danced around as the music played, throwing her head from side to side. "Sorry," she said, falling on the bed. "You must think I'm nuts."

"No," Josh said, laughing. "I think you're cute." Immediately he realized what he'd said. "I mean, um, we should go over the maps," he said quickly.

"Did you just say you think I'm cute?" Charlie asked.

"No," Josh said.

"So you *don't* think I'm cute?" asked Charlie.

"No," Josh replied. "I mean, yeah. But I didn't mean it to come out that way."

"It's okay," she said. "I think you're cute too."

Before Josh could respond, Charlie jumped up. "Stay here," she said. "I'll be right back."

Josh felt his cheeks flush as he tried to process what had just happened. He *did* think Charlie was cute, but he hadn't meant to tell her that. It had just slipped out, and now he couldn't take it back. *Now what?* he thought.

Charlie returned to the room carrying a box. She brought it to the bed and set it down. It was made of black metal, and the surface was scratched and dented. In the center of the top was a logo Josh recognized at once—a simple circle with flames in it.

"That's the Torcher symbol," he said.

Charlie nodded. "My dad was a Torcher," she told

him as she lifted the lid. "He kept some stuff."

She reached into the box and pulled out a small cyphoto album. Starting it up, she showed Josh the screen. On it was a photo of seven men all wearing Torcher uniforms. They grinned happily at the camera.

"That's his squad," Charlie said.

"Which one is your dad?" Josh asked.

Charlie pointed to a short man with black hair. He was the only one not smiling. "There," she said.

She scrolled through the pictures. Mostly they were of the men from the first photograph. Then they came to a picture showing a beautiful woman. She was leaning against a railing. Behind her Josh could see the tracks of a roller coaster, and to one side three little kids ran by in a blur, balloons bobbing on the strings in their hands. The woman was holding a cone of bright pink cotton candy.

"That's my mom," Charlie said.

"That roller coaster looks familiar," said Josh.

"It's Happy Time," Charlie said quietly. "My dad took her there when he asked her to marry him." She stared at the picture for a long time without saying anything.

"What happened to her?" Josh asked finally.

Charlie turned the album off. "She died," she

said. She put the album back in the box and took out something else. It was a medal. "My dad got this for torching a thousand z's," she said, handing it to Josh. "Isn't it cool?"

Josh examined the medal. It was round, and in the center was the Torcher logo. Beneath it was the Torcher motto: SAVED BY FIRE.

"He must have saved a lot of people," Josh said, impressed.

"You mean zombies," Charlie countered.

Josh looked at her, not understanding.

"Think about it," said Charlie. "Zombies used to be people. By killing them, the Torchers saved them from having to be monsters."

"I always thought that by the time z's turned they were pretty much not human anymore," Josh said.

"You don't know that," Charlie said, her voice oddly sharp. "Nobody really knows." She took the medal back and returned it to the box.

"Can I ask you something?" Josh said.

Charlie nodded.

"How come when you play the hologame, you always play a meatbag?"

"It's good training," said Charlie. "It helps me learn to think like a zombie, so when I play the game for real I get inside their heads."

"I don't think I want to be in a head like that," Josh told her.

Charlie looked at him. "Don't knock it till you've tried it," she said. "You might even *like* it."

Charlie got up and walked to her dresser. Opening the top drawer, she rooted around and pulled something out. When she came back, Josh saw that she was holding a small silver vial.

"What is that?" he asked.

Charlie unscrewed the top of the vial and poured two small, white tablets into her palm. "This," Charlie said, "is Z. It's something that will help you think like a zombie. At least for a little while. I take it whenever I'm playing the game."

Josh eyed the pills doubtfully. "I don't do drugs," he said.

"Don't worry," Charlie said. "It's totally safe. It's not a *drug* drug." She took one of the pills and put it in her mouth. She swallowed and stuck out her tongue. "See? Now it's your turn."

She handed Josh the second pill. He held it between his fingers, looking at it. Was it really safe? What was it going to do to him? He looked at Charlie, who laughed. "Come on," she said. "You won't regret it."

That's what they all say, Josh thought. *Right before you do something stupid.* But he had to admit, he was curious. Also, he didn't want Charlie to think he was afraid.

"It will make me think like a zombie?" he asked.

Charlie nodded.

"And that's a *good* thing?"

"Just trust me," said Charlie. "It's like nothing you've ever done."

Josh looked at her face. She was grinning. *How bad can it be?* he thought. Before he could answer that question, he put the pill in his mouth and swallowed.

10

"Josh! Dinner!"

Josh closed his eyes. He wasn't really in the mood to be with his family, but he had no choice. He'd come home early from Charlie's, totally forgetting that he wasn't supposed to be done with his fake meeting until eight. When he walked in, his parents and Emily were there. The mini-golf place had been closed for renovations, so they'd come home to have dinner and play some board games.

They were all happy to see him, but he wished he were anywhere else but there. *I should have stayed at Charlie's,* he thought. But Charlie had homework to do. She'd promised to call later to see how he was doing. "In the meantime," she'd said, "just go with it."

He'd started to feel weird on the train ride home. It wasn't anything he could put his finger on. He just started to feel kind of . . . fuzzy. The feeling had grown stronger, and now he felt slightly nauseated. The last thing he wanted to do was eat.

At the same time, though, he was starving. He hadn't realized how hungry he was, but now he was acutely aware of the rumbling in his stomach. It felt as if he hadn't eaten in days.

He checked his face one more time. Seeing nothing out of the ordinary, he left his room and went downstairs. His father was standing at the stove. The grill in the center of the range was lit, and the smoke from it was being sucked up into the silver hood that covered the stove.

"You're just in time," said Josh's father as he placed one of the steaks on the grill. It sizzled as it touched the hot metal.

Josh looked at the cooking meat, and his mouth began to water as the smell filled his nose. The scent was incredibly strong—blood and fat and meat mingled together. He swallowed hard, tasting it in his throat.

"How would you like your steak prepared this evening, sir?" his father asked him. "Medium or well done?"

"Rare," Josh answered. "Almost raw."

His father looked at him with a surprised expression. "You sure?" he asked.

"I'm sure," said Josh.

"You're the boss," his father said as he laid two other steaks on the grill.

He poked the steaks with a fork. Juice ran from the holes and fell onto the grill, popping and hissing. Each crackle released another burst of the meaty smell, making Josh swallow hard as he imagined putting the meat in his mouth and chewing it. He had to force himself not to snatch the remaining raw steak from the plate and start gnawing on it.

It must be the Z, he realized. *It's working.*

Charlie had told him that the drug made you feel wild. Now Josh understood what she meant. He did feel wild, almost animal-like. He could still think, but another part of him was growing more powerful by the minute, a part he had never experienced so clearly before. He felt his heart racing.

"Here, you take over."

Someone was speaking to him. Josh looked at the speaker, and for a moment he couldn't tell who it was. He saw a faceless body, a body that coursed with blood and smelled the same as the meat on the grill. Then his vision cleared, and he realized that he was looking at his father. He was holding the meat fork out to Josh.

"Oh," Josh said, trying to remember where he was.

"Yeah. I'll do it." He took the fork from his father and went to stand in front of the grill.

"I'm going to go help your mother set the table," his father said. "Let those cook another couple of minutes, then turn them over. Put your steak on when you flip those, and turn it after two minutes."

Josh nodded. His father left him alone, and he stood staring at the cooking meat. Once again the amazing smell overwhelmed him. He reached out with the fork and pierced one of the steaks. Juice dripped onto the grill, where it bubbled and blackened. The rest pooled on top of the meat. Josh touched it with his fingertip and ran it over his lips, smearing them with blood. His tongue flicked out and licked it off. The iron taste filled his mouth, and he wanted more.

His steak was still waiting to go on the grill. Instead of putting it on, he took a knife and cut off a large chunk. Shoving it into his mouth, he chewed it with big bites, his teeth shredding the meat into pieces that he gulped down greedily. It was amazing, and he picked up the knife to cut some more.

"Are you eating *raw* meat?"

Emily was standing in the doorway, looking at Josh with an expression of disgust. "Do you know what lives in meat?" she said. "You could totally get worms."

Josh heard her talking, but he was more interested

in the way she smelled. Like the steak, she reeked with the aroma of blood. He could hear her heart beating. No, he could *feel* her heart beating, pushing blood through her veins.

"Hello?"

Josh shook his head to clear it. Emily was pointing to the grill, where the steaks were starting to smoke. Josh looked at them for a moment, not realizing what was happening. Then something in his mind turned back on, and he understood that he needed to do something. He quickly flipped the steaks over. The sides that had been against the grill were blackened.

"Mom's going to kill you," Emily decreed before turning around and marching out of the room.

Josh turned his attention back to the steaks. He added his own to the grill and tried to ignore the smell. Something weird was definitely going on in his head, and he knew it had to be the Z. *It's your reptile brain taking over,* he told himself. He didn't know whether that was true or not, but whatever it was, it felt really weird. Weird and kind of exciting. It was as if he'd become somebody else—no, *something* else.

That thing was still inside of him, and it was growing stronger. Slowly Josh felt the part of his brain that could think clearly shutting down as the other, wild part took over. Everything grew a little hazy as his eyesight changed but his sense of smell intensified.

"Josh, are those steaks done?"

He heard his mother's voice, but when he answered her all that came out was a growling sound.

"They smell done," said his mother. "I think they're ready."

Josh managed to get the steaks off the grill and onto a plate, but the smell was almost too much for him. He had to push himself away from the counter before he tore into all four steaks. As it was, he grabbed his own steak and ran with it into the bathroom. Slamming the door, he sat down on the floor and began devouring the meat.

He held the steak in both hands, ripping at it with his teeth. It was still mostly raw, and blood dripped from the shredded pieces. He barely tasted the chunks of meat as he swallowed them, almost choking. He'd never been so ravenous in his life.

A banging on the door stopped him. "You all right in there?" his father called out.

Josh looked at the steak in his hands. Blood covered his fingers, and there were chunks of meat on the floor around him. He stopped himself from picking them up and eating them.

"I'm okay," he answered his father. He had to concentrate hard on speaking the words.

"Well, don't stay in there all night," his father said. "Dinner's ready."

Josh said nothing, but he heard his father walk away. He looked once more at the steak in his hands. There was very little of it left—mostly fat and some stringy pieces covered in blood. Looking at it made him both sick and hungry. Before he couldn't resist any longer, he dropped the remaining meat into the toilet. He scooped up the pieces on the floor and added them as well, then flushed the whole mess down. He watched the meat swirl around the bowl and disappear.

He went to the sink and turned on the cold water. Bending down, he put his mouth under the tap and let the water fill it. It washed away some of the meat taste, but not all of it. He drank some more, swallowing and trying to rinse the blood from his throat. He suddenly felt like he might throw up.

He turned the water off and looked at himself in the mirror. His pupils were huge black circles.

The wild feeling was still there, waiting. As sick as he felt, there was something really exciting about letting that other part of him take over for a little while. Everything felt more real, more raw, more alive.

If that's what being a zombie felt like, he was surprised. He'd always thought of them as being stupid, mindless things that didn't know what they were doing and didn't feel anything. But he felt so much. All he *did* was feel. Every sensation was intense beyond words. And he didn't need words because there was no reason to *think* about anything.

Next time it will be easier, he told himself. *I'll be ready.*

He washed his hands, checked his eyes to see if his pupils were any smaller (they were, a little), and got ready to join everyone for dinner. He didn't know what he was going to say about the steak, but he would come up with something. He would be funny, and they would all have a good time.

Charlie was right—there was nothing to worry about. The Z had been a little intense, but nothing too heavy. Best of all, he had *enjoyed* it, and it really had opened his mind up to what it might feel like to be a zombie. He could see why Charlie took it while she was playing the game. It really made you think like a z did.

He thought about the game tomorrow. It was going to be great. He laughed. His life had changed radically over the past few days. "And this is just the beginning," he told his reflection.

11

It was raining hard the next morning. The wind blew the water across the beach in heavy sheets, carrying with it discarded candy wrappers, empty cans, and other trash that littered the sand. The ocean lapped at the shore with dirty brown tongues flecked with yellowish foam. A dead gull, its feathers matted and torn, was dragged into the water by a wave.

Josh wiped his hair from his eyes and looked for the entrance to Happy Time. He spotted it a little way down the boardwalk—a huge grinning clown's head, its paint worn away so that it had only one eye. Josh carefully made his way along the dilapidated boardwalk. Passing through the clown's open mouth, he walked among the arcade of empty booths until he found one marked with a torn poster of a bearded lady. **OME SEE THE FREAK SHO**, it declared in big letters. To the right of the sign was a doorway covered by a dirty, yellowed curtain. Josh pushed through it and into the room beyond.

"You're late." Stash looked at Josh and popped a nut into his mouth.

"Five minutes," Josh shot back. "The train sat in the tunnel for twenty minutes. I guess the tracks were flooded."

"It's no problem," Bess assured him. She was just pulling on the heavy black boots that went with their uniforms. She gave Stash a scowl. "Besides, Scrawl isn't even here yet, so settle down."

Stash turned away and walked over to a battered old sofa upholstered in red velvet. When he sat on it, a cloud of dust rose around him. He started sneezing violently.

"Serves him right," Bess said, laughing. "What a jerk."

Josh set his backpack down and started to dress. He saw Seamus and Finnegan in another part of the room, but Freya and Charlie weren't there. He asked Bess where they were.

"They're helping Clatter bring the flamethrowers up," she said. "He keeps a locker of them in one of the lower levels."

"Have you played here before?" Josh asked as he stepped into his Torcher uniform.

"Once," Bess answered. "It's a little creepy. Most of the rides are pretty much gone, but a couple of them are still standing. They don't work, of course, but it's still weird walking around inside of them. She looked at Josh. "Don't worry, though. It'll be fun."

A curtain at the rear of the room opened and Clatter entered, accompanied by Freya and Charlie. Each of them carried a bag and set it on the ground. Freya unzipped one of them and removed three flamethrowers. She opened the other two bags and removed five more.

"Josh!" Clatter said. As he walked over to greet Josh, his coat of keys jangled merrily. "Are you ready for your first big game?"

Josh nodded. "I think so," he answered. "Who are we playing for?"

Clatter wagged a finger. "We never discuss the wagerers," he said. "You let me worry about that. You just focus on playing a good game."

Charlie came over to stand by Josh. "How are you feeling?" she asked in a whisper.

"Pretty good," Josh said. "Last night was amazing."

Charlie grinned. "Didn't I tell you?" she said.

Josh looked at her. There was something funny about her eyes. They weren't quite focusing on him.

"Are you on it now?" he asked.

Charlie giggled. "Yeah," she said.

"I thought you only use it when you play the holo-game," said Josh.

"Sometimes I take it when we're playing for real," Charlie answered. "It's even more intense then."

Josh looked around to make sure no one was listening. "Can I have one?" he asked.

Charlie shook her head. "You're not used to it yet."

"Come on," Josh begged.

Charlie leaned in close. "Don't talk about it here," she said. "And no, you can't have any. It's too risky."

Josh groaned. "You're no fun," he said, only half joking.

"Hey, guys." Scrawl entered the tent, shaking water from his coat. "Sorry I'm late. The damn train got stuck."

Josh looked over at Stash, waiting for him to say something smart. But Stash just looked down and dropped a shell onto the floor. *He's afraid of Scrawl,* Josh thought with some satisfaction. *He just thinks he can bully me because I'm the new guy. Well, we'll see about that.*

"Never mind," Clatter said to Scrawl. "Just get your team together and meet at the starting point in fifteen minutes. You know what to do."

Scrawl glanced at his watch. "No problem," he said. "We'll be ready."

Clatter looked around at the rest of them. "In that case I wish you all good luck and happy hunting," he said.

When Clatter was gone, Scrawl called everyone together. As he laced up his boots, he went over the plan for the game.

"We're starting at the entrance to the funhouse," he said. "Two teams. First team is Seamus, Finnegan, Bess, and me. Second team is Freya, Charlie, Josh, and Stash."

Josh groaned silently. Why did he have to be on a team with Stash? But at least Charlie would be with him.

"There's a total of twelve z's running around this place," Scrawl continued. "That means we each get at least one kill. The other four are up for grabs. But nobody hog them," he added, looking meaningfully at Stash. "Everybody gets a chance at the bonuses. Got it?"

Stash looked away. "Got it," he muttered.

"That's all there is to it," Scrawl said as he stood up. He turned to Josh. "Did you study the manual?"

"Yep," Josh said.

"I hope you memorized the maps," said Scrawl. "You'll need them to play this field. It's got some tricky sections."

"I'm good to go," Josh assured him.

"Put this in your ear," said Scrawl as he handed Josh device the size of a small gumball. "It's a communicator. You'll be able to hear everyone else, and they'll hear you. Keep the chatter to a minimum. You can imagine what it's like if everyone talks at once."

Josh tucked the communicator into his left ear. It fit snugly, then expanded to fill the space. There was a slight tickling sound as something bonded with his skin. "This is biotechnology," he said, surprised. "I thought only the military used stuff like this."

Scrawl grinned. "Like I told you before, Clatter has connections," he said. "Let's go."

They left the freak-show tent and walked to the end of the arcade, where a dilapidated structure with **FUN HOUSE** written across the front stood with its doors yawning open. Scrawl went inside, and the rest of the team followed.

Scrawl checked his watch. "We should be starting right . . . about . . . now," he said as the now-familiar electronic woman's voice came through the communicator in Josh's ear.

"Torchers, prepare for play," it said.

In front of them, mirrored doors swung inward, revealing a staircase going down. "Use the lights on your torches," Scrawl reminded them as he led the way.

Josh turned on his light, which produced a thin but clear beam courtesy of the halogen bulb mounted above the flamethrower's barrel. He kept it pointed down as he followed Seamus into the stairwell.

At the bottom of the stairs Scrawl stopped. "Team one, we're going north," he said, indicating a long hallway off to his left. Team two, head south."

Scrawl and his team moved out, leaving Josh, Charlie, Freya, and Stash at the foot of the stairs.

"Listen up," Freya said. "I want this to be quick and clean. We make a sweep of our quadrant, we torch anything we see that isn't human, and we collect our pay." She looked at Josh and spoke in a low voice. "Remember, there are cameras monitoring us at all times. The customers want to see action, so make sure you're always on."

Josh nodded. He understood the rules. If they performed well, the customers made bigger bets and everyone made more money. But Josh wasn't concerned just about the money. He wanted to show that he could really play.

"My guess is that we're going to have a six-and-six," Freya said as they started to walk. "Clatter almost always divides them up equally."

That means two of us will get a bonus z, Josh thought. He hoped he got one. He also hoped Stash didn't.

The tunnel they were in suddenly curved to the left and opened up into a small room filled with machinery. Freya turned to Josh. "Do you know where we are?"

Josh pulled an image of the map from his memory, trying to recall all the different sites. "The merry-go-round," he said. "We're underneath it."

"Good job," Freya said. "And ahead of us through the door on the other side?"

Stash made a spitting sound. "What is this, kindergarten?" he said. "It's the bumper cars, then the Tilt-A-Whirl, then the flying swings."

"Actually, it's the Tilt-A-Whirl, *then* the bumper cars," Josh said without thinking.

"Josh is right," Freya said.

Stash grunted and spat on the floor. Josh avoided looking at him, but he knew what the other boy was probably thinking. He chided himself, *You should have just kept your mouth shut.*

A crackling sound filled Josh's ear, followed by Clatter's voice. "Team one has located and neutralized one target," he said.

"Damn!" Stash said, slamming his hand against a piece of machinery. "They get the first-kill bonus."

"Calm down," Charlie said.

"We could have had it if we weren't standing around here chatting like a bunch of girls," Stash said angrily.

"We need to make up some time," Freya said, ignoring him. "Split up. Charlie, you come with me. Stash, you and Josh check out what's going on topside."

"Topside?" Stash groaned. "Why do I have to go topside?"

"Because I said so. Now shut up and *go!*"

Charlie and Freya headed off to the other side of the room, while Stash started climbing a ladder that ran up the side of one wall. He didn't say a word to Josh, who followed him, wishing he were with anyone else.

At the top of the ladder Stash pushed against a hatch that swung up and over. Then he put his head through the hole, looked around, and climbed out. Josh emerged after him into a gloomy tent that covered a large merry-go-round. Rain pounded on the roof and dripped through holes in the rotting canvas. In the semidarkness Josh saw the animals of the carousel sitting silently, their painted eyes staring straight ahead.

Stash still said nothing as he walked around the edge of the merry-go-round. Josh decided to walk in the other direction. The carousel was large enough that after a few steps he could no longer see Stash. Instead he focused on the merry-go-round itself. A meatbag could easily hide among the carved horses, tigers, and rabbits.

A second later he heard a whooshing sound and the clatter of broken glass. Then he heard Stash yell in frustration. As Josh started toward the other side, a figure emerged from the carousel and hobbled toward the side of the tent, where a slit in the canvas created a kind of doorway.

Josh aimed his flamethrower at the zombie. "Target in sight!" he shouted, and pulled the trigger. Just as he did, a second figure came flying out from between two horses. Startled, Josh jerked to the side so the stream of fire from his thrower missed the zombie and narrowly avoided catching the second figure, which fell to the ground bellowing in pain. Josh realized, too late, that it was Stash.

"Torcher down!" he yelled, kneeling down beside Stash.

"Get the hell away from me!" Stash shouted, shoving Josh. "You fouled my kill, you stupid noob." He stood up and ran after the zombie, who had managed to leave the tent.

Josh got up, retrieved his flamethrower from where it had fallen, and looked around. He knew he should follow Stash, but he really didn't want to be anywhere near him right now. It would be better for him if he returned to the hallway and tried to find Freya and Charlie. But he knew it was foolish to leave a Torcher alone chasing a z, especially one that might be wounded. *Besides,* he thought, *maybe this is another test.*

He heard a crackling in his earpiece, then Freya's voice came through. "Josh, what's the situation?"

Josh hesitated. He wanted to say that Stash was injured, but since Stash had run off he wasn't sure that was true. And he didn't want Freya to think he was panicking.

"We sighted a z," he said. "Stash is in pursuit."

"Good," Freya said. "Then you know what to do."

The communicator went silent. Before he could talk himself out of it, Josh pushed through the opening in the tent and found himself outside. It was raining even harder now, and he could barely see anything. But off to his right he saw a black figure entering one of the attractions. It had to be Stash.

He made his way along the arcade until he came to the spot where Stash had disappeared. "Great," he said, looking at the ride. "The Tunnel of Love."

Sighing, he ran up the ramp to the start of the ride, where a bunch of little boats that carried riders through the tunnel were gathered. The water in the imitation stream had long ago dried up, but the rain had filled it halfway. As Josh made his way to the heart-shaped opening of the ride, the water sloshed around his feet.

Josh walked carefully down the track and through the entrance. The inside of the ride was a mess. Overturned boats blocked his path, and pieces of fallen timber lay across the floor, crushing whatever they'd fallen on. Holes in the roof let in even more rain, and it was almost impossible to see anything. Josh tried using the light on his flamethrower, but it did little to help. Fortunately the flamethrower itself remained lit even in the rain.

He saw no sign of Stash or the zombie. How could they have disappeared so quickly? As far as Josh could tell, he was alone.

"Stash," he whispered. "Stash, do you copy?"

There was a hissing in his communicator, but no answer from Stash or anyone else. All he heard was static. He tapped his ear. "Stash? Freya? Charlie?"

There was no answer. Either something was blocking transmissions between the communicators or his was malfunctioning. Again he wondered if perhaps he was being tested. Maybe they'd turned off his communicator on purpose to see what he would do without it.

He worked his way deeper into the tunnel, becoming more and more certain that he had made a mistake. Stash had probably looked inside, seen no sign of the z, and left. Most likely he was looking for Josh right now and getting madder and madder. *What a great first game,* Josh thought miserably.

Then a loud creaking broke the silence, and a boat came rolling backward out of the rainy darkness toward Josh. He had to scramble sideways to avoid being hit, and just barely managed to get on the narrow walkway beside the track before the boat slid by him. It crashed into the stationary boat behind it, and Josh saw that it wasn't empty. Stash was in it, and he was being pushed over the edge by a zombie.

The zombie was a clown. Its face was painted white, with blue stars around its eyes and a big red mouth that grinned stupidly. It was wearing a red and white polka-dot suit with giant pom-pom buttons down the front, and its bushy pink hair stuck out like a cloud around its head. It had its hands around Stash's throat, and its face was hanging over his. Stash struggled, but he couldn't scream because he was being choked. Instead he writhed like a bug stuck on the end of a pin.

Josh readied his flamethrower but quickly realized there was no way he could use it without hitting Stash. Thinking quickly, he dropped the weapon on the walkway and rushed the boat. Jumping into it, he grabbed the zombie around the chest and wrenched it off Stash. The z hissed angrily and clawed at Josh's hands.

"Stash! Run!" Josh yelled.

Josh twisted to the side, still clutching the clown, and fell out of the boat. The zombie hit the floor first, with Josh on top of it. Scurrying back, Josh grabbed the barrel of the flamethrower and swung it up to firing position. He found the trigger and pulled, and the z burst into flame. To Josh's surprise, the zombie rolled over and over, trying to put the fire out. He'd never seen a meatbag do that before. Usually they just beat at the flames uselessly. This one seemed to be trying to save itself. But it was doomed.

Having taken care of the zombie, Josh rushed to the boat to make sure Stash was all right. He was sitting up, but he was holding his hand to his shoulder. "The damn thing bit me," he said, wincing in pain.

Bit? Josh thought. *Since when can animatronic zombies actually bite?* Before he could say anything, several figures emerged from the tunnel behind him. He whirled around, his flamethrower aimed at chest level.

"Weapon down!" he heard Scrawl shout.

Josh lowered the flamethrower. Scrawl jumped into the boat and took a look at Stash. Behind him, Seamus and Finnegan exchanged glances.

"I'm okay," Stash said weakly.

"You're bit," Scrawl said. "It's game over. You know the rules."

Stash began swearing, but he didn't argue. Scrawl turned to Josh. "That was a big risk you took," he said. "That z could easily have gotten you too."

Josh couldn't decide whether Scrawl was angry or not. He shrugged. "Stash needed help," he said.

Scrawl looked back at the injured player. "Yeah," he said. "He needs help."

"What happens now?" Josh asked. "Do we keep playing?"

"You do," Scrawl said. "We'll get Stash out of here. You meet up with the rest of the team. They're at the roller coaster. You know where it is?"

Josh nodded. "You're sure you don't need help with him?"

Scrawl shook his head. "We're good," he said. "You go. And hey, congrats on your first kill."

In all the commotion, Josh had forgotten about the zombie. He looked over at the smoking mess on the floor. "Thanks," he said.

12

Peering into the terrarium on Charlie's desk, Josh watched as the mechaspider spun its web. Its delicate body moved from side to side as the silk played out from its spinnerets. The mechaspider's intricately jointed legs moved in a slow ballet as the creature made its way around its web, spiraling out from the center and connecting to the glass walls of its enclosure.

"Isn't it beautiful?" Charlie said. "It's a golden orb weaver."

"It's really pretty," Josh agreed. The spider's oblong body shimmered in browns and golds, while its long legs were banded in black. A pattern of small white dots speckled its carapace.

"If it were real, I would feed it moths and bees," Charlie said.

"Have you ever seen a real one?" Josh asked her.

Charlie shook her head. "Biologists are supposedly growing them in labs from frozen eggs, but it will be a long time before most of us see real ones." She sighed. "Yet one more thing our ancestors ruined."

"My parents won't let us have any mechapets," Josh said. "My mother is freaked out by them."

Charlie laughed. "But doesn't she make imaginary animals real?" she said.

Josh laughed too. "I know. It's weird, right? But she says that at least those are real animals."

"I'm saving up for a tarantula," Charlie told him. "I know exactly which one I want. *Avicularia avicularia,* the Guyana pinktoe."

"Pinktoe?" said Josh. "That doesn't sound very spidery."

Charlie shook her head. "You should see them," she said. "They're all black except for the ends of their feet, which are pink. They live in trees and never touch the ground. That's what I like about them. They're always looking down on the world." She smiled. "I have almost enough to get one," she said. "Two more kills and it's mine."

Josh walked away from the spider terrarium and stood at one of the windows, looking out at the street. It was Sunday afternoon. This time he'd told his parents he was going out to take pictures for a photography-class project. He felt bad about lying to them again—particularly when they'd told him to have a good time—but he'd really needed to talk to Charlie.

"How's Stash doing?" he asked. It was still raining. A woman was walking by, holding the hand of a small child in a red raincoat. The woman was trying to cover them both with an umbrella, but the child wanted to walk in the rain and was pulling on the woman's arm and laughing.

"I guess he's fine," Charlie answered. "Clatter was fixing him up."

"Do people get bit often?"

"Not often," said Charlie. "But sometimes."

"Have you?" Josh asked her.

Charlie shook her head. "No," she said. "And I don't want to. The meatbags may not be real, but they can do some damage."

Josh had been thinking about what had happened, and it bothered him a little bit that Clatter's cyber-zombies could really hurt the players. Torching the meatbags was one thing. They couldn't feel pain. But Josh and the other players could, and putting them in danger like that seemed . . . strange. "Don't you worry about getting hurt?"

"It's all part of the game," said Charlie. "The

wagerers like it to be realistic."

That made sense to Josh. After all, they were pay-ing big money. The more real the game seemed, the more interested they would be. And ultimately he benefited. He thought about the money sitting in the box in his closet. He'd been shocked at how much Clatter had given him at the end of the game. It was more money than he'd ever had.

"You were lucky to get that bonus," Charlie said. "If I'd been a little quicker on the draw, it would have been mine."

The woman and the child turned the corner and disappeared. Josh looked at Charlie, who was now lying on her back on her bed, her head hanging over the side. "Sorry," Josh said. "I didn't mean to steal it."

"It's okay," said Charlie. "I'm just teasing. You played a great game. It wouldn't surprise me if clients started betting on you."

Josh felt a swell of pride at the thought that after only a couple of games he might be one of the favorite players.

"That's what you really want," said Charlie, sit-ting up. "Then, on top of bonuses, you get a bigger cut. Scrawl gets something like twenty percent of every-thing people bet on him."

Josh whistled. "That's impressive," he said.

"I'm up to ten percent," Charlie informed him. "I bet you'll be there soon. Clatter likes you."

Josh turned around. "I'm having a blast," he said. "Thanks again for recruiting me."

"Thank *you*," Charlie said. "Clatter was so impressed by your game that he gave me a bonus for finding you."

Josh gave her a stern look. "And you're not giving me half?" he said, pretending to be angry.

Charlie laughed. "No way," she said. "That's one eighth of a mechaspider. It's all mine. Besides," she added, "I told you about Z. You can consider that your bonus."

"That stuff is intense," he said.

"It's great, isn't it?" Charlie said. "Wait until you try playing a game while you're on it. It's like you and the z's are connected. You find them a lot faster."

Josh cleared his throat. "Where can I get some?" he asked, trying to sound casual.

Charlie sat up. "You're in luck," she said. "I think I can spare a couple." She got up and went to her dresser, returning with the silver vial. Unscrewing the lid, she poured half a dozen tablets into her hand, which she held out toward Josh.

Josh walked over to her and reached for the pills. As his fingers came near them, Charlie made a fist, hiding the Z from him. "I didn't say they were free," she said.

Josh looked at her. "How much?" he asked.

Charlie's dark eyes sparkled. "It'll cost you a kiss," she said.

Josh hesitated. Was she kidding? He looked at her closed fist, then back at her face. She was staring him straight in the eye, not blinking. Slowly he leaned toward her. He saw her close her eyes and open her mouth. His lips touched hers. Her mouth was soft. He kissed her quickly and pulled away.

Charlie opened her eyes and lifted one eyebrow. "I think that was worth one," she said. She opened her fist and handed Josh one pill. "How many more do you want?"

Josh kissed her again. This time he lingered longer. He felt her arms go around him, the fist holding the Z pressing against his back.

When he finally pulled away, Josh felt himself blushing. Charlie smiled. "Okay," she said. "I think that one is good for the rest of these." She tucked the Z into his hand and closed his fingers over the pills.

"Um, I don't want you to think that these are the only reason I did that," Josh told her as he put them in his pocket.

"Oh, I know," Charlie said. "I figured you just

needed a little incentive."

Josh looked down. "Okay, then," he said, not knowing what else to say.

"Besides, now Bess owes me twenty bucks," Charlie said.

Josh looked up. "She bet you I wouldn't kiss you?" he said.

"It was a sucker bet," said Charlie. "I knew you'd do it."

Josh didn't know whether to laugh or be offended. "I can't believe you bet on me!" he said.

"I *said* I knew you would do it," Charlie reminded him. "It wasn't much of a bet. Come on. Let's get something to eat."

They went down the stairs. But as they entered the second-floor workspace, Charlie suddenly stopped. A man was standing in the middle of the room, a welding torch in his hand. He turned and looked at them, and Josh saw that one half of his face was badly burned. The skin there was thickly scarred, and his eye was missing.

"Dad," Charlie said.

The man's eye moved to Josh, then back to his daughter. "Who's he?" he asked.

Charlie didn't answer. She seemed to be frozen.

"Josh," Josh said. "It's nice to meet you."

The man grunted in reply.

"I didn't hear you come in," Charlie said quietly.

"Is he one of your Torcher friends?" her father asked.

Charlie shook her head. "We have a class together," she said. "We were just doing homework."

Her father looked at Josh again but didn't say anything. He turned back to the sculpture he was working on and began welding a piece of metal to one of the outstretched arms. A hand had formed, and he was adding a finger to it.

"Let's go," Charlie whispered to Josh. They skirted the room, avoiding her father, and went downstairs.

"I'm sorry about that," Charlie said when they were out on the street. The rain had slowed to a drizzle, and they walked through the puddles left behind.

"It's okay," Josh assured her. "He seems . . ." He looked for a word to finish his sentence.

"You don't have to say anything," said Charlie.

Josh reached out and took her hand, and she let him. "What happened to him?" he asked.

He felt Charlie stiffen.

"He got bit," she said.

"By a z?" Josh asked, shocked.

"Yeah," Charlie replied.

"Then shouldn't he be—"

140

"Dead," Charlie said. "Yeah. He should be. But when he was bit, he torched himself. He burned the bite."

Josh couldn't believe it. "He burned his own face?" he asked.

"It killed the virus before it could infect him," Charlie said. "They weren't sure that it had really worked, so they kept him in quarantine for six months. When he didn't show any signs of turning, they let him out."

Josh tried to imagine what it would be like to torch his own face. There was no way he could do it.

"That's why he doesn't want me playing the game," said Charlie.

"He knows about—" Josh began.

"No," Charlie interrupted him. "Not about the real game. He thinks I only play the hologame. If he knew about the real game, I don't know what he would do."

"Well, I think I can handle being your study buddy," Josh joked.

They walked in silence for a minute. Then Charlie spoke. "I told you my mother was dead," Charlie said. "That's not true. She couldn't handle it when my father came home. They fought all the time and finally she left. I don't know where she is."

"But how could she leave you behind?" Josh asked before he could stop himself. "I mean . . . sorry."

"It wasn't all her fault," Charlie said. "My dad was really angry. Violent. But he was never bad to me," she added. "Never. My mother said I was the only one who could take care of him."

"And you don't know where she is?"

"No. It's better this way," Charlie answered.

Josh wanted to ask her how it could possibly be better, but he didn't.

"I'm sorry I lied to you," Charlie said. "About my family being normal. Remember, I told you we were the only ones on the team with boring stories."

Josh chuckled. "Oh yeah," he said.

He saw a tear slip from Charlie's eye.

"Don't start crying on me," he said.

"I'm not crying," Charlie objected. "It's the rain."

"Okay, then," said Josh. "Because I'm pretty sure that's the Seventh Rule of Torching: No crying."

Charlie laughed as she wiped her eye. "That must be in the revised edition," she said. "I'll try to remember that."

"You'd better," said Josh as they continued to walk. "You never know when there will be a pop quiz."

13

On Monday Josh was at his locker, hanging up his coat, when Firecracker appeared. "Where were you yesterday?" he asked.

Josh shut his locker. "Why?" he said. He hadn't spoken to Firecracker since the incident with their report, and things were still a little weird between them. In addition, he had a headache. He'd taken a Z the night before and spent almost all night playing the hologame with Charlie.

"I called," Firecracker said. "Your dad said you were out taking pictures."

"So?" said Josh.

Firecracker snorted. "Come on," he said. "What do you think I am, stupid?"

"You said it, not me," Josh snapped. He started to walk away.

"Hey!" Firecracker called after him. "What's your problem?"

Josh ignored him. He wasn't in the mood to talk to Firecracker. Last night he'd played a zombie for the first time in the hologame. Now he understood why Charlie liked it. The Z had really helped him get into the zombie mood. He'd seen things differently, felt things differently. Everything had been more intense—primal. He'd hunted the Torchers like they were animals, smelling them out and following the sound of their hearts beating. He'd killed four of them and gained sixteen experience levels.

But the Z had also kept him up all night, and now he was exhausted. He thought about taking half a Z this morning, but he didn't want to waste it. They had practice that afternoon, and he wanted to save it for that.

Josh managed to avoid Firecracker the rest of day, though it meant skipping lunch and hiding out in the bathroom. But that was okay—it gave him some time to rest. He'd actually fallen asleep in the bathroom stall, waking up only when some seniors dragged a freshman into the bathroom and threatened to dunk his head in the toilet if he didn't pay them off. The kid had screamed bloody murder, and Josh jolted awake thinking he was in the middle of a game.

Now the day was over and he was on the train heading to the Docklands. He couldn't wait to see Charlie and to play with the rest of the team. He also wanted to find out if Stash was okay. He didn't like the guy, but he was still a Torcher, and they had to look out for one another.

When he reached his stop, he got off and walked toward the wharf. He was thinking about the Z in his pocket, and not really watching where he was going. So when someone came up from behind and grabbed his arm, he yelled in surprise.

"It's just me," Firecracker said, holding his hands up.

Josh stared at him. "Are you following me?" he asked.

"I just want to talk," Firecracker said. "What's up with you?"

"Nothing's *up* with me," said Josh.

"Then what are you doing in the Docklands? Coming to help the homeless?" Firecracker stared at Josh, daring him to lie.

"It's none of your business," said Josh. "Just go home."

"Or what?" Firecracker asked.

Josh felt himself getting angry. "Just go," he said. "Leave me alone."

He turned and started to walk away, hoping that Firecracker would give up and go the other way. No such luck. Firecracker rushed forward to block Josh's path. "I want to know what you're doing," he said.

Josh stared at his friend. Why couldn't Firecracker just let it go? He started to push past, but Firecracker moved over and cut him off.

Without thinking, Josh shoved him. Firecracker reeled backward but didn't fall. His face reddened and he stormed toward Josh. The two collided, Firecracker pushing Josh against a brick wall. Two Zooeys who had been standing on the corner turned to stare at them.

"Get off!" Josh grunted, trying to push Firecracker away.

"Josh, come *on*," said Firecracker. "Tell me what's going on."

Josh put one foot against the wall and used it to push himself forward. Firecracker stumbled back. Caught off balance, he was an easy target. Josh punched him in the stomach, and Firecracker crumpled to his knees.

"Hey!" yelled one of the Zooeys, a boy in a duck costume. "Fighting isn't cool!"

Josh took a few steps toward the boy and the other Zooey, a girl dressed like a koala bear, grabbed the duck's hand and pulled him away. Josh turned back to Firecracker, who was standing up again, holding his stomach.

Before Josh could react, Firecracker swung at him. His fist connected with Josh's cheek, and there was a sharp crack. Pain exploded in Josh's head. He ran at Firecracker, tackling him. The two of them fell to the sidewalk, where they wrestled for position until finally Josh had Firecracker pinned beneath him.

"Get it through your thick head," Josh said, flecking Firecracker's face with spittle. "I don't want you following me."

He could see confusion in Firecracker's eyes, and for a moment he felt bad and almost broke down and told the truth. Then he remembered that if he let Firecracker know what was going on, he would be risking everything. He had to keep his part in the game a secret.

"Stay away," he said. "You got that?"

He waited for Firecracker to nod, then got up. Without looking back, he walked as quickly as he could down the street. He turned a corner and waited to see if Firecracker passed him. After a minute he took a look and saw that the sidewalk was empty. *He's gone*, he thought with relief.

Still, he took a different route to the shipyard. He didn't want to take any chances. Firecracker *wasn't* stupid. He was a good tracker, and he could easily be tailing Josh. But Josh was pretty sure he had hurt

Firecracker's pride enough that he would just leave. He hated himself for having done that to his best friend, but he'd had to—for both their sakes.

Only when he was safely in the tunnel walking to the ship graveyard did he relax a little bit. He was all right. Firecracker didn't know anything.

When he saw Charlie sitting on top of a ship's propeller, cleaning her flamethrower, he felt much better. She saw him and waved. "Hey there," she said. "I've been waiting for you."

"Yeah?" Josh said. "Why's that?"

"So I could give you this," Charlie answered, giving him a quick kiss. Josh tried for another one, but Charlie shook her head. "We have to be careful," she said. "Team romances are kind of a no-no."

Josh sighed. "I suppose I can do that," he said dramatically. Then he pretended to think of something. "*Or* I could break up with you. Then it wouldn't be a problem."

"Just *try* breaking it off," said Charlie, squinting. "Then next time you've got a z after you, I might just have to trip you."

Josh didn't say anything, distracted by the throbbing in his cheek.

"Come on. I'm just joking. Don't be mad."

"It's not that," said Josh. He hesitated, not sure

he should tell Charlie what had happened. Then he sighed. "It's Firecracker. He followed me today."

Charlie's eyes widened. "He followed you? Did he see where you went?"

"No. I caught him in time," Josh answered.

"Don't tell Clatter," Charlie said quickly. "He's super paranoid about that kind of thing. Keep it to yourself."

"All right," said Josh. "I'm going to get changed."

He left her to finish cleaning her thrower and went to the locker room. Finnegan, Seamus, and Scrawl were already there, talking, but when Josh came in they stopped abruptly.

"Hey," Josh said. "Am I interrupting something?"

Finnegan and Seamus didn't say anything, but Scrawl shook his head. "Nah," he said. "We were just talking about Stash."

"How is he?" Josh asked as he opened his locker and took his uniform out.

"Not great," Scrawl said. "He'll be fine, but his bite got infected and he won't be playing for a while."

Josh slipped into his uniform. "How does a cyberbite get infected?" he asked.

He saw Seamus and Finnegan look at each other. Then Finnegan said, "He got dirt in it. We told him to be careful, but you know Stash."

Josh snorted. "Yeah," he said. When nobody responded, he added, "Not that he isn't a good guy, or anything."

"It's okay," Finnegan told him. "We all know Stash can be a jerk."

Josh smiled. "That doesn't mean I want him to get hurt," he said.

"Like I said, he'll be fine," Scrawl said. "He's just on temporary time out. Now let's go kick some zombie butt."

The others left the locker room, and Josh sat on the bench to tie his boots. Then he reached into the pocket of his jeans and took out half a tablet of Z. He put it in his mouth and swallowed hard, feeling it go down.

When he rejoined the group, they were still waiting for Freya, so everyone was just hanging out talking. Bess came up to Josh, frowning. "You cost me twenty bucks," she said, crossing her arms over her chest. "Charlie told me all about it," she whispered. Then she made kissing sounds with her lips.

Josh looked over at Charlie. She was looking up at the ceiling, pretending to be interested in something.

"I'm going to get both of you," Josh told Bess. "You just wait."

"Ooh, I'm scared," Bess said, wiggling her fingers and miming fear.

Josh walked over to Charlie. "I thought we weren't telling anyone," he said.

"I *had* to tell Bess," said Charlie. "Otherwise I would have owed *her* twenty bucks." She laughed.

"Hey," Charlie said, looking around. "Did you take the Z?"

Josh nodded.

"Me too," Charlie said. "Let's make sure we're on the same team for practice. We'll kill!"

Caught up in Charlie's excitement, Josh forgot all about Firecracker and his earlier worries. The Z was starting to work, and his thoughts were slipping away.

"Kill," he said, grinning at Charlie. "That's just what we'll do."

14

Josh looked down the stairs. Something was moving below him; there was a slight shifting of the shadows that normally he might not notice. But the Z had worked its magic on his brain, and although his thoughts were a little hazy, he was sensing things more acutely. He sniffed, smelling something dank.

"Water," he said.

Finnegan switched on his torch's light and shone it into the darkness. A dozen steps down, the stairs disappeared into water. "Good work, genius," Finnegan said.

Ever since Finnegan had been assigned to a team with Josh, Charlie, and Bess, he'd been acting weird. Assuming it was because he had been separated from his brother, Josh was trying not to let Finnegan's comments bother him. But his patience was wearing thin.

"What's your problem?" he demanded.

Finnegan stepped back. "I don't have a problem," he said, sounding surprised.

Josh grinned. "I didn't think so. So how about you go first down the stairs, then?"

Suddenly Charlie was beside him. "Ease up," she whispered so that only he could hear.

Josh laughed. "I'm fine," he said.

Charlie grabbed his elbow. "Josh," she said. "I'm serious. Just cool it, okay?"

Josh closed his eyes and took a few deep breaths, until he calmed down a little. "I'm fine," he told Charlie.

"Josh, you take lead," Bess said. "Finn, you're rear man."

Josh glared at Finnegan. "No problem," Josh said.

He descended quickly, moving faster than he knew he should. The light mounted on his flamethrower cut through the blackness. When he reached the point where the water met the stairs, he kept going, never hesitating. The cold water slid over his boots and up his legs, and still Josh didn't slow down.

When the water was up to his waist, the stairs ran out and he was on level ground. Ten feet ahead of him the opening to a huge pipe gaped like an open mouth about twelve feet across. The metal was rusted and flaking off, and the water was speckled with tiny pieces of it.

"What is this place?" Josh asked.

"One of the intake tunnels," said Bess. "This is where the water came in to flood the main room and raise the ships to the surface. There are a dozen of them." She shone her light at the top of the tunnel entrance, where a number was etched into the steel. "This is tunnel nine."

"The worst one," Finnegan mumbled.

"The *hardest* one," said Charlie, correcting him.

"Why?" Josh asked.

"This one is still live," Bess explained. "The others were turned off years ago, but this one still works. It's connected to a line used by the city to take water from the ocean to use in the hydrogenerators that power the subway. The guys who built this place tapped into that line. They installed a valve to open and close it, but when they abandoned it, that valve was stuck halfway open. So whenever the city uses this particular line, water comes through tunnel nine too."

"What she's trying to say is that this place can flood at any second," Finnegan added.

"Not any second," Charlie countered. "You get a warning, at least if you keep your ears open."

"Right," said Bess. "When water moves through the main line, you can hear it. Then you know you have about three minutes to get out of the tunnel before it starts filling up."

"What kind of noise?" Josh asked her.

"It's hard to explain," Bess answered. "Trust me, you'll know it when you hear it."

"How often do they use the line?"

"Not often," said Charlie. "The lines are old, so they rotate between them. This one gets used maybe three times a month."

"But never on the same day," Finnegan added.

Josh looked at the water. "It looks like they've used it pretty recently," he remarked. "Look how high it is."

Bess shook her head. "It's always at least this high," she said. "Remember, the valve is stuck halfway open. When the tunnel floods, it only drains back out to the level of the valve opening."

"Why not just fix the valve?"

"Clatter thinks it makes a great training zone," Charlie said.

"And he's right," said Bess.

"Wait a minute," Josh said. "If the tunnel goes straight in and straight out, what's the big deal? We just go in until we find the z's, torch them, and get out."

Finnegan laughed but said nothing.

"It's not that easy," Charlie said. "The tunnel

doesn't just run straight through. It's in five sections, with a flood chamber between each section and the next. The flood chambers have a hatch door on each side. If the tunnel starts to flood, theoretically you can release the door closest to the main line and prevent the water from coming any farther this way."

"Theoretically?" said Josh.

"They don't always work," Finnegan said. "The machinery is old. Some of it is broken. Some of it sticks. You just never know."

"Each flood chamber has a shaft that runs up to the surface," Bess continued. "It's a way to vent water if it builds up. There's also a ladder in each shaft, kind of an escape route if you're trapped in the room."

"Not that you're likely to make it," said Finnegan. "More than likely the water will rise faster than you can climb."

"There are also some smaller access tunnels," Charlie said. "They link the twelve tunnels together. But they're really only wide enough to crawl through."

"Which the z's are really good at," said Finnegan.

Josh tried to make sense of everything he was being told. Normally it wouldn't be a problem, but the Z was making it hard to analyze everything clearly. *Hatches*, he thought. *Access tunnels. Flood chambers.*

Individually the words made sense, but when he tried to put them all together, things got a little fuzzy.

"So you're saying that the z's could be anywhere," he said finally. "Got it. Let's go torching."

Without waiting for the others, he pushed ahead through the water. His eyes quickly adapted to the darkness, another benefit of taking the Z. He watched the shadows carefully for signs of movement but saw nothing.

After about a hundred yards they came to a wall that prevented them from going forward. A circular door about six feet across and made of thick steel was set into the center of the wall.

"This is the first hatch door," Bess said, shining her light on the door. "See that lever on the right?"

Josh looked where her beam was pointing and saw a rectangular box about a foot high affixed to the wall beside the door. A metal rod extended from it at an angle.

"When you pull the lever, it activates the chains that raise and lower the door," said Bess. She reached for it. "Be ready to shoot if there's anything inside."

Josh and the others stood back, their flamethrowers held out in front of them, as Bess pulled the rod down. There was a grinding sound as the heavy door rose straight up into the ceiling.

Josh stepped through the opening and found himself in a square chamber approximately fifteen feet on each side. From the doorway, steps led down from the tunnel to the room's floor. On the opposite side of the room another set of steps went up to a hatch door that was partially open. The room was filled with water that left only three steps exposed.

"Doesn't look like there are any meatbags in here," said Josh, shining his light around. He walked down the steps and into the partially flooded chamber. When his feet touched the floor, the water was just above his waist. As he waded across the room, he noticed a ladder affixed to the wall on his left. It led to a hole in the ceiling, and he guessed it was the escape shaft Bess had mentioned.

"Where are the access tunnels you talked about?" he asked Bess. "I don't see any other ways in or out."

"They're below water level right now," Bess said. "It's different in each room. You just have to look everywhere."

They made their way to the other side of the chamber and ducked beneath the partially opened hatch door to reenter the tunnel. The next stretch was as empty as the first, and Josh found himself getting bored.

"The other team better not get all the z's," he complained.

"Don't worry," Finnegan said. "You'll get your share."

When they reached the second chamber and found it empty, Josh was annoyed. "This is a waste of time," he said as he surveyed the room. "We might as well go back."

All of a sudden a loud clanking sound filled the room, and the hatch door behind them crashed closed, falling from the ceiling as the chains rattled violently. They all swirled around and stared at it.

"How did that happen?" Bess yelled. She looked at Finnegan, who was standing closest to the control box, but he shook his head.

"It wasn't me," he said, showing her that he was holding his flamethrower with both hands.

"Somebody had to have touched something," Bess insisted. "The hatches don't just—"

She was cut off as the water exploded upward. Three zombies rose from the bottom, screeching as they clawed at the air.

"Meatbags!" Josh yelled. "Torch them!"

One of the zombies—a man in a tattered suit—lunged at Josh. With no room to use his flamethrower, Josh used it as a club instead, butting the man in the chest with it so that he staggered back and fell into the water.

The other two zombies—an old woman with gray hair and a boy in a scouting uniform—were trying to get up the stairs to where Finnegan was standing. He aimed his flamethrower at them and pulled the trigger. The two z's burst into flame, but Charlie had to dive sideways to avoid being hit as well. When she came up she was sputtering.

"Finnegan, you idiot!" she yelled as the flaming zombies swirled around her.

The man who had attacked Josh was back on his feet. This time Josh did flame him, but even on fire he kept coming. In fact, the three z's had somehow managed to get between the four Torchers and the tunnel door.

"This way!" Finnegan yelled, sloshing through the water toward the opposite door.

The four of them made it into the next section of tunnel as the burning zombies stumbled after them. One of them—the scout—fell into the water, causing a cloud of hissing steam to rise around him. The other two continued on, moaning.

"Out of the way!" Charlie shouted, pulling on the lever sticking from the hatch-door control box.

Nothing happened. Charlie pulled again. There was a grinding sound, as if the gears were trying to work, but still the door didn't budge.

"Keep going," Bess ordered, turning and heading further into the tunnel.

"What about the z's?" Josh asked as they jogged along.

"They'll burn out," said Bess. "Don't worry about them. Worry about the ones we can't see."

"It's like they were *herding* us," said Charlie. "Like they'd set a trap to get us to go this way."

"Please," Finnegan sneered. "They're not that smart. They're not *any* kind of smart."

"Then who shut the hatch door?" Charlie snapped back.

"It was an accident," said Finnegan.

"Whatever it was, we can't go back that way," Bess reminded them. "We'll have to use one of the escape shafts."

"We've never done that," said Charlie.

"There's a first time for everything," Bess said, grinning.

Josh's head ached. His sense of smell had grown stronger, and the odors of rusting steel, stagnant water, and now the stench of the burning zombies filled his nose. His heart was beating more quickly, and there was a ringing in his ears.

They burst into the third chamber, which was empty like the first.

"I don't like this," said Finnegan as they waded through the room. "I *really* don't like this. We should go back."

"Not until we complete the mission," Bess insisted. "There's one more chamber and then the final part of the tunnel. Then we're out of here."

They were halfway down the fourth length of tunnel when they heard the grating of metal on metal behind them. Finnegan, turning around, shone his light into the darkness. The beam illuminated a shut hatch door.

Finnegan ran toward the door. "Who did that?" he shouted.

"Finnegan! Get back here!" Bess's voice was forceful, but Josh sensed fear in it as well.

Finnegan stopped and stared at the hatch door for a moment before going to the control lever and pulling it. Nothing happened. When Finnegan turned around, his face was a mask of panic.

"*Now* do you think they aren't smart enough?" Charlie asked.

Finnegan walked back to them, shaking his head. "No," he said. "There's no way. They can't do this."

Josh heard himself laugh. "What are you guys afraid of?" he said. "They're just cybots. You're acting like they're really trying to kill us."

For a moment he thought he saw Finnegan and Bess exchange a look, then Bess was all business. "Josh is right. But we still want to complete the mission. The fourth flood chamber is up ahead. We'll sweep it, check out the tunnel beyond it, and finish up. I'm sure Clatter set this all up to test us. Nobody panic, all right?"

Charlie and Finnegan nodded. Josh laughed again. Despite the situation, he felt powerful. Or was he laughing at the others because he was thinking like a z? He didn't know, and he didn't care. He was having a great time.

They kept moving. In the fourth chamber they found a single zombie. Dressed in overalls, it was just wandering around holding a wrench in its hand. Charlie torched it without any trouble.

As they headed up the steps to the final length of tunnel, Finnegan stopped. "Maybe one of us should wait here," he said.

Josh turned around. "Why?"

"The hatch got shut after we left the chamber," Finnegan reminded him. "If one of us stays here, we can at least make sure no one messes with it from this side."

"That's a good point," Bess agreed. "You stay here. The three of us will go on."

"He's afraid," Josh said to Charlie as they walked into the tunnel.

Charlie nudged him with her elbow. "Don't make fun of him," she said, but Josh heard her giggle.

"Oh no!" Josh said, imitating Finnegan's voice. "A zombie! Seamus, help me!"

Again Charlie giggled, but this time Bess turned around and shushed them. "Keep it down," she ordered. "You never know when—"

A sudden rumbling interrupted her. The tunnel shook slightly, making the water slosh from side to side.

"The main line!" Charlie yelped. "It's filling up!"

"Go!" said Bess, pushing them. "Back to the flood chamber!"

Josh stumbled as he tried to run through the water. It seemed to be pulling at him, holding him back. Behind him he heard a low growling.

"The water is coming," said Charlie. "Hurry!"

They reached the chamber, where they found Finnegan standing on the steps. "Is it the main?" he asked.

"Get the hatch shut!" Bess barked. "That will stop it."

Finnegan grabbed the lever and pulled. It broke off in his hand, leaving just a stub of metal. He looked at it helplessly. Josh ran over and pushed him out of the way. Grabbing the short length of metal, he pulled as hard as he could. The jagged end of the broken lever cut into his palm, and blood ran down his wrist. The lever didn't move.

"There's no time," said Bess. "And we can't get back to the third chamber. We have to go up."

As she spoke, more water surged in through the tunnel. Finnegan let out a frightened squeak and ran for the ladder affixed to the wall beside the open hatch door. He dropped his flamethrower and started climbing, ignoring the rest of them. Josh watched his head disappear into the hole in the ceiling.

"Does he know where he's going?" he asked Bess.

"None of us do," Bess said. "Just go. We'll figure it out."

Josh waited for Charlie to start up the ladder, then motioned for Bess to follow her. Bess shook her head. "I'm the team leader," she said. "I go last. And don't argue. We don't have time."

Josh looked at the water, which was rising more quickly than he thought it would. Already the steps were covered, and even as he watched it rose another inch.

He slung his flamethrower over his shoulder and started up the ladder, ignoring the pain in his wounded hand. Ahead of him Charlie was passing through the hole in the ceiling. Josh wondered what was waiting for them there.

He found out a moment later when he emerged into a small space. Instead of going up further, as he'd expected it to, the ladder ended there, and another tunnel continued off to the left. Charlie was moving through it on her hands and knees.

Josh heard Bess come up behind him. "What's the holdup?" she shouted. "This place is about to turn into a swimming pool."

Josh moved as quickly as he could, sliding into the tunnel. He heard Bess start to follow him. Then she yelped in surprise.

"A z has me!" she called to Josh.

Unable to turn around in the tunnel, Josh bowed his head and tried to look through his legs. He saw Bess's startled face for a moment, illuminated by the light of her flamethrower. Then she was pulled backward.

"Josh!" she cried.

Josh heard the mumbled moaning of a z. It was dragging Bess back to the hole in the ceiling.

"Kick!" Josh shouted.

"I'm trying!" Bess shouted back. "It won't let go!"

Josh didn't know what to do. He couldn't turn

around. He couldn't maneuver his flamethrower in the small space. Even if he could get to it, he couldn't shoot past Bess.

He could hear Bess ramming her foot into the z. She was also shouting at it to let go. Josh looked ahead. Somewhere in the darkness Charlie and Finnegan were still crawling. Calling to them wouldn't help, though—they couldn't turn around either.

It was up to him.

Just as he was trying to formulate a plan he felt something wet against his knees. *Water,* he thought vaguely. *Water is coming in.*

Behind him Bess choked. Then she screamed. "It bit me!" she yelled.

The water was coming in more quickly now. Josh realized that the flood chamber must have filled up and the water was being forced into the tunnel. But surely *someone* must know they were trapped in there, and would somehow reroute the water. They wouldn't just be allowed to die.

"Josh! Go!" Bess called out. She choked again. "My body will block some of the water, but not for long."

"I'm not just leaving you here!" Josh yelled.

"I'm bit," said Bess, her voice softer now. "Just leave me."

"It's a *game!*" Josh said, becoming more frantic as

the water rose past his hands. "The bite doesn't matter. But if you don't move *now*, you're going to drown."

"Josh, listen to me." Bess's voice was eerily calm. "I'm the squad leader, and I'm telling you to go."

Josh started to argue, but something in Bess's voice told him not to. Besides, his survival instinct was screaming at him to move. "I'll get help," he told Bess. "We'll be back."

He crawled forward as quickly as he could. The rough metal scraped his palms raw, and he could feel the water rising quickly. It was almost up to his chest now, and in another minute or two he wouldn't be able to breathe. He tried not to think about Bess. *It's going to be all right,* he told himself, repeating it over and over as he scrambled through the black tunnel.

The tunnel seemed to go on forever. Then it opened up into a square shaft maybe three feet on each side. The shaft rose straight up, a ladder attached to one wall. Above him Josh saw a tiny point of light.

"Charlie?" he yelled. "Charlie, is that you?"

"Josh!" Charlie's voice echoed down the shaft. "Hurry! There's a tunnel up here that we think leads back to the surface."

The water pouring into the shaft was filling it up quickly. Josh grabbed the ladder and started climbing, staying just a few steps ahead of the water. When he reached the top, he saw Charlie.

"Come on!" Charlie yelled, grabbing his hand. "Where's Bess?"

Josh shook his head. Charlie froze, horror crossing her face. Then Finnegan yelled at them to hurry, and she moved. Josh followed as they ran through yet another tunnel, this one built out of brick.

"How do you know this takes us back to the surface?" Josh asked as they ran.

"There was a diagram on the wall back there," said Finnegan. "Right up here should be a set of stairs."

Moments later the stairs came into view. But blocking them was a z, a big man whose muscled body was bleeding from multiple wounds, as if he'd been tearing at his own skin. Seeing the three Torchers, he lurched toward them.

Barely thinking, Josh rushed at the zombie, tackling him and pushing him against the wall.

"Josh!" Charlie shouted. "The blood! Don't touch it! Your hands are cut!"

Who cares about fake blood? Josh thought as he fought the zombie, who was thrashing his head from side to side and trying to bite Josh's face.

He saw Finnegan run by him and up the stairs. Charlie was next. As she passed Josh, she grabbed his arm and pulled. "Come on!" she said.

Josh was staring into the zombie's rheumy eyes. It was gnashing its teeth, or what was left of them, and its tongue was lolling from its mouth. Blood and spittle flecked its chin. It was disgusting, but for some reason Josh couldn't stop looking at it. His brain slowed down, as if he and the zombie were thinking the same thoughts.

Then Charlie yanked hard on his arm and tore him away. She practically dragged him up the first dozen steps before pushing him behind her and raising her flamethrower. Josh watched as she shot a blast of fire at the z, which was trying to climb the stairs after them. Charlie kept the flame burning for longer than usual, and when she released the trigger, the zombie's skin was blackened, falling to the stone steps in bloody chunks.

"That's for Bess," Charlie whispered. Then she turned around and took Josh's hand, and they started to climb.

15

The tap on his shoulder startled Josh. He jumped and opened his eyes. Emily was standing beside his bed, looking at him curiously. Josh removed the headset he was wearing and turned it off.

"Sorry," Emily said. "I knocked, but you didn't hear me. What are you listening to?"

"Crystal Static," said Josh. "What do you want?"

Emily frowned. "What's your problem?" she asked. "You've been grumpy ever since you got home. Did one of the homeless people make fun of your clothes or something?"

"You know how Mondays can be," Josh answered. He wasn't about to tell her that he was upset because Bess had almost died in the game that afternoon. He still couldn't believe Clatter, Scrawl, and Seamus had managed to get into the sealed chamber through the tunnel and get her out. By the time he, Charlie, and Finnegan had reached the surface, Bess had been transported to the hospital, where she was recovering.

Clatter had apologized repeatedly for the mechanical malfunctions he said caused the hatch doors to lock, and Josh knew he felt terrible about the accident. He'd praised Josh for his quick thinking under pressure. But even knowing that Bess was alive couldn't help Josh shake the memory of seeing her face for what he thought was the last time. She'd looked so scared, and he'd had to leave her there alone to—he thought—die.

He shook the thoughts from his head and looked at Emily. "So what do you want?"

"I'm having trouble with my homework," said Emily. "I was wondering if you could help me."

"Can't you ask Mom or Dad?"

"I could," said Emily. "But I don't want to. Besides, they're busy."

"So am I," Josh told her.

"Busy doing nothing," said Emily. "You've been 'busy' for two weeks."

"I have a lot to do," Josh said. "You wouldn't understand."

"You mean your new girlfriend?" said Emily.

Josh sat up. "What are you talking about?"

Emily cocked her head. "So she *is* your girlfriend.

I told Stella she was wrong."

"Who's Stella?" said Josh.

"A friend of mine from dance class," Emily told him. "She said she's seen you with the same girl a bunch of times. On the train."

"Well, you can tell Stella she is wrong," Josh said.

"Oh, I'll do that," said Emily. She turned to leave the room. At the door she turned around. "I just hope Mom and Dad don't find out about her," she said. "Stella said she didn't look like a homeless person to *her*."

Emily started to leave, but Josh called her back. She turned to him, an innocent look on her face. "Yes?" she said. "Is there something I can do for you?"

"Get your homework," Josh told her.

Emily beamed and ran out. She returned a few moments later carrying her NoteTaker. Josh moved over on the bed, and she sat next to him.

"What are you having a hard time with?" Josh asked her.

"Math," said Emily.

"Ah," Josh said. "That's why you don't want to ask Mom or Dad." He looked at the problem on her NoteTaker and started to tell her how to solve it. Then he paused. "Wait a minute," he said. "Since when have you had trouble with math?"

"Since now," Emily said.

Josh handed her back the NoteTaker. "I'm not buying it."

Emily groaned. "All right, I don't need help with my homework." She kicked her feet against the bed.

"Come on," Josh urged. "What's going on?"

"Fine," Emily said, as if he'd forced her to talk. "It's you. You've been acting all weird."

Josh felt a knot of fear form in his gut. What had Emily noticed? He'd been careful not to take Z too often at home. He'd done it a couple of times, but only when he was in his room alone. Then he'd sat up all night playing the hologame.

"Yeah, well," Josh said. "I am pretty weird."

"This is weirder than normal," said Emily. "I don't really know how to explain it. And now there's this girl."

"I told you, she's just a friend," Josh reminded her.

"And you don't talk to Firecracker anymore," Emily continued.

"Sure I do," said Josh. "Just because he hasn't been over for a few—"

"Come on, Josh. Poppy told me," Emily interrupted him.

Poppy. Firecracker's little sister. *Between her and this Stella girl, they're practically a detective agency,* Josh thought. He'd been worried about Firecracker when really he should have been concerned about a bunch of nine-year-olds.

"Firecracker and I kind of had a fight," he told Emily.

"About that girl?"

"No," Josh said. "It's nothing."

"Is that how you got that bruise on your face?"

Josh put his hand to his cheek. "Nah, I walked into an open locker door."

"Poppy said he's been really sad," Emily told him, looking at his bruise doubtfully.

"Sad?" Josh echoed. "Firecracker?"

"That's what she said," Emily confirmed.

"Well, don't worry about it," Josh told her.

"You shouldn't fight with your best friend," said Emily. "They're kind of hard to find."

"When did you turn into a fortune cookie?" Josh asked her.

"When did you get a girlfriend?" Emily countered.

"For the last time, she's not my girlfriend," said Josh.

"Stella said you kissed her," Emily pressed.

He was busted. But how? He and Charlie were always careful *not* to do anything like that where people might see them who shouldn't. "She never saw that," Josh said. "Because it never happened."

"Stella said she saw you," Emily said stubbornly.

"Did she get a picture of it?" asked Josh.

He saw the expression on Emily's face falter. He'd caught her. Stella might have seen him with Charlie, but she'd never seen them kiss.

"She's still your girlfriend," Emily said. "I know she is."

"You just keep thinking that," said Josh. "But don't go telling anyone things you can't prove."

"Maybe," his sister said, clearly annoyed that she'd been beaten.

"Hey," he said. "You want to watch a holofilm after dinner? I'll even let you pick."

Emily's face lit up. "Yes!" she said. "And I know just what I want to see."

"Nothing with princesses or dancing," Josh warned her.

Emily made a disgusted face. "What do I look like, an eight-year-old?" she said. "I want to see that documentary about the sharks they found in the Hell Sea on Mars."

Josh groaned. "Haven't you seen that, like, twelve times?" he asked.

"Thirteen," Emily corrected. "But I can watch it over and over. Those sharks are amazing. I mean, come on, they practically have lava for blood. What's not to love?"

"All right," said Josh. "We can watch your stupid sharks. Now get out of here. I have some stuff to do."

When Emily was gone, Josh lay back down and closed his eyes. Why had he and Charlie been so careless? Maybe it was time for them to just tell people they were together. Charlie said it was against Clatter's rules, but maybe he would make an exception.

Then again, the mood on the team had been a little strange. Stash still hadn't come back, and not only had Bess been injured in that afternoon's game, Freya had taken a bite when a meatbag hiding underwater in one of the sewers had jumped up and grabbed her from behind. So now they were down three team members. *Maybe it's not the best time to try to bend the rules*, Josh decided.

Then there was the Firecracker situation. It had been really hard for Josh to ignore his best friend, especially since they had a couple of classes together. But after Firecracker had tried to talk to him a few times and Josh had made it clear he wasn't going to talk, they had each started pretending that the other didn't exist. In class they sat as far apart as possible, and Josh had started eating lunch in an unused classroom in the school's lower level. Sometimes he had to share it with one or two of the stoners who liked to spend the lunch hour high on virtual-reality drugs, but they were mostly okay.

He knew that he was partly to blame for what had happened between him and Firecracker. It was only natural that Firecracker was curious. But now it was too late to apologize.

Or is it? he asked himself. Why couldn't he tell Firecracker he was sorry? He didn't have to tell him everything. He could just tell him about Charlie, and say that he was afraid *she* would get in trouble if anyone knew about them. That was sort of a good explanation for Josh's behavior that day.

He got up, went to his desk, and punched Firecracker's number into the com terminal. After three notifications the screen lit up and Josh found himself looking at the face of Firecracker's uncle, who he and Poppy lived with. He was a timid, nervous man, but when he saw Josh he smiled.

"Josh!" he said, sounding relieved.

"Hi, Mr. Reilly," said Josh. "Is Firecracker there?"

A worried look crossed the man's face. "No," he answered. "Isn't he there with you?"

"No," Josh said.

"He said he was staying over at your house tonight to work on a project for school," Mr. Reilly said.

Josh didn't know what to say. Why would Firecracker tell his uncle he was staying over at Josh's house? More important, where had he *really* gone? It wasn't like him to lie to his uncle. But Josh didn't want to upset Mr. Reilly, so he said, "I remember now. He was going to stop by our friend Mac's house and try out a new game. Then he's coming here. Duh. I totally forgot."

Mr. Reilly sighed, visibly relieved. "That's what I thought," he said.

"I'm sorry I bothered you," Josh said. "Have a good night, Mr. Reilly."

"You too, Josh. Tell Peter to call me when he gets in."

"Sure thing," said Josh, and cut off the comlink. He leaned back in his desk chair.

Things weren't adding up. Firecracker wouldn't just disappear. But now that he thought about it, he hadn't seen him at school that day either. He'd assumed Firecracker was sick or had a dentist's appointment or something. Now he worried that something bad might have happened to him.

A terrible thought came to him . . . but it was the only possible answer.

"Charlie told Scrawl about Firecracker following me," Josh whispered as a cold, hard knot gripped his insides.

16

"**I**t's Josh."

"Hey," Charlie said. "I was going to send you a video message later."

"Did you tell anyone about Firecracker following me?" Josh asked her.

A flicker of fear crossed Charlie's face. She recovered quickly, but Josh had seen it. "You did, didn't you?"

"What makes you think that?" said Charlie. She cleared her throat.

"Firecracker is missing," Josh said. "And I think Scrawl has something to do with it."

"Scrawl?" said Charlie. "What would Scrawl have to do with Firecracker?"

"I was hoping you could tell me," Josh answered.

He watched Charlie's face on the com screen, waiting for her reply. She looked down. For a long time she didn't say anything. When she looked up again her eyes were clouded with fear. "I need to talk to you," she said. "Not on com. In person."

"Why can't we talk here?" Josh asked.

"We just can't," said Charlie. "Please, Josh. Just meet me. I might know something about Firecracker."

Josh hesitated. If Charlie knew something about his friend's disappearance, why couldn't she just tell him?

"Where?" he asked Charlie.

"Do you know where the Church of the Sorrowful Mother is?" Charlie answered.

"Yes," said Josh.

"Meet me there in half an hour," Charlie told him.

Josh hesitated for a moment. Should he trust Charlie? He wanted to. He *needed* to. But now he didn't know. If she had told Scrawl about Firecracker, then how could he believe anything she told him?

He looked at the clock. It was seven-thirty. If he hurried, he could get to Three Sisters Square and back before ten. He had no choice. He grabbed his jacket and knit hat and left his room. Nobody was in the living room, so he didn't bother telling anyone he was going out. He would be back before they noticed anyway.

It was raining again, and he wished he'd

remembered to bring an umbrella. He pulled his hat down, but still he got wet. He didn't care, though. He just wanted to get to the church and talk to Charlie. Hopefully she would know where Firecracker was.

He decided to take the hoverbus. Because of the rain, most people were heading underground. Only a few chose to stand at the curb getting wet. But Josh saw the blinking blue lights of a city hoverbus only a block away, so he joined the small group at the stop. He watched the bus approach, the jets on its underside emitting streams of warm air that kept it floating several feet above the street. In the cold the air turned to steam, giving the bus the appearance of an angry dragon. When it came to a stop, Josh got on and took a seat near the back door.

The ride took twenty minutes. It was raining even harder when Josh got off at Three Sisters Square, but the Church of the Sorrowful Mother wasn't far. Josh ran across the square, which was filled with penitents standing in the rain mumbling the strange chants of their religion. Their eyes were closed, and they took no notice of him as he ran up the stairs and passed through the huge stone archway above which the Mother stood, her hands covering her eyes.

Inside, the church smelled of incense and old wax. Oil lamps, centuries old, hung on long chains from the vaulted ceiling, their flames sending up plumes of black smoke. All along the stone sides of the sanctuary, stained-glass windows depicted strange scenes from the life of the Mother. Josh had studied some of them in his religious history class at school, but he had long since forgotten what they were.

Several anchorites were gathered around the circular stone altar at the front of the church. The altar was strewn with pink, red, and white roses, and the women were chanting in low voices. Josh wondered what the anchorites were saying. Supposedly they spoke a language only they understood.

He looked around for Charlie and spotted her kneeling before a low wall covered in white candles. As Josh watched, she lit one of the candles, held it in her hand as she said something, then placed it on the wall beside the others. Then she stood up and turned around. When she saw Josh, she smiled and walked toward him.

"It's for my mother," she said. "The candle. I light one for her every week."

"Oh," said Josh. He wasn't sure how he was supposed to respond.

"She was Gaian," Charlie explained. "I mean, she *is* Gaian." She smiled sadly.

"What does the candle do?"

Charlie laughed. "I don't know. Sends out light and happiness or something."

Josh nodded. Now that he was face-to-face with Charlie, he almost forgot why he was there. She was so pretty, with her wet hair shining in the candlelight. *You're here for Firecracker,* he reminded himself. *And she knows something about him.*

"So what about Firecracker?" he said.

"Not here," said Charlie, looking around. "Come with me."

She walked along the side of the sanctuary. Josh hesitated a moment. Charlie looked back and nodded for him to follow.

They passed the chanting anchorites and entered a low-ceilinged hallway built out of the same stone as the rest of the church. The hallway curved around the back of the sanctuary. Every twenty feet or so was a heavy wooden door with a small window about five feet up. Josh noticed that some of the windows were covered by solid metal plates. Charlie stopped before one of the doors with an open window, looked inside, and pushed the door open. She entered while Josh stood in the doorway, looking at the room beyond. It was small, no more than eight feet long by five feet wide, and it was completely bare.

"What is this?" he asked Charlie.

"A prayer room," Charlie said. "Come in."

Josh stepped into the room, and Charlie shut the door. She slid a heavy iron deadbolt into place and then slid the metal covering on the door's window closed.

"People come in here to pray or meditate," Charlie explained. "The anchorites sleep in these rooms at night. Well, some of them do, anyway."

"It's like being in a tomb," said Josh. He ran his hands over the stone walls. They were cold and damp. He couldn't see how anyone could sleep in such a place.

"You asked me if I told Scrawl about Firecracker," Charlie began. Josh looked at her. She wasn't looking away from him now. "I did," she said.

Josh shook his head. "Why would you—"

"He followed me," said Charlie.

Josh stood there, not sure he'd heard her correctly. "Followed you?" he said. "When?"

"A few days ago," Charlie said. "I was walking home, and he just appeared out of nowhere. He said he'd seen you talking to me on the train."

Stella said she saw us on the train, Josh thought.

"He wanted to know who I was," Charlie continued. "He wanted to know what you and I were doing together." She was talking more quickly now. "He accused me of . . . of . . . being some kind of bad influence on you."

"What did you tell him?" Josh asked.

Charlie shook her head. "He was yelling," she said. "I didn't know what to say." She looked at Josh. "So I ran."

"Why didn't you tell me?"

"I don't know," Charlie said.

Josh sighed. "But you told Scrawl."

"Yes. I just wanted him to know that someone might be trying to track us," said Charlie. "We're supposed to tell him when—"

"What did he do?" Josh said, interrupting her. "What did Scrawl do?"

"I think he just wanted to scare him," said Charlie.

"Scare him?" Josh said. "What, into not following you? Into forgetting that he saw us together? That doesn't make any sense, Charlie."

She turned away from him, saying nothing. Josh stared at her back, waiting for an answer. When she finally turned around, she was crying. "You don't understand," she said, wiping her nose with her hand. "But it's not your fault. I should have told you."

"Told me what?" Josh asked.

Charlie bit her lip. "It's not just the game that

Clatter doesn't want anyone to know about," she said. "There's something else."

"What something else?" said Josh.

Charlie crouched down and put her head in her hands. "You're going to hate me," she said quietly.

Josh crouched beside her. "I won't hate you," he told her. "But you have to tell me."

Charlie looked at him through tear-stained eyes. "It's the Z," she said, her voice hoarse. "He doesn't want anyone to know about the Z."

It took Josh a moment to put the pieces together. "You get the Z from Clatter," he said. "That's it, isn't it?"

"We all do," said Charlie. "Everyone who plays. He makes it and gives it to us."

"And he doesn't want anyone to find out that he makes it," Josh said.

"Right," Charlie said. "He gives it to us and also sells it to his customers who bet on the game. He's going to start selling it on the streets, too, and he'll make a lot of money. But if anyone finds out, he'll probably go to jail, and the game will be shut down."

Josh stood up. "Why didn't you tell me?" he asked.

Charlie stood up and pushed her hair back. "Before I tell you, you have to know something."

Josh didn't respond. "Everything I feel about you is real," she said. "Everything about *us* is real. I've never licd about that." She laughed. "Believe me, it would be easier for both of us if I were lying. But I really like you, Josh." She paused for a long moment. "You believe me, don't you?"

Josh looked at her worried eyes and her shaking hands. He did believe her. "I do," he said.

"Like I said, Clatter gives Z to everyone on the team," she said. "The only one who doesn't take it is Scrawl. He says it makes him feel sick. Anyway, Clatter doesn't make us pay for it, but . . ."

"But?" Josh encouraged her.

"But after a while he calls in a favor," Charlie said.

Josh didn't understand. "What kind of favor?"

"He makes us find a new person for the team," said Charlie. "If we don't, he cuts us off. And believe me, it isn't pretty when that happens. Bess refused to do it, and you saw what happened to her."

"Bess?" said Josh. "What are you talking about? He saved Bess."

Charlie shook her head. "No, he didn't," she said. "He killed her because she wouldn't recruit for him. He sent her into the tunnels knowing she wouldn't let the rest of us die. He didn't get to her in time, Josh. He never even tried. He let her drown."

"No," Josh said. "You're lying. He wouldn't do that.

He wouldn't let one of us *die*."

"He's done it before," Charlie said. "You don't know what he's really like, Josh. You have no idea."

Josh felt the air leave his lungs. Was Charlie telling the truth? Was Bess really dead? And was Clatter responsible? He couldn't believe it.

Then something else she'd said clicked into place. "You're telling me you recruited me as payment to Clatter for the Z?" he asked.

Charlie nodded slowly. "Yes," she said. "That's what I'm telling you."

17

Josh ran through the rain, not caring where he went. He just wanted to get away from Charlie. She followed him for two blocks, calling for him to stop, but he lost her by getting on a hoverbus and then, just as the doors were closing, pushing his way off through the back door. The last he'd seen of Charlie, she had her face pressed against the bus window, yelling his name.

His heart was pounding, and he felt like he might throw up. Charlie had used him to pay Clatter for her Z. If what she said was true, soon enough Clatter would demand that he do the same thing. And all this time Charlie had been telling him not to mention Z to anyone on the team. *She really played me,* he thought.

He looked around, trying to get his bearings. He had run eastward away from Three Sisters Square and was now a block away from Midcity Park. He could walk through it, exit through the south end, and be only a couple of blocks from his house. But how could he go home when his best friend was missing? His whole life had been sent into a tailspin.

The rain had chased most people out of the park, and the ones who remained were mainly Dusters (who never seemed to notice the weather), Boarders using the empty paths as raceways, and the occasional person walking a dog.

He stuffed his hands into his pockets, and his fingers landed on something small and hard. He pulled out the tablet of Z and looked at it. He started to throw it onto the ground, but found he couldn't do it. Despite the hatred he had for Z at that moment, the memory of how it helped him be a better player—and how it made him feel good even when he wasn't playing—made it impossible for him to just let go.

Instead, he took it.

As he kept walking, his mind slipped into a comforting fog. The part of Josh that worried about everything disappeared and was replaced by a feeling of invincibility. Nobody could hurt him. They would be *afraid* of him. The world around him became all about sensations. The rain on his skin. The smell of the air. The sounds of cars honking and voices chattering like birds. All of it swirled around in his head like a storm.

A Boarder whizzed past him, the wheels of his board *clack-clack-clack*ing on the pavement. They tossed up water behind them, and the spray caught the light from the streetlamps and dazzled Josh's eyes. The Boarder laughed, the sound rolling through Josh's head like waves. He laughed too. Everything was okay now. Charlie didn't matter. Scrawl didn't matter. Firecracker didn't matter.

Nothing mattered.

The peaceful feeling lasted until he reached the center of the park, where a group of Zooeys was dancing in the rain beneath a streetlamp. The frantic, pounding beat of techno music filled the air as the rabbits, cats, and kangaroos bounced up and down, their paws waving wildly and their heads going back and forth. Watching them, Josh began to feel afraid. The music seemed to wrap around his heart, replacing its steady pumping with jerky, painful lurches.

Anger bloomed in his mind, expanding like a flower opening to the sun. The Zooeys had ruined his moment of happiness. Their thumping music and frenzied dancing pulled at him, trying to drag him into the dizzying chaos. Josh fought it off, resisting. He had to make it stop.

With a roar he charged into the group, pushing

bodies to the ground and trying to find the source of the tormenting music. Frightened Zooeys screamed and crawled away from him as he yelled at them to shut up. He grabbed a lion by the throat and pulled him close, so that their faces were almost touching. He could feel the lion's heart beating like a drum in his mind, and smelled the stench of fear. "Where is it?" Josh shouted. "Where is it?"

The Zooey shook his head. "I don't know, man. I don't know!"

Josh shoved the lion away. Now the Zooeys were in a circle around him, staring in terror. He whirled around and around, daring them to come closer. "I'll kill you!" he screamed. "I'll kill all of you!"

And he really did want to hurt them. He ran for them and they scattered, fleeing into the dark. Watching them go, Josh began to laugh. *They're afraid of me,* he thought with delight. *They're afraid of me.* It made him feel strong. No one—nothing—could harm him.

"Hey!" a voice called out.

He turned to see three Boarders behind him. One, a boy wearing a T-shirt that said BOARD > BORED on it, shook his head. "That wasn't cool, man. They were just having fun."

Josh growled. The boy stepped back but didn't run.

"You should leave," said another Boarder, a girl with dreadlocks threaded through with beads in every color.

Josh laughed at her. She was weak. And she was telling *him* what to do.

"Maybe we should show him the way out," the third Boarder said. Not much bigger than Emily, he was stick thin.

Josh sneered at him. "Maybe you should try," he said.

He dashed in their direction. Unlike the Zooeys, though, they didn't run. They met his attack, closing in as he aimed for the smallest one. As his head butted into the boy's chest, the others tackled him. Josh fell to the pavement. His face hit the ground hard, and he felt his cheek scraped raw.

Rolling onto his back, Josh kicked and clawed at the Boarders. His fingers found the girl's hair and pulled hard. She yelped in pain, then slammed her fist into his nose. Blood spurted out. Josh could taste it on his lips, thick and metallic. The smell, too, was overwhelming, making him hungry and sick at the same time.

The first Boarder was on top of Josh now, trying to pin his arms to the ground. Josh bucked, throwing him off, and rolled on top of him. He put his hands

194

around the boy's throat and started to squeeze. He saw the boy's eyes widen in fear as his air was cut off.

Josh wanted to see him die. By choking him, he could destroy everything that was gnawing at him. His mind skipped from thought to thought, and image to image. Charlie. The burst of fire from a flamethrower. Firecracker. The melting face of a z. It was like watching a holofilm gone crazy. Only by killing the Boarder could he make it stop.

Then he was flung sideways as a shower of falling stars crossed his vision. There was a loud roaring in his ears, as if a huge unseen wave had crashed over him. He looked up and saw the skinny Boarder staring down at him. The boy was holding the end of his board in both hands and raising it up for a second blow. Josh watched as it came toward him.

Josh woke up choking. His mouth was filled with water, and he couldn't breathe through his nose. He spat, trying to clear his throat, and gagged. A horrible iron taste coated his mouth. He wiped his lips with his hand and it came away red. *That's blood,* he thought, wondering whose it was.

The rain was falling hard, and it was dark. He tried to sit up, but pain rocketed through his head. He touched his nose, and again his fingers were painted red. The rain washed away the blood, turning it pink as it dripped onto Josh's shirt. His head swam, and he thought he might pass out, so he sat quietly, just trying to breathe.

He was also cold. The rain had soaked him, and he was shivering. He rubbed his hands on his arms to warm them, but it did no good. His teeth were chattering, clicking together in an erratic dance. He blew his nose to clear it, and a thick glob of half-clotted blood splattered onto his jeans. He tried to wipe it away, but it only smeared.

He looked around at the empty park. How long had he been lying there? Had anyone come along and seen him? Why hadn't they helped? *I could have died,* he thought. *Why didn't anyone do something?*

He wondered what time it was and looked at his watch. The glass was smashed, and he could just make out the numbers. It was ten.

He forced himself to stand up. Again he saw bursts of light in his head, and he almost sat down again. But he had to get out of there. He had to get home. There was something he needed to do, although he couldn't remember what it was.

Then it came to him. What Charlie had said. About how she'd set him up to settle her debt with Clatter.

As if he were just hearing the news for the first time, Josh felt overcome by shock and anger. Charlie had lied to him, and she might have gotten Firecracker in trouble as well. Josh had to find out. He had to help his friend.

He walked slowly, trying not to jar his body too much. After a few minutes he felt a little better, although he could tell that his face was pretty badly cut up. How was he going to explain *that* to his parents?

Tell them you were knocked down, he thought.

The story would probably keep him from getting in too much trouble tonight. Then he'd just have to figure out what to do about Charlie and how to find out what happened to Firecracker.

Something else occurred to him. Once Clatter found out that Josh knew about the Z, and about what Scrawl might or might not have done to Firecracker, it was pretty much guaranteed that Josh would be next on his list of problems to solve. Which meant one thing—Josh had to get to Clatter before Clatter got to him.

18

Josh didn't go home.

He made it as far as his block, even as far as the sidewalk in front of his house, but as he set his foot on the first step, he realized with absolute certainty that if he didn't do something *now*, it might be too late. Firecracker was still missing, and Charlie had told him too much. Maybe she would just keep their conversation to herself, but maybe she would run to Clatter and tell him everything.

He turned his back on his house and walked to the corner. How was he going to find Scrawl? He didn't even know where he lived. And what if Charlie had already gotten to him? Then he would know what Josh was after.

Still, he had to try. He leaned against a light post and thought. His head was throbbing, but he forced himself to concentrate. What did he know about Scrawl?

Nothing, he thought with some surprise. *He's a blank page.* If someone had asked him a minute before what his relationship with Scrawl was, Josh would have said they were friends. But now he realized that although Scrawl was always nice to him, Josh knew very little about him. It was as if Scrawl had deliberately kept himself a mystery.

But there had to be something, some clue Scrawl had let drop, maybe in conversation. Josh tried to remember anything they'd talked about. His mind came up empty, and he felt frustration growing in him. It was stupid to think he could handle this on his own. He should just call the police and tell them what he knew.

Then, from the depths of his memories, something rose up. Something Scrawl had said to him when they met. What had they been talking about? *Comics,* he thought.

That was it—the Pageteria. Scrawl had said that he lived a couple of blocks away from it. It was in Farside, on the other side of the city. That seemed like a good place to start.

He went to the subway station and looked at the interactive map. Punching in where he wanted to go, he waited for the route to be highlighted on the map. After memorizing it, he passed through the gates, scanned his fare card, and went to the right platform. Fortunately, the train came only a minute later.

The car was sparsely populated, and by the time the train reached the first stop in Farside, it was almost empty. Josh waited until the cyberconductor called out the stop he wanted, then exited into a dingy station. Water dripped from the ceiling, and the lights flickered in protest. The white tiles of the walls were dirty and broken, and the place smelled like garbage. Josh hurried up the stairs to the street.

He walked the four blocks to the Pageteria. It was closed, but he hadn't come there to check out the collections. He just wanted to use it as a reference point for looking for Scrawl's house. But now that he was there, he didn't have a clue where to begin.

Just ask, he told himself. *Someone around here must know him.*

"Right," he said aloud. "Because there are only, like, four hundred houses around here. Why don't I just knock on all the doors, one at a time?"

He looked around. The streets were mostly empty, although a block away he saw a small group of people hanging around outside what looked like a bar. As he got nearer, he saw that it was three women talking to a man. The man had a mechabird on his shoulder—a beautiful blue and gold parrot—and the women were talking to it.

"Who's a pretty bird?" one woman said.

The parrot cocked its head. "You are," it squawked. The women laughed as the man grinned. Then the man noticed Josh standing there. "What are you looking at?" he said gruffly as the women eyed Josh up and down.

"Nothing," Josh said. "Actually, I'm looking for someone."

The man laughed. "Who isn't, kid? Aren't you out a little late for a school night? Why don't you just run on home now."

Josh forced himself to keep talking. "His name is Scrawl," he said. "I was supposed to meet him here, and—"

"Never heard of him," the man interrupted him. The parrot ruffled its feathers. "Never heard of him," it echoed.

Josh turned around. "Thanks," he muttered as he walked off, trying to think where to go next.

"Wait a minute," a voice called out.

Josh turned to see one of the women walking toward him. She was balanced on heels so high, Josh wondered how she kept from tipping over, but she wobbled only slightly as she approached. "You want to talk to Scrawl?" she asked.

Josh nodded. "You know him?"

The woman smiled. "Everybody around here knows Scrawl," she said. "But only about half of them will admit it. Let me guess—you want to talk to him about getting something."

"Umm, sort of," said Josh.

"You and half the city," the woman said. She regarded him for a long moment. "You look like a nice kid," she said. "And you look like you've had a hard night. You go on over to 1372 Barber Street. It's two blocks that way. Apartment 3D. Tell him Lola said it was okay."

She smiled at Josh, who smiled back. "Thanks," he said. "Thanks a lot."

"No problem," Lola said.

Josh watched her walk back to her friends, then walked to Barber Street. A few minutes later he was standing in front of apartment 3D. Taking a deep breath, he rang the doorbell. A moment later the door opened and he was looking at Scrawl.

"How'd you get here?" Scrawl said, clearly surprised to see him.

"Lola," Josh said. He wasn't in the mood for giving explanations; he wanted to hear some. "I want to talk to you about Firecracker. And Z."

If Scrawl was shocked, he didn't show it. He simply

nodded and held the door open. "Come inside," he said.

Josh entered the apartment. The furniture was stylish, and the walls were covered in framed artwork. Josh looked at the closest piece and saw that it was a drawing in ink of a costumed figure.

"Green Lantern," Scrawl said. "It's just a sketch, but it cost me four months' pay. It's an original Gil Kane." He handed Josh a towel. "Dry off," he said.

Josh toweled off his head, wincing a little at the pain.

"What happened to you?" Scrawl asked.

"Just a little accident," said Josh.

"I assume you didn't stop by just to say hi," Scrawl said.

Josh looked him in the eye. "What did you do to Firecracker?"

Scrawl didn't blink. "We had a little chat," he said.

"What about?" Josh said.

Scrawl shrugged. "I just asked him to stop following Charlie around."

"Huh," Josh replied. "I thought maybe you talked about Z and how Clatter is planning on selling it on the streets."

This time Scrawl did blink. But he quickly regained his composure. "That didn't come up," he said. "But it sounds like somebody's been talking to *you* about it."

"Where's Firecracker now?" Josh asked.

"How would I know?" said Scrawl.

"Don't lie," Josh snapped. "He never went home."

Scrawl had a puzzled look on his face. "He's missing?"

Josh nodded. "Yeah, he's missing. And I think you know why."

Scrawl sat down on a chair. "No," he said, although he seemed to be talking to himself and not to Josh. "He said he wasn't going to take him."

"Who said that?" Josh demanded. "Take him where?"

Scrawl looked up. "Charlie told you about the Z, didn't she?"

Josh hesitated. If he admitted it, then Scrawl might do something to Charlie. But she was the only likely source of the information, and they both knew it. "Yes," he said.

Scrawl stood up. "We have to find her," he said.

"Wait a minute," Josh protested. "What about Firecracker? And why do we have to find Charlie? She was fine when I saw her."

"When was that?" asked Scrawl.

"About two hours ago," said Josh.

Scrawl shook his head. "They could already have her."

Josh held his hands up. "What the hell are you talking about?" he said. "If you're trying to get me to forget about Firecracker—"

"I didn't do anything to your friend!" Scrawl shouted. It was the first time Josh had ever heard him lose control. All he could do was stand there, looking at Scrawl's normally cool face twisted in anger.

"Listen to me," Scrawl said in a softer tone. "There's more going on here than you know. Way more. It's not just about Z or the game. But it's gone too far now, and I can't let him hurt anyone else."

"Clatter?" Josh asked.

Scrawl nodded.

"Charlie said he killed Bess," said Josh. "Is that true?"

Scrawl looked away. "We didn't take her to the hospital," he said quietly. "We put her in the incinerator."

"And you just let him?" Josh said angrily. "You didn't try to stop him?"

"You have a little sister, right?" Scrawl asked in reply.

Josh nodded. "So what?"

"Well, so do I," said Scrawl. "Two of them. Jilly and Annie. They're nine and eleven. Do you want to know what Clatter said he would do to them if I told anybody about him, about what he does?"

Josh shook his head. "I think I can imagine," he said.

"I thought I could go along with his game," Scrawl said. "Believe it or not, he's been good to me. I owe him a lot. But I've paid him back enough. And now we're going to stop him." He took a deep breath. "But first I have to show you something you really don't want to see."

19

Josh looked down into the hole. A foul smell wafted up through it. "I'm not going down there," he told Scrawl. Scrawl was kneeling in the street, holding the manhole cover he'd removed a moment ago. "Just do it," he ordered Josh. He looked over his shoulder. "That light is going to change in about fifteen seconds, and I don't really feel like getting flattened. Now *go!*"

Josh hesitated just a moment longer, then stepped onto the first rung of the ladder. When he was halfway down, Scrawl followed him, pulling the manhole cover back over the opening. Seconds later Josh heard the sound of wheels over their heads. He reached the bottom of the ladder and stepped into a puddle of water that covered his shoes and the bottoms of his jeans.

"Nice place for a front door," he remarked as Scrawl joined him.

"That's the point," Scrawl said. "It's the *back* door.

And where better to put it than in the middle of one of the busiest streets in the city?"

Josh had to admit it was a clever idea. When Scrawl had told him they were going to go into the sewers through a hole in Broad Avenue, he was sure he'd heard wrong. But as soon as the light turned red to allow the cross traffic from Seventh Street to go, Scrawl had run out, heaved the manhole cover up, and told Josh to get in.

Josh still wasn't sure he should trust Scrawl. But following him seemed to be his only option.

"Did it have to be a sewer?" Josh asked.

"Actually, it's a storm drain," Scrawl corrected him.

Scrawl had brought two flashlights along. They each had one, and Josh used his to scan the tunnel ahead of them for anything he didn't want to step in. Several times the beam of light shone on rats, which looked at Josh and Scrawl with wary eyes and scurried out of sight beneath the piles of trash that littered the floor.

"Where are we going?" Josh asked Scrawl for the tenth time since leaving the apartment.

"I told you, you don't want to know," said Scrawl.

"I have to find out sometime," Josh objected.

Scrawl stopped. He turned and looked at Josh, his

flashlight casting a ghostly shadow on his face. "Okay," he said. "You're right. I'm taking you to Clatter's factory."

"His factory?"

"Where he makes Z," said Scrawl.

"That's insane," Josh said. "We should be getting help."

Scrawl hesitated. "I think Firecracker is there," he said. "Maybe Charlie too."

Josh felt his heart skip a beat. "Why would he have them there?"

"That's the part you don't want to know about," said Scrawl. "You'll just have to see for yourself."

He resumed the trek through the sewer. Soon the floor began to slope down, and Josh had to work hard to keep his balance. They descended at a steep angle before the tunnel leveled out again and continued on. Then they walked for another fifteen minutes, making several turns, until they came to a steel door marked with a sign that read CES CREWS ONLY.

"City Electrical System?" Josh said. "What is this, a power hub or something?"

"Or something," said Scrawl. He was typing something into a keypad to the side of the door. A moment later it opened with a hiss. Scrawl stepped inside and motioned for Josh to follow.

They were in a small room. On the side opposite the first door was another door, exactly the same. The first door shut behind Josh as Scrawl went to the second. "This is an airlock," Scrawl explained. "The two doors can't be open at the same time, and each one has a different code." He looked up at the ceiling, where a several small nozzles protruded from the smooth metal surface. "If you enter the wrong code, those emit gas," he said. "It will knock you out cold in under ten seconds."

"That would certainly keep people out," Josh said. "So why do you know the codes?"

Scrawl finished typing. "Let's just say Clatter trusts me," he said. "Well, as much as he trusts anyone."

The room Josh entered next was huge. It was also as modern looking as the sewer entrance was dilapidated. The walls were covered in polished metal, and the lighting was low and soothing. Several fans were running, and the air smelled clean and fresh.

"It's like a hospital," Josh said.

Scrawl snorted. "You're not far off," he said.

Josh could see a row of five metal operating tables on the far side of the room. As they drew closer, he saw that a body lay on one of the tables. It was a zombie. Its wrists and ankles were constrained by metal cuffs attached to the table, and another metal cuff was around its neck, holding it down.

The zombie was a teenage girl. Her long blond hair was matted, some of it clotted with dried blood from a wound on her scalp. Her skinny body was dressed in dirty jeans and a pink Hello Kitty T-shirt. Her skin was mottled with ugly bruises, and one eye was sewn shut with thick black thread. The other eye looked up at the ceiling, unmoving.

On each cuff was a small circular opening, and into each opening was inserted a long, thin needle attached to a length of clear tubing. Yellowish fluid filled the tubes, which ran beneath the table and disappeared into the floor.

"He makes the zombies here too?" Josh asked.

Scrawl nodded.

Josh reached out to touch the zombie's skin, but Scrawl grabbed his wrist. "Don't," he said.

"Relax," Josh said, irritated. "I just wanted to feel her skin. It's amazing how he makes them look so real." He pointed to the tubes. "What's that stuff, hydraulic fluid for the robotics?"

"It's blood," said Scrawl.

"Blood?" Josh repeated. "What are you talking about?"

"These are bleeding tables," Scrawl told him. "He's not pumping anything *in*, he's draining it *out*."

Josh recoiled, staring at the girl. "I don't get it," he said. "I thought you said that this is where he makes Z."

"It is," said Scrawl. "But to make Z he needs blood. Zombie blood. And this is how he gets it."

Josh waited for Scrawl to say he was joking. When he didn't, Josh pointed to the girl and said, "You're telling me that's a *real* zombie?"

"She's real, all right," Scrawl answered.

Josh stared at him. Scrawl had to be kidding. But the look on his face was deadly serious. Could he be telling the truth?

Josh laughed nervously. "You're messing with me," he said. "Right?"

Scrawl shook his head.

"There haven't been any in years," Josh said.

"There are now." Said Scrawl.

Josh looked at the zombie on the table. He couldn't believe he had almost touched it. "Where do they come from?"

Scrawl looked at him. "This is the part you *really* don't want to see," he said. "Don't freak out on me, okay?"

"I'm already beyond freaked out," Josh told him. "It can't get any worse."

"Yeah, it can," Scrawl replied. He walked toward a

door to the right of the tables. When he reached it, he paused, took a deep breath, and pushed it open.

The stench was enough to make Josh gag. At first he was so busy coughing that he didn't have time to look for the source of the smell. When he could more or less breathe again, he looked up. They were in a room lined with cells, about twenty on each side. And inside each one was a zombie.

Josh felt like he'd been punched in the stomach. "They're real?" he said. "All of them? But that's impossible. All the z's were wiped out. The virus was wiped out."

Scrawl shook his head. "That's just what the government wants people to think," he said. "They never wiped out the virus, just the people who had it. Clatter's father worked on the project. He found a way to infect people and make them zombies."

Josh crept closer to the cell that Scrawl was looking into. Inside it was a man wearing a tattered suit. His skin bubbled with lesions, and his eyes were filmed over. He opened his mouth, revealing stumps of blackened teeth and a swollen purple tongue. Seeing Josh and Scrawl, he beat his hands against the glass, coating it with blood-flecked drool.

"He's alive?" Josh asked, still unable to believe it.

"Alive as he can be," said Scrawl.

"And Clatter made him like this?"

Scrawl nodded. "Yeah," he said.

Josh looked into the next cell. There a woman with a rat's nest of hair sat in the corner, pulling her own fingernails off. Half a dozen of them littered the floor. Josh felt his stomach rise.

"But why?" he sputtered. "Why would anyone want to *make* meatbags?"

"Money," Scrawl said. "Like I said, Clatter's dad studied the zombie virus. He was a chemist. He wanted to find a way to wipe it out. But the government wanted him to do just the opposite. They wanted him to make a weapon that would turn people *into* z's. Something they could put into the water or the air or food to infect a lot of people at once."

"Biological warfare," Josh said. "That's sick."

"That's what Clatter's father thought too," said Scrawl. "He refused to do it. So they decided to give him a little incentive to cooperate. They kidnapped Clatter. He was maybe five or six. They told Clatter's father that if he did what they wanted, they would give him his kid back."

"An offer he couldn't refuse," Josh said.

Scrawl nodded. "That's right," he said. "He just wanted to save his son. He did what they asked, but they killed him. They killed his wife too. They would have gotten Clatter, but he got away. I don't know who he was before, but since then he's been Clatter."

"And now he's making zombies using his dad's technology," Josh said. "That's messed up."

"I think what happened to him made him a little crazy," Scrawl replied. "He's super smart, there's no doubt about that. But he's also twisted. He says making money off of z's is payback for what the government did to him and his parents. The more zombies he makes, the more Z he makes."

"Z is zombie blood," Josh said, shuddering at the thought. Then he remembered that he had taken some himself, and panic filled him. "Z turns people into zombies?" he said.

"No," Scrawl answered. "Don't worry," he assured Josh. "We've all tried it. It won't turn you. Clatter has other ways of doing that. Z is made from z blood, but it's a diluted form of it. Just enough to make you feel a little bit of what they feel, but not enough to turn you."

Josh slumped to the ground with his back against the door of one of the cells. He heard the zombie inside start clawing at the metal. He tried not to listen. Scrawl came and sat beside him. "How long has he been doing this?" Josh asked him.

"A couple years," said Scrawl. "It took him a long time to figure out how to do it efficiently. The first versions of Z really did turn users into meatbags. Then Clatter got it to where it only made them crazy. Now he's got it pretty much figured out."

"Pretty much," Josh said. "Great. And how does the game come into this?"

"It's another way to make money," said Scrawl. "And it's a way to get rid of z's that are too far gone. That's when he puts them into the game."

Josh didn't want to accept what he was hearing. "We've been killing . . . people?" he said. "*I've* been killing people?"

Scrawl took him by the shoulders. "You wanted to know," he said as Josh took great gulps of air. "Now you do."

"And you knew about it," Josh said. "That makes you as bad as he is."

"He helped me, Josh," Scrawl said. "He's helped all of us."

"You mean he's bought you," said Josh, thinking about Scrawl's nice apartment. Then he remembered how excited he'd been seeing his first paycheck, and he felt a little ashamed. "How many of the others know?" he asked.

"Only Seamus and Finnegan," Scrawl answered. "I know they don't look like it, but they're science geeks. He's teaching them how to make the Z and how to replicate the virus. I help him with business stuff. The others he just uses for the game."

A thought occurred to Josh. "So if somebody gets bit in the game, they're being bit by a real zombie?"

Scrawl didn't say anything.

"What really happened to Stash and Freya?" Josh asked.

"Josh, it doesn't—"

"What happened to them!" Josh yelled. "Tell me!"

Scrawl nodded toward the cells at the end of the row. "Over there," he said.

Josh got up and walked slowly toward the cells. When he got there, he steadied himself and then looked through the window. Freya—or what had once *been* Freya—lunged at him, her teeth bared. She'd torn out her hair, which lay in bloody clumps on the floor, and her bald scalp was black with dried blood. Josh looked away.

He forced himself to look into the next cell. Stash was in it, standing motionless in the middle of the tiny space. The place on his shoulder where he'd been bitten was green and gangrenous, and his skin was mottled with dark purple lesions. One of his eyes was missing, the socket where it had been like raw hamburger.

"Who are the rest of them?" he asked Scrawl.

"Different people," he answered. "People who didn't pay their wagers. Street people. Runaway kids. People nobody will miss."

"So first he infects them, then he milks them for their blood," said Josh. "It's a slaughterhouse. Like they have for animals. Only these aren't animals, they're people."

"Yes, they're people. What did you think zombies were?" said Scrawl.

"I thought those were cybers!" Josh said. "And the ones in the hologame aren't real. It's just pretend."

"Still, I bet you never really thought about who they *used* to be," Scrawl said softly. "I know I didn't."

Josh started to argue, but stopped. Scrawl was right. He knew about his aunt Lucy, and yet he had never thought of her—not even once—when he was torching the z's in the game.

Freya pounded on the window of her cell and let out a strangled scream. Josh turned away. "Is this what happens to Torchers who 'retire' from the team?" he asked.

Scrawl didn't answer, but he didn't have to. Scrawl's silence confirmed it.

"So we help him make his money, we kill his victims when he's done with them, and if we try to get out, we end up like them." He jerked his head toward

Freya's and Stash's cells.

"We need to find your friend," Scrawl said. "And Charlie, if she's here. He hasn't turned them yet, or they'd be in here. That means he's probably holding them somewhere else while he decides what to do with them."

"Well, I *was* doing exactly that," said a voice. Clatter was standing in the doorway, peering at them through his gray glasses. He smiled and nodded at Scrawl, then Josh. "However, I think you gentlemen have just decided for me."

20

"**W**here are they?"

Josh faced Clatter. The anger in him was growing quickly, particularly because Clatter just stood there grinning. Josh wanted to wipe the smirk off his face. He even started toward the man, but Scrawl grabbed him and pulled him back. "Don't do it," he told Josh. "You won't win."

"You should listen to Arthur," Clatter said. Then he addressed Scrawl. "I assume this means you've decided to end our partnership."

Scrawl said nothing. After a moment Clatter sighed. "I *am* disappointed," he said. "You showed such promise. Now, well . . ." He waved his hand around the room full of cells. "It's unfortunate."

"You're not turning me into one of those things," said Scrawl. "I'd rather die."

"That could certainly be arranged," Clatter

replied. "But the alternative is so much more interesting. No, I'm afraid I can't make an exception for you, Arthur."

Scrawl stiffened but remained silent, staring at Clatter.

"What do you want?" Josh asked Clatter.

Clatter turned his attention to Josh. "Who says I want anything?" he asked. "Am I to understand that you think this is some kind of negotiation?" He laughed.

"I want Charlie and Firecracker," Josh said firmly, though terror threatened to take control of him. Now that he knew what Clatter was doing, the possibility that he might not leave the underground lab alive seemed very real.

"You *want*?" Clatter said. "I don't think you're in any position to be *wanting* anything."

"Well, maybe I have something *you* want," Josh countered.

Clatter raised an eyebrow. "And that would be?" he asked.

"Money," said Josh.

Clatter leaned against the doorway. "Are you offering me a bribe?"

Josh shook his head. "You know I don't have *that* kind of money," he said. "But I'm worth it."

"A ransom," said Clatter.

"No," Josh said. "Not a ransom. I mean my game playing. And his," he added, nodding toward Scrawl. "We're the best gamers you have."

Clatter shrugged. "You're good," he said.

"Really good," Josh said. "We bring in more money than anyone else on the team." He didn't know if this was entirely true, but he figured it was worth a shot. When Clatter didn't contradict him, he assumed he had guessed correctly.

"Let's play a game," he continued. "Me and Scrawl against your zombies. Call in your biggest wagerers. Make a big deal about it. A match to the death or whatever."

Clatter thought for a moment. Josh held his breath, hoping his idea would work. "Go on," Clatter said.

"If we win, you let us go," said Josh. "All of us. We won't say anything about what you're doing down here."

Clatter chuckled. "Or I could just kill you and not worry about that anyway," he said.

"Except that before we came here I sent my parents a com message telling them where we were going," said Josh. "It's set to open at five o'clock tomorrow morning."

Clatter shook his head. "You're lying," he said.

"No, he isn't," said Scrawl. "My sister will get the same message. It has maps and everything. The cops would be here by six, and there's no way you could clear everything out of here by then. Even if you killed us, your entire business would be wiped out. Plus, I think there are some people who would love to get their hands on you."

Clatter looked from one of them to the other. *He's trying to decide if we're bluffing,* Josh thought. He decided to beat Clatter to the punch. "No, you don't know whether we really did it or not," he said. "But you have more to lose by assuming we didn't than you do by assuming we did."

To his surprise, Clatter grinned. "That was very well put," he said. "All right. We'll play a game. But it won't be just you and Arthur playing. Your friends will join you. All four of you must survive, *and* all the zombies will have to be killed. If you can manage that, I will let you all go."

"How do we know you'll hold up your end of the bargain?" Josh asked.

"You don't," said Clatter. "But you have more to gain by assuming I will than you do by assuming I won't. So, do we have a deal?"

Josh looked at Scrawl, who nodded.

"Excellent," Clatter said. "At this hour it will take a

little while to gather together an audience. But I think that makes it even more exciting, don't you? I'll send the message out immediately. In the meantime, I imagine you'd like to see your friends. Come with me."

He walked to one of the cells and typed a code into the keypad beside it. Josh and Scrawl stepped back as the door opened.

"Don't worry," Clatter said as he stepped inside the cell. "It's unoccupied."

Josh and Scrawl followed him into the cell; then the door slid shut and the floor began to drop. It took a second for Josh to realize that they were in an elevator. It continued down for twenty or thirty seconds, then came to a halt. The doors opened and Clatter stepped out into a tunnel very much like the one through which Josh and Scrawl had entered the lab.

Josh was surprised that Clatter had turned his back on them. *Maybe we could jump him,* he thought.

"He has weapons," Scrawl whispered just loudly enough for Josh to hear him. Josh nodded to let him know he understood, even though part of him still wanted to knock Clatter down and hurt him.

"You know, Josh, I could use someone like you on my team," Clatter said. He turned and paused. "My *other* team, I mean. I plan to introduce Z to the streets shortly. You've tried it. You know how popular it will be. The profit potential is extraordinary. Are you sure you won't consider joining me?"

"I'll never be like you," said Josh.

"You wound me," Clatter said, feigning sadness. "And here I thought I was such a role model to all of you."

They walked for a few minutes and came to a stone archway covered by an old iron grate. Behind the grate was a small room cut into the rock, and Charlie and Firecracker were sitting on the floor, not looking at each other. When they heard noise in the tunnel, they glanced up. Josh saw expressions of hope flash across their faces but quickly disappear when they saw that Josh and Scrawl were with Clatter.

"I've brought you some company," Clatter said as he removed one of the keys tied to his coat and inserted it into the ancient lock. The lock opened reluctantly, and Clatter pulled the grate open just far enough for Josh and Scrawl to go inside. He shut it behind them and locked it. "I'll go make the arrangements," he said. "I suggest you fill your friends in on what we've agreed to."

As soon as Clatter disappeared, Charlie and Firecracker started talking at the same time.

"Where did you go, and what happened to your face?"

"Dude, what the hell are these people doing?"

"I didn't mean to—"

"I was only trying to—"

"Quiet!" Josh said. "Just listen. We don't have a lot of time."

He explained to Firecracker and Charlie about the zombies and Z, and about the deal he'd made with Clatter.

"What do you mean we have to fight our way out?" asked Firecracker. "Like for real?"

"For real," said Josh.

"This is insane," Charlie said.

"Look around," Scrawl told her. "This whole thing is insane."

Charlie shook her head. "This isn't happening," she said. "It's, I don't know, a dream. Or a bad Z trip. I just have to wake up." She started beating at herself with her hands.

Josh grabbed her and held her. She struggled for a moment, then slumped against him. He felt her shake as she sobbed.

"We can do this," he whispered. "We've done it a thousand times."

"Are you telling me you guys have been playing the game with real zombies?" Firecracker asked. "And real flamethrowers? And now we're playing to get out of here alive?"

"Yeah," Scrawl said. "That's pretty much it."

"That's awesome," Firecracker said.

"It's not awesome!" Charlie yelled. "Don't you get it? We have to kill people!"

Firecracker snorted. "We have to kill *meatbags*," he said. "Big deal."

"Some of those meatbags are our friends," said Scrawl.

"Come on, man," Firecracker said.

"What's wrong with you?" Charlie said. She pulled away from Josh and shoved Firecracker against the wall.

"Hey!" he said.

"This isn't a stupid game," Charlie continued. "It never was. We just thought it was. Those *meatbags* you're so hot to torch used to be like us." She looked at Josh and Scrawl. "Some of them *were* us. And that slimeball out there has made a lot of money from people like you who think it's a whole lot of fun."

Firecracker put his hands up in defeat. "Don't take it out on me," he said. "I wouldn't be here at all if you hadn't told Freakula there that I was stalking you." He looked at Josh. "Which I wasn't. I was just worried about you."

Josh nodded. "I know," he said. "It's okay. Right

now we have to talk about our plan."

"What field are we playing on?" Charlie asked.

Scrawl shook his head. "We don't know," he said. "But my guess is he'll put us on Location Eleven."

Charlie's head whipped up. "Eleven?" she said.

Josh looked from her to Scrawl. "What's eleven? I don't remember that from the manual."

"It's not in the manual," Scrawl said. "We've never played it before."

"Where is it?" Josh asked.

Scrawl rubbed his nose. "Feverfew," he said.

"The insane asylum?" said Firecracker. "That place on the cliffs? It's been condemned for at least thirty years. It's totally falling apart."

"Exactly," said Scrawl. "We haven't used it before because it's too dangerous for the Torchers. That's why Clatter wants to use it as a field."

"So the odds are against us," Charlie said.

"Then we just have to play the best game we've ever played," said Josh. He looked at each of them in turn. "We can do it. We just have to stick together."

21

Clatter came for them half an hour later. Seamus and Finnegan were with him. The two of them behaved oddly, not looking at the four captives and rocking back and forth slightly on their feet.

They're doped up on Z, Josh thought as Clatter unlocked the cell and told them to come out one by one. Josh went first. As he exited, Finnegan took his arm and placed a handcuff around his wrist. Josh tried to pull his hand back, but Finnegan gripped it tightly, then cuffed the other wrist also.

"Just a precaution," Clatter said. "Nothing to worry about."

"Five o'clock," Josh reminded Clatter. "That's when the message goes out and the cops come."

"Oh, I think this will be over long before then," Clatter said.

The three others joined Josh, all of them

handcuffed. Clatter ordered them to follow Seamus, who led them in the opposite direction from the elevator. A hundred yards on, the tunnel opened up into a larger tunnel running perpendicular to the first one. A short flight of stone steps led down to a small landing past which a stream of dirty water flowed along sluggishly. An old wooden rowboat was tied to the platform with a rope.

"Couldn't afford a hoverboat, huh?" Firecracker asked sarcastically.

Seamus pushed him roughly down the steps, with Finnegan urging the others along behind him. "We like it old school," Seamus said, nodding at the boat. "Get in and shut up."

Josh stepped in first. The boat rocked beneath him, and with his hands cuffed he couldn't keep his balance. He fell sideways, hitting one of the boat's bench seats with a painful thud. Seamus laughed, a dull chuckle that made Josh's skin crawl. He'd always found the twins a little strange, but now they were totally creeping him out.

Charlie got in next and sat beside Josh. Firecracker and Scrawl followed, squeezing in next to them, then Finnegan and Clatter, who took the seat at the front. Seamus untied the rope tethering the boat to the platform and got in last, taking the middle bench and facing Josh. As the boat floated out into the stream, he took the ends of the two oars attached to the sides of the boat by heavy steel oarlocks and began to row.

The tunnel was lit by a string of electric lights that ran along the ceiling. The ancient bulbs were mostly dead, but a few still worked. As the boat floated along, Josh occasionally caught a glimpse of what was around them.

"This tunnel was once used by the old underground rail system," Clatter announced from the front of the boat. "Like all the old tunnels, it flooded when Antarctica melted and the seas rose. But what was a tragedy for so many has been a boon for those of us who wish to conduct business unnoticed. The tunnels run nearly everywhere one might wish to go beneath the city."

Clatter continued to talk, but Josh tuned him out. He didn't care what Clatter had to say, but remained focused on what lay ahead. Without knowing the layout of where they would be playing, the team of Torchers couldn't form a real plan. But Scrawl had seen some basic maps of Feverfew, and assuming that that's where they were going, had used a piece of broken stone to sketch out a rough idea of what it might look like inside on the floor of the cell.

Seamus made several turns, moving into various

tunnels until Josh's sense of direction was completely lost. Sometimes they flowed with the water, and sometimes Seamus had to struggle against it. They passed half a dozen platforms similar to the one from which they'd launched the rowboat, and Josh wondered what part of the city each one led to.

Finally they traversed a very long tunnel where the water flowed more quickly. *It's going out to the ocean,* Josh thought. *This is where it empties out. We must be somewhere near the cliffs; Scrawl was right.*

Seamus muscled the boat to yet another landing, and Finnegan jumped out, tying the rope to a ring set into the stone. Seamus was next, and he and Finnegan helped Clatter out of the boat. No one helped Josh and his friends, who got off as best they could.

They were marched up a series of stone stairs. These were much steeper and longer than the ones they'd come down, and Josh was breathing heavily when they reached the top. His skin was soaked with sweat, and his shirt clung to him in the clammy, cold air.

They walked through a doorway and found themselves in a dimly lit basement. Tall filing cabinets lined the rust-stained walls. The drawers on many of them were open, and sheets of paper spilled out like entrails. Josh noticed that several of the papers had small black-and-white photographs stapled to them. *Those are patient records,* he noted grimly.

They came to a set of doors. Clatter pulled a handle that protruded from the wall, and machinery in the walls ground to life. The doors opened, revealing an elevator large enough to accommodate them all. As it lurched upward, the elevator shook with the strain.

Josh watched the buttons on the elevator's control panel light up as they passed each floor. At *4* it shuddered to a stop, and the doors opened.

"Watch your step," Clatter said as he got out with a strange jumping motion. Then Josh noticed that the elevator had stopped a good six inches below the level of the floor outside. The floor itself seemed to sag, as if the ancient building had given up.

"This is where the game will begin," Clatter said. He nodded at Finnegan, who produced a key and proceeded to unlock the handcuffs. Josh massaged his wrists, which had been rubbed raw by the metal. He noticed the others doing the same.

"The rules are very simple," Clatter continued. "There are twelve zombies. Find and kill them all within two hours and you go free."

"We didn't agree on a time limit," Josh objected.

"My customers don't have all night," said Clatter. "And neither do you."

"But this place is huge," Charlie said. "There's no way we can cover it in two hours. You know that."

Clatter nodded. "You may well be right," he admitted. "But as you yourself said," he added, looking at Josh, "you *are* the best Torchers I have."

Josh pushed down the urge to rush Clatter.

"Of course, if you do *not* complete the task . . ." Clatter left the sentence unfinished. They all knew what would happen.

"We'll become zombies," Firecracker said. "Yeah, we get it."

Clatter looked at Firecracker with an expression of amusement. "For someone who has never played the game outside of his bedroom, you're remarkably confident," he said.

Firecracker returned the stare. "We're all good at something," he said slowly. "I'm sure one day you'll figure out what your something is."

Josh enjoyed watching the look on Clatter's face change. Firecracker had landed a direct hit. *You might not be the brightest guy,* he thought, *but I'm glad you're on my team.*

"Your torches are through that door over there," Clatter said, his tone decidedly less friendly. "I'm afraid we forgot to pick up communicators for you. You'll have to stay in contact the old-fashioned way.

You must remain here while we return to the control center. Do not enter the room until you hear the command to begin." He removed a watch from one of his pockets. "Who's going to be the team captain?"

Scrawl nodded at Josh. "I guess I am," Josh told Clatter.

Clatter handed him the watch. "When the game begins, this will start to count down the time remaining," he said. "As usual, there are cameras throughout the building. Your progress will be followed with much anticipation."

Clatter, Finnegan, and Seamus returned to the elevator. As the doors began to close, Clatter looked at Josh and smiled. "Good luck," he said. The sound of his laughter followed the elevator as it descended.

"No communicators," Scrawl said. "Great. He wants us to yell so the z's hear us."

"How are we going to find a dozen zombies in this place?" Charlie added. "We could spend an hour on each *floor*."

"We'll have to break up," said Firecracker. "Each of us take a floor or something."

"No," Josh told him as he put the watch on his wrist. "That's what Clatter wants us to do." He spoke quietly, knowing that if Clatter had put cameras in, then he had undoubtedly installed microphones as well.

"Remember what we agreed on—we stick together. All of us get out of here or none of us do."

Scrawl nodded. "Josh is right," he said. "We have to do this as a team."

"All right," said Firecracker. "Then what's our plan?"

"This place is basically a big square," said Scrawl. "Four corridors around a central open area that used to be a garden. It's where the patients went to go outside without being able to escape. I say we do a basic sweep pattern. Start at one corner, go around until we come back to it, then go to the next level. The place was designed so that the stairs alternate position. On floors two and four they're in the southeast corner. On three they're in the northwest. They did that so that nobody could have a straight shot out of here if they ran. We can use the stairs as a starting position."

"Are we all okay with that?" Josh asked.

Charlie and Firecracker nodded.

"I know I said we would all stick together," Josh continued. "But if we all stay on the same floor, maybe it's okay if we sweep in teams of two. That way we can cover the floor twice as quickly. Whichever team gets to the stairs first waits for the other. We've got half an hour for each floor. If the second team doesn't show up by the time thirty minutes is up, the first team—"

"Goes to the next floor," Firecracker interrupted him.

"No," said Josh. "They go find the other team. Remember, we're *all* getting out of here. Now, does anyone else have a watch?"

"I do," Firecracker said.

"Then you go with Scrawl," Josh told him. "Charlie will come with me. We'll alternate partners on each floor."

"Why?" Firecracker asked.

"So we don't get too comfortable," Charlie explained. "It keeps us fresh."

"All right," said Josh. "Now we wait for the signal."

It came five minutes later, just as Josh thought he wouldn't be able to stand the suspense any longer. A screeching sound filled the hallway, followed by Clatter's voice. It was tinny and faint, and Josh had to strain to hear it.

"Time begins now," Clatter said simply, and the air went dead.

"Go!" Josh called out, and ran for the doors.

He burst through them into a small room. Two beds were against the wall, their metal frames rusted and the stained mattresses on them bursting open. Four torches lay on one of the beds.

"Could these be any older?" Scrawl asked as he

picked one up and slung it over his shoulder.

"Another advantage for the other team," Josh joked grimly. He turned his flamethrower and checked the fuel level. It was at half of what it should be.

"Do you know how to use that?" Scrawl asked Firecracker, who was looking at his torch.

"I'm not sure," said Firecracker. "Where do the arrows go again?"

Despite himself, Josh laughed. He'd missed his friend's careless sense of humor. He suspected Firecracker wouldn't be joking once he saw his first zombie up close, but for now his attitude helped ease the tension, at least a little bit.

"Ready?" Josh asked.

"Ready," Charlie said as the other two nodded.

"Let's go find us some zombies," said Josh.

22

The first zombie was waiting for them right outside the door. Because they weren't expecting one so soon, none of them were prepared for it. Charlie, who went first, walked right into it. The zombie, a huge man in a coverall with HOWARD stitched over the pocket, wrapped his arms around her and immediately went for her neck. Charlie didn't even have time to scream.

Scrawl, following behind her, butted the zombie in the face with his torch, causing him to fall back a step or two. It was enough for Charlie to slip out of his grasp, and with a fierce yell she kicked the zombie squarely in the stomach. It doubled over, and she delivered a roundhouse kick to its shoulder. A moment later the zombie was in flames as Scrawl torched it.

"Come on!" Charlie shouted, waving Josh and Firecracker out of the room.

They skirted around the zombie. Josh saw Firecracker stop and stare at the man, who was on all fours crawling slowly toward them. Firecracker wore a confused expression as if he couldn't believe what he was seeing was real. For a moment he even started to go back toward the zombie.

"Firecracker!" Josh yelled. "Move!"

Firecracker tore himself away from the site of the flaming zombie, and the four of them moved down the hallway. "It was alive," Firecracker said as they went. "It had a name. *He* had a name."

"You can't think about it," Josh told him, although he knew this was impossible. How could they *not* think about it, especially now that they knew how the zombies had been made? But they had to try. Josh reminded himself that nobody would want to live that way, and that if he and his friends wanted to get out of there, they had to do what they had to do.

"Here's our starting point," Scrawl said as they reached the end of the corridor. "Josh, you and Charlie go right. Firecracker and I will go left. We'll meet at the stairs. Remember, we've got eleven to go."

They split up. Josh and Charlie walked side by side as they began their search. The fourth floor seemed to be nothing but patient rooms. Every door they passed opened into a room very much like the first one, with two beds and one small window covered by thick bars.

"Where would a z even hide in one of these?" Charlie asked when they were halfway down the hall and hadn't found anything.

"Could be a small one," Josh reminded her. "A kid."

Charlie looked at him. "Even Clatter wouldn't do that," she said. "Would he?"

"I don't know," Josh answered. "Until a few hours ago I wouldn't have believed any of this."

They reached the end of the first hallway without finding anything, and the second hallway seemed to be a mirror image of the first. By the time they'd checked the fourth room on that side, Josh was getting anxious. Where were all the meatbags? He looked at his watch. Ten minutes had passed. They had five left.

"This is like one of those nightmares where you're trying to get out of a place and keep coming back to the same door," Charlie remarked as they approached the next room.

The next second Josh was on the floor and a horribly disfigured face was hovering over his. He recognized it as the woman whose cell he'd looked into in the lab. She gnashed her teeth, flecking him with spit. He noticed that most of her tongue had been chewed off, leaving her with a bloody stump that twitched from side to side as she tried to talk.

Charlie grabbed the woman by the collar and pulled her back. With a ripping sound the woman's dress tore, and Charlie slipped sideways. Josh could smell the woman's breath as she bent closer and closer. It was worse than the smell in the sewers, reeking of blood and decay.

Josh heard footsteps, and suddenly the woman was pulled away from him, her bloody fingertips clawing at him as she was lifted up. He heard Firecracker yell, "Stay down!" and then felt heat on his skin as a stream of fire erupted over him. A gurgling scream filled the air, followed by the horrible stench of burning meat.

Josh rolled over and onto his knees. As he stood, he saw something on the floor and picked it up. It was a name tag, the kind that people wore at meetings or parties when they wanted to identify one another. HELLO, it said. MY NAME IS. Below this someone had printed, in perfectly even letters, ALICE.

"What is that?" Charlie asked as she peered over Josh's shoulder.

"He wants us to know their names," Josh replied. "He's reminding us that they're human." For reasons he couldn't understand, he folded the tag in half and tucked into the pocket of his jeans. "First Howard, and now Alice," he said. "I wonder who's next."

"Did you guys find anything?" Charlie asked Scrawl.

"Just our friend Howard," Scrawl answered. "Is she your only one?"

Josh nodded. "Ten more," he said.

"And three floors," added Charlie. "Why do I think most of those ten won't be on floors three or two?"

"He's saving them for us," Josh agreed. "But we still have to check every floor. He's making sure we don't have much time when we get to the end."

Charlie looked around, scanning the hallway for cameras. "Are you having fun?" she yelled. "Are you getting all this, you sick bastards?"

Josh took her arm. "Come on," he said gently. "Time's up for this floor."

They took the stairs to the third floor in single file, with Josh leading. As they descended, the condition of the walls deteriorated. Huge chunks of plaster were missing, exposing the wood beneath. Broken pipes protruded like bones from the splintered ceiling, and only a few bulbs still emitted any light. What little they did was thin and watery. Josh turned on the light on his flamethrower, but nothing happened. He clicked it half a dozen times to make sure. The others did the same, with no better results.

"Great," Josh said.

As planned, they switched partners, and Firecracker gave Charlie his watch. Josh, now with Firecracker, took the left-hand hallway. Unlike the fourth floor, the third was a mixture of rooms. The first one they came to was an examining room. The floor was cluttered with old instruments, and a tattered eye chart hung on one wall. A discarded hospital gown, stained and torn, lay across the examination table. Other than that, the room was empty.

Another exam room sat next to the first. As Josh swung the door open, a figure turned toward him. It was a man holding something in his hand. The light in the room was burned out, and it was impossible to see exactly what it was, but Josh thought he saw something wet hanging from the end.

He lifted his flamethrower as the zombie shambled toward the door. He waited until he could read the name on the man's tag—RICHARD—and then aimed at his chest. Just before he hit the trigger, Josh realized what the man was carrying was a hand. Veins and tendons dripped from the wrist where it had been broken from the arm, and on one of the fingers was a ring.

He has both of his hands, Josh thought as he stared

at the zombie. *That means that one belongs to some-one else.*

The man dropped the hand, and Josh stared at it. Something about the ring was familiar to him, although he couldn't place it. It looked like the body of a snake coiled around the finger, its head biting its tail to form a circle.

"Get down!"

Firecracker's voice startled Josh. He looked up just in time to see the zombie reaching for him. Instinctively falling to his knees, he covered his head with his hands as Firecracker's flamethrower roared into action. The zombie wheeled back, shrieking.

"Close the door," Firecracker said. "Roast him."

Josh started to do that, then saw the hand again. Trying not to think about it, he reached out and grabbed it, flinging it outside the room. Firecracker cried out in disgust. "What are you doing?"

Josh slammed the door and pressed his back against it as the zombie tried to get out by ramming his body again and again into the door. Josh could feel the heat from the flames passing through the metal, and every time the zombie hit the door, he jolted Josh forward. But slowly the hits became less and less forceful, until finally they stopped completely.

After checking to make sure the zombie was really

dead, Josh turned back to the hand. He'd been staring at it while holding the zombie back but had come no closer to figuring out why the ring triggered something in his brain. He knelt and reached for the hand.

"Don't touch it," Firecracker warned. "It's got blood all over it. You get that in you and you might as well be that guy," he added, gesturing at the closed door. Smoke was seeping out from underneath it and filling the hallway. It burned Josh's eyes.

"I don't have any cuts on me," Josh said as he reached out and pulled the ring from the finger. It came off easily, and he wiped it on his jeans. "I've seen this ring before," he said. "I just can't remember where."

A muffled scream came from somewhere else in the building, interrupting his thoughts. "Charlie?" Firecracker asked.

Josh shook his head. "No." He put the ring in his pocket, and he and Firecracker ran down the hall. Josh completely forgot about checking the rooms until they started to turn the corner into the next corridor. He stopped. "We should go back," he said to Firecracker.

The scream came again, this time louder and more frenzied. Josh looked down the hall just as someone rounded the corner, running straight for them. Whoever it was moved much more quickly than zombies usually did, with a rolling gait that carried the body forward in weird zigzagging steps.

For a moment Josh *was* afraid it was Charlie, but in the dim light it was impossible to tell. Then two more figures came around the corner. He saw flames flickering at the ends of two torches and knew the figures were Charlie and Scrawl. Which meant that the screaming figure was a z.

The zombie kept coming. Then, when it saw Josh and Firecracker standing with flamethrowers pointed at it, it stopped. It started to turn, but Charlie and Scrawl were closing in from the other side. The zombie raised its arms as if to cover its face with its hands, and that's when Josh saw that its right arm ended in a stump.

"On three!" he heard Scrawl shout. "One! Two! Three!"

All four of them fired their weapons at the zombie. It was consumed in a fireball that immediately blackened the walls and ceiling. Flames whipped around the zombie like a tornado. The creature stood perfectly still for a few seconds, then collapsed into a pile like burning leaves. Josh and Firecracker stood on one side of it, looking through the fire at Charlie and Scrawl.

When the flames died down, Charlie ran to Josh.

"She knew," she said. "She *knew* we were going to kill her. I've never seen one run away before." She choked back tears. "Josh, it was horrible."

Josh reached into his pocket and removed the ring. "Have you seen this before?" he asked Charlie.

She took the ring and looked at it. Then her hand began to shake.

"Freya," she whispered. "It's Freya's."

23

"There are eight left," Josh said as they pounded down the stairs to the second floor. He clenched his fist, feeling Freya's ring press against his palm. Rage burned in his chest. He looked at his watch. "Forty-five minutes left," he called out. They had wasted time, and it was his fault. After they torched Freya, he had fallen apart, cursing Clatter and screaming in pain and anger over what his friend had been turned into. The others, not knowing what to do, had let him yell it out.

Now he was filled with new strength. Eight z's stood between him and Clatter, and he was determined to find them. He strode down the hallway, abandoning the two-to-a-side plan and kicking in every door he saw. The second floor held more examination rooms, as well as what seemed to be offices for the doctors. They found the next zombie in one of those, standing by the wall and staring dumbly up at a framed diploma, like he was trying to read it. Josh noted the name on the z's tag—PAUL—before giving Scrawl the okay to torch him.

They found two more zombies on the floor, a woman named Gwen sitting in a kind of living room staring at an old broken television set, and a man named Virgil hiding in a closet. They each went down with barely a fight.

"I've got to say, these meatbags have been pretty tame," Firecracker remarked as they regrouped at the head of the last flight of stairs. "I've played holo-z's meaner than these ones."

"He's saving the worst for last," said Scrawl. "I guarantee it. Probably the ones who've been turned the longest. They're totally gone. Nothing inside but pure instinct to kill."

"Whatever they are, they're still people," Charlie said, shooting Firecracker a dirty look. "Remember that."

"Okay," Josh said. He checked the fuel level on his flamethrower. "We're low on firepower and we've got five more zombies standing between us and walking out of here. I don't know what we're going to find down there, but whatever it is, I'm not going down without a fight."

"I'm with you," Scrawl said.

"Me too," Charlie agreed.

Firecracker nodded. "Let's do it," he said.

"What's our time?" Scrawl asked Josh.

"Twenty-five minutes," Josh answered. "None to waste."

They went down the stairs. The first floor was different from the others. There were no examination rooms, no offices. In fact, it looked like a hotel lobby—one that had been bombed over and over again. The walls were covered with water-stained wallpaper that hung in ribbons where it had fallen away. The dusty old furniture had nearly disintegrated into piles of sawdust and scraps of velvet. A huge chandelier that had once hung in the asylum's grand foyer lay on the marble floor, its shattered crystals sparkling like diamonds in the moonlight that managed to find its way through the boarded-up windows.

"This is the only floor the families ever saw," Scrawl said as he surveyed the ruins. "The administrators wanted them to think this was more like a country club than a mental hospital."

"So where do we go?" Charlie asked.

"That way is blocked," said Josh, looking down the hallway running south. The ceiling there had caved in, and the corridor was impassable. "It looks like we

251

don't have a choice."

"He's herding us," Scrawl said. "Whatever is down this way, Clatter set it up."

Josh nodded in agreement. "Then let's get the show over with," he said.

The hallway seemed to go on forever. They moved quickly, taking turns stepping into any rooms they came to and doing a quick sweep. Josh didn't expect to find any z's there, and they didn't. *He's trying to get us to run our time out,* he thought.

Finally they came to the intersection of the north and west corridors. Like the south corridor, the west was also blocked by debris. The only option remaining was to go through a small door set in the inside wall.

"The garden," Scrawl said. "He wants us in the garden."

Josh tried the handle of the door. It turned easily, and the door swung out. Moonlight flooded the hallway, and Josh blinked a couple of times. After the darkness of the upper floors, even the weak light of the quarter moon took some getting used to.

The walls of Feverfew rose up all around the garden. The dark panes of the windows stared blankly out at the overgrown plants and the crumbling fountain at the garden's center, where headless figures stood reaching their cold hands up to the sky. The air was rich with the smells of dirt and rot.

"They could be anywhere in there," Charlie said, looking at the jungle of trees and flowers. "There's no way we can find them in time."

"Then they need to find us," said Josh.

The others looked at him, confused. "How?" Firecracker asked.

"We torch the whole place," Josh said. "The one thing they're afraid of is fire. We'll smoke them out. There's only one way in and out of here, right?"

"As far as I know," said Scrawl. "But Clatter could have made another one."

"We'll have to risk it," Josh said. "We're almost out of time."

"But how will *we* get out?" asked Charlie.

"One of us will guard the door," Josh said. "Make sure nobody locks it. The other three will set fires." He looked at Charlie. "You stay here."

"Why me?" Charlie argued. "Why not him?" She nodded at Firecracker. "He's the one with no experience."

Firecracker snorted. "What kind of experience do you need to set something on fire?" he countered.

"You're guarding the door *because* you have more experience," Josh said to Charlie. "If anyone—or anything—tries to come through that door or close it, you stop them."

"All right then," Charlie said. "Go start your fires."

The three boys headed for the trees. "We'll start in the back and move this way," Josh said. "Firecracker, you take the left. Scrawl, you take the right. I'll go up the middle. We run through, start blasting, and run back here. Got it?"

"Got it," Scrawl and Firecracker said.

"And don't forget, there are z's in there somewhere. Don't engage them, even if you see them. You'll just get stuck in the crossfire. Avoid them and get back here."

Scrawl looked at him. "You think this will work?"

"I don't know," Josh answered truthfully.

He counted down from three. At one, the three of them took off into the garden. Josh saw Firecracker and Scrawl disappear into the darkness; then he was plunging headlong through the overgrown grass. It was still wet from the rain, and he hoped it would light.

He drove that thought from his mind as he pushed past some wizened bushes. Then he was running through a patch of rosebushes. Their thorns snagged in his clothes and scraped his hands, but he ignored the pain. He could see the far wall of the garden twenty yards ahead of him. As it grew closer, he lifted his thrower.

A flash erupted from his right. Scrawl had reached the wall. *He always was the fastest of us*, Josh thought as he came to a stop and aimed the flamethrower at a clump of dead weeds. As he fired, a third blast came from the left. Firecracker had made it too.

The fire took hold, snaking up the stalks of grass and hungrily consuming it. It seemed to hesitate for a moment, then jumped to a nearby tree. The dead wood popped and exploded as the flames wrapped around the desiccated limbs. Josh watched long enough to make sure the fire wasn't going out, then turned and started running back to the door.

When he reached the fountain at the center of the garden, he bore left to go around it. As he did, a zombie leaped out of the muck that filled the basin and flung itself at Josh. It was covered in slime, and its hands grasped at Josh's arm but slipped away. The zombie fell, its fingers catching hold of Josh's leg. Josh stumbled, tried to wrench loose from the zombie's grip, and went down hard on his back. The air was knocked out of him.

The zombie awkwardly got to its feet and came at him. Josh scrambled for his flamethrower, but he had fallen on top of it and couldn't get it. He had nothing to defend himself with. *This is it*, he thought. *I lost*.

A figure charged out of the darkness to his left,

bellowing madly. The zombie, confused, stopped its forward rush. Then Josh saw Firecracker aim his flamethrower at the thing's head and fire. The zombie crackled as the flame made contact with the water soaking its skin and clothes. Steam exploded off its head, enveloping it in a black shroud of smoke and steam.

Firecracker pulled Josh to his feet. "Nice work," Josh said, grinning.

The two of them ran as fast as they could back to the doorway, where Scrawl and Charlie were standing with their throwers at the ready. "What happened?" Scrawl asked. "You guys were right behind me."

"We had a visitor," said Josh. "But we took care of it."

"You mean I took care of it," Firecracker corrected him.

"Just look for z's," said Josh. "They've got to be coming out sooner or later."

As if on cue, four zombies emerged from the smoke. They walked slowly and heavily. One, already on fire, clawed at its charred shirt. The other three headed for the four friends and the door.

"Four of them and four of us," Charlie said. "Pick your z, boys."

The four of them fanned out, each one heading

for a different zombie. Scrawl took the one that was already smoking, hitting it dead on with a blast that peeled the skin from its torso. Charlie took on a massive man who, even after being set afire, continued to walk toward her until a second blast from Scrawl took out the zombie's legs and left it a pile of melting fat.

Josh advanced on his target. To his left Firecracker was toasting his zombie, which left just one to go. For the first time Josh allowed himself to think that they really might get out alive.

Then he saw the zombie's face. "Stash," he whispered.

Stash saw him and stopped. His dead eyes stared at Josh, and his mouth began to move. His head rolled from side to side as well, and his arms twitched spasmodically. Josh raised his flamethrower. But as he took aim, he saw Stash's mouth move again. Something about it wasn't right. He wasn't just making random sounds. *He's trying to talk,* Josh realized.

Before he knew it, he was running toward his old teammate. He heard Charlie, Scrawl, and Firecracker screaming for him to stop, but he kept going, coming to a halt only when he was just out of Stash's reach. Stash turned his head, looking at Josh, and mumbled. Josh still couldn't hear him.

You have to get closer, he told himself.

Fighting every one of his natural instincts, he took another step toward Stash. Stash didn't move. Josh took another step, then another, until he was right in front of Stash. He looked into the boy's one remaining eye. It was milky, and thick yellow ooze dripped from the corners. But then, just for a moment, it seemed to clear, and Josh almost believed he was looking at the old Stash.

"Home," Stash mumbled. He pressed something into Josh's hand. Then, before Josh knew what he was doing, Stash staggered back, pretending to be hit, and fell into the flames that had engulfed the garden. Josh watched, a scream stuck in his throat, as Stash disappeared behind the wall of fire.

The next thing he knew he was being pulled back by Scrawl and Charlie. "We have to get out of here," Charlie yelled above the roar of the inferno.

Josh turned his back on the garden and followed his friends through the door. When they were in the hallway again, Firecracker shut the door behind them. "Now what?" he said. "We got them all, didn't we?"

Scrawl nodded. "Yeah," he said. "But somehow I don't think we're done yet."

"What are you holding?" Charlie asked Josh.

Josh looked at the key in his hand. "Stash gave it to me just now. But I don't know what it's for."

Scrawl took the key from Josh and looked at it for a long moment. "I think I know what this is," he said.

"What?" asked Josh.

"You know how Clatter wears that coat with all the keys sewn on it?" Scrawl said. "He doesn't just do it because it looks cool. He does it to hide things." He held the key up. "Things like this."

"What's the key to?" said Firecracker.

Scrawl held the key up. "If we're lucky—the way out."

24

"**C**latter is a genius," Scrawl said as they walked. "But he's also paranoid. He has escape routes all over the place. I think this key opens the door to one of them."

"How do you know?" Charlie asked.

"Here," said Scrawl, pointing to one end of the key, where the letter *F* was stamped. "F for Feverfew." He turned the key over, and on the other side was the number *237*. "Room 237," he said. "Whatever this key unlocks, it's in that room."

"What if it isn't?" asked Firecracker. "What if Clatter gave him the key to trick us?"

Josh thought about the look in Stash's eye when he handed over the key. A lump formed in his throat. "I don't think he did," he said.

"Okay," said Firecracker doubtfully. "Then let's get up to room 237 and see what's up there."

They headed for the stairs, but the ding of the old elevator drew their attention. The doors opened, and Clatter emerged with Seamus and Finnegan. He strode across the lobby toward where the four exhausted friends stood.

"Play along," Scrawl whispered to the others as Clatter got closer.

"I must say, you've impressed me," Clatter said. The tone of his voice was warm, but Josh heard an undercurrent of frostiness that he didn't like. "Your methods on the final test were a bit crude, but given the time constraints, rather brilliant."

"I'm glad you liked it," Scrawl said. "Now how about keeping your end of the deal?"

Clatter took a deep breath. "As much as I'd like to, I'm afraid I can't," he said. "You see, you didn't complete the game in the allotted time. You were exactly one minute and seventeen seconds over."

Scrawl shook his head. "I knew you'd never let us go," he said.

"Mmm," Clatter replied. "Your lack of faith in me is disappointing. But it's irrelevant, as you lost."

"So now what?" said Josh. "You kill us?"

Clatter feigned shock. "Of course not," he said. "They do." He nodded toward the stairs, where a dozen or more zombies were shambling toward the lobby.

"And now I will say good-bye," said Clatter. He, Seamus, and Finnegan walked rapidly toward the waiting elevator, stepping inside. As the doors shut, Clatter tipped his hat and smiled. "Good luck!" he called out.

Scrawl glanced at the zombies, then ran for the elevator. "Help me!" he yelled to the others.

Josh, Charlie, and Firecracker joined him at the doors. Scrawl looked up at the needle over the door. It was only halfway between the lobby and the basement. He shoved the grate that covered the elevator doors aside and started prying them open.

"What are you doing?" Josh said. "We have to get to the second floor."

"We can't let them get out of here," said Scrawl, trying to force his fingers into the crack between the doors. "If we don't stop him, Clatter will keep on doing what he's been doing. He'll just replace us with other players. More people will die."

"And how are we going to stop him?" Charlie asked.

"There's a hand brake on top of the elevator," Scrawl said. "The mechanics used them for stopping the car during shaft maintenance, when they rode on the roof to access the pulleys. If I can get to it, I can stop the car between floors and trap them there. That way the police will know just where to find them."

"There's no time for that," Firecracker said.

"Not if you keep arguing," said Scrawl. "Now help me get these doors open."

Firecracker and Josh took one door while Scrawl and Charlie took the other. At first the doors wouldn't budge, but then they reluctantly creaked open. Josh peered inside. He could just see the top of the elevator car.

"We'll wait for you upstairs," Josh told him. "In room 237."

Scrawl shook his head. "Don't wait," he said. "In case something goes wrong, I want you on the way to the police. Now get out of here."

Josh started to object, but Scrawl was already lowering himself into the shaft. He clung to the ladder. "Go!" he yelled. "Now!"

Josh and the others turned and faced the zombies. In order to get to the stairs, they were going to have to fight their way through, and they had no weapons left. Even then, they had no idea what waited for them in room 237. *It could be nothing,* Josh thought. *We could be walking right into a trap.* But it was their only chance.

"We can't kill them," Josh said. "So let's just get through them. Don't let them grab you, or you'll probably get bit."

"Really?" Firecracker said. "Thanks for the tip." He grinned at Josh. "Race you to the second floor," he said, and took off.

Josh watched as his friend ran straight at one of the zombies at the front of the pack, a fat man wearing a blood-spattered butcher's apron. Firecracker lowered his shoulder and hit the z square in the chest, sending him flying backward into some of the other zombies. They fell like bowling pins, and Firecracker shouted, "Strike!" triumphantly.

Charlie and Josh followed him, dodging the zombies that grasped clumsily at their clothes. Firecracker was already halfway up the first flight of stairs, calling for them to hurry. Charlie ducked under the arms of a zombie woman swinging her purse like a weapon— and Josh, who was behind her, was hit right in the face by it. He fell backward, hitting his head on the tile floor.

Stunned, he couldn't move. He saw the zombie woman's face as she leaned over him. Her milky eyes rolled back in her head and her mouth opened, revealing broken teeth. She dropped her purse and reached for him with hands covered in sores.

"Back off, meatbag!" he heard Charlie yell.

The zombie woman turned her head, snarling, as Charlie's foot hit her in the stomach. The z let out a grunt and was flung to the side. Then Charlie was grabbing Josh's hand and pulling him to his feet. His head throbbed as he stood, and for a moment he thought he might faint.

"Come on!" Charlie encouraged him. "We're almost there."

Josh forced himself to move. He saw the stairs ahead of them, clear of z's. They just had to get to the second floor. His feet moved up the steps as behind them the zombies moaned in frustration. Josh knew they would follow, and even though they moved slowly, there were a lot more of them.

As they reached the landing, a body fell in front of them, almost hitting them. The zombie—a teenage boy—twitched frantically, trying to move his broken limbs.

"Sorry!" Firecracker yelled, looking at them over the balcony. "I didn't know you were there."

Charlie and Josh stepped over the z and ran up the rest of the stairs. Josh's head still hurt, but it was clearing. When they met up with Firecracker in the second-floor hallway, he looked at the number on the nearest door.

"Room 237 is this way," Firecracker said, pointing to the left. "And we should probably hurry. Company's coming."

Josh and Charlie turned and saw four zombies coming up the stairs, moving with surprising quickness. The three friends dashed down the hall, finding the room about halfway down. They'd passed the room during their sweep of the floor, but because it was locked, they had assumed it was zombie free. Digging the key from his pocket, Josh jabbed it into the keyhole and turned it. For a moment nothing happened, and Josh's stomach sank. The four z's were getting closer.

Then there was a click and the lock slid open. Firecracker and Charlie slipped into the room, with Josh entering last. He slammed the door shut and turned the lock just as a zombie face appeared in the window, pressing its bloody mouth against the glass.

Josh turned away from it and surveyed the room. They didn't have much time. The z's would either break the glass or break the door down. Whatever was in the room Josh and the others had to find it, and soon.

But the room was empty. Completely empty. There wasn't a chair, a desk, a bed—not even any trash.

"What is this?" Firecracker said. He turned and looked at Josh. "I told you this was a trap. Now we're stuck in here, and sooner or later those things are going to get in." He pointed at the door, where the faces of two more zombies were peering in at them. They were also banging on the door, and it shook in its frame.

"Not so fast," said Charlie. "There's a closet."

"Oh, a closet," said Firecracker. "That makes *everything* better. We can just hide in there until the meatbags go away."

Ignoring him, Charlie went to the door in the wall and turned the knob. She pulled the door open, stepping back in case there were any surprises inside. When nothing jumped out, she looked in.

"What is it?" Josh asked.

Charlie shook her head. "I'm not sure," she answered.

"Well you'd better figure it out in the next thirty seconds," said Firecracker. "That door isn't going to hold."

There was pounding on the door, followed by the sound of breaking glass. Outside, the zombies' moans grew more frantic. "Like I said," Firecracker yelped, pushing Charlie into the closet as he grabbed Josh by the wrist and pulled him inside too.

There was barely room for the three of them in the closet. Not that it really mattered. As far as Josh could tell, they were simply inside an ordinary closet, an *empty* ordinary closet. There were no weapons in it, not even coat hangers. The only thing in there was a single old-fashioned lightbulb hanging from the ceiling.

The sound of breaking glass came again, and Josh peered out to see a zombie reaching through the window of the room's door and grabbing its doorknob from the inside. Soon the room would be filled with z's, and there would be no escaping them this time. There were too many of them, and without weapons Josh and his friends would be zombie food.

Acting on instinct, Josh pulled the closet door shut as the first zombie staggered into the room. Now the closet was pitch black. Josh could hear himself breathing heavily as he thought frantically for some way out.

"I'm not dying in the dark," Firecracker said, reaching up and pulling the frayed string attached to the lightbulb.

The light flickered on. A second later the floor fell away beneath them. Josh, Charlie, and Firecracker shouted in surprise as they plunged into darkness. Above them the light continued to burn but grew smaller and smaller as they fell.

A few seconds later, Josh landed with a thud on something soft. Charlie fell next to him, and Firecracker landed on top of them both. He rolled off with a grunt and sat up.

"Where are we?" he asked.

Josh looked around. They were on top of what

seemed to be a pile of old mattresses—at least six or seven of them—in some kind of cellar. The mattress they were sitting on was stained, and it stank of mold and dirt. It sagged beneath their weight, and Josh had to roll to the left to get to the side and throw his legs over the side.

That's when he saw the old ambulance. Large and white, it had a fat, round fender over each wheel and a long front end with circular glass headlamps that looked like eyes. A single red light stuck up from the roof. On the side door was painted a big red cross, and underneath that, in black, the words FEVERFEW ASYLUM.

Firecracker jumped down from the mattress and looked at the ambulance. "This thing must be at least a hundred years old," he said.

Josh climbed down from the mattress pile and helped Charlie down as well. Once on the ground, Charlie eyed the ambulance doubtfully. "*This* is the big secret of room 237?" she said.

Firecracker, who had gone around to the other side of the ambulance, called out, "The keys are still in it!" Then the door beside Josh and Charlie opened. "Get in!" Firecracker ordered.

Josh looked at Charlie. "He's got to be kidding."

Before Charlie could answer, something fell onto

the mattresses behind them. Josh turned and saw a zombie flailing around, trying to turn itself over. A second later another one fell from the hole in the ceiling, and then another.

Charlie looked at the ambulance, then at Josh. "I don't think we have a choice."

She and Josh climbed into the ambulance just as one of the zombies managed to roll off the mattresses. It lay on the floor for a moment, then moaned and got up. It turned its head toward the ambulance, where Josh was looking at it through the window.

"Can't you get this thing started?" Josh asked as the z snarled and spat out strings of bloody drool.

Firecracker was turning the key in the ignition. The engine made choking sounds but didn't start. More zombies had fallen to the floor, and now, attracted to the sound, they started congregating around the truck. There were half a dozen of them. They stared in the windows with milky yellow eyes, their faces only inches from the glass. Josh looked away.

"I don't know what to do," Firecracker said, his voice cracking. "This thing is ancient."

"The clutch!" Charlie yelled. "Push in the clutch!"

Firecracker looked at her in bewilderment. "The what?"

Charlie pointed to one of the pedals near the floor.

"You have to push that in and put the gears into neutral, otherwise you can't start the engine."

Firecracker pushed tentatively against one of the pedals with his foot. "This?" he said.

"Switch seats," Charlie ordered, climbing over him.

Firecracker scooted next to Josh. "How do *you* know how to drive this thing?" he asked as Charlie fiddled with the pedals and pulled on the gearshift that rose up from the floor.

"My father has an old Mustang," she said. "It was *his* father's, and someday it will be mine. He taught me how to drive it when I was twelve." She turned the key, and the engine sputtered. A zombie banged on the passenger-side window, which cracked.

"Go!" Josh said as the zombie hit the glass again. "Go, go, go, go, go!"

Charlie turned the key again. This time the engine rattled to life. The zombies began to bang on the ambulance, roaring angrily. The one outside Josh's window hit the glass once more and it shattered, the pieces falling all over Josh's lap. A rotting hand came through the opening, reaching for Josh's hair. He smelled the stench of decomposing flesh.

Suddenly the ambulance leaped forward, knocking a z to the ground. There was a sickening crunch as the tires ran over it. Charlie pulled on the gearshift, and the ambulance shuddered. Something inside made a grinding sound. But a moment later they were moving ahead even more quickly.

"Where are we going?" Firecracker asked as Charlie drove down what seemed to be a long corridor cut through solid stone.

"The only way we *can* go," said Charlie. "Unless you want to go back and ask for directions."

Charlie turned something on the dashboard and the headlights came on, producing two thin beams of weak yellow light that barely cut through the darkness. They could see a little way ahead, but not far enough to see the two wide doors that barred the end of the corridor. By the time they loomed into view the ambulance was headed straight for them.

"Hang on!" Charlie yelled as she urged the car forward.

A second later they hit the door. Wood splintered, one of the headlights went out, and the ambulance shook, but it didn't stop. Instead they found themselves emerging onto a road. Josh leaned out the window and looked behind them. On a bluff above them Feverfew loomed in the darkness.

"That must be how they took patients in without anyone seeing them," he said, glancing at the mouth of the tunnel they had just exited. He shuddered as he thought about the possibility of the zombies getting out through it. *We'll get to the police before they can,* he reassured himself. *They'll come block it up again.*

Charlie steered the ambulance down the narrow, twisting road that led away from the hospital. Unused for decades, the road was falling apart. Pieces of it were gone, and in other places plants grew up from cracks in the pavement. As they bounced along over bumps and ruts, Josh prayed that the old ambulance would stay together.

"If I'm right, this road connects to the Upside Highway," Charlie said. "We can take that to the police station at Citytop. That's the closest one."

"Are you kidding?" said Firecracker. "It will take forever to get through that traffic."

Charlie scanned the dashboard, pushing and pulling on knobs. The windshield wipers went on, then off. The remaining headlight blinked out and came on again.

"What are you looking for?" Firecracker asked.

A shrieking sound pierced the night, and a red light lit up the dark around the ambulance. "That's what I'm looking for," Charlie said as the siren wailed.

As she had guessed, the road did lead onto the Upside Highway. And everyone did get out of the ambulance's way. Now that they were away from Feverfew, and Clatter, and the zombies, Josh allowed himself to think about Scrawl. Was he okay? Had he trapped Clatter, Seamus, and Finnegan and gotten himself out? Josh hoped so. *He's a smart guy,* he reminded himself. *He'll be fine.*

He also thought about his family. He knew they were worrying about him. He couldn't wait to call and let them know he was okay. Even more, he couldn't wait to see them again. The first thing he was going to do was apologize to his parents for ever thinking the game was harmless fun. The second thing he was going to do was tell Emily what a great sister she was. He hadn't allowed himself to think about it during the game, but now that it was all over he realized how close he'd come to never seeing them again.

Suddenly the tiredness that had been growing all night began to overtake him. He leaned back and closed his eyes. *Maybe it's all a bad dream,* he thought. *Maybe I'll wake up in my own bed.*

He dozed for a few minutes, until the jerking of the ambulance coming to a stop woke him. "We're here," Charlie said.

When they walked into Precinct Number 42, Josh felt safe for the first time since leaving his house that afternoon. They were in a police station. They would tell someone their story, Clatter would be arrested, and they could go home. Someone else could worry about the zombies roaming around Feverfew. His career as a Torcher was over.

As they walked to the front desk, they were surrounded by a sudden flurry of excitement. Uniformed policemen ran past, paying no attention to them. There was frantic talking, and the buzzing of com units filled the air as invisible voices shouted directions.

"What's going on?" Charlie said. "Where are they going?"

Josh turned around to see what was happening. Outside, dozens of police vehicles were starting to pull out of the station lot, their lights spinning. Then he noticed the screen above the door to the building. It was tuned to a local news channel, and although Josh couldn't hear what the reporter was saying, he saw the word *zombies* scroll by on the news ticker running below the picture.

He, Charlie, and Firecracker looked at one another. "No!" Josh said.

He looked back at the screen. This time he saw the whole headline: ZOMBIES SIGHTED IN OLD TOWN. GET TO SAFETY. MORE INFORMATION TO FOLLOW. The picture showed a street in Old Town. Half a dozen zombies were lurching down the street. The camera zoomed in on one of them.

Charlie gasped. Then she sobbed. "It can't be," she said. "Josh, no. It's not—"

"It's Scrawl," Josh said.

A man approached the zombies. He was wearing a black uniform with a familiar logo on it. He pointed his flamethrower at Scrawl.

"No!" Firecracker shouted.

As fire burst from the flamethrower, Charlie buried her head in Josh's neck and sobbed. He held her close, telling her that everything would be all right.

But it won't be, he thought. *It will never be all right again.*

MICHAEL THOMAS FORD

is the author of the teen novel SUICIDE NOTES as well as several essay collections and adult novels, including JANE BITES BACK. He lives in San Francisco with his partner and their five dogs. Visit him online at www.michaelthomasford.com.

Tell It Slant

Writing and Shaping
Creative Nonfiction

Brenda Miller & Suzanne Paola

McGraw·Hill

New York   Chicago   San Francisco   Lisbon   London   Madrid   Mexico City
Milan   New Delhi   San Juan   Seoul   Singapore   Sydney   Toronto

Library of Congress Cataloging-in-Publication Data

Miller, Brenda.
    Tell it slant : writing and shaping creative nonfiction / by Brenda Miller and
Suzanne Paola.
        p.   cm.
    Includes bibliographical references.
    ISBN 0-07-144494-7
    1. English language—Rhetoric.   2. Journalism—Authorship.   3. Investigative
reporting.   4. Creative writing.   5. Report writing.   I. Paola, Suzanne.
II. Title.

PE1408.M548   2004b
808'.042—dc22   2004008443

    14 15 16 17 18   DOH/DOH   3 2 1

ISBN 0-07-144494-7

Emily Dickinson poem (p. iii) reprinted by permission of the publishers and the trustees of
Amherst College from *The Poems of Emily Dickinson*, Thomas H. Johnson, ed., Cambridge:
Mass.: The Belknap Press of Harvard University Press, copyright © 1951, 1955, 1979,
1983 by the president and fellows of Harvard College.

McGraw-Hill books are available at special quantity discounts to use as premiums and
sales promotions, or for use in corporate training programs. For more information, please
write to the Director of Special Sales, Professional Publishing, McGraw-Hill, Two Penn
Plaza, New York, NY 10121-2298. Or contact your local bookstore.

This book is printed on acid-free paper.

Tell all the Truth but tell it Slant—
Success in Circuit lies
Too bright for our infirm Delight
The Truth's superb surprise
As Lightening to the Children eased
With explanation kind
The Truth must dazzle gradually
Or every man be blind—
—Emily Dickinson

Contents

Introduction

Where to Begin

The word is the making of the world.

—WALLACE STEVENS

Here's how it happens: I'm at a party, or sitting quietly in my seat on an airplane, or milling around at a family reunion, and someone finally asks me the question: "So, you're a writer. What do you write?" It's a deceptively simple question. And seems to demand a simple response.

But in the split second before I can answer, I go through all the possible replies in my head. "Well," I could say, "I write essays." But essays sound too much like academic papers and articles. I could say, simply, "Nonfiction," but then they might think I write celebrity biographies, cookbooks, or historical treatises on World War II. I could try to take the easy way out and say I write autobiography or memoir, but people would raise their eyebrows and say, "Memoir? Aren't you too young to write your memoirs?" Besides, not all of what I write is memoir; in fact, many of my pieces are not based in private memory at all.

*All this is too much for casual party chat. I need a term that, once deployed, will answer all their questions for good. But I know that if I answer with the correct phrase—*creative nonfiction*—I'm in for a long night. My interrogator will warm up to the debate, throwing out the opening volley: "Creative nonfiction? Isn't that an oxymoron?" His forehead crinkles, and his eyes search my own, trying to understand what, exactly, I'm talking about.*

I want to tell him that I love writing creative nonfiction precisely because of this ambiguity. I love the way writing creative nonfiction allows me to straddle a kind of "borderland" where I can discover new aspects of myself and the world, forge surprising metaphors, and create artistic order out of life's chaos. I'm never bored when I write in this genre, always jazzed by the new ways I can stretch my writing muscles. But I rarely trust my listener will understand. So, more often than not, I smile and say, "Maybe I'll show you sometime." Then I execute a pirouette and turn his attention toward the view out the window or to the lovely fruit punch in its cut-glass bowl. I direct his attention to the myriad things of this world, and maybe that is the correct answer after all.

—BRENDA

When Emily Dickinson wrote, "Tell all the Truth but tell it Slant / Success in Circuit lies . . ." what did she mean by these lines? We think she meant that truth takes on many guises; the truth of art can be very different from the truth of day-to-day life. Her poems and letters, after all, reveal her deft observation of the outer world, but it is "slanted" through the poet's distinctive vision. We chose her poem as both title and epigraph for this book because it so aptly describes the task of the creative nonfiction writer: to tell the truth, yes, but to become more than a mere transcriber of life's factual experiences.

Every few years, National Public Radio checks in on a man who feels compelled to record every minute of his day in a diary. As you can imagine, the task is gargantuan and ultimately imprisons him. He becomes a slave to this recording act and can no longer function in the world. The transcription he leaves may be a comprehensive and "truthful" one, but it remains completely unreadable; after all, who cares to read reams and reams of such notes? What value do they hold apart from the author? In nonfiction, if we place a premium on fact, then this man's diary would be the ultimate masterpiece. But in literature and art, we applaud style, meaning, and effect over the bare facts. We go to literature—and perhaps especially creative nonfiction literature—to learn not about the author, but about ourselves; we want to be *moved* in some way. That emotional resonance happens only through skillful use of artistic techniques. As Salman Rushdie put it, "Literature is where I go to explore the highest and lowest places in human society and in the human spirit, where I hope to find not absolute truth but the truth of the tale, of the imagination and of the heart."

Simply by choosing to write in this genre, and to present your work as non-fiction, you make an artistic statement. You're saying that the work is rooted in the "real" world. Though the essay might contain some elements of fabrication, it is directly connected to you as the author behind the text. There is a truth to it that you want to claim as your own, a bond of trust between reader and writer. If you present a piece as fiction, you are saying that the work is rooted in the world of the imagination. Though the story may contain autobiographical elements, the reader cannot assume that it has a direct bearing on the truth of the writer's life or experience. At some point, every writer needs to decide how she wants to place herself in relationship to the reader; the choice of genre establishes that relationship and the rules of engagement.

The more you read and study, the more you will discover that creative nonfiction assumes a particular, creating *self* behind the nonfiction prose. When you set about to write creative nonfiction about any subject, you bring to this endeavor a strong voice and a singular vision. This voice must be loud and interesting enough to be heard among the noise coming at us in everyday life. If you succeed, you and the reader will find yourself in a close, if not intimate, relationship that demands honesty and a willingness to risk a kind of exposure you may never venture in face-to-face encounters.

This is not to say that creative nonfiction must be "self-centered." On the contrary, creative nonfiction often focuses on material outside the life of the author, and it certainly need not use a personal "I" speaker. It's the "creative" part of the term *creative nonfiction* that means a single, active imagination is behind the piece of reality this author will unfold. Essayist Scott Russell Sanders wrote, "Feeling overwhelmed by data, random information, the flotsam and jetsam of mass culture, we relish the spectacle of a single consciousness making sense of a portion of the chaos. . . . The essay is a haven for the private, idiosyncratic voice in an era of anonymous babble."

This "idiosyncratic voice" uses all the literary devices available to fiction writers and poets—vivid images, scenes, metaphors, dialogue, satisfying rhythms of language, and so forth—while still remaining true to experience and the world. Or, as novelist and essayist Cynthia Ozick put it, "Like a poem, a genuine essay is made out of language and character and mood and temperament and pluck and chance."

Creative nonfiction can focus on either private experience or public domain, but in either case, the inner self provides the vision and the shaping influence to infuse the work with this sense of "pluck and chance." In many cases, the essayist may find himself "thinking aloud" on the page. Then the essay becomes a continual process of unexpected discovery. The creative nonfiction writer continually chooses to question and expand his or her own limited perceptions.

Lee Gutkind, who edits the journal *Creative Nonfiction*, says creative nonfiction "heightens the whole concept and idea of essay writing." He has come up with the "the five Rs" of creative nonfiction: Real Life, Reflection, Research, Reading, and 'Riting. That second "R," Reflection, means that in contrast to traditional objective journalism, creative nonfiction allows for and encourages "a writer's feelings and responses . . . as long as what [writers] think is written to embrace the reader in a variety of ways." Imagination coupled with facts form this hybrid genre that is both so exciting and so challenging to write.

As in any creative enterprise, the most difficult challenge to writing creative nonfiction lies in knowing where to begin. One might think that creative nonfiction would provide an easy out for this question. After all, someone might chide, all the material is at your fingertips. It's nonfiction after all; the world is yours for the taking. But the minute creative nonfiction writers put pen to paper, they realize a truth both invigorating and disheartening: we are not the rote recorder of life experience. We are artists creating artifice. And as such, we have difficult choices to make every step of the way.

Memoir may seem more straightforward, but as William Zinsser articulates in his introduction to *Inventing the Truth: The Art and Craft of Memoir*, "Good memoirs are a careful act of construction. We like to think that an interesting life will simply fall into place on the page. It won't. . . . Memoir writers must manufacture a text, imposing narrative order on a jumble of half-remembered events."

We've designed this book to help you gain access to your particular stories and memories—your particular voice—while also providing suggestions for turning your gaze onto the world in a way that will allow you to find material outside of the self. We begin with memory and move steadily outward to family, environment, spirituality, history, the arts, and the world. In this way, we hope you will begin to consider both your individual life and our collective lives as material for creative nonfiction. Readers will want to read your work not because they wish to lend a sympathetic ear to a stranger, but because of the way your truth-filled stories may illuminate their own lives and perceptions of the world.

At the end of each chapter, we provide a series of "Try It" exercises. These are prompts to help you put into action the principles we've explained. Use them as starting points to creating your own brand of creative nonfiction.

PART 1

UNEARTHING YOUR MATERIAL

Remember that the writers whom we call eternal or simply good and
who intoxicate us have one common and very important
characteristic: they get somewhere, and they summon you there, and
you feel, not with your mind, but with your whole being, that they
have a certain purpose and, like the ghost of Hamlet's father, do not
come and excite the imagination for nothing. He who desires
nothing, hopes for nothing, and is afraid of nothing, cannot be an
artist.

—ANTON CHEKHOV, IN A LETTER TO
ALEXEI SUVORIN, NOV. 25, 1892

1

The Body of Memory

Memory begins to qualify the imagination, to give it another formation, one that is peculiar to the self. . . . If I were to remember other things, I should be someone else.

—N. Scott Momaday

In my earliest memory, I'm a four-year-old girl waking slowly from anesthesia. I lift my head off the damp pillow and gaze blearily out the bars of my hospital crib. I can see a dim hallway with a golden light burning; somehow I know in that hallway my mother will appear any minute now, bearing ice cream and 7-Up. She told me as much before the operation: "All good girls get ice cream and 7-Up when their tonsils come out," she said, stroking my hair. "It's your reward for being brave." I'm vaguely aware of another little girl screaming for her mother in the crib next to mine, but otherwise the room remains dark and hushed, buffered by the footfalls of nurses who stop a moment at the doorway and move on.

I do not turn to face my neighbor, afraid her terror will infect me; I can feel the tickling urge to cry burbling up in my wounded throat, and that might be the end of me, of all my purported bravery and the promised ice cream. I keep my gaze fixed on that hallway, but something glints in my peripheral vision and I turn to face the bedside table. There, in a mason jar, my tonsils float. They rotate in the liquid: misshapen ovals, pink and nubbly, grotesque.

And now my mother has simply appeared, with no warning or announcement. Her head leans close to the crib, and she gently plies the spoon

3

between the bars, places it between my lips, and holds it there while I swallow. I keep my gaze fixed on her face, and she keeps her gaze on mine, though I know we're both aware of those tonsils floating out of reach. The nurses pad about, and one of them enters the room bearing my "Badge of Courage." It's a certificate with a lion in the middle surrounded by laurels, my name scripted in black ink below. My mother holds it out to me, through the bars, and I run a finger across my name, across the lion's mane, across the dry yellowed parchment.

—BRENDA

The Earliest Memory

What is your earliest memory? What is the memory that always emerges from the dim reaches of your consciousness as the *first one*, the beginning to this life you call your own? Most of us can pinpoint them, these images that assume a privileged station in our life's story. Some of these early memories have the vague aspect of a dream, some the vivid clarity of a photograph. In whatever form they take, they tend to exert on us a mysterious fascination.

Memory itself could be called its own bit of creative nonfiction. We continually—often unconsciously—renovate our memories, shaping them into stories that bring coherence to chaos. Memory has been called the ultimate "mythmaker," continually seeking meaning in the random and often unfathomable events in our lives. "A myth," writes John Kotre, author of *White Gloves: How We Create Ourselves Through Memory*, "is not a falsehood but a comprehensive view of reality. It's a story that speaks to the heart as well as the mind, seeking to generate conviction about what it thinks is true."

The first memory then becomes the starting point in our own narratives of the self. "Our first memories are like the creation stories that humans have always told about the origins of the earth," Kotre writes. "In a similar way, the individual self—knowing how the story is coming out—selects its earliest memories to say, 'This is who I am because this is how I began.'" As writers, we naturally return again and again to these beginnings and scrutinize them. By paying attention to the illogical, unexpected details, we just might light upon the odd yet precise images that help our lives make sense, at least long enough for our purposes as writers.

The prominent fiction writer and essayist David James Duncan calls such autobiographical images "river teeth." Using the image of knots of dense wood that remain in a river years after a fallen tree disintegrates, Duncan creates a metaphor of how memory, too, retains vivid moments that stay in mind long after the events that spurred them have been forgotten. He writes:

There are hard, cross-grained whorls of memory that remain inexplicably lodged in us long after the straight-grained narrative material that housed them has washed away. Most of these whorls are not stories, exactly: more often they're self-contained moments of shock or of inordinate empathy. . . . These are our "river teeth"—the time-defying knots of experience that remain in us after most of our autobiographies are gone.

Virginia Woolf had her own term for such "shocks" of memory. She calls them "moments of being" and they become essential to our very sense of self. They are the times when we get jolted out of our everyday complacency to really *see* the world and all that it contains. This shock-receiving capacity is essential for the writer's disposition. "I hazard the explanation," she writes, "that a shock is at once in my case followed by the desire to explain it. . . . I make it real by putting it into words." Woolf's early moments of being, the vivid first memories from childhood, are of the smallest, most ordinary things: the pattern of her mother's dress, for example, or the pull cord of the window blind skittering across the floor of their beach house.

The memories that can have the most emotional impact for the writer are those we don't really understand, the images that rise up before us quite without our volition. For example, the flash of our mother's face as she sips from a cooled cup of coffee, her eyes betraying some private grief you've never seen before; or the smell of grapefruit ripening on a tree outside your bedroom window. Perhaps the touch of a stranger's hand reminds you of the way your grandmother casually grasped your hand in her own, the palm so soft but the knuckles so rough, as you sat together watching television, not speaking a word.

These are the river teeth, or the moments of being, the ones that suck your breath away. What repository of memory do you hold in your heart rather than your head? What are the pictures that rise up to the surface without your bidding? Take these as your cue. Pick up your pen, your net, your magnet, whatever it takes. Be on alert. This is where you begin.

Metaphorical Memory

A metaphor is a way at getting at a truth that exists beyond the literal. By pin-pointing certain images as *symbolic*, writers can go deeper than surface truths and create essays that work on many levels at once. This is what writers are up to all the time, not only with memory but with the material of experience and the world. We resurrect the details to describe not only the surface appearance, but also to make intuitive connections, to articulate some truth that cannot be spoken of directly.

Many writers allow early memories to "impress themselves" on the mind. They do not dismiss them as passing details but rather probe them for any insights they may contain. They ask not only "what?" but "why?" "Why do I remember the things I do? Why these memories and not others?"

Let's go back to that first memory of the tonsils, that early river tooth in the personal essay at the beginning of this chapter. For me, Brenda, as a writer it is not important *what* I remember—or even the factual accuracy of the scene—but *why* I recall it the way I do. And, I keep coming back to that incongruous jar of tonsils. I doubt the doctors did such a thing (my mother has no recollection of it), but it remains the most stubborn and intractable part of the scene. What I like about this part of my memory is its very illegibility. The best material cannot be deciphered in an instant, with a fixed meaning that, once pinned down, remains immutable. No. As essayists, we want the rich stuff, the inscrutable images whose meaning is never clear at first, second, or third glance.

I could interpret that jar of tonsils in any number of ways, but this is the one I light on most frequently. When I woke from having my tonsils removed, I knew for the first time that my body was not necessarily a whole unit, always intact. At that moment, I understood the courage that it will take to bear this body into a world that will most certainly cause it harm. Of course, as a child I realized no such thing. But, as an adult—*as a writer preserving this memory in language*—I begin to create a metaphor that will infiltrate both my writing and my sense of self from here on out.

Think back on that early memory of yours, the one that came to mind instantly. Illuminate the details, shine a spotlight on them until they begin to yield a sense of truth revealed. Where is your body in this memory? What kind of language does it speak? What metaphor does it offer for you to puzzle out in writing?

Muscle Memory

The body, memory, and mind exist in sublime interdependence, each part wholly twined with the others. There is a phrase used in dancing, athletics, parachuting, and other fields that require sharp training of the body: *muscle memory*. Once the body learns the repetitive gestures of a certain movement or skill, the memory of how to execute these movements will be encoded in the muscles. That is why, for instance, we never forget how to ride a bike. Or why, years after tap dance lessons, one can still execute a convincing shuffle-hop-step across a kitchen floor.

One cannot speak of memory—and of bodily memory in particular—without trotting out Marcel Proust and his famous madeleine. Proust dips his cookie in the lime-blossom tea, and *Remembrance of Things Past* springs forth, all six volumes of it. Because memory is so firmly fixed in the body, it takes an object that appeals to the senses to dislodge memory and allow it to float freely into the mind or onto the page. *These* memories will have resonance precisely because they have not been forced into being by a mind insistent on fixed meanings. It is the body's story and so one that resonates with a sense of an inadvertent truth revealed. As writer Terry Tempest Williams has said, the most potent images and stories are those that "bypass rhetoric and pierce the heart."

So, as far as memory devices go, you could do worse than turn to the body for guidance. The body can offer an inexhaustible store of triggers to begin any number of essays, each of which will have greater significance than what appears on the surface. Sometimes, what matters to us most is what has mattered to the body. Memory may pretend to live in the cerebral cortex, but it requires muscle—real muscle—to animate it again for the page.

The Five Senses of Memory

By paying attention to the sensory gateways of the body, you also begin to write in a way that naturally *embodies* experience, making it tactile for the reader. Readers tend to care deeply only about those things they *feel* in the body at a visceral level. And so as a writer consider your vocation as that of a translator: one who renders the abstract into the concrete. We experience the world through our senses. We must translate that experience into the language of the senses as well.

Smell

"Smell is a potent wizard that transports us across thousands of miles and all the years we have lived," wrote Helen Keller in her autobiography. "The odors of fruits waft me to my southern home, to my childhood frolics in the peach orchard. Other odors, instantaneous and fleeting, cause my heart to dilate joyously or contract with remembered grief."

Though Helen Keller's words are made more poignant by the fact that she was blind and deaf, we all have this innate connection to smell. Smell seems to travel to our brains directly, without logical or intellectual interference. Physiologically, we *do* apprehend smells more quickly than the other sensations, and the images aroused by smell act as beacons leading to our richest memories, our most private selves. Smell is so intimately tied up with *breath*, after all, a function of our bodies that works continually, day and night, keeping us alive. And so smell keys us into the memories that evoke the continual ebb and flow of experience. The richest smells can be the most innocent: the smell of a Barbie doll; Play-Doh; the house right after your mother has cleaned (the hot dust inside the vacuum, the tart scent of Lemon Pledge); or the shoes in your father's closet, redolent of old polish. Or, the smells can be more complex: the aftershave your father wore the day he lost his job or the scent of your baby's head when you first held her in your arms.

What are the smells you remember that even in memory make you stop a moment and breathe deeply, or that make your heart beat more vigorously, your palms ache for what's been lost? Write these down. Write as quickly as you can, seeing how one smell leads to another. What kinds of image, memories, or stories might arise from this sensory trigger?

Taste

Food is one of the most social gifts we have. The bond between mother and child forms over the feeding of that child, either at the breast or at the bottle, the infant body held close, the eyes intent on the parent's face. When you sit down to unburden yourself to a friend, you often do so over a meal prepared together in the kitchen, the two of you chopping vegetables or sipping wine as you articulate whatever troubles have come to haunt you. When these predicaments grow overwhelming, we turn to comfort food, meals that spark in us a memory of an idealized, secure childhood. When we are falling in love, we offer food as our first timid gesture toward intimacy.

In his famous essay "Afternoon of an American Boy," E. B. White vividly remembers the taste of cinnamon toast in conjunction with the first stumbling overtures of a boyhood crush. In "A Thing Shared," food aficionado M. F. K. Fisher uses something as simple and commonplace as the taste of a peach pie—"the warm round peach pie and cool yellow cream"—to describe a memory of her father and sister the first time they found themselves alone without the mediating influence of their mother. The food acts as more than mere sustenance; it becomes a moment of communion. "That night I not only saw my father for the first time as a person. I saw the golden hills and the live oaks as clearly as I have ever seen them since; and I saw the dimples in my little sister's fat hands in a way that still moves me because of that first time; and I saw food as something beautiful to be shared with people instead of as a thrice-daily necessity." This scene becomes an illustration of how we awaken to one another. It's less about her own family than about the fleeting moments of connection that can transpire in *all* families, in one way or another.

What are the tastes that carry the most emotion for you? The tastes that, even in memory, make you stop a moment and run your tongue over your lips and swallow hard? Write these down, as quickly as you can. Which scenes, memories, associations come to the surface?

Hearing

Sounds often go unnoticed. Because we cannot consciously cut off our hearing unless we plug our ears, we've learned to filter sounds, picking and choosing the ones that are important, becoming inured to the rest. But these sounds often make up a subliminal backdrop to our lives, and even the faintest echo can tug back moments from the past in their entirety.

For example, in his short gem of an essay, "The Fine Art of Sighing," memoirist Bernard Cooper uses a sound as subtle as a sigh to elucidate his relationship to his family, himself, and the world. He describes how his father sighs, how his mother sighs, and how he, himself, sighs. And, paradoxically, by focusing in on this small, simple act, Cooper is able to reveal much larger things: his mother's dissatisfaction with domestic life, his father's gruff sensual nature, and Cooper's ambivalence about his own body and sexuality. "A friend of mine once mentioned that I was given to long and ponderous sighs. Once I became aware of this habit, I heard my father's sighs in my own and knew for a moment his small satisfactions. At other times, I felt my mother's restlessness and wished I could leave my body with my breath, or be happy in the body my breath left behind."

Music is not so subtle but rather acts as a blaring soundtrack to our emotional lives. Think about the bonds you formed with friends over common musical passions, the days spent listening to the same song over and over as you learned the mundane yet painful lessons of love. Sometimes you turned up that song as loud as you could so that it might communicate to the world—and to your deepest, deafest self—*exactly* the measure of your emotion.

We often orchestrate our memories around the music that accompanied those pivotal eras of our lives. In his essay "A Voice for the Lonely," Stephen Corey writes movingly about how a certain Roy Orbison song can always call him back to his sophomore year of high school, to his friendship with a boy as outcast as himself. He characterizes those moments as "The right singer, the right sadness, the right silence." When you have the soundtrack down, the rest of life seems to fall into place.

Touch

Hospitals rely on volunteers to hold babies on the infant wards. Their only job is to hold and rock any baby that is crying or in distress. The nurses, of course, do not have time for such constant care, but they know this type of touch is essential as medicine for their patients' healing. As we grow, this need for touch does not diminish, and thus our raging desires for contact, our subtle and not-so-subtle maneuvers that lead us into skin-to-skin encounters with other living beings.

We are constantly aware of our bodies, of how they feel as they move through the world. Without this sense we become lost, disoriented in space and time. And the people who have affected us the most are the ones who have *touched* us in some way, who have reached beyond this barrier of skin and made contact with our small, isolated selves.

Sometimes an essayist can focus on the tactile feel of objects as a way to explore deeper emotions or memories. For instance, in his short essay "Buckeye," Scott Russell Sanders focuses on the feel of the buckeye seeds that his father carried with him to ward off arthritis. They are "hollow," he says, "hard as pebbles, yet they still gleam from the polish of his hands." Sanders then allows the sensation of touch to be the way we get to know his father:

> *My father never paid much heed to pain. Near the end, when his worn knee often slipped out of joint, he would pound it back in place with a rubber mallet. If a splinter worked into his flesh beyond the reach of tweezers, he would heat the blade of his knife over a cigarette lighter and slice through the skin.*

Such sensory details bring the reader almost into the father's body, feeling the pound of that mallet, the slice of the skin. He never needs to tell us his father was a tough man; the images do all the work for him. These details also allow us to see the narrator, Sanders, watching his father closely, and so this scene also conveys at least a part of their relationship and its emotional tenor.

Think about the people in your life who have touched you deeply. What was the quality of their physical touch on your body? How did they touch the objects around them? Why do you think this touch lingers in memory?

Sight

How do you see the world? How do you see yourself? Even linguistically, our sense of sight seems so tied up in our perceptions, stance, opinions, personalities, and knowledge of the world. To see something often means to finally understand, to be enlightened, to have our vision cleared. What we choose to see—and *not* to see—often says more about us than anything else.

When we "look back" in memory, we *see* those memories. Our minds have catalogued an inexhaustible storehouse of visual images. Now the trick is for you to render those images in writing. Pay attention to the smallest details: the way a tree limb cuts its jagged edge against a winter sky or the dull canary yellow of the bulldozer that leveled your favorite house on the street. Close your eyes to see these images more clearly. Trace the shape of your favorite toy or the outline of a beloved's face. Turn up the lights in the living room. Go out walking under a full moon. Keep looking.

For Annie Dillard, in her jubilant essay "Seeing" (from *Pilgrim at Tinker Creek*), being able to see truly is akin to spiritual awakening:

One day I was walking along Tinker Creek thinking of nothing at all and I saw the tree with the lights in it. I saw the backyard cedar where the mourning doves roost charged and transfigured, each cell buzzing with flame. . . . It was less like seeing than like being for the first time seen, knocked breathless by a powerful glance. . . . I had been my whole life a bell, and never knew it until at that moment I was lifted and struck.

What are the moments in your life that have "struck" you? How have they been engraved in memory?

Fortunately, we live in an age where visual memories are routinely preserved in photographs and on videotape. Sometimes these photos and films can act not only as triggers for your memory—reminding you of the visual details of the experience—but they can also prompt you to delve more deeply below the surface.

TRY IT

1. Write a scene of a very early, vivid memory. What calls out for further examination? Are you realistic? What are the odd details, the ones that don't seem to fit with other people's versions of the story? What in this scene seems to matter to you? Should it? What are you leaving out? If you get stuck, keep repeating the phrase "I remember" to start off your sentences; allow this rhythm to take you further than you thought you could go.

> VARIATION 1: Do you have an ideal "earliest memory"? Write this out, and see how your imagination and your memory intersect or diverge. Is there an essay in the process of memory itself?

> VARIATION 2: Talk with family members about *their* memories of the time you pinpoint as your first memory. How do they corroborate or deny your own memory? How can you create a "collaborative" memory that includes their versions of the events? How does this memory enact a family "myth"? Is there an essay about the way these divergent accounts work together?

2. In the preface to his anthology *The Business of Memory*, Charles Baxter writes, "What we talk about when we talk about memory is—often—what we

have forgotten and what has been lost. The passion and torment and significance seem to lie in that direction." What have you forgotten in your life? What are the moments that keep sliding out of reach? Write for twenty minutes, using the phrase "I can't remember" to start off each sentence. Where does such an examination lead you?

You may find that by using this exercise you can back into the scenes and images you *do* remember but never knew how to approach. You can write some very powerful essays based on this prompt, exploring material that seemed too dangerous to examine head-on.

VARIATION: After you've lighted on some events or times you can't fully articulate, do a little research. Ask others about their memories of that time. Find documents or photographs that may shed some light on the issue. Be a detective, looking for clues. After you've gathered enough evidence, write an essay that focuses on the way your memory and the "reality" either differ or coincide. Why have you forgotten the things you did?

3. How many different "firsts" can you remember in your life? The first meal you remember enjoying, the first smell you remember wanting to smell again, the first day of school, the first book you remember reading by yourself, the first album you ever bought, the first time you drove a car, the first kiss, the first time you were touched in a sexual way? How does your memory of these "first" events color your perception of yourself? What kinds of metaphors do they generate for your life story?

Smell

1. Gather articles that you know carry some smell that is evocative for you. One by one, smell them deeply, and then write the images that arise in your mind. Write quickly, allowing the smell to trigger other sensory associations.

2. Which smells in your life are gone for you now? Which ones would you give anything to smell again? Have you ever been "ambushed" by a smell you didn't expect? For example, have you opened a box of clothing from a deceased relative and had the smell of that person's house flood over you? Or, have you walked into a friend's house and smelled a meal exactly like one you remember from

childhood? Write a scene about such an incident. If you can't remember anything like that, imagine one. How do these sensory memories differ from memories of the past you'd normally conjure up? Write an essay exploring the idea that your body carries its own dormant memories.

> **VARIATION FOR A GROUP:** Each person brings in an object that carries some kind of strong smell and takes a turn being the leader. Keep the object hidden until it is your turn. The rest of the group members close their eyes while the leader brings this object to each person and asks him or her to smell deeply. After everyone has had a chance, the leader hides the object again. Each person immediately writes the images and associations that smell evoked. Share these writings with each other and see how similarly or differently you reacted to the same odor.

Taste

1. Try to remember the first meal you consciously tasted and enjoyed. Describe this meal in detail; make yourself hungry with these details. Who ate this meal with you? If you can't remember any such meal, imagine one.

2. If you were to write a life history through food, what would be the "touch-stone" moments, the meals that represented turning points for you? Which meals have you loved? Which meals have you hated? Which meals marked important transitions in your life?

> **VARIATION FOR A GROUP:** Have "food exploration" days set aside for your group meetings. On these days, one person is responsible for bringing in an item of food for everyone to taste. Try to choose foods that leave strong sensory impressions: a mango, perhaps, or a persimmon. After exploring the sight, textures, and smells, taste it. Describe this food in detail, then go on to whichever images and metaphorical associations arise. In your own life, what is most like a mango? Begin an essay by outlining which people, feelings, events, or memories this food conjures up for you and why.

Touch

1. Take an inventory of the scars or marks on your body. How were they received? How do these external scars relate to any internal "markings" as well?

2. Find an object that you consider a talisman, something you either carry with you or keep in a special place in your home. Hold it in your hand, and, with your eyes closed, feel all its textures. Begin to write, using this tactile description to trigger memories, scenes, and metaphors.

> **VARIATION FOR A GROUP:** Each person brings in such an object for a "show-and-tell," explaining the story behind the item. Pass these things around the room for everyone to examine, and then write based on *someone else's* talisman. What did it feel like in your hand? How does it trigger memories of your own?

Sound

1. Try re-creating a scene from your childhood using *only* the sense of hearing. What music is playing in the background? Whose voice is on the radio? How loud is the sound of traffic? What do the trees sound like in the wind? Are there insects, birds, animals? A hum from a factory? Rain, rivers, the lapping of a lake? What is the quality of the silence? Try to pick out as many ambient sounds as you can, then begin to amplify the ones you think have the most metaphorical significance. What kind of emotional tone do these sounds give to the piece?

2. Put on a piece of music that you strongly associate with a certain era of your life. Using this music as a soundtrack, zero in on a particular scene that arises in your mind. Try writing the scene *without mentioning the music at all*, but through your word choices and imagery and sentence structure convey the essence of this music's rhythm and beat.

> **VARIATION:** Do the same thing, but this time use fragments of the lyrics as "scaffolding" for the essay. Give us a few lines, then write part of the memory those lines evoke in you. Give us a few more, and continue with the memory, so that the song plays throughout the entire piece.

> **VARIATION FOR A GROUP:** Each person brings in a tape or CD of instrumental music that evokes some kind of strong emotion. Put on these pieces in turn, and have everybody write for at least five minutes to each track, trying not to describe the music directly but focusing instead on the images and memories the music brings up. Choose a few to read aloud when you're done, but don't mention which piece of music acted as the trigger; have the rest of the group try to guess which music corresponds to which writing.

Sight

1. What do you see when you look in the mirror? Where does your gaze land first? How does this gaze determine your attitude toward yourself and your life? Do you see your younger self beneath the present-day face? Can you determine your future self through this gaze?

2. Using a photograph of yourself, a relative, or a friend, describe every detail of the scene. Then focus in on one object or detail that seems unexpected to you in some way. How does this detail trigger specific memories? Also, imagine what occurred just before and just after this photograph was taken; what is left outside the frame? For instance, write an essay with a title such as "After [Before] My Father Is Photographed on the *U.S.S. Constitution*." (Insert whichever subject is appropriate for the photographs you've chosen.)

> **VARIATION FOR A GROUP:** Repeat the above exercise, but then trade photographs with your neighbor. Which details strike you? How does any part of the scene remind you of scenes from your own life? Perform a number of these trades around the room to see which details leap up from other people's photographs.

2

Writing the Family

One thing that we always assume, wrongly, is that if we write about people honestly they will resent it and become angry. If you come at it for the right reasons and you treat people as you would your fictional characters . . . if you treat them with complexity and compassion, sometimes they will feel as though they've been honored, not because they're presented in some ideal way but because they're presented with understanding.

—KIM BARNES, AUTHOR OF *IN THE WILDERNESS* AND *HUNGRY FOR THE WORLD*

My brother is swinging the bat and I'm bored in the stands, seven years old. My mother has given me a piece of paper and a pen that doesn't have much ink in it. I've written, "I HAVE TWO BROTHERS. ONE IS A LITTLE ONE. ONE IS A BIG ONE. WE ONLY HAVE TWO GIRLS IN OUR FAMILY. ONE IS ME. ONE IS MY MOTHER." The mothers sit all around me, their straight skirts pulled tight across their knees. My brother is swinging the bat and wiggling his hips on the other side of the mesh. "THE BIG BROTHER IS MEAN. THE LITTLE BROTHER IS SOMETIMES MEAN." Where is my father? I squint to see him near the dugout, his hands cupped around his mouth. My brother swings the bat, and the ball sails, sails, sails out of sight. Everyone stands up, cheering, but I stay seated long enough to write: "THE BIG BROTHER JUST MADE A HOME RUN AND I THINK THATS ALL I'LL WRITE. GOOD-BYE." My brother prances around the bases, casual and grown-up and intelligent, slapping the hands held out in high fives as he trots past third.

The catcher already sulks unmasked against the backstop. My brother casu-
ally taps his foot against home.

   On that scrap of paper, I naturally turn toward the people in my life as
a way to begin a description of that life. As a child, it's nearly impossible to
think of myself as an individual separate from my family. And already, as
a novice autobiographer, I see myself spurred by the impulses to document
(here is the world, defined by mother, father, brothers), to explore emotion
(oh, the harsh treatment I receive at my brothers' hands!), and to transcribe
events as they occur (a home run!). In a sense, I'll repeat these impulses over
and over throughout the years as I grow into a writer, hopefully refining
them a little bit along the way.

—BRENDA

Situating Yourself in Relation to Family

From the minute we arrive in the world, we're put at the mercy of the people
who care for us. And we might find the rest of our lives taken up with dual,
contradictory impulses: to be an integral part of this clan and to be a separate individual, set apart. Our families, however they're configured, provide
our first mirrors, our first definitions of who we are. And they become our
first objects of love, anger, and loyalty. No wonder so much creative nonfiction is written about family. How can we really get away from these people?
How have they shaped who we are in the world? And how do our particular
families reflect issues common to us all?

   The most important strategy for dealing with family is learning how you
can approach the big issues by focusing on the smallest details. It's often
tempting, especially when you're dealing with emotionally charged material,
to try and encompass *everything* into one essay. Such a strategy will leave you,
and your readers, numb and exhausted. Ask the small questions. Who was
the family member to come last to the table? Who kept (and perhaps hid) a
diary? Who had the most distinctive laugh? Sometimes these questions are
the ones that lead to the biggest answers. For example, in "Reading History
to My Mother," Robin Hemley spurs a complex essay about his mother by
focusing in first on her eyeglasses:

My mother owns at least half a dozen glasses, and I know I should have sorted through them all by now (we tried once). . . . On her dresser there are parts of various eyeglasses: maimed glasses, the corpses of eyeglasses, a dark orphaned lens here, a frame there, an empty case, and one case with a pair that's whole. This is the one I grab and take out to my mother who is waiting patiently, always patient these days, or perhaps so unnerved and exhausted that it passes for patience.

In this memoir, Hemley will detail the decline of his mother's physical and mental health as she advances in age, and he chronicles his own ambivalent responses to caring for her. This subject will lead into even bigger ideas about how we read history to one another, how we re-create our histories as part of our love for one another. Rather than approach such things head-on, Hemley wisely turns to the small, physical things first—those eyeglasses—as a way to not only create a convincing scene, but also to plant the seeds for the emotional material to come. Those mangled, mixed-up eyeglasses signal the state of mind we'll be invited to enter.

The Biographer

When we're writing about family, sometimes it's helpful to think of ourselves as biographers, rather than autobiographers. This slight shift in perspective just might be enough to create the emotional distance necessary to begin shaping experience into literature on the page. It will also allow you to take a broader view of your subject that encompasses community, culture, and history. It will still be a *subjective* account—all biographies filter through the mind and emotional perspective of a writer—but it will be an account that has managed to take a wider view.

Sometimes it's helpful to imagine our relatives as they must have been before we knew them as mother, father, grandmother, and so forth. In Paisley Rekdal's essay "The Night My Mother Met Bruce Lee," for example, she allows herself to imagine in vivid detail her mother as a sixteen-year-old girl:

Age sixteen, my mother loads up red tubs of noodles, teacups chipped and white-gray as teeth, rice clumps that glue themselves to the plastic tubs' sides or dissolve and turn papery in the weak tea sloshing around the bottom. She's at Diamond Chan's restaurant, where most of her cousins work after school and during summer vacations some of her friends, too. . . . My mother's nails are cracked, kept short by clipping or gnawing, glisten only when varnished with the grease of someone else's leftovers.

We then move from this imaginative scene into a "real" one closer to the present day; the contrast between the two allows for a kind of understanding and character development that would otherwise be impossible.

If you were to take on the mantle of the biographer, how could you begin to see the members of your family differently? How can you combine the objectivity of a researcher with the subjectivity of the biographer? You'll find that even if you haven't written a full-fledged biography, you will have found fresh ways to conceptualize those people who are closest to you.

The Obstacle Course

When we write about family, we set ourselves up for a plethora of ethical, emotional, and technical issues that may hinder us from writing altogether. It's one thing to write about your sister in your diary; it's quite another to write about her in an essay published in a national magazine. And when we set out to write about family, we are naturally going to feel compelled to break long silences that may have kept the family together in the first place. In recent years, many creative nonfiction works have emerged that take on issues of child abuse, incest, alcoholic parents, and other emotionally charged issues. When you sit down to write, you might feel obligated to write about traumas of your family history. You might feel these are the only issues "worth" tackling in literature.

Family is always an enormous subject, and as writers, we must find a way to handle this subject with both aplomb and discretion. If your family history is particularly charged, it will be even more essential for you to find the smaller details—the miniscule anecdotes—that will lead the way into a successful essay. This is not to say that you can't or won't take on the big issues. But they must arrive on the page less as issues and more as scenes, images, and metaphors that will evoke a strong response from the reader.

Permission to Speak

While drafting your essay, you must instinctively drown out the voices that tell you *not* to write. Your mother, father, sisters, and brothers must all be banished from the room where you sit at your desk and call up potentially painful or embarrassing memories. But once you know you have an essay that is more for public consumption than private venting, you have some difficult decisions to make. How much of this is really your own story to tell?

Writers deal with this dilemma in a variety of ways. Some merely remain in denial, convincing themselves that no one—least of all their families—will ever read their work. Some go to the opposite extreme, confessing to their families about their writing projects and asking permission to divulge certain stories and details, giving them complete veto power. Some, such as Frank McCourt with *Angela's Ashes*, wait until the major players have died so that they can no longer be hurt by the exposure or pass judgment on the writer. Some decide that writing about this material in a nonfiction form is just too risky and decide to present their work as fiction instead. Some writers change the names of their characters—some even go so far as to write under a pseudonym—to protect both themselves and their families.

However you choose to negotiate these tricky issues, remember that your story *is* your story to tell. Yours is not the *only* story or perspective on family or on your community, but it is a perfectly valid voice among the chorus. In her essay "Writing About Family: Is It Worth It?" Mimi Schwartz reminds us that "a memoirist, in particular, must think of truth as having a small 't,' not a big one—as in *my* truth rather than *the* truth." And if you examine this truth with a healthy sense of perspective and with literary skill, you may be surprised at the reactions you evoke among your subjects. They may feel honored to see themselves couched in a work of literature and grateful to discover aspects of you they never realized before.

Here is how Robin Hemley dealt with these issues when he wrote and published "Reading History to My Mother."

I think this is one of the few essays I haven't shown my mother. . . . I don't think that one needs to show everything one writes to those involved—sometimes one can actually do more harm than good with the full-disclosure impulse. Sometimes, one acts more out of one's own need for absolution rather than actually considering the feelings of the person to whom the dis-

closure is made. . . . We write for many different reasons, and often our best work is dangerous, edgy, and guilt-inducing. Sometimes we feel it's worth sharing with others, whether the reasons are literary or therapeutic, and I don't think we should necessarily engage in self-censorship simply because we might be unwilling to share our work with the person(s) the work deals with. . . . I'd say that my decision was made of equal measures of love and cowardice.

Love and *cowardice* might aptly describe all of us when we find ourselves writing about family or about those close to us in our communities. Complex emotions beset us in this endeavor, and we must remain aware of them before they ambush us altogether.

If we are going to write successfully about family, our motives must be more than simple exposure of family history and secrets. We must have some *perspective* on our experience that spurs the essay beyond our own personal "dirty laundry" and into the realm of literature. (See Chapter 8 for a discussion of the dangers of "revenge prose" and "the therapist's couch.")

Our role as writers can be that of the witness. We continually bear witness to those around us, and sometimes our job is to speak for those who have never spoken for themselves. When we write about our families or take on the mantle of the biographer, we are really writing (and forging) community. As Terry Tempest Williams writes, in her essay "A 'Downwinder' in Hiroshima, Japan": "I think about . . . how much we need to hear the truth of one another's lives. . . . The Japanese have a word, *aware*, which speaks to both the beauty and pain of our lives, that sorrow is not a grief one forgets or recovers from but is a burning, searing illumination of love for the delicacy and strength of our relations."

Think of yourself as a witness and your writing will take on greater weight and urgency. As you write about the other people who populate your memories and life, you will do so with a clearer sense of purpose that will elevate your writing beyond the purely personal.

TRY IT

1. Try to reconstruct the names of your matriarchal or patriarchal lineage. For instance, what is the name of your mother, your mother's mother, your mother's mother's mother, and so forth? How far back can you go? For instance, in Brenda's case, she once started an essay with the line, "I am the daughter of Sandra, the daughter of Beatrice, the daughter of Pearl." Naming them brings them to life and enables you to begin writing about them. Where do the names come from? Does your own name have any "inheritance" attached to it? What are the stories behind the names? Are you adopted? How does this affect how you construct your sense of lineage?

> VARIATION: Circle one of the names that intrigues you for whatever reason, then do some research on this person. Find photographs, letters, or birth certificates—whatever might be stored in a family archive. Begin an essay that builds a portrait of this person from the name outward.

2. Describe every member of your family in terms of a part of the body. For instance, describe the hands of your mother, father, siblings, grandparents, and yourself. How are they alike? How are they different? Push this exercise further by going for the smallest images. Look at belly buttons, fingerprints, moles, toenails, or tongues. If necessary, imagine the details. For instance, imagine your grandmother's hands as they were before she was a grandmother. Which traits emerge in your own physical makeup? Which ones do you hate? Which ones do you love? How do you imagine you will look twenty years from now? Forty? Fifty?

3. Begin an essay by imagining the life of someone close to you—a family member, friend, mentor—before you knew them. Use your imagination coupled with your experience of this person. Use any clues that may exist: objects from the past, documents, photographs, and so forth to form a portrait of this person before you were in the picture. Then complete the essay by contrasting this portrait with the person you know today. How are they different or similar?

4. Almost all families have some mythic story about someone meeting a famous person. Try to re-create a relative's encounter with a celebrity.

5. Create a picture of your family based on some simple gesture: the way they sigh, laugh, cry, or kiss. Begin with a vivid, original description of this gesture, then describe your father, your mother, yourself, or any other family members. Try to see how examining these small gestures reveals larger details about the

family. (You can track down Bernard Cooper's essay "The Fine Art of Sighing,"
located in the book *Truth Serum*, as a model if you like.)

6. Write a family story in a voice other than your own. Use the point of view of
another family member and see how the story changes or which details now
become important.

7. Write a list of the subjects you would "never" write about. What are the
silences that can't be broken? Begin each sentence with "I would never write
about" or "I am slow to write about." See if this backward maneuver might actually lead you into scenes, details, and memories you *might* be able to handle in
a short essay.

3

"Taking Place":
Writing the Physical World

If you live in a place—any place, city or country—long enough and deeply enough you can learn anything, the dynamics and inter-connections that exist in every community, be it plant, human, or animal—you can learn what a writer needs to know.

—GRETEL EHRLICH

I am writing about the first place I remember living, casting around for a way to write about it that fits in with what I've learned is acceptable in the literature of place. Elizabeth, New Jersey: people who know the city shudder and mention the rows of smokestacks craning along the side of the New Jersey Turnpike. I spent my early years there, and along with a rickety shore bungalow, it's the place I have the most visceral childhood attachment to. But when I think of the writing of childhood place I think of Vladimir Nabokov's Speak, Memory, *with the majestic beauty of pre-Revolutionary St. Petersburg; of Annie Dillard's wooded rambles in* An American Child-hood. *How do you write about a vacant lot glinting with glass, where I spent many ecstatic hours as a child, a cemetery where my brother and I played? It was as scary and luminous a childhood as any other. Does place matter only when it carries its own transcendent beauty? How do you memorialize the seemingly unbeautiful?*

After many false starts, I begin writing about my early home by reflect-
ing on the city's name. "Elizabeth," I write, "had a Queen's name. Every
land's an extension of the monarch's body, a great green I Am of the royal
person, and Elizabeth's city showed she'd been gone a long time. It was gassy
and bad-smelling as any dead woman."

The Elizabeth of the city, I learned much later, was not Queen Eliza-
beth, as I'd thought, but some other woman. No matter. It was what I
believed at the time of writing, and what I believed, for some reason, as a
child. The interest of the place was not in its beauty, its own transcendent
qualities, but the way it bounced off my life and the lives of those around
me: the character it became.

—SUZANNE

Start Looking

Where are you reading this book? Put it down for a second and look around
you; take into account what is both inside and outside the space you're in. In
your mind, run over the significance of this place. Are you somewhere that
has meaning for you because it is the place you grew up or because it is not?
Does this place represent freedom or responsibility? Is it someplace temporary for you or permanent? When you force yourself to look around carefully
and openly, do you thrill to the natural beauty or respond to its urban excitement? Or are you somewhere now you feel you could never call home?

Our responses to place are some of the most complex we'll ever experience.
Our sense of visual beauty, our psychological drive for comfort and familiar-
ity in our environment, and our complex responses to loaded concepts such
as "nature" and "home" embed place with layers of significance. Although fiction writers typically have the importance of location and setting driven into
them, it is easy for nonfiction writers to forget that they, too, must be situated physically. We find that an essayist with a wonderful story to tell—a family story, say, of a troubled Vietnam-vet father or of raising an autistic
child—will typically leave out the vital backdrop of the story: a supportive
small town, a resource-rich city, or a town in which the family's story unfolds
against a background of petty bigotry and misunderstanding.

Where We're Writing From

We, Brenda and Suzanne, landed—through various tracks—in the smallish city of Bellingham, Washington, on the Puget Sound, under a volcano called Mt. Baker that is presently giving off steam from under-earth vents called *fumaroles*. On the one hand, our lives are peaceful. We teach classes, write, attend a film or concert now and then, and work on this book. On the other hand, every few years the mountain issues this fleecy reminder that it has more control than we ever give it credit for. Under its crust is enough molten rock to turn our lives into something else entirely.

Environments tend to function as informing elements that we take for granted and edit out of our stories until they act up. We who live here may notice that people become quieter and more lethargic during our gray, rainy winter months, bursting back into exuberant life when the sun returns. Nevertheless, it takes a certain amount of awareness to relate the way our lives unfold to the fact that we live here, in the maritime Northwest, rather than somewhere else. (And in fact, when the first draft of this chapter was written, we experienced the powerful Nisqually earthquake, centered south of Seattle, which sent our computers dancing and our certainties about the ground beneath our feet shaking along with them.)

Before proceeding any further in this chapter, pull out an essay you've already written and check to see if locations and physical settings are established. Can we hear how a key conversation was heightened by the silence of a forest clearing? Do we see and smell the banyan trees of South Florida rather than the cedars of the Northwest? If you write of a town or a city, is its physical location and socioeconomic character clear?

Setting Scenes: Place as Character

In Chapter 12, "The Basics of Good Writing in Any Form," we discuss in depth the techniques of scene-setting and its importance in nonfiction. It seems useful to touch on that topic here as well. Nonfiction writers use place frequently as a primary subject. Even if you never do, however, the place where a story unfolds plays a vital role. In all the elements of setting a scene—character, dialogue, place, action—place can be the easiest one to overlook.

Would *Jane Eyre* have been the same book without her tale unfolding against the backdrop of Thornfield, that gabled mansion with its nests of crows? Would Huckleberry Finn's adventures have had the same resonance without the silvery roil of the Mississippi River? Your own story needs the same depth of field. One useful way to judge your own scene-setting is to think of place as a character unto itself. In the excerpt from the essay "Elizabeth" at the start of this chapter, the city takes on the character of a woman: an aging, decayed figure against which the children's exploits take on an incongruous irony.

Writing About Home

For nonfiction writers, particularly memoirists, the place of childhood has a critical importance. It is the primal map on which we plot life's movements. It is the setting of the rich mythology that is earliest memory (see Chapter 1), the enchanted forest in which our benighted characters wander, looking for breadcrumbs and clues and facing down their demons. If you draw your earliest place of memory—a bedroom, say, or a favorite hiding place in an apartment or a yard—you will, by the highly selective and emotional process of memory, be drawing an emotional landscape of your childhood.

Maybe you remember the deep, sagging chair that attracted and frightened you because it was sacred to your father and he sank into it in the evening, angry from the day's work. Or perhaps you remember the table where your family sat around and ate kimchi, which none of your friends ate and of which you learned to be vaguely ashamed. Maybe you recall the soft woolly smell of your covers at night or the dim blue glow of a nightlight. This is home, the place where the complex person you are came into being. And understanding the concept of home and its physical character is key to understanding the many different individuals you'll write about in your nonfiction.

When Home Is Away

Bharati Mukherjee, an Indian-American writer, says home to her is a place she has never been and that no longer exists in a national sense. At the time of her father's birth, his village was in India. Now it is part of Bangladesh. As a woman of Indian descent, she defines her home patrilineally, making her a citizen of an unknown place, bearing ethnic claims that no longer make any sense. In her essay "A Four-Hundred-Year-Old Woman," she writes:

> *I was born into a class that did not live in its native language. I was born into a city that feared its future, and trained me for emigration. I attended a school run by Irish nuns, who regarded our walled-off school compound in Calcutta as a corner (forever green and tropical) of England. My "country"—called in Bengali* desh, *and suggesting more a homeland than a nation of which one is a citizen—I have never seen. It is the ancestral home of my father and is now in Bangladesh. Nevertheless, I speak his dialect of Bengali, and think of myself as "belonging" to Faridpur.*

Later, Mukherjee writes that for her, "the all too real Manhattan [her present home] and Faridpur have merged as 'desh.'"

For most Americans, the terms *home* and *native* are probably loaded with connotations we rarely pause to tease out. We—Brenda and Suzanne—for example, celebrate different holidays. We bake our traditional breads—challah and panettone—and mark rites of passage with chopped liver or the dried fish called *baccala* without much awareness of how those foods reflect what was available and affordable in our families' countries of origin, or the poverty and threat reflected in the fact that our not-too-distant forebears came to be here. There are stories in these deeply personal, everyday connections and disconnections in American lives.

Writing About Nature

If we think of place as character, we should add that no "character" comes with as many preconceptions as nature. Drawing energy from early writers like Thoreau, American essayists have always had a particular affinity with nature writing. This country in its present national incarnation is new—the "new country" that creates by being in opposition to the "old country" of the preceding discussion. For much of its life, it has defined itself by its wilderness, by the sense of frontier to be explored and frequently controlled. And even as the American wilderness vanishes, literature faces the question of what we have lost with it, along with the buffalo, sequoia, and deep old-growth forests breathing so recently out of our past.

In his classic memoir *Walden; Or, Life in the Woods*, Henry David Thoreau's declarations become a charge to nature writers and nature seekers for generations to come: "I went to the woods because I wished to live deliberately, to front only the essential facts of life, and see if I could not learn what it had to teach, and not, when I came to die, discover that I had not lived." American literature's historic distrust of civilization (think of *Huckleberry Finn*) has created a particular reverence for nature writing in our country. Writers like Thoreau teach us that recording the experiences of the individual removed from society—one on one with the physical world that created him or her—provides an avenue to "live deep and suck out all the marrow of life."

Thoreau's approach to nature—as a way of paring life down to its essentials, finding oneself—continues in the work of writers such as Wendell Berry. In essays like "An Entrance to the Woods," Berry describes how on a hiking trip, "Today, as always when I am afoot in the woods, I feel the possibility, the reasonableness, the practicability of living in the world in a way that would enlarge rather than diminish the hope of life."

To Berry and Thoreau, nature represents life at its most basic—life at the bone. But in the literary world, few subjects are as complex in their symbolic structure as nature. To Wordsworth, it was the ultimate muse, the "anchor of his purest thoughts." To others, it's simply the ultimate power.

What does nature mean to you? For those with a nature-writing bent, it's deceptively simple to wax rhapsodic about the cathedral beauty of old-growth forests or the piercing melodies of the thrush. In other words, we tend to approach nature writing first and foremost as description. While fine description is dandy, it tends to wear thin after a while. Even if your prose about the soft rosy beauty of the alpenglow is first rate, if you don't move beyond that, readers are likely to want to put your writing down and go see for themselves.

What holds readers in the works of writers like Berry and Thoreau is the sense of a *human consciousness* moving through nature, observing it, reacting to it, and ultimately being transformed by it. Thoreau's description of his cottage at Walden Pond is instructive:

I was seated by the shore of a small pond. . . . I was so low in the woods that the opposite shore, half a mile off, like the rest, covered with wood, was

my most distant horizon. For the first week, whenever I looked out on the
pond it impressed me like a tarn high up on the side of a mountain, its bot-
tom far above the surface of other lakes, and, as the sun arose, I saw it
throwing off its nightly clothing of mist, and here and there, by degrees, its
soft ripples or its smooth reflecting surface was revealed, while the mists, like
ghosts, were stealthily withdrawing in every direction into the woods.

Notice how Thoreau embeds his basic concept of living in nature as stripping human life bare in this very description. Not only is it beautifully poetic, but we see Walden Pond looming huge in front of him, throwing off its obscuring mists, as a kind of mirror for Thoreau's consciousness, coming clear in nature and throwing off the layer of fog of human convention.

Remember Scott Russell Sanders's essay "Buckeye" from the "Touch" section of Chapter 1? Later in the essay, Sanders describes how his father, a born naturalist, once stripped the husk from a buckeye to show it to his son. "He picked up one, as fat as a lemon, and peeled away the husk to reveal the shiny seed. He laid it in my palm and closed my fist around it so the seed peeped out from the circle formed by my index finger and thumb." Here, the buckeye seems to come alive, almost hatching from the author's hand. It's an image of the life both men find in nature, as well as an image of the father coming alive in the author's memory.

When you think of your feelings about nature, think about Thoreau and Sanders, and the question of how what you see before you embodies larger forces: an aspect of the human condition or the tenderness and toughness of a person you know. Use that larger element as a way into your essay.

Writing About the Environment

In "An Entrance to the Woods," Wendell Berry goes beyond merely describing the woods or the way in which his hiking and camping experience lends perspective to his own human existence. As a nonfiction writer who is constantly pushing himself to examine with the broadest possible lens what exists at the tips of his fingers (which all good nonfiction writers do), he asks himself how he as a human being embodies the larger interaction of human and nature. It's an interrelationship that's become problematic at the beginning of the twenty-first century, as we face global warming and the last century's out-pouring of industrial pollution.

While in the woods, Berry hears the roar of a car in the distance and writes, "That roar of the highway is the voice of the American economy; it is sounding also wherever strip mines are being cut in the steep slopes of Appalachia, and wherever cropland is being destroyed to make roads and suburbs. . . ." It is a wonderful moment in the essay, of opening out and refocusing from a simple, enlightening natural experience to a critique of human intervention in the natural order that we've come to label the *ecosystem*.

Typically, a writer sitting down to compose a nature essay such as Berry's would "erase" that car motor from his or her record of this occasion, simply leave it out; it is tempting in nonfiction to pare down our experiences to those sights and sounds that make a unified whole. A passing mention of the noise as an anomaly—out of tone with the peaceful surroundings—would also be a natural move to make. It would be a far less important and less honest tack, though, than Berry's turn, which was to discuss how these woods in the essay exist in uneasy, threatened relationship to the human-dominated world around them.

Travel Writing

Often, a sense of place comes into sharp focus when we travel off our own turf and into lands foreign to us. Our survival instincts take over, and we grow alert as cats, turning our heads at the call of the *muezzin* in the mosque, sniffing out the smell of roasted lamb in the market stall, spying an old man bearing a homemade wooden coffin up the alleyways of a walled city. In the context of travel, "place" begins to seem not so much the land itself, but everything and anything associated with the land: its people, animals, food, music, religion—all the things that make up life itself.

Pico Iyer, a consummate travel writer, sums it up this way: "We travel, initially, to lose ourselves; and we travel, next, to find ourselves. We travel to open our hearts and eyes and learn more about the world than our newspapers will accommodate. . . . And we travel, in essence, to become young fools again—to slow time down and get taken in, and fall in love once more."

Your task, as a good travel writer, is to both pay attention to the details of place—in all their glorious particularities, with all their good points and bad—and to render these details in a voice that is wholly your own. You must situate yourself as both participant and observer, always ready for the unexpected, but armed with the many lenses that enable you to interpret this world for your readers in a way they've never heard before.

This mandate requires you to find a purpose for your writing *above and beyond* the travel experience itself. Otherwise, you will produce a piece of writing akin to those slide shows we all dread: the summons into a friend's living room to view her pictures of last summer's vacation. "And here we are at the Louvre," the hostess quips brightly, while her guests nod off behind her on the couch in the flickering light of the slide projector. If you expect the travels themselves to carry the weight of narrative interest, you will end up with an essay that looks disconcertingly like: "First I went here, then I went here, and look what an amazing/horrible/fascinating/soul-searing time I had!" Eventually, no one will care. They will sneak out your living room the back way, leaving you alone with your out-of-focus slides. The places themselves may be intrinsically fascinating, but if you render them into flat landscapes, you'll be left with the lame protest, "Well, you just had to have been there."

In a way, the demands of travel writing can epitomize the challenges of any kind of creative nonfiction writing. How do you shape or draft the work so that the experience becomes *more* than itself? How do you relinquish the role of the transcriber and take on the mantle of the artist? Critic Paul Fussell answers that question this way: "Successful travel writing mediates between two poles: the individual physical things it describes, on the one hand, and the larger theme that it is 'about' on the other. That is, the particular and the universal."

For instance, to come back to Pico Iyer once more, his books not only describe his travels into places as diverse as the L.A. airport, Burmese temples, and suburban Japan, but they also often become inquiries into the effects of globalization on the world's cultures. Born to Indian parents in England, then living for a long time in California, Iyer brings with him his deep-seated—almost innate—awareness of how modern cultural boundaries have begun to blur. He begins his book *Video Night in Kathmandu* with a description of how Sylvester Stallone's movie character Rambo had infiltrated every cinema in Asia during his visit there in 1985. By using this one specific example as a focus, he sets the tone and purpose for the book. "I went to Asia," he writes a few pages into the first chapter, "not only to see Asia, but also to see America, from a different vantage point and with new eyes. I left one kind of home to find another: to discover what resided in me and where I resided most fully, and so to better appreciate—in both senses of the word—the home I had left."

With this kind of sensibility, Iyer gains the trust of the reader. Here we know we are in the hands of a traveler who has experienced a place not only as a tourist, but as an intellectual, an artist, and a pilgrim. We can read his books, yes, to get tips on how to survive those twelve-hour bus trips, or we can read to enjoy the characters and scenes he re-enacts (his description of the bicycle trishaw driver in Mandalay will stay with you long after the book is done). But these details are held within a much greater context. In this way, he travels with a purpose that allows a sense of place to penetrate him and his readers on many levels at once.

You will find that good travel writers avoid the pitfalls that lead to self-serving or clichéd writing. They not only have a heightened perception, a precise attention to language, and a facility with scene-making, but also a marked *generosity* innate in the writer's stance, a perception that sees the foibles of the world and forgives them. In much of the beginning writing we see about travel, the writer falls into stereotypes about other tourists and the native people; he begins to either make fun of or put down the others he encounters on his travels. Such a stance not only becomes distasteful to the reader, but it betrays an insufficient maturity on the part of the writer to understand what is important and what is not. His attention to place becomes annoyingly myopic, and he becomes a whiner, complaining about "all those tourists" while munching on potato chips in line to the Sistine Chapel, his cameras slung about his neck. He is guilty of just what he is criticizing: the tourist mentality that sees only the surfaces and complains when the place fails to live up to expectations.

The other pitfall in travel writing is for the voice to become too much like a guidebook, commenting heavily on the cleanliness of the bathrooms in a hotel in downtown Istanbul but missing the dawn light on the Blue Mosque. As Fussell puts it: "Guidebooks are not autobiographical but travel books are, and if the personality they reveal is too commonplace and un-eccentric, they will not be very readable." As with any good creative nonfiction, the *self* must be wholly present in the work, a voice that engages us to take this trip along with you, to stand at the windows and gaze out at what you, *and only you*, choose to show us.

Witnesses to Our World

In the last chapter, we discussed the emerging sense of much nonfiction as a literature of *witness*—the sense that, in a world flooded with activity and change and information sources the public growingly distrusts (rightly or wrongly), the individual voice may provide the ultimate record. In the last decades nothing has changed faster than the environment. The world's population has burgeoned, and technology has developed the ability to clear lands, pollute the air, and drive species to extinction in record time. Your life has witnessed the eclipse of hundreds of thousands of species, even if they passed out of this world without your awareness. (The current rate of species extinction is matched only by that of the age of the dinosaur's demise, sixty-five million years ago.) Your life has also seen the destruction of much natural land and its replacement with man-made habitat, even if this fact too only barely crossed your consciousness.

For instance, if you can remember a time when Rhode Island spent winters buried under several feet of snow—now replaced by light snows and rains—you may be a witness to the phenomenon many would call global warming. Or, if you remember catching salmon or chasing frogs as a child—creatures you now see rarely if at all—you have witnessed the severe recent decline of several indigenous creatures. If you *pay attention*—if you notice the small changes that accumulate in the various places you inhabit—you become a witness.

TRY IT

1. Isolate a single room or outdoor place that to you forms the most essential place of childhood. Quickly write down every element of the place you can remember with as much detail as possible. What were the patterns of the things

you see? Are they old or new? Which odd details do you remember (e.g., a gargoyle-shaped knot in the wood, a gray rug with a dark stain the shape of Brazil, and so forth)? Now fill in an emotional tone for each detail. Did the wallpaper make you feel safe or frightened? What were your favorite things in this place to look at? Your least favorite? Why? What felt "yours" and what felt other? Assemble these specifics into an essay about the emotional landscape of your childhood, moving about the room, letting your essay function as an emotional "camera."

2. Many of us, like Mukherjee, find our sense of "desh" blends real and distant—maybe unseen—places. Is your family one of the many in this country that embodies a divided sense of home? What does "home" mean to you, your siblings, your parents? Many contemporary American families are very transient now. As one of our students, whose father had been transferred multiple times as she grew up, put it, "home is where there's a room for me to unpack my things." Think about whether there's a single place—a physical location—your family defines as "home," or what you do as you move around to bring the sense of home with you. If you're adopted, your birth family, whether you know them or not, may represent another concept of home. Consider writing an essay in which you unpack the complex layers of meaning in the word home, with specific references to all the possibilities.

3. Is there an "old country" in your family profile? How does it affect your family culture, traditions, or modes of interacting? Write about the ways your family's country or countries of origin cause you to see yourself as different from others in your area, perhaps straddling several very different cultures.

4. Examine a piece of your writing and scrutinize place as character. Is your setting a developed character? What kind of character is it: positive, nurturing, menacing, indifferent? Imagine the setting of a scene as a silent character, shaping and adding nuance to the action surrounding it.

VARIATION: Write a biography of a place. Choose a street, a forest, an airport (possibly look at Pico Iyer's essay on the Los Angeles airport, "Where Worlds Collide," for guidance), a shopping center, anyplace that has character to you, whether positive or negative. Write a profile, a "character study," of that environment.

5. Can you articulate what your own vision of nature is? If the outdoors draws you and brings you a special kind of knowledge or contentment, can you put into words what that connection consists of? What would your metaphor be of the human-nature interaction that is, in many ways, the ground of our lives here on earth? Can you think of a time when you went into a natural setting to make a difficult decision, work something out in your mind, or somehow come to feel more "yourself"? What led you to that place? Did it help you in the way you wanted?

Remember, as you articulate your sense of nature in language, that there's nothing else (besides love, perhaps!) that so easily lends itself to cliché. Tranquil brooks, awesome mountains, trilling birds—these are the stuff of hackneyed authors. Make your description fresh, original, and interesting.

VARIATION: Jennifer Price, who wrote an essay titled "A Brief Natural History of the Plastic Pink Flamingo," writes about *urban nature*, the aspects of nature that thrive in cities—nature stores at malls, even stuffed birds on women's hats. Write about nature without pursuing nature in the traditional sense. Stay in your apartment building or go to a shopping mall and observe the trees, the crow colonies, even the microclimates created by human development.

6. In this era of accelerating change, we ask you to think of your life as a piece of living history. Looking at your life as an intersection of personal history and the environment that surrounds you, to what can you bear witness? Write for about ten minutes, associating freely and spontaneously, about a place of your childhood, a place that for you defines your childhood—the porch of your house, a creek, the fire escape of an apartment, a special place in the woods. What did the place smell, taste, feel like? Include, but don't limit yourself to, the natural elements: air quality and odor, trees, wildlife (including insects).

Now write for ten minutes on what this place is like now, whether from your own current experiences of it or from what you've been told. How has it changed? What is gone now that was there before? What is there now that wasn't there before? Think of yourself as a living history of this place—what changes did you find between the place of your childhood and the place of your adulthood? Do these changes reflect any changes in your own life?

As you compare these two quick writings, see what larger elements emerge. Have you and the place of your childhood changed in tandem or gone in different directions? Are you witness to changes that reflect larger—perhaps dangerous—currents of change in our contemporary world? Think about it: even seemingly small things, like the loss of much of our amphibian life, such as frogs, will alter over time the nature of the planet we live on. Think about your writings in the largest possible sense: often this short exercise unlocks a valuable essay.

7. If you have a travel diary or journal, go back to it now and pull out sections that give highly sensory descriptions of place: the feel of the air, the taste of the food, the sounds, the smells. Type these out in separate sections, then arrange them on a table, seeing if you can find a common theme that may bind an essay together. What can you construe as the greater purpose for your travels? How can you incorporate that purpose into your travel writing? What is the one image that will emerge for metaphorical significance?

8. Take a day to travel your hometown as a tourist. Pretend you've never seen this place before and wander with all your senses heightened. Take a notebook with you and write down your impressions. How can you make the familiar new again?

VARIATION FOR A GROUP: As a group, take this trip together. Then compare notes and see how different eyes perceive different things. Take some time at the end of the day, or a few days later, to write together and see where these sensory impressions might lead.

4

Writing the Spiritual Autobiography

Be patient toward all that is unsolved in your heart and try to love the questions themselves like locked rooms or like books written in a very foreign tongue. Do not now seek the answers, which cannot be given you because you would not be able to live them. . . . Live the questions now. Perhaps you will then gradually, without noticing it, live along some distant day into the answer.

—RAINER MARIA RILKE

Before I sit down at my desk, I look out my window and notice the light as it reflects off the bay. I light a candle and a stick of incense, reaching over the small statue of a Buddha sitting on the windowsill. On a shelf above my desk sits a menorah my parents gave me for Hanukkah one year. A St. Christopher medal lies coiled in a small compartment in a drawer of my desk. Photographs of my four great-grandmothers bear witness to all this spiritual paraphernalia, gazing down at me with what I interpret as amused benevolence.

All of these things—the light off the bay, the incense, the meditating Buddha, the menorah, St. Christopher, my ancestors—create an atmosphere of eclectic spirituality that has come to inform much of my writing. From the very beginning, my writing has tended to chronicle the sometimes baffling turns my spiritual path has taken: from acting as the earnest president of my Jewish youth group, to drifting through days of Grateful Dead concerts in the eighties (convinced of the divinity of Jerry Garcia), to backpacking solo in the meadows around Mt. Rainier, to meditating in silence for weeks at a time in California farmhouses. I've settled down a bit in my

39

*staid middle age, but I've never lost that sense of spiritual quest driving the
trajectory of my life.*

*Now, writing itself seems to be the deepest spiritual act I can perform.
So I sit down at my desk. I light my incense. I look out my window and
take a deep breath. I feel the presence of my great-grandmothers cheering
me on. I write one word and then another. Who knows where it will lead?
What kind of faith can I muster to continue? I don't know. It's a little like
prayer, a little like meditation, a little like walking an unknown trail in
the high country.*

—BRENDA

The Tradition of Spiritual Autobiography

Though oftentimes invisible in our lives, spirituality seems to follow us everywhere. From the moment we're born, we're initiated into a world that relies
on many different rituals to guide us. Or, if we're born into a family more
secular, we become aware of ourselves in opposition to predominant modes
of religious belief. Perhaps that is why we've lately noticed a renaissance in
memoirs that use either religion or spirituality as a guiding narrative or
metaphor.

But the impulse to write spiritual autobiography has been around as long
as human consciousness. The form keeps adapting to fit whatever culture and
society demand of it. These works range from devotional narratives to science writing that finds spiritual fodder in the cells of the human body, but
the basic structure usually wins out. These narratives tend to focus on
moments of insight that lead the narrator in a new direction. By their very
nature, many spiritual autobiographies appear to mimic or echo classic "con-
version" stories found in religious texts: the protagonist is lost and then found,
and the narratives hinge on precise moments of "turning," either away or
toward points of reference identified as God, Allah, Yahweh, the Great Spirit,
and so on.

These conversions may also work the opposite way, especially after defining events such as the Holocaust or the terrorist attacks of September 11, 2001.
The narrator moves from a place of religious or spiritual certainty to one that
is more fragmented or full of doubt.

We can call these moments "epiphanies" (sudden insights), but they don't necessarily arrive with the bang the term suggests. They may be quiet moments, barely noticeable until the act of writing magnifies their significance. A turning point can be as subtle as Emily Dickinson's "certain slant of light" into a room, or Virginia Woolf's contemplation of a dying moth in her study.

The Quest Narrative

Full-length spiritual autobiographies essentially take the form of a *quest narrative*, propelled by burning questions, a journey toward an unclear destination. The protagonist sets herself on a path, encounters obstacles and unexpected guides, and is transformed along the way. For example, *The Wizard of Oz* could be the most traditional and metaphoric of spiritual autobiographies. The protagonist, Dorothy, driven by deep, inchoate longing, finds herself on a journey in an unknown country. Essentially alone, she must rely on guidance from unexpected sources to find her way toward a vague, promised land. She encounters many obstacles along the way, many turning points, but finally arrives at Oz, only to find the destination nothing like what she imagines. When she finally returns home, she is the same person but transformed by her quest.

Spirituality does not necessarily need to be contained in religions or places of worship. Nature writer John Muir, rather than turning away or toward an external spiritual figure or destination, includes spirituality in all of nature. In *My First Summer in the Sierra*, Muir writes, "In our best times everything turns into religion, all the world seems a church and the mountains altars." *How interesting everything is,* he muses throughout the book, a good mantra any writer can take to heart.

Personal Renditions of the Sacred

As with any strong work of creative nonfiction, the successful spiritual autobiography hinges on discovery through the writing process itself. The writer does not set out to give us predetermined answers but instead allows us some insight into the questions that drive him. Spiritual autobiographies, in particular, "find interesting" the turns in the road and the roadside attractions; they do not necessarily follow a straight line but proceed more intuitively, meandering from point to point in a way that may seem digressive, but actually forms a clear path in retrospect.

In *Traveling Mercies*, Anne Lamott's wry account of her own spiritual process, she puts it this way:

> *My coming to faith did not start with a leap but rather a series of staggers from what seemed like one safe place to another. Like lily pads, round and green, these places summoned and then held me up while I grew. . . . When I look back on some of these early resting places—the boisterous home of the Catholics, the soft armchair of the Christian Science mom, adoption by ardent Jews—I can see how flimsy and indirect a path they made. Yet each step brought me closer to the verdant pad of faith on which I somehow stay afloat today.*

If you look on your life as a series of "lily pads," the way Anne Lamott does, you may be able to begin an essay structured around these turning points in your spiritual narrative.

Once you set out to examine your own spiritual inclinations, you will find yourself with a new set of writing dilemmas. Spirituality can be an arena fraught with prefabricated rhetoric and tired clichés. As a writer, your challenge is to find a language and a form so personal that *only you* can give us this rendition of the spiritual life. You must remain aware of how your brand of spirituality has been depicted in the past and find a way to circumvent your reader's expectations and resistance. How do you even begin to discuss spirituality without immediately using language that has lost its meaning from overuse?

As we saw in the last three chapters, powerful writing always emerges from the physical, specific, and sensory details of your experience. If you decide to write about spiritual experience—whether positive or negative—you will want to look closely at the physical elements that make up your spiritual life, whether those include incense in a church, chanting in a synagogue, or the odor of cedar on your daily walk. Beginning there, ask yourself how your sense of spirituality informs your life and the lives of those around you.

You could also approach your spiritual autobiography by becoming a "layperson's expert." Poet Kathleen Norris, author of *The Cloister Walk* and other books on faith, creates a lyrical yet highly researched version of spirituality when she immerses herself in the world of a Benedictine monastery. In *Virgin Time*, Patricia Hampl makes a pilgrimage to the roots of her spirituality and presents a "travelogue" of faith that includes not only her own experience but a great deal of "expert" information.

In contrast to Norris and Hampl, who become friendly experts and guides, Anne Lamott takes on the role of the endearing screwup, a woman who tries her best, often falling short but able to recover. She becomes more of a buddy to the reader, articulating all those weaknesses we thought must be kept hidden. Lamott maintains a sense of irony throughout her writings on faith, a conversational voice that trusts the reader as much as we grow to trust her. One pitfall of spiritual writing is that it can become too heavy and self-absorbed; Lamott provides a good model for an alternative voice, one that claims no perfection in the spiritual life.

What Is Your "Koan?"

In his essay "The Mickey Mantle Koan," memoirist and novelist David James Duncan sets himself a koan, a puzzle or riddle given to Zen students by their masters, the answer to which might lead to spiritual enlightenment. In Duncan's case, the koan takes the form of a signed baseball sent to his dying brother by Mickey Mantle. The brother dies before the baseball arrives, and for more than twenty years it sits on Duncan's shelf—intriguing, puzzling, infuriating. Duncan knows the ball offers some clue to sorting out his grief about his brother's death, but he doesn't really know *how* it will do so.

In the essay, Duncan pushes at this "koan" and works it out before our eyes. He takes a simple, almost mundane object—a signed baseball—and gazes at it until it yields some answers. He approaches spirituality not on the level of the abstract but on a grassy playing field, where dirty old balls "hiss and pop" into the gloves of teenage boys:

From the moment I'd first laid eyes on it, all I'd wanted was to take that immaculate ball out to our corridor on an evening just like this one, to take my place near the apples in the north and find my brother waiting beneath the immense firs to the south. All I'd wanted was to pluck that too-perfect ball off its pedestal and proceed, without speaking, to play catch so long and hard that the grass stains and nicks and the sweat of our palms would finally obliterate every last trace of Mantle's blue ink, till all he would have sent us was a grass-green, earth-brown, beat-up old baseball. Beat-up old balls were all we'd ever had anyhow. They were all we ever needed.

When you set about to write your personal rendition of spirituality, look for the concrete *things* of the world that will help you find your own koan. What are the essential questions these objects trigger in you? These questions will help you move, as a writer, from the abstract to the concrete.

Above all, maintain *honesty*—with yourself and your reader. If it has been said before, don't say it. If you veer into platitude and cliché, veer right out of it again. If you find yourself mired in complaint, laugh your way out of it. Render the spiritual life with the same intuition and intelligence you bring to all your work. Find the details, the tone, the rhythms that will separate your voice from the choir's. Sing a solo. Be brave. Really belt it out.

Writing as a Spiritual Practice

> Writing is the only way I know how to pray.
>
> —HELENA MARIA VIRAMONTES

Often writers find that the writing process itself grows akin to spiritual practice. It requires the same kind of patience, ritual, and faith. In her book *The Writing Life*, Annie Dillard compares writing to sitting at a desk thirty feet off the ground. "Your work," she writes, "is to keep cranking the flywheel that turns the gears that spin the belt in the engine of belief that keeps you and your desk in midair." Poet Carolyn Forché has called the writer's stance one of "meditative expectancy." Natalie Goldberg, author of *Writing Down the Bones* and *Wild Mind: Living the Writer's Life*, sees writing as an integral part of her Zen practice: "Jack Kornfield, a Vipassana meditation teacher, said last week up at Lama, 'you meditate by yourself, but not for yourself. You meditate for everyone.' This is how we should write."

When we begin to see our writing in this kind of context, we can more easily maintain the patience and faith necessary for our work to be done. It's a secular practice, available to anyone who feels compelled to put pen to paper. When you write this way, you are "living the questions now" and offering up possible pathways into the ineffable.

TRY IT

1. Describe a religious or semireligious ritual that took place in your childhood with some regularity. Use quotes from this ritual as a frame within which you can describe memory, conflict, pleasure, and pain. Move your reader through this ritual with you. Using present tense and vivid imagery, show the emotion you felt about this particular rite as a child.

> **VARIATION:** Rewrite the scene in the past tense, from an adult perspective. How does your attitude toward this rite change?

2. Try to remember a moment in your childhood when you were first aware of a spiritual presence in your life. This can be anything from a moment within your spiritual tradition, a moment in nature, or a moment when you were alone in your room. Describe this experience from the child's point of view, in the present tense.

> **VARIATION:** Describe a moment when you were aware of the *absence* of a spiritual presence in your life. Where do these different moments lead you?

3. Put on a piece of music that has spiritual connotations for you: Gregorian chants, bamboo flutes, a Verdi opera, whatever puts you in a meditative mood. Write to this music without ever mentioning it at all.

> **VARIATION FOR A GROUP:** Each person brings in a piece of music; do the above, with as many pieces as you can in a writing session.

4. If you have a repeating spiritual ritual, give us one particular *scene* out of this rite. Focus on one day, one morning, or one hour that encapsulates what this ritual means to you. Try not to *tell* us what it means, but show us through the details you choose and the tone you create.

5. Imagine yourself into the mind of one of your spiritual ancestors. Which scene or image provides a turning point in your spiritual life even before you're born?

6. Do some research into your spiritual tradition. What are the controversies? How is it practiced in different parts of the world? Interview an elder, or participate in an intensive retreat. Write as both an observer and a participant.

7. Think about the koans that exist in your own life. Which objects, people, places, or situations have always puzzled you? How do these things represent emotions or ideas that you haven't yet been able to articulate? Begin an essay whose goal is to "push" at these objects until they yield some unexpected answers.

8. For the duration of one or two writing sessions, ban certain words from your vocabulary that already have spiritual connotations (*God, Lord, Allah, soul, heart,* scriptural language, and so forth). Often this kind of language becomes a crutch, enabling us to avoid going deeper into our material. Make a list of these words to keep with you. See what moves you have to make to avoid using these words. Which images or scenes arise to take their place?

> **VARIATION FOR A GROUP:** Make a group list of such words and promise to abide by the prohibition for whatever duration the group decides. When reading each other's work, make note of when such words arise and their effect.

5

Gathering the Threads of History

Everyone has his own story, and everyone could arouse interest in the romance of his life if he but comprehended it.

—George Sand

History is nothing more than a thin thread of what is remembered stretched out over an ocean of what has been forgotten.

—Milan Kundera

I am working on a short essay about a strange summer I had when my brother worked for the New Jersey Department of Environmental Protection, running tests on water samples that had been held up for years. He drives a tiny, two-seater Fiat Spider, the car of choice that year. My start: "It's my brother's Spider summer. Not dog days but spider days. My brother has a blue Fiat Spider. It has no backseat but I ride in the back anyway, rolled up in the ten inches or so under the rear window. Spiders aren't much more than human-sized tins so this is risky but it doesn't matter. Let me be a bottle rocket."

What follows is the revised beginning, after a quick search on major events of the year (1974) and surrounding years. I did this search primarily on the Internet, on Historycentral.com's "this year in history" service: "It's my brother's Spider summer. Not dog days but spider days. It's 1974 and things have been crashing. Nixon's resigned or is going to and a few years ago Apollo 13 crash-landed when an oxygen tank blew. (Astronauts in there like Spam in a can, Chuck Yeager said.) Karen Silkwood's about to crash.

My brother has a blue Fiat Spider. It has no backseat but I ride in the back anyway, rolled up in the ten inches or so under the rear window. Spiders aren't much more than human-sized tins so this is risky but it doesn't matter. I am a lost person. Let me be a bottle rocket."

When I add these historical details—the space program, the death of Karen Silkwood—my story becomes enriched and begins to expand outward: connections move back and forth, between the closeness of the car and of space capsules, the sense of questing and uncovering and yet danger that marked that time. The reference to Karen Silkwood adds a reference to those who ask difficult questions, particularly environmental ones, as this book goes on to do. The imminent resignation of President Nixon captures the sense of chaos and rebellion, embodied in these teenagers, so prevalent in our country at that time.

—SUZANNE

Our Historical, Universal Selves

As the preceding experience shows, each of us exists in both a private and a public way. We're all at once son or daughter, lover, sister, brother, neighbor—the person who must have chocolate cereal in the morning and who absently puts the milky bowl down for the cat to lick. We're also pieces of history. We are the people who witnessed the turn of the millennium; we're the first wave of the world's citizens to see their lives transferred more and more onto computer chips. We are also the people who saw the Berlin Wall dismantled, experienced the Monica Lewinsky scandal, and lived through the tragedy of September 11, 2001.

To look at what it means to exist and be human—and who we are as a species—we must look at history. That historical frame is one that may simply enrich your story. Or—as the Kundera quote shows—writing creative nonfiction focused on history might have a deep ethical implication. Sometimes using our own experience of history is a way of preventing that destructive forgetfulness that Kundera describes. Leslie Brody sums up her reasons for writing her book *Red Star Sister*, a memoir of her anti–Vietnam War activism, when she simply said, "You have a responsibility to tell history because people forget history."

The Moose at the Window

Bruce Beasley, a Pacific Northwest writer who teaches nonfiction, is having a conference with a young writer who says she has nothing to write about. The subject for this essay assignment is encountering the natural world. She claims to be utterly without experiences to use.

"We live surrounded by water and mountains," he tells her.

She insists that she likes to stay in, does not hike or camp, and has no feeling for the outdoors.

They go back and forth like this for a while, with Bruce asking question after question about her hobbies, her reaction to her alpine landscape. All are returned with a slightly desperate wail that the subject of nature contains nothing at all she can write about.

"There must be something," he says finally.

"Well," she says hesitantly, "there *was* that moose at the window."

A lost moose had wandered into this northwestern town, and moseyed about for several weeks, making it almost as far as the highway, before being removed by animal control. One morning, this writer woke up and found him—confused, curious, and hungry—staring in the window of her new apartment. The fascinating aspect of nature in her life turned out to be that it had found her—driven by the historical facts of rapid development and loss of habitat. Thinking about this moment as her subject led to a vivid and colorful essay.

Each of us needs to learn to recognize our moose at the window. We've all experienced meeting someone who claimed to be ordinary while finally slipping into the conversation that he or she had grown up on a commune, sung opera as a child, or—like one person we remember—come of age living inside the Statue of Liberty with his Park Service father. The world he grew into, literally seen through the eyes of the Statue of Liberty, is not the same world the rest of us know.

It's important for you as a writer, particularly a nonfiction writer, to think through what is different and important in your world, and what historical events formed the canvas for the fine brushstrokes of your own life. You can easily check the highlights of particular dates and years by using resources like Historycentral.com on the Web or reference books such as *The New York Times Book of Chronologies*.

The "When" in Addition to the "What"

Here is the opening of James Baldwin's famous essay about racism and family, "Notes of a Native Son":

> On the twenty-ninth of July, in 1943, my father died. On the same day, a few hours later, his last child was born. Over a month before this, while all our energies were concentrated in waiting for these events, there had been, in Detroit, one of the bloodiest race riots of the century. . . . On the morning of the third of August, we drove my father to the graveyard through a wilderness of smashed plate glass.

Notice that the author's attention operates like a moving camera, panning between familial and national tragedy. Family events come first; then, as if his gaze is forced away, Baldwin takes in the larger chaos of the country's rioting. Right at the start of the essay Baldwin carefully states the season and the year; it's a hot summer month during World War II. Part of the race frustration building up to the riots described here arose from black GIs risking their lives overseas and coming home to face the same old racism, a fact that would have been clear to Baldwin's contemporary audience. By the end of the paragraph, the rioters' smashed glass has become a "wilderness," as if that landscape equals the natural landscape about to close over Baldwin's father's body. The essay accomplishes an unforgettable weaving of personal tragedy with the period that spawned it.

Always keep in mind the extent to which history is the individual writ large, and the individual life is history writ small. Understanding what shapes how you perceive the world—and how you are perceived—is critical to using your own experiences to create strong nonfiction.

TRY IT

You will likely be the last person to recognize what's fascinating—and deeply significant—about you. Your friends will see it, and if you're lucky your family will too. If you're normal, you will brush off their interest, tell them it really wasn't so different—you just don't see what all the fuss is about that last night on board the *Titanic*.

Here's a tool to help you along: a checklist to start yourself off with, whether you choose to answer on paper, in a journal, or in the privacy of your own head. This checklist is designed to elicit a greater awareness of the historical events that have shaped your life, and also a greater awareness of your *social self*—you as conservative or liberal, member of a disadvantaged group, Buddhist, activist, Rosicrucian. While considering these questions, it's important to remember that this social self *always* functions in a cultural and historical context.

1. Many Americans born in the 1950s have powerful early memories of the day President John F. Kennedy was shot—young teachers crying in the classroom, the crackling of televisions left on throughout the day. More recently, most of us vividly remember the events of September 11, 2001. Which event of national or world importance do you remember most clearly? How did you hear of it, and what did you hear? What were other people around you doing? What was going on in your own life that this event bounced off of, resonated with, or formed a strange contrast to? Use all of your senses to re-create this memory.

2. Which aspects of your life do people around you consistently find most interesting? What questions do they ask you? What can you tell them that satisfies/dissatisfies them?

3. At a writer's conference, Leslie Brody talked about living through an unpleasant divorce while the royal wedding of Diana Spencer to the Prince of Wales dominated the news. She talked of the ironies of seeing the two events juxtaposed, and how the memories came to interfuse: the painful sundering of a marriage, the artificial romance of the royal wedding. Which news events formed a backdrop to the most emotional moments of your life? How do the two stories intersect?

4. Try to imagine your own life as someone five hundred years from now might view it. What about your life—the place you live in and the historical unfoldings you've witnessed—do you believe that person would find most interesting? (Hint: what do you find most interesting about life in the past?) How are you a privileged observer?

5. Get in the habit of thinking of yourself in the third person—seeing yourself move through the world as a protagonist—at least once a day. Narrate your daily story to yourself in the third person. As an objective listener (and, to some extent, you can be one), what interests you?

Dating a Significant Event

This is the exercise that helped Suzanne expand her description of the summer of 1974.

1. For the first part, write a description of several paragraphs about a scene or event you consider critical in your life. It should date from at least a few years in your past and can be from childhood. As in most writing exercises, write quickly and do not censor yourself. Be as specific and detailed as possible, using all your senses.

2. Now use a list of chronologies, possibly a simple one printed from an Internet site such as Historycentral.com, to date your experience with a corresponding national or world event. Don't worry if you feel you weren't thinking about the event at the time; your obliviousness to it may be part of what makes the essay fascinating.

3. Once you find a historical corollary, write as many connections, real or metaphoric, as you can. (Suzanne might have written "secrets, cover-ups, crashing, underground corruption, apathy.") In an essay, draw together the two links to show how a critical moment in your life unfolded against a corresponding moment in history. Don't feel the need to justify to yourself immediately why something feels important. If your gut tells you it's important, then surely it is.

6

Writing the Arts

Culture is like a magnetic field, a patterned energy shaping history. It is invisible, even unsuspected, until a receiver sensitive enough to pick up its messages can give it a voice.

—GUY DAVENPORT

I've put up a new picture, a photograph bought for me at an Edward Weston exhibit last April. The composition shows a young woman, all in black, posed against a high, white fence. She half turns toward the camera; her right hand lies tentatively across her heart. The shadow of a leafless tree (I imagine it to be a young oak) curves up and over this slight figure. Actually, it does more than curve; the shadow arches behind her in a gesture of protection. Almost a bow of respect.

Why do I like this picture so much? I glance at it every day, and every day it puzzles me. What draws me to those dark, shaded eyes? What holds me transfixed by the movement of gray shadows over the straight white planks, the drape of the black coat, the white hand raised to the breast in a stunned gesture of surprise?

These questions led me to write the first essay I ever published, titled "Prologue to a Sad Spring," after Weston's own title of the photograph I describe. In this essay, the photograph's mysterious title becomes a meditation on what it means to have a "sad spring," on how our lives are full of losses never memorialized in photographs. It's a short essay, with a circular design that leads the reader back to the appeal of black-and-white photography and to this particular photograph that started the rumination in the first place. Though it's a simple piece, with simple ambitions, it remains a

favorite essay in my repertoire. It feels almost like a gift, an ephemeral con-
nection between myself and the woman in this photograph, a distant com-
muniqué between a writer and a photographer who would never meet.

—BRENDA

The Visual Arts

With old glass-plate daguerreotypes—the earliest form of photography—if
you tilt the plate just slightly, the image disappears and the photograph
becomes a mirror, an apt metaphor for how the creative nonfiction writer can
approach art. Through a close observation of particular paintings, sculptures,
or photographs, you can reveal your own take on the world or find metaphors
in line with your obsessions. At the same time, you will elucidate that artwork
in such a way that the piece will forever after have a greater significance for
your reader.

For example, in the essay "Inventing Peace," art historian and journalist
Lawrence Weschler closely analyzes a Vermeer painting to understand what
is happening during the Bosnian war crimes tribunal in The Hague. He compares the serene, almost dreamlike settings of Vermeer with the atrocities the
judges in The Hague, just minutes from the Vermeer exhibit, hear about every
day. One particular painting, *The Head of a Young Girl*, intrigues him. He
explicates this painting for us:

> *Has the girl just turned toward us or is she just about to turn away? . . .*
> *The answer is that she's actually doing both. This is a woman who has just*
> *turned toward us and is already about to look away: and the melancholy of*
> *the moment, with its impending sense of loss, is transferred from her eyes to*
> *the tearlike pearl dangling from her ear. . . . The girl's lips are parted in a*
> *sudden intake of breath—much, we suddenly notice, as are our own as we*
> *gaze back upon her.*

Weschler closely studies this painting, interpreting the details as he unfolds
them for us one by one. He creates a *speculative narrative* that brings this
painting to life. In a speculative narrative, the writer infuses a painting or any
situation with a story that arises both from fact and imagination. For instance,
it is clear in Weschler's description that the *facts* of the painting exist as he
relates them—the parted lips, the pearl earring—but he allows himself to

speculate on the *meaning* of those details. He brings his own frame of mind to bear on the portrait; this interpretation sets up the themes for his piece.

Throughout the essay he brings in other voices—art historians, the judges at The Hague, other art patrons, journalists covering the tribunal—until we have a view of Vermeer, and this painting in particular, shaped by Weschler's sensibility and by the context in which he chooses to place the painter. In the end, the image of the girl turning away mirrors an image of one of the war criminals, Dusko Tadic, looking up at a television camera, and then turning away. Both images come to be about loss and the ravages of history:

> *Inventing peace: I found myself thinking of Vermeer with his camera obscura—an empty box fronted by a lens through which the chaos of the world might be drawn in and tamed back to a kind of sublime order.*

As you can see, though the topic is external to the self, Weschler does not sacrifice personal voice. To the contrary, the "I" remains a guiding force throughout the essay: ruminating, reflecting, and questioning his own fascination.

It's important to remember that while nonfiction work about painting is flourishing right now—such as Terry Tempest Williams's *Leap* or Mark Doty's *Still Life with Oysters and Lemon*—photography, sculpture, and installations are all rich subjects for your writing as well. As Tolstoy wrote, art is a language that communicates "soul to soul," on a level that bypasses the intellect. As a writer turning your gaze to the rich, metaphorical world of art, you enter into this dialogue and add to our understanding of the world and ourselves.

The Moving Image Arts

The term *arts* also refers to the moving image arts—television, film, video. A vital and probably the most visible part of our cultural expression, the moving image arts have been somewhat underrepresented in nonfiction and are due for more serious reflection. Remember that although you can find plenty of top-quality film and TV, the art itself doesn't have to be great to warrant your attention. In a brilliant essay titled "Upon Leaving the Movie Theater," Roland Barthes simply writes about the experience of cinema—the darkness of the theater, the unfolding of a narrative in a giant lighted square—as a way of exploring pleasure and our fascination with images.

Remember Paisley Rekdal's "The Night My Mother Met Bruce Lee," from Chapter 2? The essay invokes pop culture images of the Chinese and the Chinese-American, particularly the narrator's mother, whose school guidance counselor advises her not to go to Smith, "hinting at some limitation my mother would prefer to ignore." At the same time, a cook in the restaurant where the mother works tells her he comes from Hong Kong and hence is "*real* Chinese." Rekdal embeds that sense of cultural limbo—appearing Chinese to a white guidance counselor but an assimilated American to a recent immigrant—in the artifice of kung fu movies. In the essay, mother and daughter bond watching the martial arts film *Enter the Dragon*:

> *Bruce Lee narrows his eyes, ripples his chest muscles under his white turtleneck.*
>
> *"I knew him," my mother tells me. "I worked with him in a restaurant when I was in high school."*
>
> *"Really?" This is now officially the only cool thing about her. "What was he like?"*
>
> *"I don't remember. No one liked him, though. All that kung fu stuff; it looked ridiculous. Like a parody."*

Rekdal pays close attention to the film itself in this piece; her prose follows the film's use of lighting—the way Lee's chest "seemed outlined in silver," mirroring the way Rekdal's mother's face "twists into something I do not recognize in the television light." It's as if the cultural distortion created by the movie and movies like it distorts the mother even in the eyes of her daughter. Note that Rekdal has been careful to look at the techniques of the films in question and use them throughout her essay—not just the kung fu itself, which becomes picked up by the restaurant chef, but kung fu films' visual style of bright color and exaggerated gesture.

Films can comment on our own lives and on the history surrounding them. And film and television can capture a cultural moment. Think of how at times movies such as *Thelma and Louise* or TV shows such as "Seinfeld" seem to speak for the feelings of large numbers of people in our society, generating catchphrases and images that become embedded in our collective consciousness. These arts define us personally as well, as Rekdal shows.

As you draft an essay using the moving image arts, think of how you can use those artistic techniques for your own purposes. Can you borrow the visual style of the work in question? Can you write an essay in which you model on scenes in the work you've viewed?

You can also take a more analytical approach to television and film, exploring what they mean in terms of culture and society. For example, Bill McKibben, in his book *The Age of Missing Information*, performs an experiment in which he has friends record every channel on a Virginia cable network for twenty-four hours, then he goes about analyzing what he sees to create a portrait of the American mind-set: what we learn—and, more importantly, what we *don't* learn—from what surrounds us on TV. McKibben, who doesn't own a television himself, spends several months watching these videotapes of a single day's television programming:

> *I began spending eight or ten hour days in front of the VCR—I watched it all, more or less. A few programs repeat endlessly, with half-hour "infomercials" for DiDi 7 spot remover and Liquid Luster car wax leading the list at more than a dozen appearances apiece. Having decided that once or twice was enough to mine their meanings, I would fast-forward through them, though I always slowed down to enjoy the part where the car-wax guy sets fire to the hood of his car.*

As you can see, even though McKibben has set himself a huge, intellectual task, he does not sacrifice his personal voice or his sense of humor to do it. He contrasts what one can learn from a day of television to what one can learn from a day in the woods, providing highly specific examples of each mode, and revealing his own personality at the same time. He turns his attention and powers of observation on something as common as television and enables us to perceive its greater meaning.

Music

As we mentioned in Chapter 1, music can key us into powerful memories that define the self. And music can also serve as a medium to channel some of the most vital issues of our time. We still look back at the 1960s antiwar movement by looking at the music that sprang out of it (and what 1960s documentary would be complete without footage of Country Joe and the Fish's "I Feel Like I'm Fixin' to Die Rag"?). Music is a vessel that holds the emotions of its time.

As an example, let's consider David Margolick, Hilton Als, and Ellis Marsalis's book *Strange Fruit: The Biography of a Song*. "Strange Fruit," a song written for blues singer Billie Holiday, tells the horrendous story of Southern lynchings. Through the lens of this song Margolick, Als, and Marsalis weave together the tales of Holiday's short, heroin-addicted life: the white communist sympathizer who wrote the song, the struggle for civil rights, New York café society, even the history of lynching. This single song contains within it a story that branches out and out to speak of two extraordinary human beings as well as the thorniest problem in American history—race.

Another approach might be to mine your obsession with a particular musician or type of music. For example, in his book *But Beautiful*, Geoff Dyer creates improvisational portraits of eight jazz musicians, getting into their heads, using their points of view. His language and prose style take their cue from jazz, running riffs and hitting discordant notes, as he tries to capture the essence of these musicians on paper. As he explains in the introduction: "When I began writing this book I was unsure of the form it should take. This was a great advantage since it meant I had to improvise and so, from the start, the writing was animated by the defining characteristic of its subject." He calls his book "imaginative criticism," and he uses fictional elements along with the facts of these musicians' lives. The result is a speculative narrative, one that roots itself in music and sings itself on the page.

Literature: The "Reading Narrative"

A fascinating new subgenre of nonfiction has flourished in the last few years— we've titled these works "reading narratives." These essays show the author in different ways reading another piece of literature and using it as a springboard for his or her own actions and reflections. Like writers who use the visual arts, authors of reading narratives are somehow grappling with another artist's aesthetics as a means of probing deeper into their own. Though reading narratives sound simple, they aren't; in good hands, they present a beautifully counterpointed music of two different lives, aesthetics, and meanings. Phyllis Rose's book *The Year of Reading Proust* is an excellent example, as the author reads all of Proust's *Remembrance of Things Past* while using it as a means to chronicle her own life, comparing her Key West to Proust's Balbec, the characters inhabiting her life to those in his.

Most of us can remember at least one "eureka" reading moment. That moment may give us permission to do things differently in our own work: use a new voice, dig deeper, or consider new subject matter as potentially ours. These "eureka" writers are our literary mentors, whether we realize that or not. And what we read may spur us on in many different ways—other authors inspire us, give us permission, and also irritate us in ways that stimulate us to try something new. You can try writing a "literary history" of yourself, one that tracks your life through the many different books you've read and loved.

TRY IT

1. Begin an essay by describing a piece of art that has always intrigued you. Feel free to interpret the details, creating a speculative narrative about what is happening in the painting or what was going through the painter's mind. Find other interpretations from art scholars and begin to create an essay that approaches this artwork from several different angles.

2. Write an essay in which you parallel your interpretation of a particular artwork or artist with events going on in the world around you.

3. Write an essay in which you parallel your interpretation of a particular artwork or artist with events unfolding in your own life.

4. Think about a film that you love, that you could watch any number of times. Look closely at the conventions and physical experience of film, and question your obsession. In what ways are you comforted by the artifice of film? Where do you suspend your sense of its unreality and where do you take comfort in it? Where did you first see the film, and what has it represented to the larger cul-

ture? If you like, you can substitute something from television, but for this exercise you should go for a quality piece.

5. Think about television commercials that stick with you. How do they define the eras they appear in? How have they shaped you, perhaps in terms of social relationships, signs of status, body image?

6. Write a review of a film or a television show, using specific details that reveal your own voice and vision and that place the show in a larger context.

7. Write an essay that uses popular television or radio shows to establish the time and place of your piece. What were the shows you watched as a child? How did they establish the routine of your day? Why do you think those particular shows hooked you?

8. This prompt expands on uses of music presented in Chapter 1. Identify the piece of music that's been most important to you in your life. First, try to write down why it means so much to you, and when and where you can remember hearing it. If there are lyrics, write down all you can remember, and list adjectives that describe the melody.

Now try tracing all of the cultural connections of the song, as the authors of *Strange Fruit* did. This may or may not take a little bit of research.

9. Try to imagine your way into the head of a musician you love. Create a speculative narrative that combines fact and fiction to bring that person's music to life on the page.

10. Think about your reading life. What piece of writing has "taken the top of your head off," to use Emily Dickinson's phrase? Write a reading narrative in which you enter into dialogue with this writing—feel free to quote it. How has this reading experience changed you and helped you to redefine your life and your mission as a writer?

11. Write a history of your life through the books you've read. What was your favorite book at age five? Age ten? Age sixteen? Age twenty? Write these out in sections, rendering in specific, sensory detail the memories these books inspire in you.

7

Writing the Larger World

Like Flemish miniaturists who reveal the essence of humankind within the confines of a tiny frame, McPhee once again demonstrates that the smallest topic is replete with history, significance, and consequence.

—From a review of John
McPhee's *Oranges*

The first nonfiction book I remember reading and going back to read again was Lewis Thomas's The Lives of a Cell. *I read it while sitting in my little rented room in Arcata, California; I was a senior in college, a nascent Buddhist brimming with questions about the world and my place in it. Thomas had me thinking about mitochondria—mitochondria!—and the topic had called into question every perception I thought was sound. No longer was I a separate organism, contained within my skin, but a mere continuance of a single cell that erupted eons ago in the primordial soup.*

What got to me about these "Notes of a Biology Watcher" was not the information itself (had I read the same information in the encyclopedia I doubt it would have affected me so), but how that information was presented. Thomas was no mere biologist, but a philosopher and a poet; his sensibility permeated the information and made it real, made it personable. As I became more and more interested in creative nonfiction, I found this same kind of voice in many of the writers I loved: E. B. White, John McPhee, Tom Wolfe, Joan Didion, to name just a few. These authors brought their "I" to the world, without becoming self-centered; their focus often remained determinedly outward without sacrificing the voice that made their work unique.

Recently, National Public Radio aired a story about the recent spate in nonfiction books that focus on topics one might not expect to find interesting: orchids, tulips, mosquitoes, clouds, ether, and something as diminutive and common as dust. People are reading these books on the bus, at the beach, in a chair by the window; they're coming to the breakfast table and saying to their loved ones, "Did you know about . . . ?"

—BRENDA

Turning Outward: Finding Your Material Outside the Self

Your own private world—if you inhabit it long enough—will become claustrophobic, not only for yourself but also for your readers. In Chapters 5 and 6, we showed how placing yourself in the contexts of history or art can help diffuse some of the inward-focus of creative nonfiction. In this chapter, we encourage you to direct your gaze outward, not leaving the self behind but perhaps sublimating the self to newly discover the subjects the world has to offer.

Lee Gutkind, founder and editor of the journal *Creative Nonfiction*, believes that one of the genre's essential missions is "to gather and present information, to teach readers about a person, place, idea or situation combining the creativity of the artistic experience with . . . research. . . . Read the books and essays of the most renowned nonfiction writers in this century and you will read about a writer engaged in a quest for information and discovery."

A good creative nonfiction writer will be attuned to the things of the world that beckon for examination. In this chapter, we've broken down the categories into a few that interest us, but as with all the prompts we provide in this book, these are mere gateways for your own creative instincts.

Science

A friend said recently that every time he opens up a newspaper these days he reads something that hits his view of the world with a thunderbolt: Stephen Hawking announces that we must use genetic engineering to evolve faster or computers will make us extinct; there may be infinite parallel universes; a religious group is working to clone human beings.

When you write about science in creative nonfiction, it becomes much more than a recitation or analysis of facts but a means of probing the deepest levels of our common existence. Right now we live steeped in startling scientific and technological advances. These changes signal more than quirky facts to recite; they invade our deepest assumptions about who we are. Here's where literary nonfiction writers become almost essential for our very survival.

We need Lewis Thomas to help us take in the infinite complexities science has found in cell behavior. We need Ursula Goodenough (also a cell biologist), who in her *The Sacred Depths of Nature* creates a sophisticated theology out of an examination of cellular life. We need Oliver Sacks, writing books like *The Man Who Mistook His Wife for a Hat*, to teach us how humans cope and remain whole while a myriad of neurological forces buffet them. Michael Pollan, in *The Botany of Desire*, plants genetically modified potatoes in his garden and maps out the exact nature of genetic modification and its implications for agriculture, as well as how it feels to grow these potatoes, classified by the EPA as "pesticides," not food. (Hint: he doesn't eat them.) Writer-scientists like Stephen Hawking take us by the hand through a changing cosmos that barely makes sense to physicists now.

The Layperson's Approach. Many personal essayists, such as Annie Dillard, draw heavily on scientific knowledge without being classified as science writers, per se. These authors may flesh out a personal experience with facts that enrich the narrative and that may also be alive with metaphoric significance. Dillard's well-known essay "Total Eclipse" begins with the bald declaration, "It had been like dying, that sliding down the mountain pass." She approaches this experience with a voice that is personal and vulnerable. She writes of the experience of a total eclipse as something that continually threatens to overwhelm her and the other onlookers. The intensity of her reactions ("God save our life," "the last sane moment I remember") continues to emphasize that vulnerability. This passion is matched by that of the cosmos she constantly fits herself into, one in which light and darkness exist in a constant dance of existence and extinguishing.

> *The Ring Nebula, in the constellation Lyra, looks, through binoculars, like a smoke ring. It is a star in the process of exploding. Light from its explo-*

*sion first reached the earth in 1054; it was a supernova then, and so bright
it shone in the daytime. Now it is not so bright, but it is still exploding.*

Because Dillard insists on switching back to the world of cosmic activity from
the world of human activity, we see her sense of being "obliterated" by the
eclipse as a coherent response to a cosmos where darkness can signal an ultimate end. Hers becomes a thinking reaction to the universe we're tied to so
intimately.

The Expert's Approach. Richard Selzer's perspective is different. He is an
essayist and also a practicing surgeon, and rather than recording his own vulnerability in his essay "The Knife," he records the fearful power his practi-
tioner's skills give him. Selzer implies again and again that perhaps no human
is fully equipped to have the life-and-death power of the surgeon: "A stillness
settles in my heart and is carried to my hand. It is the quietude of resolve lay-
ered over fear." As he operates, he records the following: "Deeper still. The
peritoneum, pink and gleaming and membranous, bulges into the wound. It
is grasped with forceps, and opened. For the first time we can see into the
cavity of the abdomen. Such a primitive place."

Selzer performs a matching "surgery" on his own emotions, delving deeper
and deeper into the emotional and philosophical aspects of his role. "Here is
man as microcosm, representing in all his parts the earth, perhaps the universe." Or: "And if the surgeon is like a poet, then the scars you have made
on countless bodies are like verses."

You don't have to be a veteran of the surgical theater to have a topic you
can approach as an informed voice. If you have mastered computer technology, been part of a field camp, dissected something, or learned to fix a car,
you have a subject you can write about with both expertise and poetry.

Sports Writing

It is astonishing how much we reveal about ourselves, personally and as a society, through sports. Think of the social implications of being a "tomboy" or
a "klutz," then think of the way sports figures embody our cultural idealiza-
tions. There's a reason a great basketball player or Olympic gymnast can use
his or her image to sell almost any product going. Reflecting about sports has

yielded much great writing on the topics of our societal concepts of success and failure, masculinity and femininity, and race, as well as a way of experiencing through words one of life's great visceral excitements.

David Halberstam, one of the editors of *The Best American Sports Writing of the Century*, describes the sports writing he presents as a portrait "of the nation itself during the explosive period" of the twentieth century. His coeditor Glenn Stout calls ours a "golden age" of sports writing. Both editors—seasoned writers themselves—credit the upsurge in this form to authors like Gay Talese and Tom Wolfe, who refused to sacrifice breadth and literary flair in their sports journalism. As Stout puts it, describing the Best American Sports Writing series, "at least once or twice in every edition it was proven, unquestionably, that the best 'sports writing' was . . . just good writing that happened to be about sports." Keep this in mind as you go through the exercises at the end of this chapter. Think about how your own sports obsessions reflect yourself and your culture and what larger questions—of race, violence, and gender—come into play in the sport you choose to write about.

Joyce Carol Oates's book *On Boxing* uses the sport to reflect on larger questions. Sports writing is a field still dominated by men; it's a little surprising to see a woman writing about sports, especially such a traditionally masculine sport as boxing. She begins the essay by complicating this kind of masculinity:

> *No sport is more physical, more direct, than boxing. No sport appears more powerfully homoerotic: the confrontation in the ring—the disrobing—the sweaty heated combat that is part dance, courtship, coupling—the frequent urgent pursuit by one boxer of the other in the fight's natural and violent movement toward the "knockout."*

Oates punctures most readers' basic beliefs about boxing, using specific observations of movements in the ring—movements mirrored by her jumpy, fragmented writing—to do so. She observes the embrace the fighters exchange after the fight and goes on to ask, "Are men privileged to embrace with love only after having fought?" Oates makes the bold statement that this proves man's greatest passion "is for war, not peace." You might disagree with her conclusions, but the essay uses a close observation of a sport Oates loves to ask questions about gender roles, the nature of love and intimacy, and our human instincts.

The Myriad Things Around Us

Can you imagine writing an entire book about a color? The writing of the *Oxford English Dictionary*? The flight path of a single type of butterfly? How about those clingy grains you thoughtlessly shake off your feet at the beach? Lovely, profound, and popular books have been published in the last few years about such seemingly small things.

Poet Theodore Roethke wrote, "All finite things reveal infinitude." William Blake wrote "To see a world in a grain of sand, / and heaven in a wild flower." These thoughts are not just poets' ideas but philosophical truths nonfiction writers have been among the most successful at plumbing. On the one hand, Annie Dillard's *For the Time Being* is a book about everything, and, on the other hand, a book about—sand. At least sand—a solid substance that flows and functions like water—forms a starting point for her long theological look at the flux of the world, Hasidism, and God.

OK, you might say, perhaps sand is interesting, but color? As Simon Garfield, author of *Mauve: How One Man Invented a Color That Changed the World*, discovers, mauve had a lasting impact on the culture of its day (and ours). The color was discovered by an eighteen-year-old chemistry student, who found it in a test tube in the course of trying out something else. The first synthetic color, mauve soon became a status symbol flaunted by royals, including Queen Victoria. (Contemporaries decried the aristocratic passion for mauve by calling streets pocked by wearers as having a case of "mauve measles.") And, naturally, the invention of synthetic color changed the textile industry and the economies of the day.

Hindus speak reverently of "Indra's net"—a web of interconnectedness with a jewel at each intersection that can be used to embody the interconnectedness of the world. Gifted writers like Dillard and Garfield find the "webs" attached to the subjects that draw them—the flowing and flux suggested by sand, the accident of a test-tube residue changing the fashions and industry of a nineteenth-century imperial power.

As a writer, once you begin to look closely at what's around you—recognizing both the closest details and the larger ways each thing fits into the "Indra's net" that holds us all together—nothing will seem less than a fruitful subject for your writing.

The Essay of Ideas

The essay has long been *the* form for exploring the workings of the human intellect. Running the gamut from argument to rumination, authors have always used the essay as a vehicle for both developing and expressing ideas, holding political debates, and delving into personal philosophy. Many of us have bad memories of writing "themes" in high school; the five-paragraph essay that rigidly prescribed the way an intellectual essay could work: thesis, three supporting paragraphs, and a tepid conclusion. Here, in the realm of creative nonfiction, you can redeem the essay of ideas and return it to its rightful place in the literary arts.

As with all good creative nonfiction, it's important to make the essay specific to you and your particular voice. Writing about abstract concepts does not need to be dull or dry; on the contrary, here is an opportunity for you to use the techniques of vivid writing to illuminate difficult and obscure topics. You will seek to uncover the scenes, the details, the images, and the metaphors that make for a memorable essay.

For example, in the essay "The Semiotics of Sex," Jeanette Winterson begins a highly complex discussion of aesthetics, art, and ideology with a scene in a bookstore:

> *I was in a bookshop recently when a young woman approached me.*
> *She told me she was writing an essay on my work and that of Radclyffe Hall. Could I help?*
> *"Yes," I said. "Our work has nothing in common."*
> *"I thought you were a lesbian," she said.*

With this brief scene, Winterson provides a compelling example that wholeheartedly admits the "I" into the intellectual discussion to follow. Rather than dryly elucidate her thesis in the first paragraph, *then* provide a support for that thesis, she does the opposite; she finds a scene that encapsulates her argument and she renders that scene in a way that reveals her personality, her voice, and her concerns.

It is the combination of a personal urgency with intellectual musings that makes the essay of ideas thrive. Remember "Notes of a Native Son" from

Chapter 5? Baldwin focuses on the death of his father, but issues of race and violence pulse through the essay, creating a political argument much more effective than any pundit's analysis.

Paradoxically, when you write about abstract concepts—ideas—it is even more important to pay attention to the concrete details that make such things comprehensible. The good essay of ideas will be a mix of argument and reflection—knowledge and experience—so that in the end the reader has gained some insight into both the ideas and the mind behind them.

TRY IT

1. Scientific facts are often rich in metaphor, as is scientific language. Great science writing draws the material facts of the universe into the process of reflection on the human experience. How would it inform your writing to know that doctors call the two coverings of the brain the "hard mother" (dura mater) and the "tender mother" (pia mater)? How does it change your sense of your own experience to know that physicists believe there may be an infinite number of parallel universes, containing what ours contains, in somewhat different form?

To speed you in the process of exploring the metaphorical value of scientific facts, do a twenty-minute freewrite on any of the following bits of information. Write whatever associations or suggestions come into your head. Which of your own experiences crop up when you think of these facts?

- The human body contains a vestigial tailbone.
- Our galaxy contains a black hole into which our solar system, including earth, will ultimately collapse.
- Stephen Hawking has said that if humans don't begin to use genetic engineering to modify themselves—including incorporating computer technology—computers will evolve past us and possibly cause our extinction.
- Clones are, for little-known reasons, abnormally large.

Before you begin your freewriting session, whether in a class or a writing group or alone, add to this list any facts that have stuck in your mind as suggestive, fascinating, or just bizarre.

After your freewriting session, assuming the material interests you, try expanding it into an essay this way: use a human story (it can be your own or someone else's) to intersperse with the scientific material. At some point in the essay, you must expand on the science, but promise yourself it will not dominate.

2. Identify an area of expertise you have. (We *all* have them!) Detail that work, as Richard Selzer does so carefully in "The Knife." Examine your role and the larger significance of it, as well as the role this specialized activity plays in human culture and your own life. Think of how it makes you feel, what aspect of your humanity it accentuates.

3. Examine a sport in terms of the imagery of its body movements, dress, rituals, and rules. Do any of these seem to defy our stereotypes of this sport? What social significance can you draw from what you see? How do you connect to this sport emotionally?

4. Think of a way in which a sport has had significance in your own life or that of someone close to you. Are there ways in which this personal experience and the sport, or a sports player's career, have run parallel? How? Can you think of a time when a sporting event had an emotional impact on an important event in your own life?

5. Freewrite a list of things you deal with on a daily basis and don't think about very much. Don't be choosy; jot down whatever pops into your head: paper, fluorescent lighting, mosquitoes, slugs, flush toilets. Then select one item from your list.

What are the larger metaphysical (that is, dealing with the properties of the universe at large) connotations of your item? Look at it if you can. Let's say you have chosen a piece of white paper. What does your paper suggest? What are the implications of its smoothness and whiteness? Of writing on pressed trees? Of writing within a square frame? Don't censor yourself but simply go with your impulses. Be weird. Be funny. Find the universe in the particular "grain of sand" in front of you.

Next, uncover a few facts about your item. They may be things you already know, or that classmates or group members can tell you (having a group discussion can really launch a great freewrite here; we trivia buffs are many!) or that you can look up quickly on the Internet. (See Chapter 11, "The Basics of Personal Reportage," if you're stymied.) Then do a second freewrite, focusing on details about your item that feel interesting or suggestive. Again, don't censor yourself. Feel free to be silly, and to be broad.

6. Make a list of the abstract concepts on which you have some opinions: racism, politics, gender wars, and so forth. Now circle one of these, and come up with a list of some specific examples from your own experience that elucidate these abstract concepts in a concrete way. How can you gain *authority* to talk about these issues? How can you demonstrate to the reader that you have firsthand knowledge of these topics?

7. Collect newspaper stories and magazine articles that strike you over the course of a few weeks. Gather these headlines together and begin to explore *why* these particular stories grab your attention. Begin to do a little research on the details of these stories to see if they could lead to a larger essay.

PART 2

THE FORMS OF
CREATIVE NONFICTION

The best work speaks intimately to you even though it has been
consciously made to speak intimately to thousands of others. The bad
writer believes that sincerity of feeling will be enough, and pins her
faith on the power of experience. The true writer knows that feeling
must give way to form. It is through the form, not in spite of, or
accidental to it, that the most powerful emotions are let loose over the
greatest number of people.

—JEANETTE WINTERSON

8

The Particular Challenges
of Creative Nonfiction

Of course a picture can lie, but only if you yourself are not honest or
if you don't have enough control over your subject. Then it is the
camera working, not you.

—ANDRÉ KERTÉSZ,
PHOTOGRAPHER

*I'm writing an essay about my grandmother. I'm not sure why I'm writing
this; there are just certain scenes and images that haunt me and I have to
get them down on paper: my grandmother immobilized in a hospital bed,
the ties of her hospital gown undone around her collarbone; my mother crying quietly in a restaurant as she tells me she can't bring herself to care for
her mother in her home. As I write, I have to make several questionable
choices: do I really remember massaging my grandmother's back that day in
the hospital? Now that I've written it, the scene's taken on the stamp of truth,
seems to have replaced any "real" memories I might have of that day. And
do I relate the scene of my mother's shame; is it really my story to tell? Can
I imagine a scene between my mother and my grandmother, the difficulty
of touch between them?*

*In the end, several months later, I decide to leave in the massage scene—
it has an emotional truth to it, a resonance that indicates to me the memory is valid, not only for the essay but for myself. But I delete the scene with
my mother in the restaurant; though the facts of this moment are more readily verifiable, I've decided that it oversteps some boundary I've set up for*

73

myself. That part is not my story to tell—I don't have the authority or the permission—and it feels too risky. I also, therefore, need to cut the scene where I imagine my mother and grandmother together in our family home. This is a difficult cut—I love the writing in that section—but it needs to go because the scene no longer fits in with the trajectory of the essay.

Yet I know that none of this writing has been wasted. Through writing the scenes I eventually eliminated, I came to understand what was important for this particular essay: to focus my attention on the metaphors of touch, the difficulties of such simple gestures within the family. I also learned how I draw the theoretical lines for myself, how I choose to go about negotiating the ethical land mines of creative nonfiction.

—BRENDA

Find Your Form—Find Your Slant

We began this book with a nod to Emily Dickinson and her mandate to "tell all the truth but tell it slant." Part 1, we hope, has helped you find out just what kinds of "truths" you may have to offer. Now your job is to find a way to "tell it slant," to find the forms that will contain these truths in the most effective and interesting ways. As a writer of creative nonfiction, you must continually make artistic choices that will finesse life's experience into art that will have lasting meaning for others.

Through a careful attention to form, you will be able to create art out of your own experience. Understanding *how* we are structuring our experience forces us to be concrete and vivid. Ironically, the more particular you make your own experience—with sensory details, compelling metaphors, and luscious rhythms—the more fully a reader will feel the personal story along with you. By experiencing it, the reader begins to *care* about it, because your experience has now become his own.

We hope that you will come to find that form is your friend; that by placing your allegiance in artifact over experience, the material becomes just that: raw material that you will use to fashion art, rather than the intractable stuff of memory and experience. To come back to our friend Emily Dickinson, in a letter to Thomas Higginson, she said, rather cryptically, "My business is circumference." By this she means perhaps that she circled her life, encompassing every hummingbird, every fly, every bit of bread into her art. All creative nonfiction writers should take heed. Observe your life from every angle—

cocking your head, squinting your eyes—then fashion what you see through a voice that is yours and yours alone. Tell us the truth, but shape it in a way that wakes us from our doldrums and startles us into a new grasp of our strange and remarkable lives.

A Few Caveats About Writing from Life

Creative nonfiction is a tricky business. On the one hand, you have the challenge—and the thrill—of turning real life into art. But on the other hand, you have to deal with all the issues that come attached with that "real life." When a fiction writer wants her character to remember the first time she ate ice cream, she can enter the problem imaginatively: place the character at Coney Island with a melting chocolate cone or at a birthday party with a neat scoop on a slice of cake. Can you do the same thing when you're writing from your own memory, even when you don't exactly remember the scene? A fiction writer is able to create the set amount of characters necessary for the story's action; can you do the same thing with the characters you encounter in your own life and research? When a fiction writer needs dialogue, she writes dialogue. As a nonfiction writer, can you make up dialogue you don't remember verbatim? When you're writing essays based on research, how much of your imagination can you use? Does "nonfiction" mean "no fiction"?

The self inhabits the prose of creative nonfiction, whether or not you write directly about your own experiences. It is this "I" that picks and chooses among the facts. This "I" re-creates those essential scenes and makes crucial decisions about what to include and what to exclude. The "I" decides on the opening line that will set up the voice of the piece, the essential themes and metaphors. The "I" gives the essay its *personality*, both literally and figuratively. The essential question, then, is how do you create a piece inhabited by the self without becoming self-centered? And how do you negotiate all the ethical and technical obstacles that come with writing from real life?

The "I" and the Eye: Framing Experience

A useful way of looking at how creative nonfiction employs the "I" is to align the genre with photography. Both photography and creative nonfiction operate under the "sign of the real" (a phrase coined by literary theorist Hayden White); both operate *as though* the medium itself were transparent. In other words, when you look at a photograph, you are lulled into the illusion that you see the world as it is—looking through a window, as it were—but in reality you are being shown a highly manipulated version of that world. The same is true with creative nonfiction. Because it operates under the sign of the real, it can be easy to mistake the essay as presenting life itself, without adulteration.

But both photography and creative nonfiction actually function just as subjectively as fiction and painting, because the personal "eye" is the mechanism for observation, and the inner "I" is the medium through which these observations are filtered. As Joan Didion puts it, "No matter how dutifully we record what we see around us, the common denominator of all we see is always, transparently, shamelessly, the implacable 'I.'" The minute you begin to impose form on experience—no matter how dutifully you try to remain faithful to history or the world—you're immediately faced with a technical dilemma: how do you effectively frame this experience? What gets left outside the confines of this frame? Are some frames more "truthful" than others? And the way you decide to frame the world directly reflects the "I" and the "eye" that perform this act of construction.

Wallace Stegner, in his book *Where the Bluebird Sings to the Lemonade Springs*, posits that our task as writers is "to write a story, though ignorant or baffled. You take something that is important to you, something you have brooded about. You try to see it as clearly as you can, and to fix it in a transferable equivalent. All you want in the finished print is the clean statement of the lens, *which is yourself*, [emphasis ours] on the subject that has been absorbing your attention." A good photograph will mirror the inner vision of the photographer, just as a good essay will reflect the unique sensibility of the writer, whether or not that writer focuses on material interior to the self.

The Persona of the First-Person Narrator

Just as the details of the world and experience may be framed or constructed by a mediating "I," so too is that "I" a fabrication for the purposes of the essay. We are not the same on the page as we are in real life, and we must be aware that the "I" is just as much a tool—or a point of view or a character—that we manipulate for particular effects. The "I" on the page is really a fictional construction, reflecting certain parts of us, leaving others out, or exaggerating certain aspects for the purposes of the essay at hand.

For instance, Bernard Cooper is not *always* obsessed with the sound of sighs, as he is in his essay "The Fine Art of Sighing," just as David James Duncan often has other things on his mind besides the baseball sent to his brother the day after the brother died, which he describes in his essay "The Mickey Mantle Koan." But, for the time span of the essay, they create themselves as characters with these obsessions that focus the piece and create its reason for existing at all.

In *The Situation and the Story*, memoirist Vivian Gornick writes about finding her voice in creative nonfiction. "I began to read the greats in essay writing—and it wasn't their confessing voices I was responding to, it was their truth-speaking personae," she writes. "I have created a persona who can find the story riding the tide that I, in my unmediated state, am otherwise going to drown in." The narrating "I," the persona you create, is the one who has the wherewithal to rescue experience from chaos and turn it into art.

The Pact with the Reader

As you create this persona, you also establish a relationship between yourself and the reader. In creative nonfiction—more so, perhaps, than in any other genre—readers assume a real person behind the artifice, an author who *speaks* directly to the reader. Just as in spoken conversations, it's a symbiotic relationship. The reader completes this act of communication through his attention to the author's story, and the author must establish right away a reason for the reader to be attentive at all. For this relationship to work, however, the author must establish a certain level of trust.

Simply presenting your work as an "essay" rather than a piece of fiction sets up certain assumptions. The reader will be engaged in a "true story," one rooted in the world as we know it. Because of this assumption, the reader needs to know he is in good hands, in the presence of, in Vivian Gornick's words, a "truth-speaking" guide who will lead him somewhere worthwhile. The reader needs to know he won't be deceived along the way, led to believe something that turns out to be patently untrue. Philippe Lejeune, in his seminal work *On Autobiography*, calls this the "pact with the reader." The essayist pledges, in some way, both to be as honest as possible with the reader *and* to make this conversation worthwhile. Without this pact, true communication becomes impossible.

As essayist Patricia Hampl puts it, "You tell me your story, I'll tell you mine." Without this understanding, we become more like the people you occasionally see in the park: men and women talking to themselves, rehashing past wrongs, their arms gesticulating wildly in the air. We don't really *listen* to such a narrator; in fact our impulse is to turn and walk in the opposite direction.

So, *how* does a writer establish this kind of pact with the reader? In the introduction to *The Art of the Personal Essay*, essayist Phillip Lopate writes that "part of our trust in good personal essayists issues, paradoxically, from their exposure of their own betrayals, uncertainties, and self-mistrust." When we reveal our own foibles, readers can relax and know they engage in conversation with someone as human as they are.

Good writers can also establish this pact through their skillful manipulation of the techniques that make for vivid writing (see Chapter 12). If we know we are in the hands of a literary artist—one who won't let us down with clichés or a weak infrastructure—then we're usually willing to go wherever he or she leads. We assume that the writer has shaped the material for its best literary effect, while at the same time remaining as true as possible to the "facts" of the world and history. Let's take a look at some famous essayists and see how they establish a pact with the reader early on in their work, combining craft with content:

Joan Didion ("Goodbye to All That"): "That first night I opened my window on the bus into town and watched for the skyline, but all I could see were the wastes of Queens and the big signs that said MIDTOWN TUNNEL THIS LANE and then a flood of summer rain (even that seemed remarkable and exotic, for I had come out of the West where there was no summer rain), and for the next three days I sat wrapped in blankets in a hotel room air-conditioned to 35° and tried to get over a bad cold and a high fever. It did not occur to me to call a doctor, because I knew none, and although it did occur to me to call the desk and ask that the air conditioner be turned off, I never called, because I did not know how much to tip whoever might come—was anyone ever so young? I am here to tell you that someone was."

E. B. White ("Afternoon of an American Boy"): "Seeing him, I would call 'Hello, Parnell!' and he would smile and say 'Hello, Elwyn!' and walk on. Once I remember dashing out of our yard on roller skates and executing a rink turn in front of Parnell, to show off, and he said, 'Well, quite an artist, aren't you?' I remember the words. I was delighted at praise from an older man and sped away along the flagstone sidewalk, dodging the cracks I knew so well."

Margaret Atwood ("Nine Beginnings"): "1. *Why do you write?* I've begun this piece nine times. I've junked every beginning. I hate writing about my writing. I almost never do it. Why am I doing it now? Because I said I would. I got a letter. I wrote back *no*. Then I was at a party and the same person was there. It's harder to refuse in person. Saying yes had something to do with being nice, as women are taught to be, and something to do with being helpful, which we are also taught."

Bernard Cooper ("The Fine Art of Sighing"): "You feel a gradual welling up of pleasure, or boredom, or melancholy. Whatever the emotion, it's more abundant than you ever dreamed. You can no more contain it than your hands can cup a lake. And so you surrender and suck the air. Your esophagus opens, diaphragm expands. Poised at the crest of an exhalation, your body is about to be unburdened, second by second, cell by cell. A kettle hisses. A balloon deflates. Your shoulders fall like two ripe pears, muscles slack at last."

What do you find in common with these four very different essayists? Though they write about quite divergent subjects, and from widely varying points of view, they've all constructed an "I" voice that speaks directly to the reader, and they all give the reader some evidence that it will be worthwhile to remain in this conversation. In her long, breathless sentences, Joan Didion reveals her embarrassment and timidity at being in a city where she knows no one and is unsure of the social conventions. Not only does she reel us in because of the details (we get to be on that bus with her), but she also laughs at herself and invites the reader to laugh with her. "Was anyone ever so young? I am here to tell you someone was." These two sentences establish that Didion has perspective on her experience. She has garnered some wisdom in the time between then and now, and so we won't be subjected to a rendition of raw emotion; rather the material will be shaped and presented by someone who is able to distance herself from the "I" who is a character in her story, and the "I" who narrates that story many years later.

E. B. White gains our trust because he is able to vividly describe a scene of childish delight and in such a way that we experience it along with him. Though we may never have had White's exact experience, he keys us into an experience that might be termed universal. Surely we've all experienced some moment of joy such as his, some moment when we were recognized by someone we admired. And if we haven't, White makes us wish we had, with his strong verbs ("dashing," "executing," "dodging"), and his powerful sentence structure that leaps and dodges and ends in a sigh of nostalgic satisfaction. White, like Didion, also shows us that he understands the difference between creating an "I" character in the story and a narrating "I" with the skills to render this story effectively. The line "I remember the words," while deceptively simple and commonplace, alerts the reader to the older writer's presence in the scene, looking on and rediscovering it along with the reader.

Margaret Atwood uses the form itself to establish that we're in good hands. She uses the interview question as a reason for writing in the first place, and then confesses that she'd rather do anything but write the essay we have in our hands. The tension between the question (which recurs nine times throughout the essay, an insistent voice that spurs the writer and reader on) and her tentative answers to that question, provide dramatic suspense for an essay that could easily, in other hands, become clichéd or predictable. Also, by confessing her difficulty with writing, she allows us to relate to her experience. It's as though she's giving voice to the doubts we all carry in our heads, a daring move that we silently applaud. She creates a persona, forthright and strong, who is able to say the things we ourselves might find difficult.

Bernard Cooper reaches out a hand and tugs us into his essay by starting off with the second-person point of view. "You feel a gradual welling up of pleasure." He makes us a participant in his essay by re-creating a sigh on the page. Read the passage aloud and see if you can keep from letting out a long, hearty sigh. And the "you" makes an assertion that's difficult to deny. The experience he creates on the page does indeed become a universal sigh, exhaled in common with thousands of others.

All these writers, along with the multitude of creative nonfiction writers we admire, must immediately make a case for taking up a reader's time and attention. In doing so, they also take care of the "so what?" question that plagues writers of creative nonfiction and of memoir in particular. Why should anyone care about your personal story or your perspective on the world? What use will the essay have for anyone outside of yourself? By engaging you in their essays through vivid details and an authentic voice, through imaginative uses of form and structure, these essayists show that the personal can indeed become universal. We care about their stories because they have become *our* stories. They have verbalized for us what has previously remained silent or have at least rephrased these issues for us in such a way as to make them new. That's what we're after as readers of literature: a fresh articulation of the world so that we might understand it more thoroughly. These essayists do so through both personal revelation and careful crafting of their prose.

The Permutations of "Truth": Fact Versus Fiction

If you set out to establish a pact with the reader—to gain his or her trust—then you must make some critical decisions about how—or whether—you will employ fictional elements in your nonfiction writing. As we've noted earlier, the simple act of writing and the construction of the narrative voice are essentially creative acts that impose a form where none before existed. Beyond that, what kinds of fictions are allowable and what are not in creative nonfiction? Just how much emphasis do we put on "creative" and how much on "nonfiction"?

Some writers believe that nothing at all should ever be knowingly made up in creative nonfiction. If you can't remember what color dress you wore at your sixth-grade graduation, then you better leave that detail out or do some studied research to find the answer. If you had five best friends in high school who helped you through a jam, then you better not compress those five into one or two composite characters for the sake of efficient narrative. On the other hand, some writers believe that small details can be fabricated to create the scenes of memory, and they knowingly create composite characters because the narrative structures demand it. Some writers willingly admit imagination into factual narratives; others abhor it and see it as a trespass into fiction.

It's interesting to note that when a writer publishes a piece of fiction that contains highly autobiographical elements, no one flinches; in fact, such blurring of the boundaries is often presumed. But to admit fictional techniques into autobiographical work creates controversy and furious discussion. The nature of that essential pact with the reader—that sense of trust—demands this kind of scrutiny into the choices we make as nonfiction writers.

We believe that every writer must negotiate the boundary between fact and fiction for him- or herself. What constitutes fabrication for one writer will seem like natural technique to another. But what we can do here is show how some writers employ fictional techniques and the effects these choices have on your credibility as an essayist.

Memory and Imagination

If your work is rooted in memory, you will find yourself immediately confronted with the imagination. Memory, in a sense, *is* imagination: an "imaging" of the past, re-creating the sights, sounds, smells, tastes, and touches (see Chapter 1). In her essay "Memory and Imagination," Patricia Hampl writes, "I am forced to admit that memoir is not a matter of transcription, that memory itself is not a warehouse of finished stories, not a static gallery of framed pictures. I must admit that I invented. But why?"

We invent because our lives and the world contain more than simple facts; imagination and the way we imagine are as much a part of ourselves as any factual résumé. In creative nonfiction, the creative aspect involves not only writing techniques, but also a creative interpretation of the facts of our lives, plumping the skeletal facts with the flesh of imagination. Personal history sometimes demands this kind of elaboration for its full significance to emerge on the page. Hampl continues, "We find, in our details and broken and obscured images, the language of symbol. Here memory impulsively reaches out its arms and embraces imagination. That is the resort to invention. It isn't a lie, but an act of necessity, as the innate urge to locate personal truth always is."

Look back to the tonsil story that precedes Chapter 1. There's no real way to verify either the fact or fiction of the tonsils floating in a jar on the bedside table. What I, Brenda, can do with this image is admit the bizarre and unlikely nature of this mental picture that imagination has called forth in conjunction with memory. I can say "Why do I remember this jar of tonsils at my hospital bedside?" In so doing, I readily admit the imagination into memory and can then proceed to construct an essay that both interprets the image for metaphorical significance and allows it to become a jumping-off point for a longer meditation on the topics this metaphor suggest. I do not discount or omit this image because its factual veracity is in question; rather I relish the opportunity to explore that rich boundary zone between memory and imagination. And I do so in full view of my audience, disclosing my intent, and so maintaining my pact with the reader.

Emotional Truth Versus Factual Truth

Mimi Schwartz in "Memoir? Fiction? Where's the Line?" writes, "Go for the emotional truth, that's what matters. Yes, gather the facts by all means. Look at old photos, return to old places, ask family members what they remember, look up time-line books for the correct songs and fashion styles, read old newspapers, encyclopedias, whatever—and then use the imagination to fill in the remembered experience." If we allow imagination into memory, then we are naturally aligning ourselves with a stance toward an emotional or literary truth; this doesn't mean that we discount factual truth altogether, but that it may be important, for *literary* purposes, to fill in what you can of the facts to get at a truth that resonates with a different kind of veracity on the page. Facts only take us so far.

Schwartz continues, "It may be 'murky terrain,' you may cross the line into fiction and have to step back reluctantly into what really happened—the struggle creates the tensions that makes memoir either powerfully true or hopelessly phony. The challenge of this genre is that it hands you characters, plot and setting, and says, 'Go figure them out!'—using fact, memory, and imagination to re-create the complexity of real moments, big and small, with no invented rapes or houses burning down." Here, Schwartz herself draws the line. We may reconstruct certain details, imagine ourselves into the stories *behind* the facts, but certain facts, such as a rape or a house burning down, cannot be invented. Or as novelist and memoirist Bret Lott puts it in his essay "Against Technique," "In fiction you get to make up what happens; in creative nonfiction you don't get to mess with what happen*ed*."

Take a look at the case of a highly publicized memoir, *Fragments: Memories of a Wartime Childhood*. In this lyrical narrative told from a child's point of view, Binjamin Wilkomirski re-creates scenes from his experience as a child survivor of the Holocaust. He recounts his father's execution in graphic detail, scenes of rats scurrying over piles of corpses. The prose is beautifully rendered, and some scenes move the reader to tears. But shortly after publication of this memoir, critics began to question Wilkomirski's veracity. One journalist did some investigation and found evidence that showed the writer had never been in a concentration camp at all. Birth certificates and adoption records showed him born in Switzerland in 1941 and adopted into a family shortly thereafter. However, Wilkomirski stood by his memories which were recovered, he said, in therapy. To him, these memories were as real—they carried just as much emotional truth—as the factual history.

Few people would argue that Wilkomirski hadn't crossed that ethical line for creative nonfiction. Though we've presented arguments that claim emotional truths can be just as veracious as facts, it is not acceptable to appropriate or wholly invent a history that has little or no relation to your own. You still need to use your own history as a scaffolding for the emotional truths you will uncover. While *Fragments* exemplifies this dictum in fairly obvious terms (to appropriate something as horrific and emotionally charged as the Holocaust leaves little room for debate), you need to see how it might operate in smaller ways within your own nonfiction writing. There are facts and then there are *facts*. Which ones are hard and fast?

For example, Annie Dillard has been brought to task simply for claiming to own a cat she never had. Her book *Pilgrim at Tinker Creek* begins with the line "I used to have a cat, an old fighting tom, who would jump through the open window by my bed in the middle of the night and land on my chest." Later in the paragraph she writes, "And some mornings I'd wake in daylight to find my body covered with paw prints in blood; I looked as though I'd been painted with roses." This image becomes important to her spiritual explorations throughout the book, and nowhere does she really acknowledge that the cat is a literary device or a fiction constructed for this purpose. For many readers, this constitutes a breach of contract; though Dillard uses the fictional cat to good effect, the fact that she has deceived the audience in some way undermines her credibility for the rest of the book. "How can we be sure of anything she says from here on out?" these readers would cry. Other readers are willing to exonerate Dillard for this fiction, claiming that it is not an important detail, and the cat is meant as a metaphorical device. After all, the book's subtitle is *A Mystical Excursion into the Natural World*. In the realm of mysticism, even nonexistent fighting toms might materialize to be our spirit guides.

What do you think? Where do you draw the line for your own work? Does Dillard undermine her pact with the reader? Would you be comfortable inserting such fictions in your own nonfiction writing?

"The Whole Truth?"

Sometimes you'll be troubled not by "facts" that are made up, but by those that are omitted. In essay writing, it's nearly impossible to tell the "whole" truth. Of necessity, you'll find yourself needing to pare away certain details, events, and characters to create an essay that makes narrative sense. For example, if you're writing about something that happened in school when you were ten years old, you'll have to decide just how many members of your fifth-grade class will make it onto the stage. Who is important and who is not, for this particular essay?

This is an easy one: you'll naturally choose to flesh out the one or two characters closest to you at the time. More difficult will be knowing when and how to omit the characters that felt important in real life but just get in the way once you land them on the page. For example, Bernard Cooper included his brothers in his early book *Maps to Anywhere*, but when he wrote the essays collected in *Truth Serum*, he made a conscious decision to leave his brothers out. This left him open to criticism from reviewers who said he deceived his audience by implying he was an only child. Here is his reply to them, from his essay "Marketing Memory":

I had three brothers, all of whom died of various ailments, a sibling history that strains even my credulity. . . . Very early in the writing of Truth Serum *I knew that a book concerned with homosexual awakening would sooner or later deal with AIDS and the population of friends I've lost to the disease. . . . To be blunt, I decided to limit the body count in this book in order to prevent it from collapsing under the threat of death. . . . There is only so much loss I can stand to place at the center of the daily rumination that writing requires. . . . Only when the infinite has edges am I capable of making art.*

"Only when the infinite has edges am I capable of making art." Perhaps that should be a credo we creative nonfiction writers etch on the walls above our desks. For that is what we're up to all the time: creating those edges, constructing artful containers that will hold some facts and not others.

These "edges" might also be formed by choosing to create "composite characters," or to compress events in time. A composite character is a fictional construction; the author blends the traits of several characters into one or two, thereby streamlining both the cast of characters and the narratives needed to take care of them. Compression of time means that you might conflate anecdotes from several trips home into one composite visit. As a writer and a member of a writing community, you'll want to think about these devices—and talk about them—to see how they conform to your own writing ethics.

Cueing the Reader

As you continue to develop your own guidelines for the permutations of truth in creative nonfiction, you'll find that you'll create your own tools for negotiating some of these tricky areas. Some simple ones to keep in mind, however, are *taglines* that let the reader in on what exactly you're up to. Phrases such as "I imagine," "I would like to believe," "I don't remember exactly, but," "I would like to remember," or even a simple "Perhaps," alert the reader to your artistic agenda. Once you set the terms of the discussion—once you situate the reader in that boundary zone between fact and fiction—then you most likely will be free to go wherever you wish.

For example, what would have happened if Annie Dillard said "I never owned a fighting tom, but I would like to imagine. . . ." Or she might have disclosed where she received the image: "I once had a friend whose fighting tomcat left paw prints of blood on her chest. I wish I had such a creature. . . ." For Dillard, this kind of tagline may have lessened the literary effect of the passage. But it would certainly diffuse any accusations against her credibility as well.

Cueing the reader can be accomplished even more subtly. If you have trouble writing a scene for a family event because it happened ten years ago, try beginning it with a line like, "This is how my father sounded," or, "This is what Sundays were like at my house." Then watch the pieces fall into place. These statements are unobtrusive, but they make it clear that you're not claiming to provide a verbatim transcript of an event.

Writers can also directly tell the reader what they're up to. Full disclosure lets readers know what we're in for. In a daring move, Lauren Slater titles a book *Lying: A Metaphorical Memoir*. Though this book is full of details that prove to be untrue, notably her descriptions of having epileptic seizures, Slater stands by her work with an obvious defense. The title tells us, quite bluntly, that she's fabricating metaphorical experiences. Though you may or may not buy this as a reader, you can't claim that she didn't warn you.

Pitfalls to Avoid: Revenge Prose and the Therapist's Couch

Ironically, while creative nonfiction can be a tool of self-discovery, you must also have some distance from the self to write effectively. You must know when you are ready to write about certain subjects and when you are not. If you are crying while crafting a piece of nonfiction, the tears will smudge the ink, ultimately making your work unreadable. If your hand shakes with anger while writing, the words will veer wildly across the page with no sense of control or design.

This is not to say that creative nonfiction is devoid of emotion; on the contrary, the most powerful nonfiction is propelled by a sense of urgency, the need to speak about events that touch us deeply, both in our personal history and those that occur in the world around us. The key to successfully writing about these events is *perspective*. Earlier in the chapter, we aligned creative nonfiction with photography. Perspective is the way a photographer chooses to frame and compose her photograph, and it is just as vital when you approach the tough subjects for personal essays. Perspective defines the difference between a journal entry meant only for private venting and the essay designed for public consumption.

As readers, we rarely want to read an essay that smacks either of the therapist's couch or revenge prose. In both cases, the writer has not yet gained enough perspective for wisdom or literature to emerge from experience. In therapist's couch prose, the writer is still weighed down by confusing emotions, or feelings of self-pity, and wants only to share those emotions with the reader. The depth of these emotions does not allow for a literary design to emerge. In revenge prose, the writer's intent seems to be to get back at someone else who has wronged him. The offender does not emerge as a fully developed character but only as a flat, one-dimensional incarnation of his awful deeds. In both cases, it is the writer who comes out looking bad, because he has not stepped back enough from the person or events to gain perspective.

As a writer, it is important for you to start recognizing when you can write about certain material and when you cannot. Perhaps it will take another twenty years before you are fully ready to deal with traumatic events in your childhood. It might take years before you're really able to deal with the breakup of your marriage. Or perhaps you will be able to write about a *small* aspect of the experience, focusing your attention on a particular detail that leads to a larger metaphorical significance outside of the event itself. For instance, remember David James Duncan and his koan of the signed baseball? He deals with the death of his brother years after the fact by focusing his attention on that signed baseball sent to his brother by Mickey Mantle. This baseball leads him to a philosophical rumination on the nature of life itself. This *peripheral vision*—this ability to sidle up to the big issues by way of a side route—is the mark of an accomplished writer, one who has gained enough perspective to use personal experience in the service of a larger literary purpose.

The best writers also show a marked generosity toward the characters in their nonfiction, even those who appear unsympathetic or unredeemable. For example, Terry Tempest Williams, in "The Clan of One-Breasted Women," writes an essay that is clearly fueled by anger, but it does not come across as personally vengeful or mean-spirited. Most of the women in her family died of cancer, an illness that could have been caused by the government's testing of nuclear weapons in her home state. By channeling her energy into research, she shows herself as someone with important information to impart, aside from her own personal history. She creates a metaphor—the clan of one-breasted women—that elevates her own story into a tribal one. By directing her attention to the literary design of her material, she is able to transcend the emotional minefield of that material. "Anger," she has said, "must be channeled so that it becomes nourishing rather than toxic." Her work is passionate, yes, but not shrill in a way that might lose her readers.

The Warning Signs

In your own work, always be on the lookout for sections that seem too weighed down by the emotions from which they spring. Here are some warning signs. Read the piece aloud and see if the prose has momentum. Where does it lag and become plodding? Those are the sections that probably haven't been refined enough to avoid melodrama. And seek out any sections that too directly explore your feelings about an event rather than the event itself. Where do you say words such as "I hated," "I felt so depressed," "I couldn't stand"? The "I" here will become intrusive, repeating itself into infinity: a monologue of old grievances.

If you find yourself telling the reader how to feel—and in a tone that's more like aggrieved chatter at a bar than convincing narrative—then you're probably headed right into revenge prose. You don't want to end up sounding like this, "And then you know what else that no-good jerk did? You won't believe this, even after *I* was the one to put him through medical school, and *I* was the one to bear his children, he says *he* needs some space, can you believe that? Space? What the hell does he need *space* for?" Channel your creative energy, instead, into constructing the scenes, images, and metaphors that will allow the reader to have her own reactions, *apart from the ones you had at the time*. On the page, your life is not just your life anymore; you must put your allegiance now into creating an artifact that will have meaning outside the self.

Try It

1. Have an individual or group session in which you plumb your own sense of nonfiction ethics. What would you do and what wouldn't you do? Would you re-create a scene or invent dialogue for someone without a clear cue to the reader? Would you invent a fact? It's useful to proceed in your writing with a defined sense of your own boundaries.

2. Practice writing cueing lines. This can be fun to do in a group, while passing one another's essays around or just writing inventive cueing lines to pass ("If I dreamed this scene, this is how I would dream it.") Sharing ideas will get you in the habit of using cueing lines creatively.

3. Try writing out a memory in scene from the perspective of at least two people who were present (members of your family, perhaps). Get their memory down as accurately as you can by questioning them, and write it as carefully and lovingly as you write your own. Think of this as an exercise in the quirks of individual perspective. If you like the results of this exercise, try juxtaposing pieces of each narrative, alternating the voices, to create a braided essay.

4. Try compressing time by creating one scene out of several similar events. For instance, take moments from several Christmas dinners and create one specific scene that encapsulates all of them. What do you gain and/or lose by doing this to your material?

9

The Personal Essay

After a time, some of us learn (and some more slowly than others)
that life comes down to some simple things. How we love, how alert
we are, how curious we are. Love, attention, curiosity. . . . One way
we learn this lesson is by listening to others tell us true stories of their
own struggles to come to a way of understanding. It is sometimes
comforting to know that others seem to fail as often and as oddly as
we do. . . . And it is even more comforting to have such stories told
to us with *style*, the way a writer has found to an individual
expression of a personal truth.

—SCOTT WALKER, EDITOR, *ESSAYS,*
MEMOIRS & REFLECTIONS

*I am a young woman in college, beginning to write. One day I pick up
Annie Dillard's book* Pilgrim at Tinker Creek. *A book-length, meditative
personal essay,* Pilgrim *documents the speaker's observations of the natural
world around her home in Virginia. It is at once deeply individual, as she
looks at the "rosy, complex" light that fills her kitchen in June, and deeply
philosophical, as she draws everything into relationship with the galaxy that
is "careening" around her. It is a bold book, drawing on the seemingly small
in order to embrace the entire world. More important to me at the time,
the speaker is a young woman in her twenties, the author herself. She's not
speaking with the authoritative male voice I have come to associate with the
essay. She speaks as Annie Dillard, with only the authority of our shared
human experience.*

> *I was fascinated to learn later that Annie Dillard originally began* Pilgrim at Tinker Creek *in the voice of a middle-aged male academic, a metaphysician. She didn't trust her own young woman's voice to engage and convince her audience. Other writers persuaded her to trust her voice and abandon the constructed one, and the book won the Pulitzer Prize, proving that the personal essay form is a broad one. It only requires that you be alert, perceptive and human.*
>
> —SUZANNE

The Personal Essay Tradition

The personal essay is "the way a writer has found to an individual expression of a personal truth." When Scott Walker wrote those words in 1986, the personal essay was making a comeback. The reading public seemed hungry for a form that engages us the way fiction does but that also teaches us something about the way real life works. While the phrase "creative nonfiction" had not yet come into popular use, "personal essay" seemed adequate to convey that sense of combining a personal voice with a factual story.

In the West, scholars often date the essay tradition back to the sixteenth-century French writer Michel de Montaigne. *Essays*, composed in Montaigne's retirement, lay much of the groundwork for what we now think of as the essay style: informal, frank (often bawdy), and associative. His book moves easily from a consideration of the classical author Virgil to pieces like "Of Thumbs." His title *Essays*, playing on the French verb meaning "to try," gives us the term we now use routinely in nonfiction writing. The essay writer "tries out" various approaches to the subject, offering tentative forays into an arena where "truth" can be open for debate.

Phillip Lopate, editor of the historically astute anthology *The Art of the Personal Essay*, puts it this way: "The essayist attempts to surround a something—a subject, a mood, a problematic irritation—by coming at it from all angles, wheeling and diving like a hawk, each seemingly digressive spiral actually taking us closer to the heart of the matter."

Prior to Montaigne, as Lopate's anthology illustrates, plenty of writers worked in what we would now consider a personal essay mode. Just a few examples include Sei Shonagon, a tenth-century Japanese courtesan who created elaborately detailed lists that revealed much about herself and her place in the Japanese court; the Japanese monk Kenko's meditative rumi-nations translated as *Essays in Idleness*; or Roman emperor Marcus Aurelius, whose book *Meditations* embodies an aphoristic essay style, creating pithy "slogans" as advice to those who will succeed him. The Stoic philosopher Seneca the Younger and the Greek biographer Plutarch both wrote "essays in disguise" in the form of letters that ruminated on a range of subjects, from noise in the marketplace to the proper comportment to maintain in the face of grief.

After Montaigne, British essayists such as Charles Lamb and William Hazlitt made the essay form their own. According to Lopate, "it was the English, rather than Montaigne's own countrymen, who took up his challenge and extended, refined, and cultivated the essay." Lamb wrote about intensely personal material. (His sister killed their mother and wounded their father; Lamb, himself, suffered a nervous breakdown.) But, he used a fictional per-sona that gave him some distance from his subject. Hazlitt wrote more in the style of Montaigne, creating essays with titles such as "On Going a Journey" and "On the Pleasure of Hating." At the same time in America, Thoreau was writing his journals and *Walden*, works that would form the foundation of American nature writing taken up by writers such as Edward Abbey and Annie Dillard.

As an essayist, you should take it upon yourself to study the tradition, not only for general knowledge but to situate yourself within that literary lineup. How does your own writing work with or against the stylistic tendencies of a Joan Didion, say, who in turn has a voice that emerges in direct dialogue with the voice of essayists such as George Orwell? Lopate's *The Art of the Personal Essay* is a good place to start, but also look at works of your contempo-raries to see how the essay is evolving in your own generation. The literary magazine *Fourth Genre: Explorations in Nonfiction* publishes some of the best contemporary writers in the form, as do the journals *Creative Nonfiction* and *River Teeth: A Journal of Nonfiction Narrative*. You should also avail yourself of the Best American Essays series. The editor, Robert Atwan, culls a selec-tion of the strongest essays published by American magazines in each year, and a guest editor pares those down further to a select few. While we will all have our own definitions of *best*, it is useful to read these anthologies to see what your contemporaries are up to. By reading widely, you will learn not only what is possible, but what has still to be discovered.

You may find, as Lopate has, that "at the core of the essay is the supposition that there is a certain unity to human experience." The personal essay carries the implication that the personal, properly rendered, is universally significant or should be. Montaigne echoes this. "Every man has within himself the entire human condition." At the same time, Lopate writes that "the hallmark of the personal essay is its intimacy. The writer seems to be speaking directly into your ear, confiding everything from gossip to wisdom." These two poles—intimacy of voice and universality of significance—go to the heart of the personal essay tradition. The essay speaks confidingly, as a whispering friend, and these whispers must be made meaningful in a larger context—capturing a piece of larger human experience within the amber of your own.

The Way Essays Work

What makes an essay an essay? How can you recognize one when you see it? When we study fiction writing or poetry, certain elements of form are easy enough to identify, such as plot or character development in short stories or lineation and rhythm in poems. Essays can be analyzed the same way, but the task is complicated by the wide variety of styles and forms encompassed by the term "personal essay." Many of these forms overlap with content, and perhaps you've already experienced several of them in the first section of this book. You've already been writing memoir, for example, when you focus on selected memories for a particular metaphorical or narrative effect. You've already started a nature essay when you described some aspect of the environment around you. Perhaps you've already tried the travel piece or a biographical sketch of someone close to you. Perhaps you've sidled up to the spiritual autobiography or the essay of ideas. All of these are forms, defined more by content than craft.

When we turn our attention to craft, we can begin to see some stylistic qualities that help to define the essay form. In his essay "A Boundary Zone," Douglas Hesse describes the difference between essays and short stories in terms of movement. In any narrative prose piece, some sense of forward movement emerges. Visualized as a horizontal line, this line keeps the story moving forward. Some essays read almost like short stories. In the well-known essay "The Fourth State of Matter" by Jo Ann Beard, the horizontal line is a shooting at the author's workplace at the University of Iowa. She begins the piece before the shooting and continues through the event and its emotional aftermath. Three other strands also propel the essay forward: a dying collie, a divorce, and squirrels inhabiting her attic. All these form miniplots, very much like a short story. She uses dialogue freely and re-creates scene with vivid, specific details. And the essay itself reads like a short story because of the present-tense voice (a narrator), and the sense of horizontal story lines unfolding and intersecting at the same time.

In contrast, a more essaylike narrative might have a stronger vertical line to it, the reflective voice that comments upon the scenes it re-creates. David James Duncan works in this mode. In "The Mickey Mantle Koan," the forward, horizontal line of the narrative—the brother's death—is interrupted, or balanced, by his ruminations on the koan of a signed baseball arriving after his brother's death. This reflective voice runs underneath the horizontal line, creating a sense of movement that delves below the surface of narrative.

Once you begin seeing essays in terms of their movement, you can decide how your own work might fit or work against the categories of personal essay. At one extreme, we have the short-story style that engages us with plot, subplots, and scenes. At the other extreme is the analytic meditation that engages us through the power of the writer's interior voice. Where do you fall on this grid? How can you expand your talents and write essays that create their own definitions?

Memoir

Remember, most essays use elements of different literary approaches. For instance, one piece by John McPhee might contain within it nature writing, science writing, and memoir. But for purposes of scrutinizing our own work and understanding our traditions, we can discuss nonfiction in terms of categories, bearing in mind all the while that we don't want to allow ourselves or the writers we admire to be limited by those categories.

A nonfiction category strongly linked with the personal essay is memoir. *Memoir* comes from the French word for *memory*; no writer of any stripe is prescient enough to put everything he or she wants to record into notes, therefore drawing on memory is an essential part of what we all do. Some readers confuse anything written with a first-person "I" that draws on personal experience with memoir, though new journalists like Joan Didion and Tom Wolfe indulge freely in both without necessarily being memoirists. And some writers, reacting to criticism that the form has become overly confessional and overly prevalent, avoid the term memoir when that's exactly what they're writing.

To be memoir, writing must derive its energy, its narrative drive, from exploration of the past. Its lens may be a lifetime or it may be a few hours. In "Total Eclipse," Annie Dillard recollects a past event, but her narrative drive—the punch of the piece—is metaphysical meditation, not memoir. On the other hand, in his "Afternoon of an American Boy," E. B. White writes a piece of pure memoir. His lens is small; he recalls a period in his teenage years when he first got up the courage to ask a girl out to dance—"that precious, brief moment in life before love's pages, through constant reference, had become dog-eared."

William Zinsser, who edited *Inventing the Truth: The Art and Craft of Memoir*, says, "Unlike autobiography, which moves in a dutiful line from birth to fame, memoir narrows the lens, focusing on a time in the writer's life that was unusually vivid, such as childhood or adolescence, or that was framed by war or travel or public service or some other special circumstance." In other words, memoirists need not have had fascinating lives, worth recounting in every detail. (Those kinds of books, as Zinsser notes, are generally considered autobiography.)

Memoir mines the past, examining it for shape and meaning, in the belief that from that act a larger, communal meaning can emerge. Memoir can heal, it can warn, and it can provide spiritual direction. Spiritual memoir—like the writings of Kathleen Norris and Andre Dubus, among others—falls in the last category. Memoir can open societal lines of communication on subjects previously held taboo. For example, Richard Hoffman's memoir of child sexual abuse, *Half the House*, eventually led to the prosecution of a child molester.

In his essay "Backtalk," Hoffman provides a defense of the surge of memoir as a corrective to a culture that has accepted the verb *to spin* to mean deliberate distortion of our news. "The ascendance of memoir . . . may be a kind of cultural corrective to the sheer amount of fictional distortion that has accumulated in [our] society." For those of you interested in the memoir form,

Hoffman's words may provide a useful starting point; think of yourself as an "unspinner," a voice striving to undo some of the cultural distortion you see around you.

Though memoir is the nonfiction form most closely associated with an "I," it can be written in second or third person; Judith Kitchen uses third person in her brief memoir "Things of This Life," for instance. These kinds of techniques—experiments with point of view, use of different tenses (past, present, future), finding just the right metaphorical image to anchor the piece—all serve to help the memoir elevate itself out of self-centered rumination and into the arena of art.

Literary or New Journalism

In 1972, for an article in *New York* magazine, Tom Wolfe announced "The Birth of the 'New Journalism.'" This new nonfiction form, Wolfe claimed, would supplant the novel. It allowed writers the luxury of a first-person voice and the use of literary devices—scene, imagery, and so forth—in the service of reporting. In other words, Wolfe's new journalism marries traditional journalism with the personal essay. Wolfe cited such new journalists as Hunter S. Thompson, then writing a first-person account of his travels among the Hell's Angels.

Wolfe emerged as one of the leaders of the new journalism, along with other writers such as Joan Didion, Gay Talese, and Norman Mailer. Wolfe rode buses with LSD guru Ken Kesey and his Merry Pranksters to write *The Electric Kool-Aid Acid Test*, all the while using his first-person voice liberally and appearing in his trademark starched high collars and white suits, a character in his own right. Wolfe's insistence on the primacy of his own experience in the act of reporting comes through even in his titles, like this one of an essay about Las Vegas (surely one of the loudest cities in the country): "Las Vegas (What?) Las Vegas (Can't Hear You! Too Noisy) Las Vegas!!!!" New journalism does stress the act of reporting; its practitioners have done some of the most intense reporting in the nonfiction world. But they also avail themselves of literary techniques and a personal voice.

As research becomes more crucial even to very personal nonfiction, such as Terry Tempest Williams's *Refuge* or Andrew Solomon's *The Noonday Demon* (a heavily researched but intimate look at depression), the line between other forms of nonfiction and new journalism blur. And, in the age of instant information on the Internet, traditional journalism becomes more interpretive and less formulaic. Think of it as a healthy blurring of the categories that can sometimes stifle the evolution of forms.

The Meditative Essay

Composing his essays, Montaigne referred to himself as an "accidental philosopher." The term *essay* carries a double meaning of both *trying* and *proving* or *testing*. To essay an action means to attempt it; to essay a substance, particularly a metal, means to test it, weigh it, and try to determine its composition. The essay itself enfolds this dual nature of the term—essays typically approach their subjects tentatively, allow readers the luxury of seeing the author roll ideas around in his or her mind, *test* conclusions rather than presenting them.

The essay form lends itself to tentative, meditative movement, and the meditative essay derives its power from careful deliberation on a subject, often but not always an abstract one. Some meditative essays announce their approach in their title, like Abraham Cowley's *Of Greatness*. In "Total Eclipse," Annie Dillard recalls the event of the eclipse in great detail before switching to her true subject, a metaphysical meditation on our relationship to the universe:

> The mind wants to live forever, or to learn a very good reason why not. The mind wants the world to return its love, or its awareness; the mind wants to know all the world, and all eternity, and God. The mind's sidekick [the body], however, will settle for two eggs over easy.

Another example of the meditative essay is Richard Bausch's "So Long Ago." Bausch's meditative intent comes through in the essay's opening, where he addresses the reader in a conversational tone that both engages us and signals that he's about to take us step by step through his thoughts:

Indulge me, a moment.

I have often said glibly that the thing which separates the young from the old is the knowledge of what Time really is; not just how fast, but how illusive and arbitrary and mutable it is. When you are twenty, the idea of twenty years is only barely conceivable, and since that amount of time makes up one's whole life, it seems an enormous thing—a vast, roomy expanse, going on into indefiniteness.

Time—and how we perceive it—is an abstract and slippery subject. Bausch's confiding voice, leading us into his meditation as if we're going into a difficult but rewarding conversation, engages us from the outset. He weaves memories, notably a funeral, among his meditations on the larger importance of time and history. "We come from the chaos of ourselves to the world, and we yearn to know what happened to all the others who came before us. So we impose Time on the flow of events, and call it history."

Without specific events, it's hard to imagine such an abstract meditation holding our interest. The best meditative essayists instinctively make this technique their own. They probe concrete events until they yield up the deeper meanings that lie buried below the surface.

The Sketch or Portrait

One of the most popular essay forms of the nineteenth century, the sketch or portrait held ground partly because of the lack of other forms of communication—the average person traveled little and, even after the invention of photography, saw far fewer photos than we see today. Writers like Dickens stepped into the breach, offering verbal snapshots of cities, foreign countries, and people.

Today we have newspapers, TV, even the Internet, but the power of language to provide not just verbal pictures but emotional ones keeps the portrait an important form. Immediately after the September 11th attacks on the World Trade Center and the Pentagon, the *New Yorker* magazine commissioned a handful of writers to capture that day in short verbal portraits, collectively titled "First Reactions." The editors realized something crucial about that world-changing event: photos may best hold the searing image of the buildings, but a writer can also capture the reality of "stumbling out of the smoke into a different world" (Jonathan Franzen).

The character sketch is also an integral part of the portrait form. Originally a kind of verbal photograph, portraits still can capture individuals in a way visual forms cannot, using imagery and description to leap from someone's surface to their essence. Maxine Hong Kingston's "No Name Woman" forms at once a largely imaginary portrait of the author's disgraced aunt and a portrait of her very real mother:

> *If I want to learn what clothes my aunt wore, whether flashy or ordinary, I would have to begin, "Remember Father's drowned-in-the-well sister?" I cannot ask that. My mother has told me once and for all the useful parts. She will add nothing unless powered by Necessity, a riverbank that guides her life. She plants vegetable gardens rather than lawns; she carries the odd-shaped tomatoes home from the fields and eats food left for the gods.*

What a world of information is packed into this formidable portrait! We see Kingston's mother sketched before us in terms of telling actions—choosing the practical over the ornamental, refusing to waste food, even for presumably religious reasons. We're prepared by this sketch for the tension mother and daughter experience over the suppression of the aunt's story, and the way that story reflects their own uncommunicative relationship.

Humor

Of all the audience responses writers may want to elicit, none is harder to gauge than humor. It's hard to argue about the sentimental value of people falling in love or the tragedy of war, but we all tend to have a comedy vocabulary peculiarly our own. Emily Dickinson, who lends our book its title, had a peculiar habit of roaring with laughter over the obituaries every day. The use of humor in the personal essay dates back to Montaigne and earlier. Let's look at some specifics of what we as a species tend to find funny.

Incongruity

In *How to Write*, Stephen Leacock said, "Humor may be defined as the kindly contemplation of the incongruities of life and the artistic expression thereof." The juxtaposition of odd or unexpected things makes up a lot of what we find comic.

In his essay "The Drama Bug," humorist David Sedaris falls in love with theater and affects a Shakespearean speech that becomes hilarious in juxtaposition with the ordinary events occupying his teenage years. Over a chicken dinner with family, he proclaims, "Methinks, kind sir, most gentle lady, fellow siblings all, that this barnyard fowl be most tasty and succulent." Humor writers like Sedaris are constantly mining their lives for incongruities to use in their work.

The Twist

Like the incongruity, the twist arises from simple surprise—a verbal rug pulled out from under the reader. In *The Deer on a Bicycle: Excursions into the Writing of Humor*, Patrick McManus describes how he fell in love with writing. "I bore down on my next essay with a diligence and concentration previously unknown to me in any academic subject. The effort paid off. A D-minus!"

Given that McManus is detailing the discovery of his vocation, we expect bells to go off with this essay of his—the D-minus comes as a funny (and self-deprecating) surprise. Anne Lamott also offers the reader wonderful twists; hers help ground a spiritual discussion that threatens to become overly solemn. "I believe that every plane I get on is doomed, and this is why I like to travel with Sam [her son]—so that if and when the plane goes down, we will at least be together, and almost certainly get adjoining seats in heaven— ideally, near the desserts."

Life's Irritations

Patrick McManus offers a wonderful piece of advice: write humor out of your bad experiences, not your good ones. Think about it. Which would make a better essay, your best family car trip, with snacks and singing "Kumbaya," or the worst, with your father muttering oaths over a flat tire while your little sister screams for a bathroom or else? What was awful then is probably hilarious now. Some of life's most irritating things—telemarketers, computerized voice answering systems, HMOs—yield some of its most reliable humor.

Exaggeration and Understatement

Exaggeration or hyperbole is a classic American form of humor, dear to practitioners like Mark Twain, who once swore that in a tour of Europe he'd seen the equivalent of a "barrelful" of nails from the True Cross. While the exaggeration is evident, Twain's comment makes a point about the number of false religious relics on display in Europe at the time. Sedaris clearly exaggerates in the long-winded pseudo-Elizabethan speeches he delivers in "The Drama Bug"; no one could remember their own monologues that precisely. (And surely his family would have swatted him with the barnyard fowl before listening to all of that!) Lamott is another comic exaggerator. It's a device she uses again and again to great effect, as when she describes a reading in which "I had jet lag, the self-esteem of a prawn, and to top it off, I had stopped breathing. I sounded just like the English patient."

Self-Deprecation

One characteristic that Sedaris and Lamott have in common is the self-puncturing qualities of the authors. They laugh at themselves so freely we feel encouraged to laugh with them—and, if we're honest with ourselves, we all have a gold mine of material in self-deprecation. No one knows our foibles better than we do. If you look at the Lamott quote—the "self-esteem of a prawn. . . . I sounded just like the English patient"—you'll note that she's laughing above all at how seriously she took herself at the time of this bookstore reading. Most comics exemplify Rodney Dangerfield's "I don't get no respect" attitude. They mine their own insecurities and attempts to make themselves larger—like Sedaris adopting the fake Shakespearean diction—to laugh at themselves and encourage us to laugh at those qualities in them, and in the process, at the whole human condition.

TRY IT

1. Write a short piece of memoir using a particular event. Write quickly and then examine the piece in light of the distinctions between the intimate and the universal. Where do you speak as though the reader is a friend, listening at your side? Do you need to reveal more of yourself, of your feelings? And where is the universality of your experience? You may want to trade with a partner to uncover the answers to these questions. You can seek out E. B. White's "Afternoon of an American Boy" as a model for this prompt.

> **VARIATION:** With Richard Hoffman's comments in mind, write a memoir of an event that seeks to "unspin" some kind of official version of it.

2. Write a journalistic story, perhaps about a colorful place nearby or an event in your community (a protest? a festival?) that uses reportorial style to capture the story but also includes your own presence as a character. Use literary devices to describe the people you see; use metaphor to paint their lives. Take advantage of literary devices, while respecting the factuality of journalism.

3. Write a sketch of a person or a place. Focus on keeping your work vivid and simple—a language portrait. Think of it as being intended for someone who cannot meet this person or visit this area.

4. Write an essay titled "On _____." Fill in the blank yourself and use the title as a way to explore an abstract concept in a personal and concrete way. All of us have abstract questions we would secretly love to write about. Why are we here? What does it mean to love a child? Why does society exist in the form it does?

5. Write down the abstract question you would most like to explore. Then freewrite a group of events you somehow associate with that question: a brush with death, giving birth, living in a different culture. Meditate on the question, alternating your meditations with the actual event.

6. Practice writing deliberate incongruities, twists, exaggerations, and understatements. What is the strangest sight you've seen over the last year? Was it a

Hare Krishna at an airport talking on a cell phone? A Santa Claus withdrawing money from an ATM? What experience in your own life led to the most unexpected conclusion, à la McManus's D-minus essay?

7. What irritates you? Write a few paragraphs on the most constant irritants in your life, whether it's telemarketers, the fact that you have almost the same phone number as the local pizzeria, whatever. Write dialogue and scene; strive to be funny. At the same time, think, as previously, of larger subjects this irritant suggests.

8. Actor Billy Bob Thornton constantly pokes fun at himself for his phobias and obsessions, notably a fear of flying and of antique furniture (!). True or not, these self-lampoons are extremely funny. What are your most humorous foibles? What do friends and family lampoon you about? What do these foibles say about you, and our human aspirations?

10

The Lyric Essay

I go out of my way, but rather by license than carelessness. My ideas
follow one another, but sometimes it is from a distance, and look at
each other, but with a sidelong glance . . . I love the poetic gait, by
leaps and gambols.
—MICHEL DE MONTAIGNE

I find myself thumbing through an encyclopedia of Jewish religion I hap-
pened to pick up at the library. As I turn the pages of this marvelous book,
I'm struck by how little I, a Jewish woman who went to Hebrew school for
most of my formative years, know about my own religion. I start writing
down the quotes that interest me most, facts about the Kaballah and ritual
baths and dybbuks and the Tree of Life. I've also started noodling around
with some other stories: a recent trip to Portugal and the news I received
there of my mother's emergency hysterectomy; notes on the volunteer work I
perform at the local children's hospital; and musings about my on-again,
off-again yoga practice. As I keep all these windows open on my computer,
the voice of the encyclopedia emerges as an odd, binding thread, holding
together these disparate stories in a way that seems organic. I begin to frag-
ment the stories and to move these fragments around, finding the images
that resonate against one another in juxtaposition.

I feel like a poet, creating stanzas and listening for the rhythms of the
sentence, using white space, reading aloud to determine when another quote
from the encyclopedia is necessary to balance out my personal story. Some-
times I have to throw out whole sections that no longer fit, but this editing
leaves room for new segments, new phrases, new images that build and

transform over the course of the essay, weaving in and out, but always grounded on the thread of prayer and the body. It takes some time, this shuffling gait, but finally I have an essay, "Basha Leah": a spiritual self-portrait in the form of a complex braid.

This lyric essay allows for the moments of pause, the gaps, the silence. The fragmentation feels correct to the piece: it allows for the moments of "not knowing," the unspoken words that seem truer than anything I could ever say aloud.

—BRENDA

What Is the Lyric Essay?

Lyric. Essay. How do these two terms fit together? At first these words may seem diametrically opposed. *Lyric* implies a poetic sensibility concerned more with language, imagery, sound, and rhythm over the more linear demands of narrative. *Essay,* on the other hand, implies a more logical frame of mind, one concerned with a well-wrought story, or a finely tuned argument, over the demands of language. When we put the two together, we come up with a hybrid form that allows for the best of both genres.

To put it simply, lyric essays do not necessarily follow a straight narrative line. The root of the word *lyric* is the lyre, a musical instrument that accompanied ancient song. Lyric poetry and essays are songlike in that they hinge on the inherent rhythms of language and sound. Lyric essays favor fragmentation and imagery; they use white space and juxtaposition as structural elements. They are as attuned to silences as they are to utterance. In its thirtieth anniversary issue devoted to lyric essays, the *Seneca Review* characterized them as having "this built-in mechanism for provoking meditation. They require us to complete their meaning."

The writer of the lyric essay brings the reader into an arena where questions are asked; it is up to the reader to piece together possible answers and interpretations. Fragmentation allows for this type of reader interaction because the writer, by surrendering to the fragmented form, declines a foregone conclusion. Writer and literary theorist Rebecca Faery notes, "In the essays that have in recent years compelled me most, I am summoned, called upon. These essays are choral, polyphonic; there are pauses, rests. . . . The rests in these essays are spaces inviting me in, inviting response."

The lyric essay requires an allegiance to intuition. Because we are no longer tied to a logical, linear narrative or argument, we must surrender to the writing process itself to show us the essay's intent. In so doing, we reveal ourselves in a roundabout way. When we write in the mode of the lyric essay, we create not only prose pieces but a portrait of our subconscious selves, the part of us that speaks in riddles or in brief, imagistic flashes.

Part of the fun of the lyric essay will be making up your own form as you go along. But, for the sake of argument, we will break the lyric essay down into four main categories that seem to encapsulate the lyric essays we see most often: prose poem (or flash nonfiction), collage, the braided essay, and a form we've dubbed the "hermit crab."

Prose Poem or Flash Nonfiction

For the introduction to their anthology *The Party Train: A Collection of North American Prose Poetry*, the editors begin with this piece by S. C. Hahn called "If My Father Were to Ask":

> *"What's a prose poem?" I would turn my face and look into the distance away from our farm house, into a wild copse of trees which runs from the road's edge and on up the hill to the far fields. Box elder, green ash, and black locust tangle in a net of branches, tied together by thorny greenbrier. I know of a coyote den beneath one old box elder tree, on the edge of a gully cutting through the copse. If I were to stick my hand into the hole, I could feel cool wet air and perhaps the playful teeth of pups.*
>
> *"Remember when you plowed the fields in the spring," I say to my father, "and the air behind you filled suddenly with sea gulls?" I can see him inhale the aroma of memory: the green and yellow tractor, the motor exhaust and dust, steel blades of the plow sinking into the earth and turning it, the smell all sexual and holy, worms and grubs uncovered into sunlight, then an unexpected slash of white as the gulls materialize behind the plow, a thousand miles and more from any ocean.*

What is a prose poem? Well, maybe it's the feeling you get when you're standing in a landscape you know well and love, a landscape where you can imagine what lies hidden behind the trees or beneath the ground. Maybe the prose poem is the "aroma of memory" and all the sensual details they evoke. Or maybe the signature of the prose poem is the unexpected surprise at the end, the improbable appearance of sea birds above the plowed fields of the heartland.

Maybe the prose poem is all these things, but most importantly, the prose poem speaks to the heart rather than the head. The prose poem is about what is possible, not necessarily what has already occurred. Even the title, "If My Father Were to Ask," privileges imagination over experience. The father has not asked the question, but what if he did?

In this way, the terms *prose poem* and *flash nonfiction* could be nearly interchangeable. Flash nonfiction is a brief essay—usually less than a thousand words—that focuses on one particular image. It is tightly focused, with no extraneous words, and it mines its central image in ways that create metaphorical significance. The language is fresh, lyrically surprising, hinged on the workings of the imagination. Lawrence Sutin, in his innovative book *A Postcard Memoir*, writes discrete pieces of flash nonfiction as he meditates on the old postcards in his collection. Though the pieces themselves are longer than anything one might write on the back of a postcard, they maintain that same kind of compactness, that intent to be concise and say only what is important for the moment at hand.

This form is fun to both write and read. A new online magazine *Brevity* "publishes concise literary nonfiction of 750 words or less focusing on detail and scene over thought and opinion." W.W. Norton has issued two volumes of short nonfiction, edited by Judith Kitchen and Mary Paumier Jones, called *In Short: A Collection of Brief Creative Nonfiction* and *In Brief: Short Takes on the Personal*. In the introduction to *In Short*, Bernard Cooper elucidates the stance of the lyric essayist working in the flash nonfiction form: "To write short nonfiction requires an alertness to detail, a quickening of the senses, a focusing of the literary lens, so to speak, until one has magnified some small aspect of what it means to be human."

Collage

Do you remember, as a child, making collages out of photographs, images cut from magazines, bits and pieces of text gathered from ticket stubs, documents, or newspaper headlines? Often, these mosaics represented the self in a way that no other form could quite accomplish. Our teachers gazed down at us lovingly as we showed them these renderings, our selves displayed in fragments made beautiful by their juxtapositions.

The collage essay works in the same way. It brings together many different fragments and assembles them so they create something wholly new. *Juxtaposition* becomes the key craft element here. One cannot simply throw these pieces down haphazardly; they must be carefully selected because of how they will resonate off one another. In this way, you act as a painter might, scrutinizing how this particular blue will shimmer against this particular yellow. You must listen for the echoes, the repetitions, the way one image organically suggests the next.

The writer must also provide some kind of grounding structure for the reader to hold onto. Going back to those collages you made as a child, they would be useless collections of fragments without the poster board and glue used to hold the pieces in place. The supporting architecture for a collage essay can take the form of numbered sections, or it can be subtitles that guide the reader along. Or the structure may be as subtle as asterisks delineating the white space between sections. The title, subtitles, or an epigraph (opening quote) can provide a hint of direction for the reader.

For example, in his short essay "My Children Explain the Big Issues," Will Baker relies on the title and the subtitles to hold together four stories about his children he has culled from memory. The subtitles—"Feminism," "Fate," "Existentialism," and "East and West"—do all the explaining he needs to do; they act as bridges, or supports, that allow Baker to write what appear to be four disparate fragments and turn them into one cohesive essay. Without the title or the subtitles, these stories would remain charming vignettes, but they would not carry the impact or hold the focus necessary for an essay. The collage structure works well here because each fragment is allowed to stand on its own while still working in concert with one another. The architecture of the piece works on a subtle level. We think we are reading over the title and subtitles, barely noticing them, but they work on our subconscious throughout our experience of the piece.

Collages work through repetition but not in a monotonous way. You must *transform* your recurring motifs from beginning to end. You must make transitions but not in the conventional way. In the collage essay, transitions occur through the strategic placement of images, stories, and phrases. How does one story lead to the next? Which image can you pick up from the last section to begin the next? Which phrase can act as a repeating and variable mantra throughout the piece? You must trust yourself and your readers to make sense and meaning out of the gaps between steps, the pauses between words, but you must also act as a guide on this pilgrimage, a pathfinder who directs with a touch we barely notice.

The Braided Essay

On the Jewish Sabbath, we eat a bread called challah, a braided egg bread that gleams on its special platter. The braided strands weave in and out of one another, creating a pattern that is both beautiful and appetizing. We eat a special bread on the Sabbath because this day has been set aside as sacred; the smallest acts must be differentiated from everyday motions.

The braided challah is a fitting symbol for an essay form closely allied with collage: the braided essay. In this form, you fragment your piece into separate strands that repeat and continue throughout the essay. There is more of a sense of weaving about it, of interruption and continuation, like the braiding of bread, or of hair.

In his prize-winning essay "After Yitzl," poet Albert Goldbarth braids several different strands together to create a highly textured essay. Written in numbered sections that at first seem to have little to do with one another, the essay works through a steady accretion of imagery and key repetitions; it speaks in a voice that grows loud, then whispers, that cuts itself off, then rambles. The strands include, among other things, a sleepy conversation in bed with a lover, a fabricated "previous life," facts about Mormon religion and Piltdown Man, a story about a cult called the "Unarians," and stories about his own (real) ancestry. The sleepy conversation provides the overall "container" for the essay, an architecture that holds the fragments in place and provides forward momentum to the piece. But by fragmenting this narrative, Goldbarth allows for the other strands to have equal weight. He returns to the conversation over and over and repeats phrases from the other strands, so that the essay never seems to veer off topic.

And that topic slowly reveals itself. The essay turns out to be about how we fabricate our own pasts, constantly and continually; how memory itself is a myth; and how we create ourselves anew in the stories we tell. The braided form allows this theme to emerge organically, to accrue in the reader's mind until it takes on the aspect of an inevitable truth. He explodes his prose to put it together again in a new pattern that is inordinately pleasurable.

The braided form also allows a way for research and outside voices to intertwine with your own voice and experience. When you write a braided essay, find at least one outside voice that will shadow your own; in this way the essay will gain texture and substance.

The "Hermit Crab" Essay

Where we—Suzanne and Brenda—live, in the Pacific Northwest, there's a beautiful place called Deception Pass. Deception Pass is prone to extreme tides, and in the tide pools you can often find hermit crabs skulking about. They look a little like cartoon characters, hiding inside a shell, lifting up that shell to take it with them when they go for cover. They move a few inches, then crouch down and stop, become only a shell again. Then they tilt, waver, and scurry away.

A hermit crab is a strange animal, born without the armor to protect its soft, exposed abdomen. And so it spends its life occupying the empty, often beautiful, shells left behind by snails or other mollusks. It reanimates these shells, making of them a strange, new hybrid creature that has its own particular beauty, its own way of moving through the tide pools and among the rocks. Each one will be slightly different, depending on the type of shell it decides to inhabit.

In honor of these wonderful creatures and the transformative habitat in which they live, we've dubbed a particular form of lyric essay the hermit crab essay. This kind of essay appropriates other forms as an outer covering, to protect its soft, vulnerable underbelly. It is an essay that deals with material that seems born without its own carapace—material that is soft, exposed, and tender, and must look elsewhere to find the form that will best contain it.

The "shells" come where you can find them, anywhere out in the world. They may borrow from fiction and poetry, but they also don't hesitate to armor themselves in more mundane structures, such as the descriptions in a mail-order catalog or the entries in a checkbook register.

For example, in her short story "How to Become a Writer," Lorrie Moore appropriates the form of the how-to article to tell a personal narrative. The voice of the narrator catches the cadence of instructional manuals, but at the same time winks at the reader. Of course these are not impersonal instructions but a way of telling her own story. And by using the literary second person, the reader is unwittingly drawn along into the place of the narrator and a natural interaction develops:

> First, try to be something, anything, else. A movie star/astronaut. A movie star/missionary. A movie star/kindergarten teacher. President of the World. Fail miserably. It is best if you fail at an early age—say, fourteen. Early, critical disillusionment is necessary so that at fifteen you can write long haiku sequences about thwarted desire.

Though "How to Become a Writer" is fiction, the story can act as a fine model for innovative lyric essays in the how-to mode. What are the aspects of your life that you could render in how-to form? How will the second-person address enable you to achieve some distance from the material and thus some perspective? These types of essays can be quite fun to write; the voice takes over and creates its own momentum.

In his essay "Primary Sources," Rick Moody appropriates the form of a footnoted bibliography to write an autobiography. In "Nine Beginnings," Margaret Atwood takes on two different forms; ostensibly it is a question/answer piece with only one persistent, annoying question. But the title also suggests the form of crumpled first drafts, fished out of the wastebasket. Nancy Willard has written an essay called "The Friendship Tarot" that begins with a sketch of a tarot card layout; she then goes on to insert her autobiographical story into the interpretation of that layout. Several writers have fashioned essays in the form of "to-do" lists. Sei Shonagon has written her lists of "Depressing Things," "Adorable Things," and so forth. The possibilities are endless.

Look around you. The world is brimming with forms that await transformation. A recipe for making soup, handed down by your grandmother, can form the architecture for an essay that fragments a family narrative into the directions for creating something good to eat. An address book that shows the many different places you or your family has lived can begin to shape the material of memory and history. A table of contents, an index, an itinerary, a playlist—all these speak with recognizable voices that might work as the right container for your elusive material.

By taking on the voice of an exterior form for your internal story, you automatically begin the process of creating an artifact out of experience. The form, while it may seem restrictive, actually allows you a great deal of possibility. Suddenly the second-person voice or the third-person perspective is available to you. You're able to take a step back and view your experience through a new lens. Often the form itself will lead to new material you never even suspected.

Think in terms of *transformation*. The word itself means to move across forms, to be changed. Think of the hermit crab and his soft, exposed abdomen. Think of the experiences you have that are too raw, too dangerous to write about. What if you found the right shell, the right armor? How could you be transformed?

TRY IT

1. Go back to one of your own pieces and turn it into fragments. Take a pair of scissors to it and cut it up into at least three different sections. Move these around, eliminating what no longer fits, juxtaposing the different sections in various ways. How can you make use of white space? How can you let the images do the talking for you?

2. Wander the streets of your town looking for random objects. Gather as many of these as you like, then bring them back to your desk and start arranging them in a way that is artistically pleasing. Then write for several minutes on each object and see if you can create a fragmented essay that juxtaposes these elements in the same way.

> VARIATION FOR A GROUP: Go out and gather objects individually, but come back together as a group to sift through the pile. Use each other's objects to create three-dimensional collages. Then write for one hour to create a collage essay using these objects as a guide.

3. Write an essay that has fewer than five hundred words. Give yourself a time limit—a half-hour, say—and write about one image that comes to mind or an image that has stayed in your memory from the last couple of days. Use vivid, concrete details. Do not explain the image to us but allow it to evolve into metaphor. If you are stuck, open a book of poetry and write down the first line you see as an epigraph (an opening quote). Write an essay using the epigraph as a starting point for either form or content or imagery. If you write more than five hundred words (about two pages), you must trim and cut to stay under the limit. Find what is essential.

VARIATION FOR A GROUP: Each person should bring in a line of poetry as an epigraph and offer it to a partner. Write for fifteen minutes, and then pass this epigraph to the next person. Write again for fifteen minutes. Continue this process for as long as you like. Try shaping one of these experiments into a complete essay of fewer than five hundred words.

4. Study a painting or a photograph that you have looked at often. What is it about this image that appeals to you so much? Begin a short essay, fewer than a thousand words, that focuses on some unexpected detail that catches your eye in this artwork. Explore this detail for metaphorical significance.

VARIATION FOR A GROUP: Each person brings in a postcard of an artwork; these are all set on a table in the front of the room. Each person browses these postcards and chooses one that appeals to him or her on an intuitive level. Begin writing. You can do this as many times as you like until an image sparks a piece of writing that interests you.

5. Structure an essay around a journey of some sort, using brief, discrete sections to build a collage. This can be a journey to somewhere as commonplace as the mall, or it can be more romantic. What kind of purposeful journey can you imagine taking, such as a pilgrimage to a sacred place?

6. Choose at least three distinctly separate time periods in your life. Begin each section with "I am _____ years old," and freewrite from there. Stay in the present tense. After reading what you've written, see if you can start finding any thematic connections or common images that would link the sections together.

7. Experiment with transitions and juxtaposition. Find one image to repeat in the essay from start to finish, but transform this image in some way so that it has taken on new characteristics by the end of the collage essay.

8. Go back to an essay that's been giving you problems. Look for the one image that seems to encapsulate the abstract ideas or concepts you're trying to develop. Find at least one outside source that will provide new information and details for you. Explode the essay into at least three different strands, each focused on different aspects of that image, and begin weaving.

9. Write an essay in the form of a how-to guide using the second-person voice. You can turn anything into a how-to. In Lorrie Moore's book *Self-Help*, she has stories titled "How to Talk to Your Mother" and "How to Be the Other Woman."

10. Choose a field guide to the natural world as your model ("A Field Guide to Desert Wildflowers," for example, or "A Field Guide to the Atmosphere.") Write an essay in the form of a field guide, inserting your own experience in this format.

11. Write an essay in the form of an interview or as a series of letters.

12. Brainstorm a list of all the forms in the outer world that you could use as a hermit crab essay model. We've done this with groups that have come up with lists of sixty entries and more! The possibilities are endless. Examples of what they came up with include crossword puzzle clues, horoscopes, fortune cookies, letters to the editor, and missing kids flyers. Choose one of these forms and begin an essay, using your own material to flesh out the "shell." Let the word choices and tone of your shell dictate your own approach to your topic. How would the vague cheeriness of fortune-cookie fortunes or horoscopes inform your family or relationship tale?

13. Write a list of the topics/issues in your life that are "forbidden" to speak about, the things you could never write. Choose one of these, and then begin to write about it in a hermit crab form.

11

The Basics of Personal Reportage

Facts in all their glorious complexity make possible creativity. The best nonfiction writers are first-rate reporters, reliable eyewitnesses focused on the world, not themselves, and relentless researchers with the imagination to understand the implications of their discoveries.

—PHILIP GERARD

Working on a book that combined memoir with environmental writing, I found in many areas I was overwhelmed with information. Pesticide research, industrial waste, radiation, and the course of the Cold War: books, papers, old newspapers piled up and slid off my desk, defying all attempts at organization. In other ways, though, I found questions that had no answers: questions about the root causes of environmentally related disease, family stories that were irreconcilably different in everyone's telling. It was an enormous relief to sit at my desk one day and realize that the lack of answers—the evasions, the uncertainties, the whole process—was a story in itself. I continued to research as doggedly as I could, but when I came up blank again and again, I began asking that emptiness whether it had a story to tell. One day I conclude the tale of a particularly frustrating phone call with these words: "I make telephone calls, hour after hour. Mostly I listen to message machines. EPA sends me to DEP, which sends me to ATSDR, which sends me to the County Board of Health, which says it has no records."

By the time I wrote this passage, I had tried to write around what I couldn't uncover, in many awkward and unsuccessful ways. I avoided subjects I needed to confront, or I tried to fake a knowledge I didn't have. I

finally realized—with a liberating shock—that the reader needed to con-
front my own frustrations and uncertainties just as I had, in order to under-
stand this story. The reader needed to hear and see the whole inquiry, even
the phone calls that petered out into more avenues of possibility without
certainty.

—SUZANNE

Cultivating the Need to Know

It should be clear by now that many of the methods we recommend for you
to use to expand your subject horizons—placing yourself in history, in the
world, braiding, and so forth—are probably going to involve research of some
sort or another. Our view of research doesn't mean hours in a library poring
over dry technical works, unless that's something you want to do. Anything
that takes you out of the realm of what you already know is research. All writers need to expand the ideas that feed them—the "flood subjects," as Emily
Dickinson called them—that form those subjects dearest to us for meditation and writing. Our "flood subjects" may never change—if you write about
nature, for example, or children, or medicine, you probably always will—but
we can and must expand the ground they cover.

Annie Dillard used to teach at our institution, Western Washington University. Science librarians still joke about her weekly forays into the science
section and the way she tottered up to the checkout desk with armloads of
reference books. Insects, sand, eclipses—nothing escaped Dillard's interest.
The range of her interests is evidenced by her essay titles, such as "Death of
a Moth" or "Living Like Weasels."

Porosity

Perhaps we can equate openness to research with openness to incorporating
the world around us and its events into our own life meditations, a kind of
artistic *porosity* to the world around us. Porous materials, such as fabrics,
absorb what comes in contact with them. The best nonfiction writers have a
special porosity to what is around them; they're unable to ignore even a moth
they happen to notice.

Not everyone will want to do full-blown investigative journalism. It's worth remembering that sometimes the best research we can do involves going somewhere we wouldn't normally go and talking to people we wouldn't normally talk to—and of course, really listening. Are you writing an essay about someone who lifts weights? Get a day pass to a gym and absorb the culture of weight-lifting—how lifters push themselves, how muscle curves out of itself when flexed. Imaginatively, see your subject there.

If you want to write about your childhood, don't settle for your memories but look at all the media that shaped your world. Check out magazines from the early years of your life from a library; watch Nickelodeon reruns from that period on television; or go to Historycentral.com and look up the key songs, plays, films, and news events of those years. Confront primary sources, such as documents, photos, films, newspapers, even gravestones; you will often find discrepancies between stories people tell you and the facts you uncover, discrepancies that reveal a lot about your stories and your subjects.

If you are writing about your parents, think about them as human beings at that earlier time—what messages were they hearing? How did those messages help shape them into the people they were?

Using Fact as Metaphor

Factual research will most often be used for what it is: fact. Water may contain a certain complex of chemicals; weight lifting may have such-and-such an effect on the body. These facts can become the basis of an essay that explores the physical wonders and limitations of our world. At times, however, fact will also function as metaphor, informing the essay both on its own terms—information about the physical world the reader may need or find interesting—and as a basis for comparison for a more intangible part of the piece.

One novice writer, Jen Whetham, wrote an essay, "Swimming Pool Hedonist," chronicling how swimming and swimming pools have defined her and held her milestones: learning to trust, early sports success, even a first sexual encounter. The first draft of the essay began by saying "My earliest memory is at a swimming pool," and included a passing reference to the odor of chlorine. That odor turned up again and again, and so Jen researched the chemistry of chlorine; she came up with this section in her final version:

> *My skin has always smelled like chlorine. . . .*
>> *Chlorine is missing one electron from its outer shell: this makes it highly attractive to other molecules. Chlorine's extreme reactivity makes it a powerful disinfectant: it bonds with the outer surfaces of bacteria and viruses and destroys them. When it kills the natural flora on human skin, the reaction creates the stuffy, cloudy smell we associate with chlorine.*
>> *Chlorine marks us in ways we cannot see.*

The essay goes on to use the touchstone of chlorine—odorless, changing forever what it contacts—as a metaphor for all the invisible ways life touches and changes us, and how we touch and change one another. It is a subtle and nuanced use of fact as fact and fact as metaphor.

Researching a Key Fact or Detail

Peter Balakian set out to write a family memoir in his book *Black Dog of Fate*. Yet, as he probed memories of life with his immigrant family in New Jersey—communal meals, days spent at his grandmother's helping her as she baked—he began to notice that the real story of his family lay in a subject they did *not* discuss: their now-vanished homeland of Armenia, including the fate of family members who had remained there. Finally, by asking questions of his family and doing his own historical research, Balakian came to grips with the real story haunting him: the massacre of the Armenians by the Turks early in the twentieth century. The massacre was so successful it gave Hitler the confidence to conceive of the Holocaust.

In Terry Tempest Williams's "The Clan of One-Breasted Women," the close of her book *Refuge*, Williams begins to examine the larger forces that may be contributing to her family's high breast cancer rate. In the following excerpt, you can see her seamless and organic movement from personal history into researched analysis. She has, as this dialogue begins, told her father of a recurring dream she has of a flash of light in the desert.

"You did see it," he said.

"Saw what?"

"The bomb. The cloud. We were driving home from Riverside, California. You were sitting on Diane's lap. She was pregnant. . . . We pulled over and suddenly, rising from the desert floor, we saw it, clearly, this golden-stemmed cloud, the mushroom. The sky seemed to vibrate with an eerie pink glow. Within a few minutes, a light ash was raining on the car. . . ."

Williams goes on to tell us that "above ground atomic testing in Nevada took place from January 27, 1951, through July 11, 1962." Williams provides an analysis of the political climate of the period—the growth of McCarthyism and the Korean War—summarizes litigation stemming from the tests, and returns seamlessly to her own story. She clearly researches the dates of the bomb testing as well as the wind patterns during those years, but she weaves those facts unobtrusively into her own narrative.

Working with Immersion

Immersion refers to the technique of actually living an experience—usually briefly—to write about it. The late George Plimpton, who was writer and editor of the *Paris Review*, lived for a while as a football player to research the book *Paper Lion*. Lee Gutkind, writer and editor of the journal *Creative Nonfiction*, has done a great deal of immersion writing: he has lived as a circus clown and has followed transplant doctors and umpires on their rounds. Several years ago Robert Sullivan lived for months with the Makah Indian tribe and observed their hunt for gray whales in his book *A Whale Hunt*.

Writers differ in their approaches to immersion research. Gutkind writes of the writer's need to become invisible, almost a piece of furniture in the room with the subject(s): "I like to compare myself to a rather undistinguished and utilitarian end table in a living room or office," he writes. Didion, on the other hand, is always a presence in her research, one whose shy, questioning self forms another character in the piece.

Several years ago a woman we know read about an adult nightclub in Seattle; it was one of the only such clubs in the United States owned and run entirely by women, with a woman-friendly and safe atmosphere. She visited the club, whose dancers were mainly college women and single mothers. Her immersion experience resulted in an essay uncovering a fascinating side of a business generally viewed as exploiting and degrading to women.

Developing Interview Skills

You'll find as many interview styles as there are writers in this world. Writer Gay Talese's polished assurance invites confidence. On the other side of the spectrum are writers like Joan Didion and John McPhee, both of whom describe themselves (or are described by others) as so shy and unsure that interviewees tend to underrate them. It's important to remember artistically as well as ethically that when you conduct research and interview people, their words may ultimately be used in ways they won't like. Didion puts it bluntly, "Writers are always selling somebody out."

Regardless of your style, there are some tips that will help any interview go more productively. Most researchers ask a few "throw-off" questions—those with simple and unimportant answers—to relax their subjects before moving on to more difficult questions. And, as far as that goes, the toughest questions should be saved for last. If someone shuts down because you asked why he or she supported the Iraqi War, for example, you don't want that confrontation to ruin the entire interview. Begin with the simplest and least emotional information, and move forward from there.

Always begin an interview with a list of questions you want to ask; a prepared list will prevent you from forgetting to ask something important because of nerves or simple absentmindedness. Also, end interviews with an open-ended question that will direct you to your next research source. For example, "What do you think is the best place to go for information about the war?" "Are there other people I should speak to about this subject?"

Philip Gerard advises that you always strive to use interviews to find primary sources. "An interview may be a great start," he says, "but will that person also let you read his or her diary, letters, business correspondence?" Gerard tells the story of a F. Scott Fitzgerald scholar who found the most valuable document in studying Fitzgerald turned out to be the writer's tax returns, chronicling his inflated lifestyle and his debt.

Above all, put your questions out there, pause, and really listen. Have your list of questions ready, but be prepared to change course when you get an answer—or a partial answer—that intrigues you. If your subject says casually, "Well, of course John wasn't around then because he was in jail for a while," follow up on that point right away; don't continue with your checklist. You may forget to come back to it, or the person you're speaking to may regret having let it slip. Listen carefully, and follow up on what you hear.

Developing Print Research Skills

Here, we'll explore three commonly used and easily accessed print research sources—the library, the Internet, and primary sources, such as legal documents and statistics.

The Library

The best thing about libraries, we think, is reference librarians. The smallest library contains an overwhelming wealth of information. There are newspapers from all over, going back many years; reference books from the obvious, World Book–type books to dictionaries of chronologies and disasters; specialized encyclopedias; works on microfilm; and tapes and videos. When you know just what you want, the computer or card catalogue will steer you to it. When you don't—say you have a general question about molecular physics or weather or genealogical research—reference librarians will point you to the right sources and help you find what you need.

We went to several of our favorite librarians for advice on how to use the library's resources most effectively. Western Washington University's Paul Piper's first tip was to develop a relationship with your research librarian—introduce yourself, and try to keep working with the same person. He or she will get a sense of what you want and keep a lookout for materials you can use. Piper also recommends spending time articulating to yourself what you're really looking for. He remembers well a patron who asked for books on dogs, then, after wasting quite a bit of time in the dog section, complained she couldn't find anything about the life cycle of the flea there! Dogs are dogs; fleas are fleas. Articulate your interest to yourself as clearly as you can.

Al Cordle, a reference librarian in Portland, Oregon, gave us this piece of advice: "I have a favorite technique for locating books in my library. I always go to the online catalogue and type in one or two keywords to describe my topic and the word *dictionary* or *encyclopedia*. Almost without fail I find specialized reference books devoted to my research topics." Cordle notes that keyword searches, as opposed to subject searches, can be more successful because the search engines operate more flexibly with keywords. Keyword searching should be an option offered by any library computer's toolbar. "So, for example," says Cordle, "if I type *encyclopedia* and *Native Americans*, I may come up with *Encyclopedia of Minorities in American Politics*, *Native Americans: An Encyclopedia of History, Culture, and Peoples*, and *The Encyclopedia of North American Indians*."

Even without the help of a reference librarian, libraries are not hard to navigate if you keep in mind that most print information can be tracked through master sources found in the library's reference section. To begin, articulate to yourself as specifically as you can what information you're looking for. If you had to ask one question to move forward on this writing project, what would it be? Once you have that specific question (or questions) in mind, identify the major reference works that might help you.

If you delve deeply into reference sources covering books and periodical literature, you will come across print sources that sound tantalizingly perfect for your research but that your library does not hold and aren't available on online archives either. Go to the information desk and inquire about your library's interlibrary loan policy. Almost anything, including out-of-print books and old newspapers on microfilm, can be borrowed through interlibrary loan. You may have to wait a few weeks for the text to appear and do a lot of reading rather quickly once it arrives, as these items generally can only be kept for several weeks. But knowing you've solved a puzzle or put together information no one else has by tracking little-known sources is part of the thrill of research.

The Internet

Most researchers agree the Internet forms the most important new research tool we have now, offering access to trillions of pages of material at the touch of a finger. This massive access also forms the Internet's biggest drawback: the large volume of unsorted material it turns up. Still, it's one of the best quick sources of information available now, especially for facts that don't hold too much ambiguity. If you want to know the migration habits of the gray whale, a quick search will get this information for you, along with maps and sound (if your computer has speakers) that will enable you to hear the grays making their way along the coast. This is quite a large payoff for very little effort.

Reva Basch, coauthor of *Researching Online for Dummies*, breaks down the areas in which Internet research is most useful. The first is to get background information on a subject, and the second is for fact-checking. AskJeeves and Refdesk.com are both highly recommended sites for fact-checking, and a site like the Library of Congress's American Memory (memory.loc.gov/ammem /amhome.html) will give you an excellent overview of any subject that could be considered historical, such as Watergate, or more recent topics like the last election. American Memory, like many other resource sites, even houses video and audio clips.

A number of search engines track what's published in thousands of print sources, and many offer abstracts or summaries of the articles—some offer complete copies. Check your library for its list of online resources to see what specialized search engines you can use there if the right engines aren't available on your home computer (assuming you have one). A few to look for: Infotrak, which is an exhaustive list of periodical publications; PDQ, which offers in many cases abstracts and complete articles; and Northern Light's Special Collections (northernlight.com), which gives access to many specialized magazines. (Northern Light charges a small fee, but your library may offer it for free.)

If you can think of an institution that would house information you need, consider checking its website. Museums, government organizations, the Library of Congress, all offer immense amounts of information on the Web. You might, for instance, wonder what the Smithsonian Institution in Washington, D.C., a premier science source, could tell you about eclipses. Use a search engine to access the Smithsonian's site, then follow its navigation instructions to access its online resources. You can often figure out Web addresses even without search engines; if you want information on nuclear energy, you might start with the U.S. Department of Energy. Put their abbreviation (DOE), with the .gov suffix used by all government agencies, after the basic World Wide Web address of www, and voila—there it is.

There are services available on the Web, called research services, that find articles for free and then make money by charging you for copies. One that uses a powerful search engine and does not require an initial fee, recommended by *Rules of Thumb for Research*, is Colorado Alliance of Research Libraries (CARL) at carl.org. If you find a helpful-looking article, you can either pay the small fee charged by CARL for a copy, or try to find the article through a local library.

You can begin playing with Internet research—assuming you haven't done this already—by choosing a good browser and search engine and typing in key words or phrases that capture your interest. Give this process a dry run just to see how it feels—choose a subject that has either interested you for a long time, or something you take absolutely for granted, maybe "the molecular structure of DNA" or "the electoral college." (We don't think much of the vagaries of how we vote, we just do it.)

Learn to scrutinize both the search engine summaries and the sites themselves for clues to how useful or downright flaky they are. The suffixes .edu and .gov, for instance, indicate sites run by educational institutions (edu) and the U.S. government (gov). A number of sites run by leading-edge universities like MIT have pages on the molecular structure of DNA, as does the World Book online (worldbookonline.com); the identities of these sources are clear from their URLs, or Web addresses. Several government sites, denoted by their .gov suffix, have good explanations of the electoral college. Lots of sites will also come up that you'll probably want to give a pass—sites not relevant to your question, personal online diaries, even stories about alien DNA! Or maybe these are another essay altogether.

Remember that computers are literal creatures. The woman searching for information on fleas can stumble through an explanation by looking for dog books, however much time she may lose approaching the subject that way. No search engine, however, can intuit the leap from "dog" to "flea." Phrase your search as precisely as you can without narrowing it down too much. "AIDS in Africa" will result in hundreds of thousands of sites; "AIDS in unwed mothers between the ages of twenty-eight and twenty in the lower Volta delta" probably won't yield any. And try alternative terms to see if you uncover more or better results—both "FBI" and "Federal Bureau of Investigation," for example.

Primary Sources

One writer we know wanted to research a point in family history about which he'd heard conflicting stories—his grandparents' marriage and the birth of his mother. Visiting the courthouse in the county where the marriage took place, he requested his grandmother's marriage license and was handed a license to a marriage other than the one to his grandfather. Intrigued, he recovered copies of both marriage licenses, wedding announcements that ran in the newspapers of the time, and his mother's birth certificate—and discovered his grandmother had been pregnant and just divorcing when she married his grandfather. Back in the 1930s both events would have prompted a great deal of scandal. Tensions in family relationships suddenly fell into place.

You may not discover anything quite so interesting, or you may find something far more interesting, but the fact is, courthouses keep records of births, adoptions, marriages, divorces, deaths, and more. Anyone can request copies; you visit the courthouse in the proper town or county, ask to see the directory of records, and request copies of what you want. Or you register with an online service like Courtlink (lexisnexis.com/courtlink), which, for a fairly low fee, can generally obtain legal documents on file anywhere in the country. If you're researching a topic in a particular town, you might want to try the historical society; most towns have them, and they keep all sorts of documents, including deeds of sale, photographs, and frequently, diaries and old publications. Old newspapers, too, teem with information, and are kept in local libraries on microfilm. You may want to back up your family interviews with research into what really happened.

There are so many other print sources of information they're hard to list here. The Government Printing Office, for example, has reports and statistics available on everything imaginable, from Congressional testimony to government-sponsored research. The Television Archives housed at Vanderbilt University contain tapes of television broadcasts, including news broadcasts as well as programs, going back to the earliest days of television. You can also request written transcripts of old broadcasts. It's possible, through intelligent research, to immerse yourself completely in another place and time.

Winnowing Down

Here's an example of the genesis of a research-driven essay. Jennifer Price, author of the essay "A Brief Natural History of the Plastic Pink Flamingo," commented that she had "no desire to write about the flamingo until I learned the guy who invented it was named Featherstone, he and his wife wore matching outfits every day that his wife sewed, and they had a poodle named Bourgeois." These stray facts convinced Price the lawn flamingo, brainchild of an eccentric inventor, might hold a story she wanted to tell.

In the course of investigating the American phenomenon of lawn flamingos, Price learned that people from film directors to *New Yorker* editors held cherished collections of the birds, and that one lawn flamingo had been kidnapped; its kidnappers sent back photographs "from" the bird as it traveled the world, against backdrops like the Eiffel Tower in Paris. "I couldn't believe one lawn ornament could represent so much," said Price, who stumbled into this story through a casual bit of research.

From those beginnings, where we fall in love with a piece of information, essays begin; the shaping that follows, however, can be difficult. At this early stage of research, Jennifer Price had to ask herself which story she really wanted to tell, Featherstone's or the flamingo's. (As the essay title indicates, she chose the latter.) The toughest thing about research is learning to sort through what you find, particularly now, in the midst of the Internet explosion and the Information Age. Imagine you're Jennifer Price, feeling just a tickle of interest in writing an essay about pink plastic lawn flamingos. A search on a powerful search engine—google.com—takes several seconds and unearths almost three hundred sites, each one loaded with lawn flamingo information.

Without looking any further, you can scan the search engine summaries and learn all these facts: lawn flamingos were initially designed using photographs from *National Geographic*, they've stirred up dissent when used to create Nativity scenes at Christmas, and the creator of them got an award from the satirical *Journal of Irreproducible Results.* This quick scan creates practically an essay in itself, without bothering to click on the sites and learn even more.

What do you do with it all? First of all, keep close to you the initial impulse that made you want to do this research—the first fact or hint that gave you a sense you had a subject for an essay you could live with, even grow obsessive about, for a while. It's important to avoid the temptation to drop into your essay everything you learn that's strange or amusing. Jennifer Price began her essay with an interest in flamingo creator Don Featherstone, but she found, sorting through her material, that it was the flamingos' borderline between artifice and nature that captured her.

What is closest to your own heart, your own obsessions? What in this research do you feel most qualified and eager to talk about? Sit with your papers, including interview notes, in front of you, and circle or highlight the material that feels most to draw you or belong to you. You can try making piles in order of urgency: what you must write about, what you probably should include, what's more iffy.

Once you've done some basic highlighting and sorting, if you are working on a piece with a great deal of research—not just a key fact, like the eclipse shadow—it helps to create a computer file or notebook page with a list of material you want to use. Put facts in an order that feels like it might correspond to the order you'll use them in, but don't burden yourself by treating this as an outline. Your writing should always stay fluid, flexible, and open to your best intuitive leaps. Consult the list as you draft, to see if there are any exciting facts—those that help explain, that offer metaphorical possibilities, and so forth—which you've forgotten.

TRY IT

1. Pull out an essay you've been working on, one that has promise but doesn't feel quite finished yet. Make a list of facts that inform this piece—none of these facts needs to be present in the work but implied, either through location, time, action, or characters. Here's a sample opening paragraph, and the list it generates.

It is 1963 and I am watching, for what seems like the hundredth time, Lee Harvey Oswald collapse as he is shot by Jack Ruby. I am wearing my Winnie the Pooh pajamas and listening to the ice clink in my mother's glass as she drinks another gin in the kitchen. I've told her I'm watching "Rocky & Bullwinkle" but by this time of night she's too far gone to pay attention.

This is a very promising start: emotional without any trace of self-indulgence, nicely detailed. Here's a list of possible research areas:

- Kennedy assassination: political climate of the time? Bay of Pigs?
- Media in the early 1960s
- Post-war Midwest (unstated in the opening, but this is the location)
- Alcoholism, particularly during this period. What was the medical view of alcoholism? The social view? How was alcohol portrayed in the media of the time?

Going down the list, the author decides that alcoholism is the most promising avenue for further study. She begins by looking at advertisements and films from the period, seeing how alcohol is portrayed: as an everyday diversion, the province of sophisticates and James Bond–types. She explores medical textbooks dating from the 1960s to probe how alcohol dependence was viewed then. She finds it a much more character-driven view, less a disease model, than today. Finally, she browses Alcoholics Anonymous literature to see how a sense of the disease of alcoholism has evolved.

The final step is highlighting information worth using and then working it into the author's story without a change of voice: it's important not to sound textbook-y, as if another author has come in to serve as newscaster. Compare two moves this author could make next, given below:

In 1963, more than half of Americans, current experts agree, use alcohol to excess, and 75 percent of films show characters drinking alcoholic drinks.

Or:

Everybody is in love with James Bond this year, who drinks martini after martini in his movies without any change in behavior. James Bond has

made "shaken, not stirred" a mantra for this martini-smitten culture.
My mother simply eliminates the vermouth.

2. The next time a strange fact grabs your attention write it down or, if it appears in a newspaper or magazine, cut out the source. Ask yourself why this fact seems to demand your attention. Write an essay based on this fact, using additional research if necessary. If you're trolling for odd facts, try almanacs or *Harper's Index*, which holds a plethora of bizarre tidbits, like the fact that the Pentagon spends $100 a minute on Viagra.

3. Chances are you've already had at least one terrific immersion experience, even if you didn't call it that: maybe it was the wedding you attended where the bride and groom were Goths who married in black robes with white talcum on their faces. Maybe it was the time your uncle dragged you along to a meeting of the local Elks Club. Fascinating immersion experiences exist all over. Do you live near a hospital? A casino? A group of Wiccans? A Society for Creative Anachronism? Ask them if they would mind you observing them a while for an essay. Keep notes, use a tape recorder, or both.

Decide, before you begin your immersion experience, how you see your role. Will you take the approach of Didion and acknowledge your presence in the events you write about, or, like Gutkind, try to keep yourself out of the narrative? Adjust your presence accordingly.

4. To hone your interview skills and create a body of information you'll almost certainly want to come back to, try family interviews. These interviews are generally far less intimidating than tracking down your local physicist to ask questions about the implications of the Big Bang. Families also tend to be repositories of fascinating hidden information—uncles who had more money than they should have, cousins who disappeared in disgrace.

Start with a question you have always wanted to get an answer—or a clearer answer—to. It may be the life story of the family scapegrace, an immigration story, or a detailed picture of a parent's early years. Make a list of questions; keep them fairly simple. If you're pursuing the story of a family member in legal trouble, your questions might include what year that trouble first occurred, full details of it, how family members responded, and so forth.

Ask your questions of two or three different family members—preferably including several generations, such as a cousin, a parent, a grandparent—and make note of the discrepancies between their versions of events. Unless your family is very different from most, there will be plenty. Follow up on your initial interviews with further questions, to see if you can explain differing versions of the story.

This second round of questions will tell you a lot about the person/event you're researching, and it will also tell you a lot—maybe even more—about the structure of your family. Typically, families have keepers-of-the-family-name types, who minimize or dismiss what seems "improper." They also have tell-all types—those who collect stories and relish relating them. You may want to meditate on who plays these roles in your family (does the answer surprise you?) and, of course, who you are in the hierarchy of things.

PART 3

HONING YOUR CRAFT

Let men and women make good sentences. Let them learn to spell
the sound of the waterfall and the noise of the bathwater. Let us get
down the colors of the baseball gloves, the difference in shade
between the centerfielder's deep pocket and the discreet indentation
of the catcher's mitt. . . . Let us enlist the Vocabulary, the Syntax, the
high grammar of the mysterious world.

—STANLEY ELKIN

12

The Basics of Good Writing in Any Form

I was delighted to find that nonfiction prose can also carry meaning in its structures and, like poetry, can tolerate all sorts of figurative language, as well as alliteration and even rhyme. The range of rhythms in prose is larger and grander than it is in poetry, and it can handle discursive ideas and plain information as well as character and story. It can do everything. I felt as though I had switched from a single reed instrument to a full orchestra.

—Annie Dillard

People need maps to your dreams.

—Allen Gurganus

I am working with a group of novice nonfiction writers, and we're about two-thirds of the way through our time together. My students have plumbed their lives in ways they never thought possible: as environmental records, as living history, as a movement through various forms—scientific, spiritual, cultural, aesthetic—of inquiry. They sort themselves through the door of my classroom with varying degrees of eagerness, and pull out their notebooks, pens cocked and waiting. They're used to coming in and interrogating themselves in different ways: Who are they really? How have they lived? Today, however, I know I'm going to make them groan. Instead of prompts like writing about the explosion of Mount St. Helens or the World Trade Orga-

nization riots in Seattle, I have them pull out a piece of their own prose and count the number of words in each sentence for three paragraphs. I also have them jot down comments on the kinds of sentences they use: simple declarative (basic subject-verb), complex, fragmented, and so forth. They do the assignment, because it would be even more boring to sit and do nothing, I suppose. Suddenly a little exclamation breaks out from a corner of the room.

"Ohmigod!" says one young woman. "All of my sentences are eleven words long!"

This young woman has been concerned about what feels to her like a flatness or lifelessness to her prose. Here, in one rather mechanical but not painful exercise, she's put her finger on the reason, or one of the reasons. On further analysis she discovers that she has a penchant for writing one simple declarative sentence after another: "I drive to the forest in April. My car is almost ready for a new clutch. The forests are quiet at that time of year." The metronomic beat of same sentence structure, same sentence length, has robbed her otherwise sparkling essays of their life.

For the sake of comparison, listen to the difference created in those three sample sentences by a little more rhetorical inventiveness: "In April, a quiet time of year, I drive to the forest. My car almost ready for a new clutch."

—SUZANNE

Scene Versus Exposition

Generally speaking, scene is the building block of creative nonfiction. There are exceptions to this statement—more academic or technically oriented writing, the essay of ideas perhaps—but overall, the widespread notion that nonfiction is the writer's thoughts presented in an expository or summarizing way has done little but produce quantities of unreadable nonfiction. Scene is based on action unreeling before us, as it would in a film, and it will draw on the same techniques as fiction—dialogue, description, point of view, specificity, concrete detail. Scene also encompasses the lyricism and imagery of great poetry. We have, as the Dillard quote at the head of this chapter indicates, access to the full orchestra. We need to learn to play every instrument with brio.

Let's begin by defining our terms. *Expository* writing, as the term implies, exposes the author's thoughts or experiences for the reader; it summarizes, generally with little or no sensory detail. Expository writing compresses time: *For five years I lived in Alaska.* It presents a compact summation of an experience with no effort to re-create the experience for the person reading.

On the other hand, *scene*, as in fiction, uses detail and sensory information to re-create experience, generally with location, action, a sense of movement through time, and possible dialogue. Scene is cinematic. Here is a possible reworking of the above sentence, using scene: *For the five years I lived in Alaska I awoke each morning to the freezing seat of the outhouse, the sting of hot strong coffee drunk without precious sugar or milk, the ringing "G'day!" of my Australian neighbor.*

The latter version of this sentence clearly presents the reader with a more experiential version of that time in Alaska, with details that provide a snapshot of the place: the slowness of time passing is stressed by the harsh routine of the coffee and outhouse; we get a sense of scarcity of supply; the neighbor even has a bit of swift characterization. Of course, for an essay in which Alaska is totally unimportant the expository summation might be the better move. But if you find yourself writing nonfiction with very little scene, you are likely to produce flat writing readers have to struggle to enter.

Remember "The Knife," by author/surgeon Richard Selzer? This essay moves fluidly between scene and exposition; Selzer forces us to *live* the awesome power and responsibility of the surgeon before allowing himself the luxury of meditating about it.

> *There is a hush in the room. Speech stops. The hands of the others, assistants and nurses, are still. Only the voice of the patient's respiration remains. It is the rhythm of a quiet sea, the sound of waiting. Then you speak, slowly, the terse entries of a Himalayan climber reporting back. "The stomach is okay. Greater curvature clean. No sign of ulcer. Pylorus, duodenum fine. Now comes the gall-bladder. No stones. Right kidney, left, all right. Liver . . . uh-oh."*

Selzer goes on to tell us he finds three large tumors in the liver. "Three big hard ones in the left lobe, one on the right. Metastatic deposits. Bad, bad."

Like fine fiction, this passage contains a clear setting—the hospital room, characterized appropriately enough by sound rather than appearance: the silence of life and death. There is action mimicking real time, containing the element of surprise. We learn along with the surgeon about the patient's metastasized cancer. There's dialogue, as the surgeon narrates to himself, to his surgical assistants, seemingly to the fates, his discovery of the patient's mortality. And, like fine poetry, this piece of writing also organizes itself through imagery: the "quiet sea" of the passive patient's breathing versus the labored voice—like a "Himalayan climber's"—of the surgeon emphasizes the former's loss of control.

Selzer's passage would be easy to change to an expository sentence: *Often in surgery I found unexpected cancer.* But the author's final purpose—an extended meditation on the relationship of human and tool, soul and body—would fall flat. The reader, lacking any feel for the grandeur and potential tragedy of exploring the body, would dismiss expository statements such as, "The surgeon struggles not to feel. It is suffocating to press the feeling out," as merely odd or grandiose.

There are several other moves worth noting in this passage. One is that, like the sample Alaska sentence given above, Selzer's surgical description is *representative scene*. In other words, he doesn't pretend this operation occurs at one specific time and place, but it represents a typical surgical procedure, one among many. Another technique to note is his use of the second person for a speaker that is presumably himself. Second person—the *you* rather than the *I*—is a point-of-view choice, discussed in more detail further on in this chapter.

In contrast, here's an example of a specific, not representative, scene, from Jo Ann Beard's essay "The Fourth State of Matter." The scenes comprising the essay all occur at very specific moments in time. Here is Beard at work, with her physicist colleagues having a professional discussion around the chalkboard:

> *"If it's plasma, make it in red," I suggest helpfully. We're all smoking illegally, in the journal office with the door closed and the window open. We're having a plasma party.*
>
> *"We aren't discussing plasma," Bob says condescendingly. He's smoking a horrendously smelly pipe. The longer he stays in here the more it feels like I'm breathing small daggers in through my nose. He and I don't get along;*

each of us thinks the other needs to be taken down a peg. Once we had a
hissing match in the hallway which ended with him suggesting that I could
be fired, which drove me to tell him he was already *fired, and both of us*
stomped into our offices and slammed our doors.

 "I had to fire Bob," I tell Chris later.

 "I heard," he says noncommittally. Bob is his best friend.

This is a very pinpointed event, not representative but presumably unlike
any other moment in Beard's life. Notice how much suggestive detail Beard
packs into a short space. These characters break rules, argue, and exist in complex relationship to one another. Her relationship with Bob is established in
this scene—a relationship that seems suffused with a genuine but relatively
harmless tension, given their ability to issue dire threats to each other without consequence. The dialogue sounds real and secures the characters, capturing the nuanced pretense of Bob's stressing the "plas" part of the "plasma."
Chris, the man in the middle, seems to have heard all this bickering before.

We all tend to use too little scene in creative nonfiction. We especially forget the possibilities of representative scene. Even when we're reporting a typical rather than a specific event, use of scenic elements, as in Selzer's surgery,
conveys a sense of character and situation far more effectively than does
summary.

Specificity and Detail

Scene forces us to use specificity and detail, elements that get lost in the quick
wash of exposition. Even in discussing the largest ideas, our brains engage
with the small workings of the senses first. And the specificity of a piece of
nonfiction is generally where the sensory details lie: the aroma of honeysuckle,
the weak film of moonlight. While it is possible to go overboard with detail,
generally in drafting it's best to keep going back and sharpening as much as
possible. You leaned not just against a tree but against a weeping silver birch;
the voice at the other end of the phone sounded like the Tin Man's in *The
Wizard of Oz*. Your readers or writing group can tell you when you've gone
too far. When you write scene, your job is to mimic the event, create an experiential representation of it for the reader.

Look at the examples given before, and think about how much the details add to those scenes: the hushed silence of the hospital room and three hard tumors on the right lobe of the liver in Selzer's essay. In Beard's, we see the bickering but ultimate acceptance of this close group of coworkers. We sense the author's ambivalent position in the group—shut out of their "talking physics," as she tells us earlier—but also her authority within the group. We sense, in the hyperbolic description of Bob's pipe smoke ("like daggers"), a bit of foreshadowing of a coming tragic event.

In *The Elements of Style*, William Strunk, Jr., explains that the one point of accord among good writers is the need for detail that is "specific, definite, and concrete." (We also address this point in Chapter 1.) Concrete detail appeals to the senses; other writers call such details "proofs." If Selzer told us readers that sometimes in surgery he found cancer, we might abstractly believe him, but it's hard to associate that fact with real life and death. In this passage, we're convinced by the specifics: three hard tumors on the liver, the surgeon's voice mumbling, "Bad, bad."

Abstract language—the opposite of relying on concrete detail—refers to the larger concepts we use that exist on a purely mental level, with no appeal to the senses: *liberty, justice, contentment,* and so on. These terms may contain the implication of sensory detail (you may flash on "warmth" when you hear "contentment," but that's a personal reaction that wouldn't make sense to, say, a penguin), but they are in themselves broad categories only. Of course, within the details you use emerges a wealth of abstract information. Beard could have summarized her relationships with her coworkers; Selzer could have presented a few expository sentences about soul and body, surgeon as God. We want experiences, not lectures; we want to enter into events and uncover their meanings for ourselves.

Paying attention to concrete detail and the input of our own senses also helps save us from the literary pitfall of cliché, an expression or concept that's been overused. Frequently, clichés are dead metaphors, so overused we don't pay attention anymore to the comparisons they contain. (Do you actually think of a yellow metal when you hear "good as gold"? Do you even realize this phrase comes from a time when the gold our country held validated our money?) If Beard had described Bob's pipe tobacco as smelling like "dirty socks," or "killing" her nose, she would have been indulging in cliché. Instead, she used the information of her senses to create a fresh image.

Chances are, you know more than you need to know to write effective scene, but your natural expressiveness has been stifled, often by misguided advice from academic writing classes. Next time you work on a piece of creative nonfiction, hear yourself talking through the story to friends in a crowded coffee shop or club. There's plenty to divert their attention: music, people-watching, smoke, and noise. Which details do you use to hold their attention? Do you imitate the look of someone's face, the sound of a voice? Do you screech to demonstrate the sound of car tires on asphalt? Your reading audience will be equally distractible. Think about how to render these attention-grabbing devices in your prose. You may want to consult Chapter 1, "The Body of Memory," to remind yourself how to use sensory detail.

Developing Character

Character development, like learning to write effective dialogue, is part of writing scene. It's another particularly easy-to-miss demand of good creative nonfiction. After all, *we* know what our parents, children, or lovers look like. Unconsciously, we tend to assume that everyone else does as well.

Suzanne has, by marriage, a very funny grandmother. She wasn't intentionally funny, but nonetheless the mere mention of her name tends to bring down the room when the family's together. The family bears in mind, as courteous people, that we need to break through our uncontrollable giggling and clue other listeners in to the source of our amusement: "Well, she came from a tiny town in south Georgia and talked about nothing all day long but her ar-ther-itis and her gallbladder that was *leakin'* plus she lied compulsively and pursed her mouth in this funny way when she did. . . ." After a few minutes of this our auditors understand why we find her so endlessly amusing. This kind of filling in, also natural in conversation, is the essence of character development.

Nothing demonstrates the power of fine characterization like studying writers who, in a few strokes, can help us apprehend someone sensually (through sight, sound, or feel) as well as give us a sense of their essence. The follow-

ing are examples of quick, effective character development from essays we
love:

- **Albert Goldbarth in "After Yitzl":** "My best friend there shoed horses.
  He had ribs like barrel staves, his sweat was miniature glass pears."
- **Lawrence Sutin in "Man and Boy":** "In the case of my father and
  myself, I had the fullness of his face and his desire to write, which
  had been abandoned when he came to America with a family to raise.
  . . . He was a middle-aged man who was sobbing and sweaty and his
  body was heavy and so soft I imagined his ribs giving way like a
  snowman's on the first warm winter day."
- **Judith Kitchen in "Things of This Life":** "Mayme would step onto the
  platform wearing a dark purple coat, her black braids wound tightly
  around her head. Her skin was too soft and wrinkly. When you kissed
  her cheek, it wobbled, and you wished you didn't have to do that."

Details that give a sense of the essence of an individual—in all his or her
typicality (commonness with their type; grandmothers typically have soft and
wrinkly skin) and individual, specific glory (sweat like miniature pears)—are
hard to define, but blazingly effective when you come upon them. Think,
when you write about someone close to you, how you would characterize that
person in a stroke or two for someone else.

Dialogue

It can be difficult to allow ourselves to use direct dialogue in creative nonfiction. After all, memory's faulty; we can't recall conversations word for word,
so why try? The answer is that we need to try, because insofar as nonfiction
attempts to be an honest record of the observant mind, dialogue matters. We
recall voices, not summaries; we observe scenes in our head, not expository
paragraphs.

Dialogue generally moves action forward. Selzer quotes himself finding the
metastasized cancer, and Beard gives a sense of the dynamics of her office.
Dialogue must characterize and capture the voice of the speaker, however,
not simply give information. The latter is called in fiction writing "informa-

tion dumping," and it occurs when you have people say things like, "Well, Carmen, I remember you told me you were taking the cross-town bus that day only because your white 1999 Volvo had developed a gasket problem." Information dumping is less of a problem in nonfiction because this genre is reality based (and people really *do not* talk that way). But, if you cue your readers that you are re-creating a conversation, it may be tempting to lard the dialogue with information you can't figure out how to get in any other way. Don't do it.

Everyone has a natural cadence and a dialect to his or her speech. We nearly always speak in simple sentences, not complex-compound ones. We might say, "When the rain comes, the grass grows," which has one short dependent clause beginning with the word "when"; we aren't likely to say, "Whenever it happens the rain comes, provided the proper fertilizer's been applied, grass grows, unless it's been masticated by cows grazing thereon"—a simple sentence or *main clause* ("the grass grows") festooned with wordy subordinate clauses. We frequently speak in sentence fragments or ungrammatical snippets—e.g., the how-are-you question "Getting along?" instead of the grammatically correct "Are you getting along?" One exception to these rules of natural speech might be a person who *is* pompous and wordy. Perhaps you're writing dialogue to capture the voice of a stuffy English professor you know. In that case, go to town. Just bear in mind that what bores you will bore others fairly quickly. In the case of people who are boorish, dull, or otherwise hard to listen to, give readers a sample of the voice and they will fill in the rest. A little goes a long way.

One final caveat: beware of elaborate taglines, which identify the speaker, such as "he said," "she argued," and so forth. In dialogue between two people taglines are often dispensable after the first two. Even when you must use them, stick as much as possible to "said" and "asked," two fairly invisible words in the context of dialogue. It's an easy mistake to make—and a difficult one to overlook as a reader—to have all of your characters "retort," "storm," or "muse." And make sure the words themselves contain tone as much as possible. (Tone can also be conveyed in a character's gesture, as in Beard's colleagues casually breaking the rules by smoking in their office.) Don't follow each speech tag with an adverb such as "angrily," "sadly," and so on. If you feel the need to use those words, ask yourself why the dialogue itself doesn't seem to contain those feelings.

Point of View

Every story is told by a storyteller (even in a piece with multiple speakers, one speaker dominates at a time), and every storyteller must be situated somehow within the frame of the work. This situating is called *point of view* (POV), and we express it through choice of pronouns. To put it simply, the tale can be told by an "I" (first-person POV), a "you" (second person), or a "he" or "she" (third person). Though it may seem at first blush as though all nonfiction must be told in first person, skillful writers do use the techniques of second- and third-person POV to wonderful effect in nonfiction. And the more the genre stretches its limbs, takes risks, and remakes its rules, the more such untraditional devices appear, and the more aware we become as writers of what they can do.

Of the three point-of-view choices, second person is the rarest, in nonfiction as well as in fiction and poetry. It's not hard to figure out why: second-person POV calls attention to itself and tends to invite reader resistance. Imagine recasting "For five years I lived in Alaska" as "For five years you lived in Alaska." That's exactly what a POV shift to second person would do; it places the reader directly in the shoes of the author, without narrative mediation. Clumsily used, second person screams out for the reader to say, "No, I didn't" with an inner shrug of indignation and stop reading. Skillfully used, however, that blurring of line between reader and author can be very powerful.

Here's a sentence from "The Fourth State of Matter" again, a classic first-person approach: "It's November 1, 1991, the last day of the first part of my life." Compare that with a short passage from Richard Selzer, who uses second person liberally throughout his essay. Watch the careful way he slips from first- to second-person POV, as if inviting the reader to experience the fearfulness of a surgeon's power:

> *I must confess that the priestliness of my profession has ever been impressed on me. In the beginning there are vows. . . . And if the surgeon is like a poet, then the scars you have made on countless bodies are like verses into the fashioning of which you have poured your soul.*

In contrast, Judith Kitchen's essay "Things of This Life" uses third person throughout the piece to create a sense of freshness and excitement in a childhood memoir:

> *Consider the child idly browsing in the curio shop. She's been on vacation in the Adirondacks, and her family has (over the past week) canoed the width of the lake and up a small, meandering river. . . . So why, as she sifts through boxes of fake arrowheads made into key chains, passes down the long rows of rubber tomahawks, dyed rabbits' feet, salt shakers with the words "Indian Lake" painted in gold, beaded moccasins made of what could only in the imagination be called leather, is she happier than any time during the past week?*

Kitchen, further along in the essay, tells us, "Now consider the woman who was that child." It seems at first an odd choice, to write about the self as if it were someone completely apart, a stranger. But as Kitchen unfolds her sense of her life as "alien," a space she's inhabiting that raises questions she still can't answer ("How can she go on, wanting like this, for the rest of her life?"), the strategy becomes a coherent part of the architecture of the essay.

Imagine the paragraphs it would take to explain such an alienation from the self—a sense of distance from one's own desires—and the relative powerlessness such an explanation would have. Annie Dillard writes in our introductory quote that she "delighted" to learn that nonfiction, like poetry, can carry meaning in its structures. Kitchen here has wisely chosen a structure to convey her feeling—a feeling open only to the clumsiest articulation.

Image and Metaphor

Janet Burroway, in her text *Writing Fiction*, describes metaphor as the foundation stone "from which literature derives." Image—any literary element that creates a sense impression in the mind—and metaphor—the use of comparison—form the heart of any literary work. Notice how, trying to impress this importance upon you, we strain to make strong metaphor: metaphors are the foundation stones of a building; they're the pumping hearts of literary writing. The ability to make metaphor is the most basic constituent of human thought and language. Yet, too often we leave direct consideration of these devices to the poets.

While essays can be organized many ways—through topic, chronology, or passage of time—organization through image and metaphor has become much more common. Clustering thoughts through images and loose associations (and metaphors are, at the most basic level, associations) seems fundamental to the way the human mind works. You may mentally jump from a look at a leaky faucet to a memory of watching the 1970s TV show "Charlie's Angels" because of the name of the actress Farrah Fawcett. You may then glide effortlessly from that thought to a sense memory of the powdered hot chocolate with marshmallows your mother made for you on weeknights while you watched television. As we grow more aware of and sophisticated about the way human consciousness operates, it makes sense that our literature will come closer to these basic thought rhythms. In the Beard excerpt we used earlier in this chapter, within a few sentences we see images of daggers and hissing and the use of the word *fire*. The imagery in this essay tells its own story—of a deadly event about to overtake the lives of these people.

You can often find clues to your own imagistic or metaphoric organizations when you recall the sensory association a thought or experience calls to mind. If the summer your best friend was killed in a diving accident always comes back to you with a whiff of honeysuckle, stay with that image and explore it in writing for a while. Does it lead to concepts of sweetness, youth, temptation, the quick blooming? If you let yourself write about the image alone for a while—not rushing to get to the subject your mind may insist is "the real story"—a more complex, more true, series of themes in your story will probably emerge.

The Rhythm of Your Sentences

It's a well-known fact that sentences must contain some variation. You must have become acquainted with this fact already. It's clear if you read a certain kind of prose. A work must use different kinds of sentence structures. Different kinds of sentence structures help alleviate that numbing feeling. It's a feeling you don't want your readers to have.

The previous paragraph contains six sentences, each composed of about ten words, and each is a simple sentence, beginning with a subject and its verb. Unlike this sentence you're currently reading, none begins with a clause. None is short. None, unlike the twenty-five-word sentence introducing this second paragraph, engages us for very long. Read both of these paragraphs together. Do you sense a difference? Do you, as we do, begin to go blank by the middle of the first paragraph, and finally feel some relief at the second one?

Notice that the second paragraph in this section of the book, while clarifying many of the ideas that the first paragraph contains, varies sentence structure and length. It also varies voice. One sentence uses the *vocative* or *command* voice ("Read both paragraphs together"), two are cast in the *interrogative* voice—they ask questions. Clauses like "Unlike this sentence" and "as we do" appear at the beginnings, middles, and ends of sentences to break up that repetitive simple structure.

There's a reason children and parents howl at each other, "Stop *saying* that!" Nothing's more boring than a voice repeating "Clean your room!" over and over again. Or the acquaintance who says "like" again and again, or the child banging out "Chopsticks" on the piano for the hundredth time. Nothing drives us quite as numbly mad as repetition does. Sentence structure is the poetic line, the bass and rhythm, of your prose. Riff, experiment, break it up.

TRY IT

1. Go through a piece of your writing and find a passage of summary that could or maybe even should be in scene. Don't fret right now about whether scene is absolutely necessary here: the point is to develop the skill of automatically asking yourself whether that option will help you.

Sometimes we stymie ourselves by imagining we must remember *everything* or we can't describe *anything*. So work with what you do remember. You may forget the look of a room but remember the sound or smell of it (think of Selzer's defining silence in that hospital room). Or create a bridge, such as writing a few sentences about how this is what a dialogue sounds like in your memory as you try to re-create it, giving yourself permission to fill in what you don't remember word for word. Remember that almost any device for reconstruction is fine, as long as you let readers in on what you're doing.

2. To get a feel for writing scene, re-create an event that took place in the last week—one with characters you can delineate and dialogue you can remember. It doesn't have to be important—it probably will help if it isn't. The point is simply to write two to three pages in which a location is established through description, people are characterized and talk, and something happens.

3. Finally, when you feel confident of your basic skills, remember a scene out of your own life that does contain the utmost importance. For everybody this will be different. It could be something as obviously important as the birth of a child or an argument leading to the end of a marriage; or its importance could be subtle but real to you—a conversation leading to a new closeness or a new distance between you and someone critical in your life. The point is, you must have a strong sense memory of this scene, one you can play back in your head over and over again; and it must matter to you.

Write the scene with as much fidelity as possible. Have the people in it enter and leave, describe what you saw, heard, and felt. If you still remember exactly how your mother asked, "Where were you last night?" describe the question in all the sensory detail you can muster, along with the wrench in your gut that came with it. Don't question right now why what matters matters. Trust your intuition, and tap into all of the passion you have invested in this scene.

Now question yourself. Why was a certain gesture or inflection so important? Why did you spend most of this conversation staring at a loudly ticking clock on the wall? Why did you notice the caramel color of your drink? The chances are that, like Selzer and Beard, your emotional story is locked into the details you remember of your life. When you begin to question the scene in this way, scrutinizing every detail, you'll probably discover an essay waiting to be written about this crucial moment.

4. Write a portrait or character sketch. Think of someone close to you and try to convey their essence, through clothing, sound, dialogue, gestures, and so forth, in two or three paragraphs. Don't aim to write scene; this portrait doesn't need to contain action, merely characterization.

When you're reasonably finished, trade your piece with a writing partner. Read each other's sketches and then elaborate on the person described, giving an overall, abstract sense of that individual's personality. How close did you come? Discuss with your partner ways this sketch could be refined: important details that may have been omitted, or others that could be misleading. Is this character sketch on its way to becoming an essay? Articulate to yourself why this character matters, why she is different, or why he is intriguingly typical.

5. Write a page or two of dialogue. Practice for this by using your notebook to record snippets of speech verbatim: exchanges with classmates, friends, spouses, parents. Pay attention to the syntax of speech. How much is grammatically correct or incorrect? How much slang or dialect appears in different speakers' voices? When you feel ready, write a page or two of typical dialogue—you can record it and write it down, or try to re-create it—with someone fairly close to you. Do the same partner swap with this dialogue you did with characterization, and see how much of the person you're describing comes through in his or her voice.

6. The only way to fully understand point of view is to experiment with it. Pull out an earlier essay of yours, or write a simple paragraph about some subject you've thought about as a likely one. Then recast the point of view, from first to second or third. Force yourself to keep going through at least one paragraph; don't look at the clunkiness of a sentence such as "For five years you lived in Alaska" and give up. Push through, and open yourself up to moments when the point of view works, when you feel interesting possibilities arise. (You can also refer to Chapter 10, "The Lyric Essay.")

Traditionally, point-of-view *shifting*—moving from the narrative position of one character to another within a piece—has been a problem area for fiction writers. Unintentional shifting is a common error for young writers; masterful shifts can make a story, as in Flannery O'Connor's famous shift to the Misfit's point of view at the end of "A Good Man Is Hard to Find." As nonfiction expands its reach, we see point of view shifting in this genre as well. Richard Selzer does it, as we've shown earlier in this chapter. See if such a switch can enrich a piece of your own writing.

7. Do a quick diagnostic of two to three paragraphs of your own prose (less might not be representative enough). How long do your sentences tend to be? How do you structure them? Do you vary voices or speech acts, such as questioning, stating, and commanding, or do you simply use the declarative or simple statement voice? Challenge yourself to approach a piece of prose in a way you haven't in the past—more short sentences or sentence fragments, perhaps, or more shifts in voice. See how this change alters your work, and opens up the possibilities of the essay.

13

The Writing Process and Revision

The writing has changed, in your hands, and in a twinkling, from an expression of your notions to an epistemological tool. The new place interests you because it is not clear. You attend. In your humility, you lay down the words carefully, watching all the angles. Now the earlier writing looks soft and careless. Process is nothing; erase your tracks. The path is not the work. I hope your tracks have grown over; I hope birds ate the crumbs; I hope you will toss it all and not look back.

—ANNIE DILLARD

In graduate school, I once submitted a workshop story that nobody liked— not one person. I remember one woman in particular: she dangled my work in front of her and said, her lips curling in distaste, "I don't understand why this story even exists!" Of course, at the time, I huffed and I puffed, and I spoke derisively of this woman at the bar that night. My friends cooed words of support, patted me on the back, and scanned the bar for more lively companionship. But even as I walked home that night, I could tell that her comment, though poorly worded, had something in it I needed to hear. It has stayed with me throughout the years, and now, when I'm at the final stage of revision, it's her question I hear in my head: Why does this essay exist? *I go back to work with a grim determination. No longer do I coddle the newborn prose, but hold it up roughly, probing for weakness, drawing blood. I try to identify and slash out all that is mere indulgence and platitude.*

At this stage in the writing process, the draft becomes nothing more than a fruitful scavenging ground. Right now, as I write, I'm in the middle of

Wyoming, and down the road a huge junkyard lies at the intersection of two minor highways. Against the rolling fields of wheat grass, this junkyard rises as ten acres of glinting metal, bent chrome, colors of every hue. One of my fellow colonists, a sculptor, began buying scraps to incorporate in her work: gorgeous landscapes with ribbons of rusted metal juxtaposed across blue skies. Now I've come to see the junkyard as a place of infinite possibility. What useful parts still hum in the innards of these machines? How will they be unearthed? What kind of work would it take to make them shine?

—Brenda

The Drafting Process

Writing is easy; all you do is sit staring at a blank sheet of paper until the drops of blood form on your forehead.

—Gene Fowler

When you first sit down to work, you may have no idea what the writing will bring. Maybe it even scares you a little, the thought of venturing into that unknown territory. Perhaps you circle your desk a while, wary of the task at hand. You pick up your cup of coffee in two hands and gaze out the window; you remember a letter you meant to write, an e-mail you meant to answer. You get up and check the mailbox, picking a few dead leaves off the coleus plant in the window. You sit down. You get up and change your shirt, appraise yourself in the mirror a long time, and come back to your desk. Maybe you pick up a book of poetry and read a few lines, put it down. You pick up your pen and write a word, then another. You go back and erase. You begin again.

Or maybe you are the type of writer who can sit down and start writing without hesitation, training yourself to write at least one full paragraph before stopping. You know you'll go back and trim and revise, so you just keep the words coming. You give yourself one hour, and you don't move from your chair in all that time. That hour, if the writing goes well, turns into two or three. You work steadily and pile up the pages.

Either way, the important thing to know, for yourself, is your own style. In the first case, to the untrained eye you may appear engaged in nothing but mere procrastination; certainly you are not writing. But if you know yourself well, you understand that this puttering is essential to your writing process. Some thought has been brewing in your brain now for several days, perhaps weeks, or months. This idea needs your body to occupy itself while the essay forms itself into something fleshy and sturdy enough to survive outside the mind and on the bleak terrain of the page. Or, in the second case, you act more like an athlete in training, knowing that routine and discipline are essential for your creative process. You write quickly because that's the only way for you to outrun your inner critic. Neither way is "correct." The only correct way to write is the way that works for you.

The writing process is just that: a *process*. You must have the patience to watch the piece evolve, and you need an awareness of your own stages. You must know when you can go pell-mell with the heat of creation, and when you must settle down, take a wider view, and make some choices that will determine the essay's final shape.

First drafts can be seen as "discovery drafts"; much of the writing you did from the prompts in Part 1 will fall into this category. You are writing to discover what you know or to recover memories and images that may have been lost to you. You are going for the details, the unexpected images, or the story line that reveals itself only as you go along. The best writing you do will have this sense of exploration about it; you allow yourself to go into the unknown, to excavate what lies beneath the surface. It's important to allow yourself permission to write *anything* in a first draft; otherwise you might censor yourself into silence. The first draft is the place where you just might light upon the right *voice* for telling this particular story; once you're onto that voice, you can write for hours.

No matter how good (or bad) this material seems at first glance, most often it will need some shaping and revision before it is ready for public eyes. Writer Natalie Goldberg calls revision "envisioning again," and this gets at the heart of true revision: you see your work in a new light and rework it for a specific effect. Revision, perhaps, is an acquired taste, but you may find that revision actually becomes the most "creative" part of creative nonfiction. At this stage you've already produced the raw material; now you have the opportunity to dig into it with your sleeves rolled up, all your tools sharpened and at the ready. It is in revision that the real work begins. The short story writer Raymond Carver often wrote twenty to thirty drafts before he was satisfied. "It's something I love to do," he said, "putting words in and taking words out." Or listen to Vladimir Nabokov: "I have re-written—often several times— every word I have ever published. My pencils outlast their erasers."

Global Revision Versus Line Editing

Revision can often be mistaken for line editing. There is a time, naturally, for going back to your prose to fine-tune the grammar, change a few words, and fix typos. But first you need to look at the essay as a whole and decide what will make this essay matter. What is the *real* subject of the piece? Where does the voice ring out most strongly? What image takes on more metaphorical significance than you realized? What now seems superfluous, mere deadweight that hinders the essay's momentum?

It's beneficial to take some time between drafts at this stage of the process. After that first, heady flush of creation settles down, you'll better be able to pinpoint the areas that sing and those that fall flat. You'll be able to notice an unexpected theme that emerges organically through the imagery you chose. You'll hear how the ending may actually be the beginning of your piece. Or the beginning may make for a better end. At this point you need to see the work as a fluid thing, with infinite possibilities still to come. What you may have intended to write may not be the most interesting part of the essay now. Be open to what has developed in the writing process itself, and don't be afraid to cut out those areas that no longer work.

Ask yourself this question: what is the essence of the topic *for this particular essay*? Many times it's easy to think that we have to put in everything we know or feel about a topic in one essay. For instance, if you're writing about a big issue, such as sexual abuse in childhood, you may be tempted to write a gigantic essay that incorporates every incident, every feeling you ever had, and the entire cast of characters involved. Or if you're writing about a life-changing travel experience, you might feel you need to put in every stop along the way. You have to figure out what is necessary for this essay *and this essay alone*. You will write other essays about the topic, don't worry. As writer Natalie Goldberg put it, "Your main obsessions have power; they are what you will come back to in your writing over and over again. And you'll create new stories around them."

You may keep only a small portion of the original work, perhaps even just one line. But by doing this kind of pruning, you enable new, more beautiful and sturdy growth to emerge. Take comfort in knowing the old work may find its way into new essays yet to come. Keep a file on your desk or in your computer called "fragments." If it's hard for you to let go of a section completely, put it in this file and know that you will call it back sometime in the future, in a new incarnation. Time and again, we have found new homes for those bits and pieces of prose that just didn't work in their original homes.

The Role of the Audience

When you're writing a first draft, it's often necessary to ignore any concept of audience just so you can get the material out. An attentive audience, hanging on your every word, can be inhibiting at that stage of the writing process. But when you're revising, some concept of audience will help you gain the necessary distance to do the hard work that needs to get done. This audience can be a single person. What would your writing teacher from high school—the one who drove you into writing in the first place—think of this essay? Where would she say you're being lazy or timid? What would your most trusted friend say about that last paragraph? Sometimes by merely placing yourself in another person's perspective, the problems of the piece become readily apparent and you can fix them with ease.

Or the audience can be much larger. Many times, having some kind of reading venue or publication in mind can focus your attention in a way that nothing else can. Many towns have open-mike readings in cafés or bookstores where beginning and experienced writers are invited to read their work to an audience. If you are brave enough to commit yourself to reading one night, you will find yourself in a fever of revision, reading the piece aloud many times and getting every word just right. Or, you might decide that you're ready to start sending your work out for publication. Find one journal and read as many copies as you can, then revise your piece with this publication in mind. You'll surprise yourself with the focus you can generate once the piece leaves the personal arena and goes public.

Three Quick Fixes for Stronger Prose

After you've done the hard labor on your essay, you'll want to do the finish work, the small things that make the prose really shine. (We don't mean to suggest these two processes are mutually exclusive; naturally you will find yourself adjusting the prose as you go along.) We have three quick fixes that make any piece stronger: "search and destroy," "the adjective/adverb purge," and "the punch."

Search and Destroy

The most overused verbs in the English language are variations of *to be*— these include *is, are, were, was,* and so forth. While these verbs are necessary (note how we just used two of them in the last two sentences), often you can sharpen your prose by going over the piece carefully and eliminating as many of them as you can. To do this you will need to look closely at the words surrounding the *to be* verbs; often you can find a stronger verb to take its place or a more juicy noun. Even when you eliminate an *is* here or a *was* there, the resultant prose will seem much cleaner and lighter. It's the kind of work the reader won't notice directly (except for word nuts like us), but it will immediately professionalize your prose.

Take a draft of an essay that is nearly finished. Go through it and, with a red pen, circle all the *to be* verbs. Go back and see if you can rework any of those sentences to replace them with verbs that feel more "muscled," have more impact to them. Sometimes you'll find you don't need the sentence at all, and you'll have eliminated some deadweight. If you're working in a group, exchange essays with one another and do the same thing. Suggest new lines that eliminate the *to be* verbs.

The Adjective/Adverb Purge

Often, adjectives can be your enemy rather than your friend. Adjectives or adverbs can act as crutches, holding up weak nouns or verbs, and they actually water down your prose rather than intensify it. As with the search-and-destroy exercise above, the point here is not to eliminate adjectives and adverbs altogether, but to scrutinize every one and see if it's necessary for the point you want to get across.

Take an essay you think is nearly finished and circle every adjective and adverb. Go back and see if you can rework the sentences to eliminate these words and replace them with stronger verbs and/or nouns. Or you can take stronger measures. For at least one writing session, ban adjectives and adverbs from your vocabulary. See how this exercise forces you to find more vivid nouns and verbs for your prose.

The Punch

Professional writers develop a fine ear for language. Writers are really musicians, aural artists attuned to every rhythm and nuance of their prose. And when you study the writers you admire, you'll invariably find that they tend to end most of their sentences, all of their paragraphs, and certainly the closing line of the essay, with potent words that pack a punch. They do not allow their sentences to trail off but close them firmly and strongly, with words that leave the reader satisfied. When you work toward strong closing words in your sentences, the prose also takes on a new sense of momentum and trajectory, the sentences rearranging themselves in fresh ways to wield that satisfying "crack."

Read your essay aloud, paying attention to the sounds of the words at the ends of sentences and paragraphs. Do they ring clearly and cleanly, firmly ending your thought? Or do they trail off in abstraction? Circle any words that seem weak to you; then go back and rework these sentences for better closing effects. Pay particular attention to the word you use to end the entire essay. How do you leave your reader? What will he remember?

An Example of the Writing Process

We asked the writer Bernard Cooper for his thoughts on the writing process. Here is what he had to say:

A friend of mine once said that she needed two things in order to write: paper, and Liquid Paper. This was before she used a computer, of course, but I think her statement illustrates the importance of revision, the necessity to change and perfect what one has written down. I edit relentlessly— have already revised this very statement. My prose itself tends to come in short bursts, while the bulk of my time is involved in trying different words and sentence structures and punctuation so those word-bursts say exactly what I want them to. Revision seems to me the writer's most crucial task; you are given the chance to make your work as powerful as possible. "Words are all we have," said novelist Evan Connell, "and they'd better be the right ones." Anyone who has written for long knows the pleasure in finding the word that makes a description suddenly more vivid, or finding the structure that makes a sentence more taut, surprising, rhythmic, or funny.

When you write well, revision becomes not a chore, but the essence of the writing act itself. What came before cleared the way for what is to come; no writing is ever wasted, no time spent at the desk useless. Writing creates its own rhythm and momentum, and you must be willing to go with it, to become absorbed in the task, to let go of the writing you once thought precious. It's exhausting work, requiring stamina and rigor, but the rewards keep you going.

At one time or another, many writers experience what they call "gifts"— essays or poems or stories that seem to come effortlessly, full-blown onto the page with little revision or effort. But as the poet Richard Hugo put it, "Lucky accidents seldom happen to writers who don't work. . . . The hard work you do on one poem is put in on all poems. The hard work on the first poem is responsible for the sudden ease of the second. If you just sit around waiting for the easy ones, nothing will come. Get to work."

TRY IT

1. Take a writing session to observe everything you do around writing. What is your routine? How does it serve or sabotage you? What keeps you from writing? What helps you? What happens when you change your routine?

2. Do you have an inner critic that immediately censors or criticizes your writing? Take a piece of paper and draw a line down the center. On the right side of the paper, begin writing, perhaps from one of the writing exercises in Part 1. On the left side, write down any critical thoughts that come to mind as you write. (Don't worry if the session becomes only critical thoughts; it happens all the time!) Do this for about five or ten minutes, then go back and read what the critic has to say to you.

On a new sheet of paper, begin a dialogue with your inner critic. How does the critic both enable and sabotage your writing? For example, you may realize that the critic is merely trying to protect you from the harsh criticism the world might heap on you; rather than a hostile presence, the critic may actually be quite benevolent.

3. Take out a piece you wrote at least a month ago. Read it aloud, either to yourself or to a kind audience. Make note of the paragraphs that feel full and rich and those that are not as strong. Are there any areas that surprise you? What is the essay *really* about? What can be cut out and saved for another time? What needs to be included that was left out at first?

Here are some specific questions to ask yourself as you go about the global revision process:

- Is there one image that can be used as a cohesive thread throughout the piece? How can you amplify this image and transform it from beginning to end?
- Have you chosen the most effective point of view for telling the story? What happens when you experiment with third person? Second person?
- Look closely at the beginning paragraph of your essay. Do you begin in a way that draws the reader in? Often, the first few paragraphs of a rough draft act as "clearing the throat." Is the true beginning really a few pages in?
- Look closely at the end of the essay. Do you end in a way that leaves the reader with a compelling image? Often it's tempting to "sum up" the essay in a way that can be wholly unsatisfying to the reader. Can you end on an image rather than an idea?
- How do the beginning and ending paragraphs mirror or echo one another? The first and last paragraphs act as a frame for the piece as a whole. They

are, in a way, the most important places in the essay, because they determine everything that happens in between. If you make an effort to connect
them in some way—repeating a key image from the beginning, bringing
back on stage the major players for a final bow—you will find a stunning
finish to the piece.

14

The Writing Group

The fiction that artistic labor happens in isolation, and that artistic accomplishment is exclusively the provenance of individual talents, is politically charged and, in my case at least, repudiated by the facts. While the primary labor on *Angels* has been mine, more than two dozen people have contributed words, ideas and structures to these plays.

—Tony Kushner

I have just received a joyous e-mail from my friend Dan, telling me he has placed his latest manuscript with a university press he admires. It is an outpouring of both personal and group pride. My husband and I have been part of Dan's writing life for more than a decade, since the two of us met him in graduate school. That was fourteen years ago.

Originally, a group of six graduate students comprised our workshop. I can't remember whose casual suggestion it was that we begin meeting in a special room in a Charlottesville tavern that's always been something of a grad student hangout. The small room holds old Moët & Chandon Champagne posters crammed on every wall, curvy Art Deco women holding bottles. Each piece we put up for discussion we distribute the week before and talk about for twenty minutes to half an hour. The feedback is smart, bracing, encouraging. We find both value in everything and room for the writing to flower into something even finer. And, of course, there's always time for chat and catching up before and after the workshop part of our get-togethers. In addition to our workshop meetings, we soon celebrate each other's successes, throw each other parties, help each other search out publication venues.

*Now, almost a decade and a half later, we have mail and e-mail. We
still share our work, albeit less regularly and much more slowly. We still feel
a kudo for one of us is a kudo for the group, as we have nurtured, edited,
and prodded each other for much of our writing careers. Between us we've
gone from beginners at the art of literary writing to having published twelve
books. And all of us know, as Dan's e-mail shows, we couldn't have done it
alone.*

—SUZANNE

The Need for Feedback

Tony Kushner, in the quote introducing this chapter, states the case strongly
but not, we think, too strongly. Writers need feedback. The myth of writers
as loners who follow their vision and remain true to their inner muse, buck-
ing rather than embracing outside help, is very much a myth. It was created
largely by the writers of the British Romantic period, whose artistic mytholo-
gies we still cling to, though those writers themselves used one another unceas-
ingly as idea sources and sounding boards. Virtually all writers do. "I write,"
said Terry Tempest Williams, "in a solitude born out of community."

The modern writing workshop or writing group is not an innovation but
a form of learning that can be traced back as long as literature and the arts
have flourished. You can use this chapter to find ways to create your own
workshop group—one with members you trust, who can grow with you and
your work—or to get the most productive working relationship you can out
of the group you have. Even if this desire seems improbable now, trust us: if
you keep writing, you will want caring and responsive readers.

Setting Guidelines for Discussion:
A Practice Approach

In the following section on learning to give useful responses, we will provide
very specific suggestions for shaping workshop discussion. You may use or

adapt these as your group sees fit. For now, it is a good idea to have a preliminary talk with your peers about what does or does not work for you as a group in receiving feedback. You can and should discuss the entire process of workshopping, come up with a procedure, and devise your own workshop etiquette—a collective sense of what is OK and not OK in talking about your writing. Logistical questions to discuss include how far in advance you will share your work, whether you will read pieces aloud at any point, and whether you want to include written comments or limit yourself to oral critique.

It is essential to find a method of discussion with which the group feels safe and comfortable; don't flounder around trying to shape your valuable writing without first defining what helps you. To guide this process, find an essay, perhaps from a literary magazine, for practice. Read the piece and offer comments as you would in a workshop setting, and together monitor the discussion for responses that seem diminishing, unconstructive, or unhelpful. You may want to ask the group to rule out feedback based on "I do like," "I don't like" formulas. These are by their very nature subjective comments and hard to use in the revision process. All of you together can watch out for unhelpful critical language—"stinks," "lame," "one cliché after another."

Of course we don't advocate only praise; those words probably do hold suggestions for revisions that need to be made. What's important is that you work together as a group to find more constructive approaches. "This doesn't come up to the level of the rest of the essay," "I'm not seeing this scene yet," or "The language here could be more original" might be suitable comments to replace the offending ones.

Even when you hear responses that feel appropriate, use this practice session to sharpen them. If someone says he or she can't quite get a feel for a character, question why that is and try to formulate the most specific response possible. "I can't quite see David because he's never described and never speaks until you find him crying in the kitchen." Try reformulating your feedback comments two and three times to make them as specific as possible. Practice together until you feel good about one another's feedback style and the comments flowing from your discussion feel supportive, encouraging, and full of ideas to take back to your writing desk.

The Agenting Approach

One workshop strategy we have had great success with is the agenting approach. It is a role-play method. All the members of the writing group agree to function as one another's literary agents for the duration of the group.

Literary agents take on their author-clients because they believe in them. Agents feel certain they can sell their clients' essays and books. They derive their income from sales of their authors' work, so their faith in their authors is concrete and tangible. At the same time, agents become valuable critics and editors. They must bring their clients' work to the publishing market in its finest possible form.

As literary agents, then, you believe absolutely in one another and in the value of the group members' writing, and the fact that it can be brought to a final, polished form worthy of publication. At the same time you have an interest in making the essay or book extract the best it can be. And so you will provide substantial encouragement and substantial feedback.

As an agent your comments are always couched in terms like, "I think this will really work once the dialogue feels more authentic/Jack has a fuller character/we know where Luke ended up." Like an agent, you will always begin your responses by citing what *does* work, and, where appropriate, providing ideas for transferring that success to less polished parts of the essay.

When beginning this approach, it can help to write out comments in the form of letters—the type of communication you'd likely get from a literary agent. These letters will begin with an affirmation of your faith in your client; a summary of what works well in the piece; and a careful, detailed listing of what needs to be addressed before the piece is finally ready. These letters can be used to fuel discussion and passed to the author at the end of a workshop session. A wonderful side benefit of the agenting approach can be, when you reach a phase in your group relationship where lots of revision has taken place, you can decide to devote an hour or two to browsing at the periodical section of a bookstore or a library, finding suitable publication venues for one another's work.

Avoid broad comments and responses that simply provide your evaluation, your stamp of approval: "I liked this," "I couldn't get into this." Use language that reflects your awareness that your opinion is simply your opinion, not the word of a literary judge speaking from on high. Try to use language that addresses the problem: "This feels sketchy to me," not "This is weak writing." Be as specific as you possibly can. Always include in your discussions a session, either at the beginning or the end, where you only talk about what works well in the piece. It's too easy for workshop conversations to become centered wholly on the negative.

Here are a few more guidelines to consider.

- Don't use pointlessly critical language.
- Don't be subjective or start talking about your own experience unless there's a specific reason to, such as an expert knowledge you can add to the work at hand. ("I've worked at an emergency room and I don't think it would be painted bright pink," not "I've worked at an emergency room; isn't it weird?")
- When you give praise, see if you can add even more to your comment by suggesting another place where the same writing tactics can help the essay. Do provide revision suggestions freely, along with support and encouragement. The other side of the workshop coin from the pick-it-all-apart session is the lovefest, which ultimately disrespects the writer's ability to bring his work to a higher level, and does him no good.

Remember always that as you give to others in your group, you will get back. You have a deep commitment to their growth as writers and to the productive workings of the group as a whole, so always act accordingly. Also, we often learn the most about our own writing while listening carefully to critiques about someone else's work. What is true for that person struggling with a satisfying ending is probably true for you as well. Don't assume that the only time you learn anything is when your own piece is up for discussion.

Here are a few tips for making the group work.

- **Agree to distribute copies of writing to be workshopped no less than forty-eight hours in advance of your meeting.** Provide photocopies or laser-printed copies, not handwritten ones that will be hard to read professionally. Even with all the goodwill in the world, things come up, and with less than two days to prepare comments, members will come in scanning the essays as they go, a frustrating experience for reader and author.

• **Set an amount of time you will spend on each essay, with a five- or ten-minute degree of flexibility.** Twenty minutes to half an hour usually works.

• **Have one of you agree to facilitate the discussion.** Facilitating means making sure the conversation stays within or lasts until the assigned period. Facilitators can also throw out topics or questions as necessary (each piece under discussion can have a different facilitator). We remember one poorly run graduate workshop in which the instructor simply allowed the group to go on as little or as long as it liked, leading to discussions that ranged anywhere from five minutes to an hour. That's a frustrating, insulting experience for an author, so agree in advance to monitor your time and keep comments on track.

A Workshop Checklist

Here is an intuitive way to read an essay to be discussed:

1. Jot down the scenes, descriptions, and images that stick with you: the "Velcro words and phrases," as writer and teacher Sheila Bender put it. Put the essay down and make note of the first thing you remember about it. Generally these passages are the ones that not only are the best written, but the most key to what the essay is doing at a deep level.

2. Identify the emotional tones of the essay and its prose. You may sense the pleasure of a friend's visit, of a hike, the anxiety of sentences that all begin with "I think" or "I believe." Do you get the sense of over formality in a phrase like "I am perturbed"? Do you wonder why the author calls her mother by the definite article, "the mother"? Does it feel somewhat chilly? In all cases, are these feelings ones the author intended to convey, or do they seem unintentional and perhaps working against the movement of the essay?

3. Identify your curiosity. Make note of where specifically you want to know more. "I want to know more about that distant definite-article mother," "about that feeling of perturbation in the pit of the stomach," "about the author's uncertainty," "about the rest of the family," and so forth. Which locations/characters would benefit from more description? Which characters' voices do you want to hear? Where do you want to know more about the

author's responses and feelings? These curiosities help locate places for expansion.

If you need help going deeper with your comments, here are some **content questions** to consider:

- What is the organizing force of the essay, and does it sustain the piece? If this essay has a clear narrative (a story to tell), is the story clear? If it is a lyric essay organized around images, do the images keep it going?
- Are characters effectively presented and fully developed?
- Is dialogue believable, important to the overall essay, and used where it needs to be? Does it help shape character?
- Are there places where exposition should be replaced by scene for greater reader involvement or scene replaced by exposition for greater compression?
- Is the point of view working well? Would it help to try another point of view, e.g., substitute first person for second?
- If this is a meditation or essay of ideas, is there an ideology behind it? Is it presented clearly? Is it presented in a way that respects the reader, rather than becoming preachy or heavy-handed?
- Are the images used fresh and interesting? Do they work together in a way that supports the essay?
- Is the language fresh throughout, avoiding sentimentality and cliché?

Here are some **form questions** to keep in mind:

- Does the form of the essay add to/enhance its content?
- Is the organization effective? Look closely at elements such as collaging, the use of white space "jumps" between material, and whether the piece's organization is purely chronological, following the order in which events happened, or something else.
- Does the piece begin and end in a way that feels satisfying? Note that "satisfying" does not necessarily mean providing closure, or full answers to any questions it might raise. Does the essay open in a way

that makes you want to keep reading, and end in a way that provides some sort of aesthetic stopping point?

These samples will help you with **diction questions**:

• Does the language seem appropriate to the subject? Is it at times overly fussy or formal or overly slangy and flip?
• Does the essay contain any archaic or outmoded language—a trap we all fall into in literary writing—that doesn't belong?
• Are the sentence structures and rhythms appealing and effective?

We suggest you use these questions when you read, picking and choosing as seems appropriate, rather than marching through them one by one in the group. Facilitators can also keep this checklist handy, as a way of sparking conversation when it begins to lag.

Creating Your Own Writing Group

The veteran publisher Stanley Colbert wrote, "Your journey to the best-seller list begins with a single reader." All of the people you come in contact with who share your interest in writing and literature are resources for forming a writing group.

Who are your friends or acquaintances who love to write? If you've never talked with them about forming a response group, try it. Most writers spend their lonely computer or typewriter time dreaming of an audience of enthusiastic readers—chances are, you will be proposing something they'll regard as a dream come true. If you're shy about your writing and find it hard to think about sharing it with your cat, let alone a group, try this. Look at the questions in the intuitive list, given previously in this chapter. Now think of a piece of your writing and imagine answers to those questions. Chances are the thought of hearing a list of your Velcro scenes and images, the places you've made a reader curious, will actually seem pretty pleasant.

The fact is, when we worry about sharing our work, we imagine ourselves handing an essay to someone and saying, "What do you think?" and standing, knees trembling, for the final judgment. Well, first of all, no one has the all-knowing literary judgment to do that (a contemporary of poet John Milton, author of *Paradise Lost*, wrote of him, "His fame is gone out like a candle in a snuff and his memory will always stink"). Second of all, delivery of verdicts is not what writing groups are for, and you should never let yours drift into that destructive habit. Remember, you can and should exert control about the feedback process, and talk about it as a group until you get it right.

Kate Trueblood, an author and teacher of writing, formed a group with three other writers she knew who seemed compatible. Though the group was friendly and supportive, the workshop did spend a few meetings having to fine-tune their discussion style. "At first it was a little jumbled and unfocused, and feelings were hurt," Kate remembers. The group communally generated a list of rules that's kept them going successfully for many years now. "We talk about what's successful first, then acknowledge amongst ourselves when we're moving to critique. We work from global issues to smaller issues. And each time we pass out a manuscript we designate what kind of feedback we want, and what stage the work is in."

If you don't know anyone interested enough or compatible enough to form a workshop group with you, you still have another excellent resource—your local bookstore. It's a well-kept secret that many bookstores have active writing groups that meet regularly and often welcome new members. Our town has a writing group that meets once or twice a month at a local Barnes & Noble. New members join by making a phone call to the group's founder and coordinator, who makes sure they are serious and committed to the group's style before letting them in.

If you find your bookstore(s) does not have a workshop group, start one. Ask to speak to the store manager of a bookstore you like or, in a larger store, the community relations coordinator. These folks will generally help you, by posting signs and advertising in store newsletters and calendars, to find other folks in your community interested in sharing their writing. From the interviews we've done with bookstore personnel, the response will almost certainly be strong: there are a lot of writers seeking readers out there. From the bookstore's point of view, it's a way to lure literature lovers into their store on a regular basis. From your point of view, it's heaven: a group of peer reviewers, and a comfy place to meet.

Most of all, be excited about one another's work, and your own. Use your writing group as a place to generate writing as well as to critique it. Set aside time to create writing prompts together, or agree to try separately to tackle a difficult subject, providing each other support as you go along. Have writing time together with music that inspires you playing in the background. Meet at museums. Bring a piece of writing each week you've fallen in love with and share it, then talk about what it can teach you.

Remember that a group of writing friends once sat in the house during a thunderstorm and challenged each other to write a ghost or horror story, and then met again to share their efforts, one of which was Mary Shelley's classic *Frankenstein*. It was a book that would never have been created any other way.

Last Words

Lately I've been reading the selected poems of William Stafford, which includes some of the poetry he wrote the year before he died. Stafford was in the habit of getting up every day at 4 A.M. He wrote, by hand, during the dark, quiet hours in his study. He wrote about the simple things, the small things, in a voice that carries with it that sense of early morning meditation.

I don't know if Stafford was cognizant of his approaching death (he was eighty years old, after all, and perhaps at some point we can no longer deny that particular specter at our door), but the poems written during those final days have the quality of "last words": stripped of artifice, speaking from a self that wants only to understand and be understood. These are poems that want us to pay attention—not to abstract ideas and philosophies, not to idle worries or regrets, but to the world as it unfolds before us, every minute, every day. And as I read these poems I'm thinking that all of our writing, perhaps, could be written with this kind of disposition: with the tenor of "last words," the essays we would leave behind if no further writing were possible.

—Brenda

These days, whenever I visit one of my friends, her twelve-year-old daughter begs for my stories. My own son, at four-and-a-half, is already too jaded to listen to me for very long. But suddenly, my Baby Boom, New York–area history fascinates Elisabeth. I find it hard to come up with enough anecdotes to satisfy her curiosity. She's fascinated that I saw the Rolling Stones and the Grateful Dead when they were young bands; she fires questions at me about Apollo 11, or how I watched Richard Nixon's motorcade once as his thick makeup sweated down in the heat. She wants to know about the antiwar protests and race riots I grew up with. These are topics she's studying in school, and I reach deep into that trusty and unquestioned valise—my life—to find material to satisfy her.

It's hard to believe. Our lives—secret, banal, and full of Kleenexes and bus schedules as they are—form stepping-stones to the future and vital links to the past. What we have lived through and done will define the world as it exists hundreds of years from now. We are the only witnesses to this our time, which is as wondrous and banal as any moment in history, and which carries its full complement of world-changing events: wars fought, great art made, rights hard won. Value your own life and the experiences you've had: they are priceless. At the same time, learn to love the world you live in. Hike urban streets, mountain trails, or better yet, both. Go to places you've never thought of going before; talk to everyone you meet with the assumption that his life is just as interesting as yours. Fall in love, be passionate, and the stories of your time will be yours to tell.

—SUZANNE

Regaining Passion

Sometimes when you're in a writing class or studying writing intensively, it's easy to temporarily lose the passion that brought you to writing in the first place. It's easy to feel as though you've taken all the magic out of it, and you sit at your desk, bored or resistant, unable to find one thing worth writing about. Especially when you write creative nonfiction, it's easy to feel as though you've "used up" all your material, plumbed all your memories, reflected on everything there is to reflect about. Your mirror has lost its luster, your pen run dry of ink.

When this happens (and it happens to all of us), you must do whatever it takes to refill the well. This might mean just taking some time out to roam the city or spending a week on the couch with your favorite books and comfort food. It might mean making a date with your writing group or deciding to write poetry or fiction for a while instead. The important thing to remember is *it will come back*. Your passion for writing will always return, doubled in force, after its period of dormancy. The writing life is one of patience and faith.

As you've read through this book, you've received all kinds of writing prompts to trigger new work; you've read about techniques; you've learned a bit about the philosophical and ethical challenges of creative nonfiction. You've perhaps learned new ways to approach your own memories, research interests, and ideas. Now, with all this knowledge still settling inside your head, we will tell you one last thing:

Forget it all.

Don't forget it forever. But just forget it for now. Take a moment to be quiet in the space where you do your best work, at the time when the muses are most present. Try to remember what it's like to be a beginner; regain what the Zen masters call "beginner's mind," open to all possibility. When you're ready, we offer you this one last

Try It

1. What are your "last words"? What would you write if you knew your time was up?

2. What would you notice in the world around you? What's important for us to hear?

Bibliography

What Should I Read Now, and Where Can I Find It?

Read, read, read. Read everything—trash, classics, good, and bad,
and see how they do it. Just like a carpenter who works as an
apprentice and studies the master. Read! You'll absorb it. Then write.
If it is good, you'll find out. If it's not, throw it out the window.

—WILLIAM FAULKNER

There's no getting around it. Reading and writing go hand in hand. You cannot be a good writer without also being a good reader. You *must* read widely,
with the eye of a writer, engrossed not only in the plot or the characters or
the descriptions, but attuned to the craft that makes these things come alive
on the page. You read to hear other writers' voices, but you also read to tune
up your *own* voice, to remember what gets you excited about writing in the
first place. Through reading, you continually learn the craft all over again.

Throughout *Tell It Slant*, we refer to many fine essays to illustrate key
points in writing creative nonfiction. Space and money prohibit the inclusion
of those essays in this book, but we've compiled a handy list for you to keep
in mind the next time you're prowling the bookstore. This is by no means a
comprehensive accounting of great creative nonfiction! Such a list would be
long and wide, but we hope to give you at least a place to begin.

175

Atwood, Margaret. "Nine Beginnings." In *The Writer on Her Work*, edited by Janet Sternberg. New York: W.W. Norton, 1991.

This essay is written in the form of an interview with one question: "Why do you write?" The title and form also suggest that the reader is privy to first drafts fished out of the wastebasket. In a way, we are pulled into the "interview" as well, forced to think about our own reasons for writing. Though Atwood initially resists answering the question, she does, in fact reveal quite a bit about herself and her writing, ending in a section that could be taken as a complete writing philosophy.

Baker, Will. "My Children Explain the Big Issues." In *In Short: A Collection of Brief Creative Nonfiction*, edited by Judith Kitchen and Mary Paumier Jones. New York: W.W. Norton, 1996.

In this short essay, Will Baker gives us several vignettes about his children. These sections all have subtitles using abstract concepts such as fate, feminism, and so forth. The author himself makes no commentary on the small scenes; instead the reader must put together meaning based on the title and the subtitles. Like Atwood's "Nine Beginnings," this essay is a good model for looking at how writers use unconventional means to deal with transitions from topic to topic, or from scene to scene.

Baldwin, James. "Notes of a Native Son." In *Notes of a Native Son*, revised edition. Boston: Beacon Press, 1984.

In this famous essay, originally published in 1955, Baldwin not only articulates part of his autobiography, but he also sets this autobiographical material against the backdrop of history (the race riots) and the issue of racism. As Henry Louis Gates, Jr., put it, Baldwin "named for me the things you feel but couldn't utter. . . . Jimmy's essays articulated for the first time to white America what it meant to be American and a black American at the same time."

Bausch, Richard. "So Long Ago." In *The Business of Memory*, edited by Charles Baxter. St. Paul: Graywolf Press, 1999.

Why do we remember the things we do? How are they distilled to stories in our minds and the stories we tell others? Is memory the "truth?" Bausch is primarily a fiction writer, so you might explore the fictional techniques at work in this essay: the use of scene, dialogue, narrative voice, and so forth. We are listening to a story: a story about the nature of story and memory. This personal, intimate stance seems as necessary to the essay as its content.

Beard, Jo Ann. "The Fourth State of Matter." In *The Boys of My Youth*. Boston: Little, Brown and Co., 1998.

This essay first appeared in the *New Yorker*'s special fiction issue for 1996, and many people assumed it to be a short story rather than an essay (some bookstores also wanted to display her subsequent collection of essays *The Boys of My Youth* in the fiction section rather than in nonfiction). What makes an essay read like an essay? What makes a story read like a story? What is the line between truth and fiction? Is there one? Do you read a piece differently if it's presented as fiction? These are the kinds of questions you can think about as you read this stunning piece.

Berry, Wendell. "An Entrance to the Woods." In *Recollected Essays 1965–1980*. San Francisco: North Point Press, 1981.

Wendell Berry is a farmer in Kentucky. He's also a poet (a famous one at that) but his primary orientation revolves around finding a home for himself in nature. His observations are not mere glorification but a profound call to awaken the reader to the encroachment of "civilization" on nature. You do not need to agree with Berry's politics to appreciate this particular style. Connections arise intuitively, through language.

Cooper, Bernard. "The Fine Art of Sighing." In *Truth Serum*. Boston: Houghton Mifflin Co., 1996. (Also reprinted in *In Short*.)

This short, perfect essay can illustrate many different aspects of effective creative nonfiction. It appears at the exact center of Cooper's collection *Truth Serum*, when he moves from essays that deal mainly with his childhood and into ones that deal with his adulthood as a gay male. The recurrent theme of the body runs throughout this collection. Cooper explores how he struggles to come to terms with his sexuality, with his fear of AIDS, and his relationships with men and women. The structure of "The Fine Art of Sighing" allows Cooper to approach big subjects in a *peripheral* way, sidling up to the issue of the body through the smallest gesture of the sigh.

Didion, Joan. "Goodbye to All That." In *Slouching Towards Bethlehem*. New York: Simon and Schuster, 1968.

Didion might be called a foremother of creative nonfiction. This essay is one of Didion's most well-known pieces; the title may be an allusion to Robert Graves's autobiography (published in 1929) in which he describes his experience as a young man in World War I. For both writers—Didion and Graves—the phrase "Goodbye to All That" sums up, in almost a breezy voice, the dismissal of youth from the perspective of the older (and wiser?) self. Didion is a novelist, journalist, and screenplay writer, as well as an essayist, and all these skills come to bear in her creative nonfiction writing. You can try imitating the long sentence in the first section that starts, "When I first saw New York." The long sentence tends to elicit strong details and memories that may otherwise remain hidden.

Dillard, Annie. "Total Eclipse." In *Teaching a Stone to Talk: Expeditions and Encounters*. New York: Harper & Row, 1982.

Annie Dillard gained fame as a creative nonfiction writer with her book *Pilgrim at Tinker Creek*, a book-length meditation on the spirituality and metaphysics inherent in nature. Dillard often turns toward the natural world in her attempts to make sense of the ideas that haunt her. In this essay, an eclipse becomes more than an eclipse; it becomes a terrifying metaphysical journey. From her personal perspective, Dillard also gives us many facts about eclipses embedded in the narrative.

Duncan, David James. "The Mickey Mantle Koan." In *River Teeth: Stories and Writings*. New York: Doubleday, 1995.

As we described earlier in the book, a "koan" is a Zen puzzle, a riddle given to a disciple by the master as a way of spurring enlightenment. Zen monks often work these koans for years, and the answers to them are most often illogical, defying logic or reason. In this essay, Duncan approaches a difficult subject—the death of his teenaged brother—by focusing on a small object that is peripheral to the main story: a baseball signed by Mickey Mantle. This object becomes his koan, something he doesn't quite understand. He uses the opportunity of the essay as a way of working out this koan on the page.

Fisher, M. F. K. "A Thing Shared." In *The Art of Eating*. New York: Collier Books, 1990.

In 1943, M. F. K. Fisher wrote, "There is a communion of more than our bodies when bread is broken and wine drunk. And that is my answer, when people ask me: Why do you write about hunger, and not wars or love?" Fisher is known primarily as a food writer, though her work takes on many more topics than food. She has written about highly personal subjects such as her divorce from her first husband and the death of her second. Her books often include recipes interspersed among the prose. Fisher shows how memories of particular tastes can be the key to highly charged memories.

Goldbarth, Albert. "After Yitzl." In *A Sympathy of Souls*. Minneapolis: Coffee House Press, 1990.

This braided essay explores how we create our own ancestries. Goldbarth is known primarily as a poet, and one who incorporates all manner of disciplines into his work: science, pop culture, film, and so forth. (He's also known as a collector of kitsch; he supposedly has the largest collection of 1950s outer-space toys in the state of Kansas!) His propensity for gathering disparate images is evident in this essay and may initially cause you some consternation. (His indulgent delight with language may also invite resistance!)

Hemley, Robin. "Reading History to My Mother." In *Fourth Genre: Explorations in Nonfiction*, edited by Michael Steinberg. East Lansing, MI: MSU Press, spring, 2001.

In this essay, Hemley approaches a difficult topic—taking care of an aging parent—through the form of a braided essay. He also uses a photograph as a way of entering a past not his own, and he publishes the photo along with the essay. Hemley once told us this essay seemed to come together almost magically, every piece falling into place. He wrote it while he was trying to figure out some complex issues surrounding his mother, and so it carries that kind of urgency, that quality of attention to intuition.

Iyer, Pico. "Where Worlds Collide." In *The Fourth Genre: Contemporary Writers of/on Creative Nonfiction*, edited by Robert Root and Michael Steinberg. Boston: Allyn and Bacon, 1999.

Pico Iyer is a huge fan of Van Morrison. We mention this because much of his work, though ostensibly about travel in the physical world, is also about interior, spiritual travels, journeys "into the mystic," as Morrison would put it. (Iyer has also spent quite a bit of time in monasteries.) This particular essay takes a commonplace locale, the airport, and transforms it through his attention to detail. He makes the familiar exotic; he makes us really *look* at sights we might readily pass over in our quest to get somewhere else.

Kingston, Maxine Hong. "No Name Woman." In *The Woman Warrior*. New York: Knopf, 1976.

This story within a story sets up a series of tensions, as various characters interact with the story of the aunt. "No Name Woman" serves as a brilliant introduction to the way family stories become mythological. They become springboards to the family members' feelings about themselves and one another. It also works as a meditation on the reliability of memory itself.

Kitchen, Judith. "Things of This Life." From *Only the Dance*. Columbia, S.C.: University of South Carolina Press, 1994.

This elegiac essay presents a writer connecting the curbed desires of adulthood with the seemingly limitless desires of childhood, and as such, it is an essay that unfolds through intimate detail. One of the most arresting choices Kitchen makes is to narrate this essay in the third person, a technique that we often forget is available to us even when writing about ourselves.

Lamott, Anne. "Why I Don't Meditate." In *The Best Spiritual Writing 1998*, edited by Philip Zaleski. San Francisco: HarperSanFrancisco, 1998.

This essay teeters on a fine balance between slapstick humor and its serious message of opening up and trying to connect, rather than letting life's difficulties and your own anxieties shut you down. It is about Lamott's lack of ability to meditate, much as she wants to, and her gradual opening up to a substitute path that serves her just as well.

Mukherjee, Bharati. "A Four-Hundred-Year-Old Woman." In *The Writer on Her Work*, edited by Janet Sternberg. New York: W.W. Norton, 1991.

Mukherjee invokes the haunting image of her father's native village in what was then India, now a place annexed to another country, for a descriptive yet philosophical meditation on the nature of home, or "desh." Mukherjee uses her upbringing—born in a place that no longer exists, taught in a Western school that inculcated in its students a culture foreign to their own—as a metaphor for the transplanted lives of many contemporary people.

Price, Jennifer. "A Brief Natural History of the Plastic Pink Flamingo." In *Flight Maps*. New York: Basic Books, 1999.

This essay is a well-researched and charming look at a quirky subject, plastic lawn flamingos. Though these flamingos might seem hardly worth such consideration, the author ties their swelling popularity in the mid-twentieth century with Americans' evolving attitudes toward nature—the desire to experience it in tamed, altered form. She pulls in periodicals and advertisements of the period, explaining how the lawn birds first became so popular—representing a serious commitment to a particular kind of "artificial nature"—then made the transition to the sort of jokey relic we call "kitsch."

Rekdal, Paisley. "The Night My Mother Met Bruce Lee." In *The Night My Mother Met Bruce Lee.* New York: Pantheon Books, 2000.

Rekdal, who is Chinese-Norwegian, spends much of her book exploring her relationship with her mother, whose ancestry is Chinese. She probes the deeper questions associated with being biracial, here seen in the delicate way she observes Chinese culture both from the inside and the outside. It's a beautiful example of how to deepen an essay by fully imagining the life of a person close to you, a person you seek to understand.

Sanders, Scott Russell. "Buckeye." In *Writing from the Center.* Bloomington, IN: Indiana University Press, 1995.

This short essay contains so much. It is both a character sketch and an extended memory, as the author uses the buckeyes he's saved from his father's pocket to conjure his father up in specific childhood scenes. The father is characterized physically—particularly through his laborer's hands—and in his voice. The essay relies on scene, detail, and dialogue to establish its beautiful, elegiac tone.

Sedaris, David. "The Drama Bug." In *Naked.* Rockland, MA: Wheeler Pub., 1997.

Nobody handles relationships quite like Sedaris, who manages to present his family in all of their rough-edged gruffness, yet keep his tone ultimately affirmative—of the possibilities of intimacy, of family. Sedaris also has a wonderful hand with dialogue; his remembered Shakespearean soliloquies are hilariously exaggerated. All of his books are available on audio; his reading style adds considerably to the humor of the essays.

Selzer, Richard. "The Knife." In *Mortal Lessons: Notes on the Art of Surgery*. New York: Simon and Schuster, 1976.

Not only a vivid description of the feeling of surgery from a practicing surgeon and a fine scientific piece, but "The Knife" is also an extended experiment in point of view. Beginning impersonally—"One holds the knife"—the essay shifts quickly to a first person—"I am still struck with a kind of dread"—and then second, as the author moves deeper into this dangerous surgery: "You turn aside to wash your gloves." Selzer removes the normal barrier between the reader and the experience, putting us in the position of fighting to save this desperately ill patient.

Sutin, Lawrence. *A Postcard Memoir*. St. Paul: Graywolf Press, 2000.

This book is a memoir/lyric essay told in the form of meditations triggered by the author's antique postcard collection. The postcards appear in black and white next to the texts they prompt, and the postcard pieces move out from stories of the author's parents—damaged survivors of the second World War—to his own childhood and finally his own parenthood: a journey through time and places, which postcards represent, but with a sometimes brutal realism that seems the opposite of postcard sentimentality.

White, E. B. "Afternoon of an American Boy." In *Essays of E. B. White*, reprinted edition. New York: Perennial, 1999.

White's essay is a flawless piece of memoir: a personal reminiscence crafted into a literary work that is neither self-indulgent nor limited. He captures the awkwardness of early acquaintance between the sexes, escorting a girl he admires to a tea-dance. At the same time he pokes nuanced fun at a scourge of the mid-twentieth century, the House Un-American Activities Committee (HUAC), whose eventual chairman was the older brother of White's teenage crush.

Williams, Terry Tempest. "The Clan of One-Breasted Women." In *Refuge: An Unnatural History of Family and Place*, second edition. New York: Vintage Books, 2001.

Williams opens this essay with a bold declaration—"I belong to a Clan of One-Breasted Women." It sounds grand, tribal, until we learn she is talking about coming from a lineage of women all of whom have undergone mastectomies. Williams's father reveals to her that her dreams of a flash in the desert are part of a real memory: that of seeing aboveground bomb testing in the 1950s. The fact of the testing, and the heavy fallout on Utah, is the chip of information Williams needs to question her family's high legacy of cancer.

Woolf, Virginia. "The Death of the Moth." In *The Death of the Moth and Other Essays*, reprinted edition. New York: Harcourt Brace Jovanovich, 1974.

This short, intensely poetic recounting of a moth's dying at the author's window is rich in connotations: the attempts to preserve a life through writing, as Woolf is doing, versus the "bead of pure life" that is the moth, flickering out in its brief and record-less existence.

Suggestions for Further Reading

Lopate, Phillip, ed., *The Art of the Personal Essay*. New York: Anchor Books, 1994.

An anthology of classic essays from antiquity to the twentieth century, providing an excellent historical overview of the form.

D'Agata, John, ed., *The Next American Essay*. St. Paul: Graywolf Press, 2003.

An anthology that takes up where Lopate's anthology leaves off, including experimental work that complicates the term "essay."

Root, Robert and Michael Steinberg, eds., *The Fourth Genre: Contemporary Writers of/on Creative Nonfiction.* Boston: Allyn and Bacon, 1999.

An excellent collection of essays by a variety of contemporary writers in the genre.

Kitchen, Judith and Mary Paumier Jones, eds., *In Short: A Collection of Brief Creative Nonfiction.* New York: W.W. Norton, 1996, and *In Brief: Short Takes on the Personal.* New York: W.W. Norton, 1999.

Both these volumes collect a wide array of "short-short" essays, providing the reader with a variety of approaches to the form.

Zinsser, William. *Inventing the Truth: The Art and Craft of Memoir.* Boston: Houghton Mifflin, 1987.

Interviews with several writers of memoir that elucidate some of the key issues that come up as soon as we begin to write in this genre.

Index